THE
RAGMAN'S
MEMORY

THE RAGMAN'S MEMORY

ARCHER MAYOR

THE MYSTERIOUS PRESS

Published by Warner Books

A Time Warner Company

Mysterious Press books are published by Warner Books, Inc.,
1271 Avenue of the Americas, New York, NY 10020

 A Time Warner Company

The Mysterious Press name and logo are registered trademarks of Warner Books, Inc.

Printed in the United States of America
First Printing: December 1996
10   9   8   7   6   5   4   3   2   1

Library of Congress Cataloging-in-Publication Data

Mayor, Archer.
    The ragman's memory / Archer Mayor.
        p.   cm.
    ISBN 0-89296-636-X
    I. Title.
    PS3563.A965R34   1996
    813'.54—dc20   96-23331
                                                              CIP

To Molly,
For her encouragement, her faith, and her honesty—
with heartfelt thanks for a wonderful friendship.

~THE~
RAGMAN'S
MEMORY

Chapter One

"Joe? You've got a visitor."

I looked up from the paperwork spread across my desk. Harriet Fritter, the squad's administrative assistant, stood in the doorway with a half-smile on her face.

I glanced at the calendar thumbtacked to the wall before me, wondering what appointment I'd forgotten. There was nothing under today's date.

Harriet stepped aside and gestured to a small, skinny girl with large, thick, wire-rim glasses, looking very serious. I guessed her to be about twelve years old. Her shoulder-length, straight dark hair was still dusted with the snow that had been falling heavily outside for the past twenty-four hours. She was holding a small brown grocery bag tightly with both hands.

"Lieutenant Joe Gunther, this is Norah Fletcher."

I half-rose from my chair and shook the girl's slim hand. She had a firm grip, which both surprised and pleased me. "Miss Fletcher. Please have a seat. Would you like to take your coat off?"

I gestured to my guest chair as Harriet faded from view.

Norah Fletcher declined to remove her overcoat, and sat nervously on the edge of the seat, the brown bag between her knees.

"How can I help you?" I asked.

Her dark eyes rose from her rubber boots, which were creating small puddles on the carpeting. She studied me with great intensity. "I know about you from newspaper stories, and I thought you should see this. My mom said I shouldn't, but I think something's wrong." She thrust the paper bag out to me.

I took it from her gingerly, noticing its light weight, and placed it on my desk. "What is it?"

Her eyes narrowed slightly, with a child's surprise at my not tearing into the package without pause. "It's a bird nest, but I want you to look at it before I say any more."

I was impressed, both at her poise and her unusually mature strategy. Still, yielding to a cop's instinct to control, I prolonged Norah Fletcher's anticipation.

"May I call you Norah?"

She nodded without comment.

"If your mother was against the idea, how did you get here? You live nearby?"

"I walked from school. My mom thinks my lunch was in there." She nodded toward the bag.

It was mid-afternoon. "Doesn't she expect you back home?"

She hid any irritation at my delay, refusing to join the game I was only half-consciously playing. "I walk to the library every day. She picks me up there after work. She's a secretary."

"Where's home, Norah?"

"Hillcrest Terrace—off the Guilford Street Extension."

"Just you and your mom?"

She nodded, with the smallest flicker of a smile. "And Oreo. My cat."

Maybe it was this resurfacing of the child from behind the serious face that made me abruptly cave in. I reached for the bag. "Let's take a look."

I peered into the dim opening, saw a cluster of dry grass and twigs, and poured it out into the hollow of my hand.

"It's a chickadee nest," Norah explained. "I have a birdbox on a post in my backyard, near the field. A couple of chickadees have been using it for years. I clean it out because they like to build a new one each year. That's why it looks a little weird—kind of boxy."

I placed the nest on my desk and poked it with my finger, studying how the birds had woven their intricate home together. Its outer sides had retained the distinct shape of a surrounding small box.

"Turn it around," Norah urged, for the first time showing a little impatience.

I did so gently, rotating it on the tabletop without picking it up. As its far side came into view, I better understood Norah's interest in what I'd seen as a perfectly normal abandoned nest.

The overhead fluorescent lighting caught it first, revealing among the scratchy, dull-colored hay a swatch of something smooth and reflective. I leaned forward to look at it more carefully.

"It's human hair," she stated with certainty.

I didn't argue with her. It appeared she was right.

I sat back, opened my desk drawer and withdrew a Tiger Milk bar, which I offered her. "You must be hungry."

She nodded and took the bar with another fleeting smile. As she peeled back the gold wrapper, I thought about her discovery, and what it might mean to us.

The fact that human hair was intertwined within a nest didn't come as a surprise. My own mother had cut my brother's and my hair outdoors so the birds could use it during the spring, and my father had once had a hunk of hair painfully plucked out by a bird while he was working in one of our fields.

But these memories brought me no comfort here, nor did they prompt me to dismiss Norah Fletcher's concern with some patronizing lecture on symbiotic relationships.

For the long, thick twist of discolored strands was no mere

tuft of cut or plucked hair. It was bound at its base by a small, withered, leathery patch of scalp.

*   *   *

The snow had stopped falling by the time we gathered in Norah Fletcher's backyard on Hillcrest Terrace, high above Brattleboro, Vermont. The street marked the abrupt end of the town's urban expansion to the southwest. On one side, in front of Norah's home, was a modest, middle-class neighborhood, clinging to the side of a steep hill, and overlooking the town, the distant mountains, and the interstate slicing through it all. On the other side—neatly sheeted in glistening, pristine white—was a vast, empty, featureless field that stretched up and away to the horizon like a frothy, frozen sea.

Separating Norah's backyard from that barren field, a split-rail fence stood guard like the shaky railing of some decrepit ancient ship—a faint and picturesque reminder of how much of Vermont remains dominated by its natural surroundings, despite the ambitions of urban developers and condo builders alike.

Norah, her mother, Ann, my second-in-command, Sammie Martens, and I stood in a cluster by the back door under the pale gray sky, and silently took in the implications of Norah's discovery.

"If there is a body out there," Sammie muttered bluntly, "it'll be a neat trick finding it."

Ann Fletcher shook her head, resting her hand lightly on her daughter's shoulder. "Birds use hair all the time in their nests. I told Norah that. I asked her not to pester you people."

Norah didn't react. She remained motionless, looking out at the wooden birdhouse that was nailed to an upright by one of the fence posts outlined like a ship's crow's nest against the fathomless pale expanse beyond it. She didn't shake off her mother's hand, which was there more in support than as a rebuke in any case, but I could sense the restless energy between them—of single parent and single child, strained by the mutual need to be independent, yet united by the strong bonds of steady companionship. Ann had told me earlier, when we'd dropped by her office to pick her up, that Norah was a loner—a studious perfectionist who preferred the tranquillity of her own company to the chaotic tumble of her schoolmates—and that she sometimes lacked the benefit of other people's opinions in forming her own thoughts.

A loner myself, I sympathized with the child.

"We're glad she did pester us, Mrs. Fletcher. You're right about the hair. We've even found marijuana growers collecting it from barber shops to ward off deer. But what Norah found wasn't cut."

I let the unstated implication float in the frigid air, interlaced with the mist from our breathing.

"Oh," Ann Fletcher finally murmured.

"Norah," I asked the girl, "from what you've told me, I guess you monitor those chickadees pretty closely."

She kept her eyes on the fence. "I watched them every day." Her tone reflected her sorrow that such constant friends had become involved in something so grim.

"When did they build the nest?"

She didn't hesitate. "Early July. That's late for chickadees. I tried to look up why, but I couldn't find it anywhere. Maybe it was because June got so hot all of a sudden, after May was so cold. They might've gotten confused. Or they could've tried to nest someplace else that didn't work out, so they came back here. I don't know."

That all sounded reasonable to me, who had but a layman's knowledge of such things. I waved a hand toward the fence like a genial host. "Let's get right up to it."

We shuffled through the thick, soundless snow up the tilting yard until we were standing around the birdbox, nailed about head-high on its pole. There were several small evergreens planted in a row parallel to the fence, their presence further emphasizing the emptiness before us. Far to our right, however, coinciding with the end of the block, I saw a straight line of dark, prickly, bare-branched woods running along one side of the field—up and over the crest of the hill, vanishing from view to the south.

Norah caught my look. "That's their territory. They never

nest too far from woods. A single pair needs at least two or three acres. This box is a little far away, but I coaxed them here with some good food, and I lined the box with sawdust. They like that . . . at least they did."

I put my own hand on her shoulder and gave her a small squeeze. "They'll be back. This kind of thing only bothers us."

"I guess so."

Sammie—small, muscular, and energetic, an ex–Army Ranger prone to action—was becoming restless with my tempered approach. She leaned her elbows on the railing and nodded toward the field with her chin. "How many acres do you figure?"

"About fifty," Ann Fletcher answered from slightly behind us.

I turned to her, wondering if her hanging back was the product of embarrassment for having downplayed her child's discovery, or fear of what it might yield. "Is it used for anything?"

She shook her head. "No. It's owned by someone from Florida. They have a big house on the other side. It used to be farmland, but it just sits there now."

"Do people use it for picnics or hikes or anything?" Sammie asked.

"The children play along the edges sometimes, and go exploring in the woods. But nobody I know goes out into the middle."

"It's a little scary," Norah added softly.

"How so?" I asked.

She looked up at me for the first time since we'd arrived here. Her eyes were magnified by the thick glasses, giving her a dreamy quality. "It's just so big, and it's tilted so you can see everything in the valley," she pointed north, beyond her house. "It makes you kind of dizzy—and it's hot and buggy in the summer."

I kept my eyes on hers, probing for any knowledge possibly lurking below the surface, conscious or not. "What do you think happened out there, Norah?"

Next to me, I could hear her mother's small intake of breath.

The child answered in the form of a question, "Someone died?"

"Besides the hair in the nest, is there anything else that makes you think that?"

I sensed Ann Fletcher's alarm, her yearning to speak on her daughter's behalf. But there was something else, too—a hesitation that spoke of her concern that Norah might know more than she'd previously let on.

But Norah looked genuinely baffled. "I don't understand."

I shrugged slightly, privately relieved. "Something you saw, heard—"

"Smelled," Sammie finished abruptly.

Norah wrinkled her nose, dissipating the tension. "No. I would have remembered that."

I turned to Sammie. "Better get a team together. We can't do anything with that," I gestured toward the snow-covered field. "But maybe one of the neighbors can tell us something. And try to find somebody from Fish and Game. If Norah's chickadees used the hair, maybe some other animals were busy, too. We need to know where to look."

Sammie shook her head. "That could take some time. They're already short-staffed in this area. I heard about a guy who's trained dogs for this kind of thing."

I knew the man she meant—the owner of specialized, so-called cadaver dogs. I'd called him at his office in Maine before coming here, and now passed along what he'd told me. "Too cold. A body out there doesn't smell any more than what's in your freezer."

"Miss Evans might be able to help," Norah said quietly.

We both looked at her.

"She's my science teacher—a naturalist. She's the one who got me interested in birds. She knows all sorts of stuff."

I glanced at Ann Fletcher, who nodded reluctantly. "That's true. She's very good—Christine Evans. I could give you her number."

"Give it to Detective Martens here. She'll be organizing all this."

Sammie and Norah's mother walked back to the gray house, their gestures exaggerated by having to wade through the deep snow. Norah was back staring at the field, her gloved hands resting on the railing—the pensive loner, I reminded myself. I wondered what was going through her mind.

"You really think somebody's out there?" she asked as I took up position next to her.

"We may not know for sure till the spring, but your birds got that hair from somewhere—either the field or the woods—and when I showed it to him, our forensics expert confirmed it came from a human. Of course, it might've been someone old and sick with no family, who just chose this spot to die in peace. That happens sometimes."

She startled me then with a child's typical lack of lasting melancholy, "It's kind of neat."

I didn't argue the point. From her perspective, that's exactly what it was. But even had I wished it, I couldn't be so detached. My curiosity wasn't restricted to the fact that the mysterious shank of hair had once belonged to someone alive. I had to discover the cause of death, and odds were it hadn't been as benign as the picture I'd just painted for Norah.

Chapter Two

Christine Evans stood by the birdbox in Norah Fletcher's backyard, her large, parka-clad body planted like a challenge to the inscrutable landscape beyond the fence.

"Birds are near the bottom of the pile when it comes to stripping a carcass," she said, her flat-footed vernacular tinted with the nasal tones of a native Bostonian. "The larger animals come first—bears, dogs, foxes, raccoons, possums, skunks. You wouldn't believe the pecking order."

She suddenly swung away from the view and fixed me with an inquisitive stare. "You're sure the hair didn't belong to some longhaired animal?"

J. P. Tyler, our small squad's forensics expert, looked frail and anemic next to Evans's energetic, pink-faced bulk. He shook his head in response. "It's human. It has traces of purple dye, like from a punk hairdo."

She accepted that with an unsentimental grunt. "Doesn't matter. It's all the same to our furry and feathered friends. Anyhow, I think you're right—you probably will find other remnants if you know where to look."

She indicated the rest of the block with a sweep of her

arm. "Under garages, in old tool sheds, culverts, storm drains—hiding places like that. Animals don't travel great distances with food, but they like to feel secure when they chow down."

She then pointed toward the woods lining the field. "That's the other place to search, but I wish you luck. Every nook and cranny is fair game. The only good news is that you won't have to look too far into the trees. The first few dozen feet ought to do it."

"What if that's where the body is?" I asked her. "Couldn't the hair have been the only thing to make it out this far?"

She shook her head. "I'd stick with your first idea," she answered. "The body's in the field, and I bet it's not too far off. Chickadees are efficient that way. They're not going to fly far to gather nest materials, especially a thick hunk of hair, and they'd be nuts to bypass the field for the woods."

Sammie Martens said to Tyler, "I guess we got our marching orders. Better ask everyone we interview if we can poke around their properties, as well."

They left to coordinate the small army of officers we'd summoned for the neighborhood canvass. Christine Evans pushed out her lips pensively, and added an afterthought. "Until the snow melts, you might have to be happy with what you've already got."

*　　*　　*

We didn't find much. The interviews were a bust. Like Norah and her mother, nobody on the street had seen, heard, or smelled anything amiss during the previous summer. No one had gone missing, no one with purple hair had been seen hanging around, and no one had made a discovery similar to Norah's. At the last house on the block, however, nearest to where the field met the woods, we did find a man who'd lost his dog to a hit-and-run the previous August, and whose abandoned doghouse contained a small collection of fragmented, gnawed-upon shards with an ominous bony look to them.

Not that we were immediately impressed, including Tyler,

much to his later discomfort. Finding bones in a doghouse, after all, was not unheard of, and this owner admitted that bones were a treat he'd regularly supplied his pet. It was more in the interest of thoroughness, therefore, that we asked Christine Evans to give us her educated opinion.

She'd been in Norah's house throughout most of the search, keeping the Fletchers company while remaining available to us. As a result, she brought them both with her to check out what we'd found, her benignly domineering style reminding me of a Scout leader conducting a nature trip. Still, despite Ann Fletcher's apparent tacit approval, I wondered about prolonging Norah's exposure to what she herself had set in motion.

Evans, however, obviously believed otherwise. Arriving at the doghouse, she gathered Norah next to her before its arched doorway, and played the beam of an officer's borrowed flashlight onto the pale ivory gleam of the scattered fragments, starkly revealed amid the otherwise pitch-black shelter.

It took her about thirty seconds to reach a conclusion. "Most of those are animal bones, but that small piece in the far corner is part of a human zygomatic arch, where the mandible hinges to the rest of the skull." She touched Norah's cheek to demonstrate.

"Wow," Norah murmured, easing my concern.

"Can we get a closer look?" Evans asked, shoving her head deeper into the opening.

I threw a questioning glance at Tyler.

"We're all set—photographs and measurements are all done."

Behind him, the late dog's owner, an older, bare-headed man with a red nose and a frost-dusted mustache, added, "It doesn't have a floor. You can tilt it back."

"Good," Evans laughed. "I was wondering how I could squeeze in there."

Four of us followed the owner's advice, and tilted the doghouse back, exposing its littered dirt floor like the innards of some large, wooden clam.

The light had dulled, the sun fading early in the winter months, so the contents of the small dwelling, now surrounded by four snowbanks instead of the walls that had once protected it, were suddenly illuminated by a half-dozen flashlights, whose bright, hovering disks swept across the hard-packed surface like theatrical spotlights.

"How big was your dog?" Evans asked the homeowner.

He held his hand out just below his waist. "Big—he was a mastiff. Really powerful."

She looked at the rest of us. "Domesticated dogs especially tend to go after the skulls—they remind them of balls."

Tyler, his embarrassment at missing the identification washed away by her enthusiasm, crouched by her other side and leaned over the exposed site, adding, "He probably buried what he didn't crush up. You can see how the earth is disturbed near the back."

Side by side in the snow, Evans and Tyler began conferring like old colleagues, pawing at the frozen earth like hampered archaeologists, trying to piece together what they could.

Tyler glanced over his shoulder, his frustration plain. "We need hammers and picks to get through this crap."

Norah Fletcher's quiet voice floated up in the wake of this comment, reminding us that these scattered shards were more than mere parts of a puzzle. "So it really is somebody?"

Tyler, as was typical when his focus was jarred by some emotional consideration, looked startled and self-conscious. Evans, on the other hand, proved how good a teacher she could be. She sat back on her haunches and draped a burly arm around the thin girl's waist, explaining to her in a near whisper the intricacies of human anatomy and of animal behavior, replacing some of the sudden chill in the air with a broader appreciation of what life sometimes throws in our faces.

By the time she'd finished, and after Norah's pale face had regained some of its studious poise, a patrolman appeared with two trenching tools and a hammer he'd borrowed from a neighbor. Evans took advantage of the interruption to get up and escort Norah to where Ann Fletcher was standing uncomfortably on the fringes of our little group.

"I think we've probably had enough science for one day. Besides, I happen to know you've got homework," Evans said, as Norah slipped her gloved hand into her mother's.

Norah merely nodded, the full impact of the doghouse's contents lingering despite her teacher's best efforts.

As they turned to go, I stepped before them and crouched down so Norah and I were eye-to-eye. "I appreciate what you did. When we find out what happened here, it'll be because you cared enough to come forward. Not many people are that observant, or show that much responsibility."

A subtle pride radiated from behind those large glasses. She murmured, "You're welcome," before looking down at the ground. I no longer felt so badly about exposing her to more than what might have been appropriate. Good experiences sometimes come in odd packages, something I sensed even Norah's mother might agree with.

I straightened and shook Ann Fletcher's hand. "Thank you."

"I tried to stop her," she answered apologetically, still obviously distressed at how events had snowballed.

"You were being protective. What she did does you credit—you obviously taught her well."

She smiled slightly, which was all I wanted to see. "Goodbye, Lieutenant."

*   *   *

Tyler appeared at my elbow. His earlier frustration at the frozen ground had faded. "I didn't mean that literally, about the pick and hammers. It'd be too destructive. We can throw a tent over the whole thing, put a space heater inside, and have the ground totally thawed within twenty-four hours. That okay?"

I turned back toward the site. "Sounds good to me. God knows how long this has been here. Anyone else come up with anything yet?"

Sammie appeared from around the back of the nearby garage. "Stennis found what looks like chicken bones on the shelf of one of the storm drains, and Lavoie got a long bone from a culvert. Both were photographed in place and bagged. Evans thinks the long bone's from a deer. The crime lab'll tell us for sure. I also called the State's Attorney's office on the cell phone."

"They sending anyone over?" I asked.

Sammie shook her head. "Said we could brief them later."

We returned to where Christine Evans was back on her knees scrutinizing the dirt before her. "There may be more," she said, pointing with a gloved finger. "See that scat?"

Sammie's face turned sour as she focused on several two-inch-long, dark, twisted droppings, their ends distinctively marked by pointed, upturned spirals.

"What about it?" I asked skeptically.

"It's from a fisher—part of the marten family—related to the weasel. They don't like open ground, but they're bold enough to come onto human property." She suddenly flashed a disarming smile at the largely ignored homeowner who was standing beside me. "Speaking purely scientifically, it's a good thing your dog died when it did. Had he lived, he not only would've pulverized these fragments, but no fisher in his right mind would've had the guts to forage anywhere near here. As it is, this scat tells us there may be more to find, and maybe where to look for it."

"The fisher took something?" I asked.

"The scat's a little old, so it wouldn't've been recently, but it's a good guess."

I noticed Tyler nodding, a pleased look on his face. This was turning into his kind of investigation.

"You said they avoid open country," I said. "Does that mean we need to search the woods for where this one might've gone?"

Evans rose to her feet, steadying herself by placing her hand on J.P.'s shoulder. "Yes, but it shouldn't be too hard to find. Look for a large, craggy, crevice-filled old tree—probably just a few hundred feet from here. You may not find much, though. Fishers aren't very big. On the other hand, they aren't bone gnawers, either. This one would've gone for whatever meat was still attached to a smaller fragment. Find out where he had his meal, and I think you'll find the bone it was attached to."

I glanced up at the sky. The fading light was sufficiently offset by the quickly vanishing storm clouds. "We've got maybe an hour and a half before it gets too dark," I told the others. "Let's see if we can find the right tree."

It took barely half that time. Sammie pulled the entire team together and strung them out in a line facing the woods, whose dark latticework of intertwining bare branches was off-set by a bright frosting of snow. Entering the forest was like infiltrating a dense and eccentric crystalline structure whose very size and darkness muffled and absorbed our movements. The sensation forced my thoughts back to the body lying under the cold, impersonal snow, lost and forgotten.

There were a couple of false starts—trees whose appearance could have fit Christine Evans's description. But when we found the real thing, there were no doubts. Barging through a tight cluster of skinny saplings, our arms crossed before our faces for protection, several of us stumbled into a clearing dominated by a crippled monster of a beech tree. Gnarled, bent, lightning-shattered, but determinedly alive, it half-lay across the land like a wounded elephant, holding itself up on a tripod of enormous branches, each the thickness of a normal full-grown tree.

"Jesus," Sammie murmured in awe.

There was a moment's stunned silence as we absorbed the majesty of the scene, and were touched by the Herculean effort this tree had made to survive.

"Wow," Christine added. "I've got to get some kids out to see this."

"This what you were after?" I asked her.

But she was already looking for ways to ascend the staggered trunk into the sprouting of branches high overhead. Sammie summoned the others on the radio, and soon Evans, Sammie, and I were surrounded like circus acrobats by a semicircle of small, upturned faces. The three of us had split up at the first major junction, to pursue our own separate tangle of twisting branches, looking for any hole, crevice, or half-rotted crack, all the while keenly aware of the tree's slippery surface and the long drop to the ground.

It was because of this latter distraction that I almost missed what I was after, only returning to a narrow split in the wood beneath me because I thought I'd seen a glimmer, as from the reflection of a single cat's eye.

I straddled the thick branch nervously, wondering what I'd seen—and wary of something suddenly bursting from out of the hole. Cautiously, I played my light down into the darkness, leaning forward only as I became convinced that what I'd found was safely uninhabited.

The crack I was poised over opened onto a large rotted-out cavity beyond. Playing the light around inside, I saw the debris of steady animal use—acorn hats, bits of vegetation, clumps of matter I couldn't identify, and the by now familiar pallor of a neatly cleaned piece of jawbone. But the bone hadn't been the glimmer that had caught my eye—embedded within it, as bright as an ember, was a single gold tooth.

This discovery suddenly personalized the remains we had found, and settled like a weight in my chest. From the moment I'd seen that huge, empty, ominous frozen field, I'd been fending off a sense of foreboding. For despite my hopeful words to Norah Fletcher, it had not struck me as a reasonable spot for some old vagrant to choose as his final resting place. It had reeked of a dumping ground. Now, for no particularly rational reason, this tooth, in all its jaunty clarity, struck me like the confirmation of a homicide.

*   *   *

Gail Zigman, my best friend and companion for many years, and my housemate for the past ten months, was the newly anointed legal clerk for the Windham County State's Attorney's office. It was in that capacity that she was watching me quizzically from across her boss's conference table, a pen poised over the pad before her.

It was the State's Attorney, however, who'd asked the question. "Are you going to be able to keep a lid on this until you have more to go on?"

I shook my head. "The paper's already called us, and Ted McDonald waylaid the Chief during a break at a meeting he was attending at the high school. So it's already gotten out. We're going to have to give them some explanation."

Ted McDonald was the corpulent, fast-moving news director of the town's single radio station—WBRT—a home-grown good ol' boy whose laid-back manner belied a surgical ability to extract information.

Jack Derby, newly elected barely a year ago, betrayed a forgivable concern. "How're you going to present it?"

"I don't have too many options—"

I was interrupted by a knock on the door. Chief of Police Tony Brandt stepped into the room. He took a chair by the door, keeping the three of us at arm's length. From the tone of his voice, I could tell it hadn't been one of his better days, with or without Ted McDonald. "I apologize for being late. I was getting an update from Sammie Martens, who was nice enough to stick around and let me know what the hell was going on."

Sammie had already called ahead to warn us. "Sorry, Tony," I said. "To be honest, there wasn't much to talk about. That's why we didn't drag you out of your meeting."

He took the apology without comment. "So I gathered. I take it McDonald picked this up on the scanner?"

"I guess," I answered. "I was just saying I didn't see any harm in giving them the straight poop—maybe someone'll come forward with a missing person report."

"We've got nothing at all so far?" Brandt persisted.

"I sent the hair, the bone fragments, and the piece of jaw with the gold tooth up to the crime lab to see what they can find. We're guessing it's somebody young. Tyler looked at the hair under his microscope and detected traces of purple dye, so maybe it was a punker, male or female. Also, the jaw included three other teeth, but no wisdom tooth—he said it hadn't erupted yet—another possible sign of someone younger. 'Course, if you want to play a worst-case scenario, there's nothing to say all three samples don't come from different bodies."

"Swell," Derby murmured.

"That's not what you're going to tell the press, are you?" asked Gail. For years, she had been a selectman in this town, before a midlife reevaluation—precipitated by a traumatic sexual assault—had led her to revive a twenty-year-old, never-used law degree. That background made her as politically savvy as anyone I knew, a fact Jack Derby hadn't missed from the moment she'd applied for the six-month clerkship.

I shook my head. "No, no. I'll play it straight. But I have a bad feeling about this. The gold tooth will probably lead to a dentist, and the X rays to an identity, but I doubt it'll end in a whimper. Young people don't generally wind up dead in a field without some help."

"Sammie said there was a design on the tooth," Tony commented.

"Yeah," I answered slowly. "That *is* something I'm going to leave out, but I hope it'll make finding the identity easier." I leaned far over the table and borrowed Gail's pad, tearing a back page out of it before giving it back.

"The tooth I found in the tree is the first bicuspid on the right side of the maxilla, or upper jaw, according to Evans. That's the one right beside the canine, heading back toward the molars. And the gold isn't a filling. It's a colored aluminum cap, covering the whole tooth. The design faces outward, it's been crudely scratched onto the cap's surface, like with a knife point or something sharp, and it looks kind of like this."

I held up my quick sketch of a utility pole with two crosstrees stuck into the mathematical symbol for infinity. "Ring a bell with anyone?"

The rest of them either shook their heads or remained silent.

"It looks astrological, but I've never seen it before," Gail said. "I could ask around."

I slid the piece of paper over to her. "Thanks."

Jack Derby removed his tortoiseshell half-glasses and rubbed his eyes, looking like a tired college professor after a long day of reading term papers. He blinked at us blearily before asking, "Why not release the design? Wouldn't that be helpful?"

"Maybe," Tony Brandt admitted. "But not until we figure out its meaning," he added with an ironic smile. "We've had enough surprises already."

"The paper and Ted'll be happy enough without it," I said. "Especially if we make it look like we're being open and co-operative."

The silence greeting that last remark was revealing. We all knew from experience that a distracting cloud of politics, posturing, and publicity would soon be complicating our lives. The truth, and how much and which parts of it were revealed, would become hostage among those who could make the most currency from it—including everyone around this table.

*   *   *

I walked Gail to her car behind the bank building where the SA had his office. The total clearing of the clouds had made the night air so cold it felt brittle, an impression accentuated by the harsh shadows thrown out by the parking lot lights. Gail's car was a shimmering white under a thick layer of sparkling, crystalline snow. It was now almost ten o'clock.

"You didn't want to send those samples to Hillstrom instead of the crime lab?" she asked me.

Beverly Hillstrom was the state Medical Examiner, an old and trusted colleague with the persistence of a bloodhound, and the usual first recipient of any corpse—or parts thereof. "It was her choice. The lab's the only one in Vermont that can do a DNA analysis, and that's what's going to give us the

most exact information. She said she'd drive down to Waterbury and take a look at the samples before they start chop-
ping them up—kill two birds with one stone. I got the distinct
impression neither she nor the lab people were overworked
right now. Our good luck—this would've taken a week or
more otherwise. Now they're saying they'll get back to us in
forty-eight hours."

I took Gail's briefcase while she brushed the snow from her
car door with her mittened hand, and groped for her key in
her purse.

I hefted the bag. "This thing weighs a ton."

She let out a weary sigh as she fitted the key to the door.
"Homework. Between the clerkship, boning up for the exam
this February, and a correspondence bar review course I just
started, I feel like I'm drowning in this crap. Tell you one
thing—if I do pass the bar and get a job, it'll feel like a vacation."

She took the briefcase back from me and tossed it heavily
onto the passenger seat, retrieving a combination brush and
ice-scraper to clear off her front and rear windows. "You coming home now? We could grab a sandwich before I hit the
books."

I shook my head. "Got to talk to the newsboys. It's only an
hour or so before deadline, and I want to make sure we get
our two cents in."

She smiled tiredly. "Some couple. We saw a hell of a lot
more of each other when we lived apart."

I kissed her cheek. "Things'll get better. I'll check in on you
when I get home."

I saw her out of the parking lot before I cut back through
the alleyway to Main Street, and began walking toward the
spire-bristling, one-hundred-year-old, red-brick Municipal
Center where my own office was located.

Despite the arctic cold, it was a beautiful night. The traffic
was all but nonexistent, the snow had softened the harsh con-
tours of the century-old industrial-era downtown, and I knew
from experience that the usual nocturnal criminal activities

would be held in check by the pause that typically followed winter storms.

My own mood didn't match the surrounding peacefulness. The discovery of stray body parts was the obvious cause, but there was more. I had been a cop in Brattleboro for over thirty years, and while a town of twelve thousand people—albeit swelling to over forty thousand during the day—was hardly the crime capital of New England, I'd seen my fair share of uncivilized behavior.

Too much, perhaps. I thought back to Gail's face in the harsh light of the parking lot. "Sexual assault" didn't describe what she'd been through. We'd caught the man responsible, and Gail's recovery had made her psychologists glow with self-satisfaction, but she'd changed in the process. Not intellectually, nor emotionally, nor even sexually, but she was no longer the same person I'd known before the attack. An intense ability to focus had been subtly upgraded to a quasi-obsessive drive. She was fueled by complex passions now— to be the best at her work, to see justice done, to put a stop to what had happened to her. There was a grim determination in her eyes that made me yearn for the untainted enthusiasm of old.

I knew that much of her original nature would return in time. It was still early—not even a year—and she was probably overloading her plate to dull the lingering fears and insecurities. She'd spent the past few months in South Royalton, at the Vermont Law School, taking an intense refresher course in criminal proceedings. The bar exam was a month and a half away, which meant endless hours of hitting the books. And she'd jumped when she'd heard of the six-month clerkship in Derby's office.

On top of her therapy sessions . . . and our moving in together.

I stopped opposite the darkened library and looked back down Main Street stretching out to the south like an abandoned urban canyon, sand-bagged with snowbanks. I'd known Brattleboro all my life, although raised on a farm seventy miles north. It was a vibrant, lively, querulous place—

populated by a life-saving mixture of blue-collar and retired hippie—and I'd seen it survive the economic body blows that had decimated other New England towns. But whether it was my years taking their toll, the price I'd seen Gail pay for who and what she was, or the fact that I'd just spent the afternoon watching a teacher turn the discovery of a few body parts into a learning experience for a child, I was feeling a sense of loss and despair.

I didn't know what had led to that person ending up dead under the snow off Hillcrest Terrace. I wasn't sure I'd ever find out. But I had to make the attempt, to give those few scattered remains a little life after death, so they could speak for themselves.

I realized then what my trouble was—what was making my other sorrows that much sharper. It wasn't so much that someone had died. I didn't have enough details yet to have an opinion on that. It was that he or she had died quite some time ago, and that only a few birds and other scavengers had taken notice of it.

A life, it seemed, should amount to more than that. It was the chance this one hadn't that saddened me the most.

Chapter Three

In general terms, Brattleboro, Vermont, is divided into four distinct sections: the downtown, with its old New England, red-brick heart; the equally aged but wood-built residential neighborhoods radiating to the south, west, and north, with the Connecticut River, and thus the New Hampshire border, forming the eastern boundary; West Brattleboro, once a separate entity, but now a slightly jilted satellite, relegated to the far side of the interstate; and the Putney Road, a strip of low-profile shopping plazas, fast-food joints, supermarkets, gas stations, and businesses, that sliced north through the no-man's-land between Brattleboro and the Dummerston town line.

It was along this latter blighted avenue that I drove to reach the newspaper office before deadline. Regardless of the stoicism we routinely showed in public, both the SA's office and the police were acutely aware of how crucial it was to treat the media as a guarded confidant. Too many times, we'd suffered the price of being close-mouthed and secretive. It was better to share some of what we knew—while downplaying the drama—than to be dogged at every step by a bunch of reporters imagining a major story was being kept just beyond their reach.

Several decades earlier, the Putney Road had been farmland, much of it owned by an old and canny operator named Benjamin Chambers. Less a farmer than an instinctive broker of almost anything salable, Chambers had taken a gamble on where and when Interstate 91's umbilical cord would eventually connect the state to the rest of the country—thereby christening Brattleboro as the "Gateway to Vermont"—and had managed to buy, trade, and some said steal a mosaic of properties lying directly in its path. By the time the federal grand plan became reality in the sixties, old man Chambers was sitting on a pot of gold.

Never had gold looked so unattractive. I was struck as always by the contrast between Brattleboro's northern residential section, which featured some of our oldest, stateliest homes, and where the Putney Road "miracle mile" began. It was like having a McDonald's sharing a wall with a grand Victorian mansion.

On the other hand, Putney Road was also where a great many locals did their shopping or came to work, not only from Brattleboro, but from towns all around. It had helped make Brattleboro a hub community, and its commercial vitality had carried the town through times that had steadily eroded nearby places like Springfield, Vermont, and Greenfield, Massachusetts. In fact—almost emblematically—one of the state's largest employers, a gigantic wholesale groceries supplier, occupied the northernmost end of the road. None of that made the strip any less of an architectural eyesore, but it highlighted the reality that had Brattleboro been only old bricks, elegant homes, and quaint shops, it would have been belly-up years ago.

About midway up the street, however, the dark side of the more-commerce-the-better philosophy loomed into view on my left. Like a missing tooth in a hundred-watt smile, a dark, abandoned building site interrupted the seamless string of fluorescent signs, bright windows, and glowing, snow-covered parking lots.

A proposed fifteen-million-dollar hotel/convention center complex—not as big as the two in far-off Burlington, but the only one of its size in the whole southeast quadrant of Vermont—its developer, Gene Lacaille, had run into financial difficulties and had dropped it, half-built, into his bankers' lap.

It was painful proof that the Putney Road money machine was not a guaranteed thing. As I drove by the lifeless site, still filled with equipment but clotted with untouched snow, I imagined a cluster of high-echelon bankers burning the late-night oil downtown, wondering how in hell to extricate themselves from this one.

I drove on for another half mile, and turned left onto Black Mountain Road. The *Brattleboro Reformer,* where I was scheduled to meet both its editor—Stanley Katz—and his radio rival Ted McDonald, had its low-profile office building tucked away on a small bluff between the shoulder of Interstate 91 and an overpass bridge. I had under forty minutes before they started rolling the presses at eleven.

The parking lot was almost empty. A morning paper, the *Reformer* was only fully staffed during the mid-afternoon overlap period when the nine-to-five workers and the news crew shared the same roof for a few hours. By this time of night, only the hard core remained—the night reporters, an editor or two, the press operators, and the backroom people responsible for getting the product delivered. It was a thin crowd, and sometimes a rowdy one, befitting a bunch whose days ran upside down.

I parked in a poorly plowed visitor's slot and began slogging my way toward the front door, marked by a peeling flagpole and a huge, dead, snow-capped potted plant. The walkway hadn't been shoveled, but compressed by countless footsteps, which had also made it hard, uneven, and slippery. A year ago, the building, if not the product, had been in better shape. A Midwest conglomerate had poured money into the place, hoping to create a *USA Today* of Vermont—with glitzy colors, bite-sized articles, and screaming headlines, jammed into a tabloid-sized paper designed to be read in a subway . . .

Except that the more the old *Reformer* was twisted out of shape, the more subscribers switched over to the more traditional *Rutland Herald*.

Several months ago, the employees, facing either layoffs or bankruptcy, had banded together, rounded up a few local backers and several banks, and had bought the paper. Now it was its old broadsheet self, printed in conservative black-and-white, and operating on a shoestring. Watering plants, painting flagpoles, and even hiring someone to shovel the walk had all fallen under the heading of needless expenses. But an era of crazed flatlander yuppiness had been survived, and I wasn't about to fault the staff's hard-won victory with complaints of a petty broken neck. So I chose my footing carefully and made my way slowly to the front door.

Beyond the double glass doors of what had been a sharp-looking modern building fifteen years earlier, the air in the large, central newsroom was stale and motionless—the ventilation kicking in only intermittently to save money. The rug beneath my feet was soiled and worn, the lighting turned off except where strictly necessary, and the trash cans overflowing for lack of a janitor. The effect suggested a futurist movie where everyone worked in shabby, fluorescent boxes on a planet where everything was dying and energy was at a premium. Supporting the notion, the only people I could see were sitting in a centralized cluster of desks, hunched before computer terminals, their faces bathed in a lifeless, electronic shade of blue.

I watched them in silence for a few seconds, impressed that they had worked so hard for such a seemingly dismal result, and remembered how Katz had once said that newspapering demanded equal parts love and dementia.

As a cop, I had little use for newspeople. I thought they were sloppy, cynical, exploitative, self-righteous, and thin-skinned. But I realized I was probably wrong, since their view of us was as lazy, close-minded, arrogant, and paranoid. Whatever the truth, we were stuck with each other, and had no choice but to cooperate.

A door opened to one of the small conference rooms lining

the far wall, and a thin, pale, exhausted-looking man in a rumpled shirt leaned out and fixed me with dark-rimmed eyes. "Joe. Come on in. Ted's already here."

I crossed the room, aware of several faces looking up from their screens to murmur greetings. I waved back to them collectively and shook Stanley Katz's hand.

"I'd offer you coffee, but we've gone through our nightly allotment. Budget crunch—sorry." He ushered me over the threshold, closing the door behind us.

A small conference table occupied the center of the room, and sitting at its far end was a man as fat as Stanley was thin, placed like a Buddha awaiting an audience. His pudgy hands were wrapped around a Dunkin' Donuts coffee cup, which he raised in salute as I nodded my greetings. "Gotta plan ahead, Joe. These guys don't have a pot to piss in."

"We don't have time to piss, Ted," Katz shot back. "We got to do more than supply five minutes of gossip for every hour of canned music."

But he was smiling as he said this. Having once told me he thought Ted McDonald was a fat slug "woodchuck"—the local pejorative for a dim-witted native-born—he'd also frequently conceded that Ted had integrity—and a network of informers he envied.

I sat opposite them both. "I wanted to let you know what was really going on, since for the past several hours, Ted's been reporting we found a body off Hillcrest Terrace, and that foul play is suspected."

"It's not?" Stan asked. "We have a source that said it is, too."

I rubbed my forehead tiredly. "They're jumping to conclusions. We have a sample of hair recovered from an old, abandoned bird nest, attached to a piece of upper jaw. Most of it's probably human—Waterbury's checking that out—but we don't know who they belong to, how long they've been lying around, or how they got there to start with. So far, there is absolutely no evidence of foul play."

Both men stopped scribbling in the pads they'd each produced. "Jesus, Joe," Ted said first, perhaps stung at the suggestion that he'd hyped up the story. "Isn't it a little unlikely someone went all the way up there to die of natural causes?"

"Maybe," I agreed, "but right now, that's as good a scenario as any. There have been no reports of missing persons, no reports of anything odd going on in the neighborhood, and nothing to indicate violence."

"You going to tear up that field?" Katz asked.

"We have no idea where the rest of the body might be, or even if there is a rest. It might've been taken apart by animals and carried into half a hundred burrows and dens by now. We found the jaw fragment in an old tree, ten feet off the ground. We're going to see what we can find out first by checking with other New England departments and NCIC, and then circulating X rays of the teeth to all surrounding dentists. The State Police crime lab and the ME are working to see what they can get from the little we sent them, and once they do, we'll put that into the system as well. It's a much more effective approach than tearing around with a bunch of snow shovels."

Katz looked up from his notes. "How did you find out about this in the first place?"

"An observant, helpful citizen," I answered blandly.

"Who shall remain nameless," he murmured with a smirk.

"Correct. Off the record?"

They both nodded.

"It was a child. She found the hair in a bird nest near her home—thought we'd be interested."

"Enterprising," Ted said. "Wish I could talk to her."

"I don't doubt it, but she's pretty shy, and a little shook up right now—that's why we're keeping her under wraps, okay?"

They both nodded again. I didn't doubt they'd honor the request.

"You said you found the jaw in a tree," Katz picked up. "How'd you know to look there?"

"We brought in a naturalist as a consultant. She gave us pointers on where scavengers might take their . . . what they found."

Katz smiled at the hesitation. "And she doesn't have a name either."

"She might," I conceded. "I'll call and ask her tomorrow if she wants to be identified."

"What about the bones? What were they? Arms, legs . . . ?"

"Probably human skull fragments, found in a doghouse, which is being thawed right now so we can dig under it to check for more. A generalized canvass will continue tomorrow at first light, to see if we can find anything else."

"I love it," Katz barely whispered, bent over his pad, his need for income-stimulating stories rising to the surface.

"Can you give us a vague idea of what you've got? Male, female, old, young?" Ted asked, sounding a little exasperated, but whether with me or his colleague I couldn't tell.

Again I shook my head, instinctively hedging. "We can't determine that in-house. We're hoping the crime lab can tell us."

Katz was looking skeptical again. "You don't have anything on your books that might fit this? I thought you guys were on the computer to each other all the time, exchanging information."

"We are, but not everybody who disappears goes missing. This might've been a homeless person, or a runaway from some town that's not on the network, or someone from a family that doesn't give a damn. It's not a flawless system."

"You do have a pretty good handle on what's happening locally, though," Ted persisted. "Is the implication that whoever this is, they're from out of town?"

I answered slowly. "That would be an educated guess, but we're covering all bases."

"I love it when they get specific like that," Katz murmured, not bothering to look up. He finished writing and sat back in his chair. "When will the lab be reporting back?"

"Maybe a couple of days."

"So that's it?"

I spread my hands. "For the moment. We'll let you know when we get more."

There was an awkward silence. McDonald was going over his notes, but Katz just sat there, staring at me. The "courts-

'n'-cops" reporter back in the old days when the paper was locally owned by a small New England chain, Katz had honed a reputation of not giving a damn who he antagonized on his way to a story. As a result, although his articles had been more accurate than not, his personality had made the point moot. The police department wouldn't have agreed if he'd written that water was wet.

Times and events had mellowed him—the paper changing hands, his quitting and briefly working for the *Herald,* then being wooed back as editor and discovering what it was like to be responsible for more than a single story. Over the past two years, he'd been battered by boardroom struggles with absentee owners, plagued by a rising turnover rate, and had watched both morale and readership dwindle as the paper had lurched toward bankruptcy. It was then, I knew from my own private sources, that he'd mortgaged his house to become one of the *Reformer's* new owners—as committed now as he'd once been cynically detached.

And yet, the expression he was giving me harked back to long ago, when the assumption was that every word I uttered was a bald-faced lie.

"What's your problem?" I asked him finally.

"No problem. I was just wondering why the personal approach for what could've been put into a press release or a phone call. Makes an old bloodhound curious—like there's more to all this."

My mind turned to the gold tooth with the enigmatic engraving, and the traces of purple hair dye, both indicative of the complex chasm of mutual need and distrust that would forever stretch between us.

I gave him a pitiful look. "We've got as many questions as you do. I just thought you'd like to have what we had before deadline. It's up to you if you want to believe we're sitting on Jimmy Hoffa's corpse."

I stood up as Ted McDonald laughed, dissolving the brief tension. "I'll make sure you're kept up-to-date."

*　　*　　*

The house Gail and I bought last year was on Orchard Street, a winding, wooded, uphill drive north of the main road linking Brattleboro to West Brattleboro. It was an enormous building, with an attached barn, a garage, and a deck out back with an equally gigantic maple tree growing through it. Gail had been a Realtor for twenty years, since dropping out of the commune that had first brought her here, and this house reflected why she'd been so successful. For a childless couple long set in their ways, who had rigorously maintained separate quarters throughout their relationship, this house had all the amenities—his and hers upstairs wings, a large enough kitchen for two people to avoid traffic jams, and lots of space, inside and out, that allowed for either companionship or privacy. The only thing missing—temporarily, I hoped—was the spirit that made a home of a house.

The rape had ended Gail's desire, even her ability, to live alone, and had coincided with my interest to build on our relationship. But shortly after the move, she'd left for law school, and was now so busy hitting the books, I barely saw her. After all that had contributed to our finally moving in together, this work-driven result had left me feeling oddly bereft. I knew my melancholy was largely selfish, and understood the forces that were driving her so hard. I also knew that with time, things would settle down, her confidence would return, and both our lives would be enriched for the changes she was making.

But that didn't stop me from feeling lonely now and then.

I parked in the garage beside the barn, comforted despite these thoughts by simply being here, and crossed the driveway to the house in the bright glare of floodlights triggered by my arrival. Gail had acquired an understandable mania for security, rigging the place with lights, shutters, an alarm system, and deadbolts.

Sadly, even in rural Vermont, this degree of self-protectiveness was looking only slightly ahead of its time. The first stop off the interstate from the overpopulated south, Brattleboro, in many people's opinion, had slid from being gate-way of Vermont to doormat in a scant thirty years. With its uninspiring but steady economy, its generous welfare checks, and its plethora of services for the poor, the town was a nat-ural for those fleeing urban blight. We had seen an alarming growth in homeless people, youth gang members, domestic violence, and petty crime. Also, where just fifteen years ago the police department had dealt with a single murder every few years, not a twelve-month period went by now without at least one homicide and several near misses.

Gail's behavior might have aroused my skepticism once, re-gardless of her reasons. Now it never occurred to me to chal-lenge it.

I used two keys to enter by the kitchen door, and saw that she'd fixed a sandwich on a plate for me, with a note reading, "Come up and visit. Am contemplating suicide."

I peeled back the top slab of whole wheat, unsure of what lay underneath. I recognized fake bacon strips made from soy, and some lettuce and tomato, but there was another item that escaped me. Too hungry to care, I sank my teeth into it and retrieved a Coke from the fridge. Food was not an area where Gail and I shared much common ground. She was a lacto-vegetarian, and I was someone who ate anything that had stopped moving. But since I didn't care in any case, I ended up eating well without having to think about it, while still enjoying the occasional Spam and pickle sandwich.

I balanced the soda can on the plate and walked through the darkened house, drawn by the gentle glow from the stair-well. As I rose into the warmth and light of the second floor, I could hear a man's muffled voice emanating from Gail's clus-ter of rooms at the far end of the hall, beyond our master bedroom.

This was where her choice of homes had been especially inspired. We each had three rooms at either end of the house that we could manage as we wished. She'd turned hers into exercise, meditation, and study areas. I'd made all of mine a Salvation Army warehouse.

I knocked at her office door and entered. Gail was sitting

in a large armchair, her feet up on an ottoman. A portable computer was in her lap, and an instructional video was running on a small TV set placed on a chair before her. A professorial type droned in front of a blackboard, pausing occasionally as the camera cut to a piece of text. Gail was fast asleep.

I hesitated, my hand still on the doorknob, knowing she both needed the rest, and would want to be woken up.

She solved my dilemma by opening one sleepy eye and giving me a small smile. "Caught me."

I tilted my head toward the TV. "Must be the company you keep."

She located the remote by her thigh and froze the professor with his mouth open.

I leaned over and kissed her. "Thanks for the sandwich."

"How did it go at the paper?" she asked, arching her back and stretching her arms high above her.

"All right. Ted was his affable self. Katz thought we weren't giving him all we had."

"Which we weren't."

"Who's your friend?" I asked of the immobilized video.

"That's the bar review course I told you about. I either do it by mail using these things, or attend classes in Burlington or South Royalton. Not much of a choice. It's not that bad—you just caught me at a bad time."

"You going to call it quits?"

She gave a weak laugh. "Fat chance. I think I'll give Mr. Energy here a rest, but I've still got a stack of discoveries to process on the Miller case from Bellows Falls. The defense is already claiming we're stalling."

I bent forward and kissed her again. Her lips parted under mine and her fingers slid up the inside of my leg. My plate still precariously balanced in one hand, I slipped the other under her sweatshirt.

She moaned softly and broke off, her face flushed and her eyes bright. She was pulling at my belt. "I think I've come up with a way to recharge my batteries."

*   *   *

There was a large skylight over our bed, tonight a frost-rimmed window onto a glittering spray of bright, hard stars. It struck me as a meaningful asymmetry—this framed picture of merciless cold, and Gail's warm naked body stretched out on top of mine. I enclosed her in a gentle bear hug, appreciative of how the day had balanced out.

It was the wrong move to have made. Her head rose sleepily from the crook of my neck, and she peered at me through a veil of long brown hair. "Better hit the books."

I knew not to argue. I massaged her shoulders briefly, slid my hands down her back, and let her go. Reluctantly, she slid off me and sat on the edge of the bed, using the moonlight from above to select her clothes from among the trail of entangled pants, shirts, and underwear stretching toward the door.

"What's the plan for tomorrow?" she asked, crossing the room and dressing, piece by piece.

"Resume the canvass and the search, get a preliminary list of all the hairdressers that use permanent purple dye, work the computer in detail—get the groundwork ready for when we hear back from the lab."

She stopped abruptly, halfway into her pants. "Damn, I forgot. I got a lead on that symbol you described. I ran it by a friend of mine who's seriously into astrology and the occult. She said your sketch looked like the symbol for the Church of Satan in San Francisco."

"Great," I murmured dourly.

"Yeah. I thought you'd like that. Supposedly, it appears in something called the *Satanic Bible*. I don't know where you'd get a copy of that, or even if you want to. She said it was a popular symbol among teenagers—a tattoo and graffiti favorite—so your victim may have known nothing about the church."

She sat back down on the bed and pulled on a pair of thick woolen socks before leaning over and giving me one last kiss. "That useful?"

"Could be. I'll let you know next time we pass in the night."

She gave me a dirty laugh. "See you in twenty-four hours then," and she vanished out the door.

Now the skylight merely looked cold, and I gathered the covers around me. No matter how trivial or common that Satanic symbol might be, I knew it meant trouble. As soon as the press and the politicians got hold of it, the heat on this case would increase—along with the troubles we'd have conducting a nice, quiet investigation.

Chapter Four

I have only four people on my detective squad. Last year, the town manager chose to treat the homicide of a fifth member as a form of natural attrition, and didn't replace him. We not only lost a friend and colleague, but got saddled with his workload as well.

Besides Sammie Martens and J. P. Tyler, our forensics man, I had Ron Klesczewski and Willy Kunkle. Ron was young, sensitive, dependable, painfully earnest, and a whiz at keeping paperwork organized and flowing—the man to have as coordinator in the middle of a big case. Originally my second-in-command, he was handicapped by enough self-doubt that he'd finally opted to return to the security of the rank and file.

Willy was the exact opposite: arrogant, insubordinate, willful, and I suspected, physically abusive in the field—although none of his snitches had ever complained and none of us had ever caught him. Willy kept his own hours, only reluctantly attended staff meetings, and made his contempt for most people well known—excluding J.P., whose scientific bent he both respected and depended on. He was, nevertheless, remarkably good at his job. Badly dressed, infrequently shaved, and burdened with a useless, withered left arm—the gift of a sniper years ago—Willy Kunkle lived among the derelicts he occasionally sent to jail. But I trusted what lay underneath his unappealing exterior without reserve. What drove him cut deeper than career, ambition, or even everyday morality. He was fueled by private demons so rooted and complex that I never doubted his steadiness or dependability. I was stuck with Willy for as long as I could stand him.

It was Willy Kunkle I sought out concerning the small bombshell Gail had dropped on me late last night.

The center of the detective squad's main room is a cluster of four modular cubicles, constructed of head-high, interlocking, sound-absorbent panels. Each detective has space enough for a desk, a chair, and maybe a corner in which to pile paperwork—not an environment conducive to loitering. Predictably, that's where I found Kunkle, leaning back in his chair, his feet up on an impressively littered desk, holding a mail-order weapons catalogue open before him.

He gave me an instinctively peevish look, which I ignored.

"You know any Satanists around town?" I asked him, knowing an unusual initial approach was often the best way to catch his interest.

His eyebrows rose. "There are some," he answered with rare caution.

"You ever seen this symbol before?" I showed him the sketch Gail had used in her research.

He frowned slightly. "This the engraving on the tooth?"

Kunkle had not been involved in yesterday's discovery or subsequent neighborhood canvass, and yet it didn't surprise me he knew the details of the case. Knowing everything that was going on inside the department, regardless of how trivial, was second nature to the man, and a telling facet of his personality.

"If you go to the far side of the playground in Crowell Park," he said, "there's a six-foot retaining wall at the top of the drop-off leading down to Beech Street. It's a good hideout in summer—the condoms, syringes, and beer cans tell you that—but one part of the wall has a ton of this shit spray-painted on it—pentangles, upside-down crosses . . . This one, too."

"You know what it means or who put it there?"

He shook his head. "Could've been the town treasurer. We got so many wackos in this town—Buddhists, Hindus, Moslems, who the fuck knows. The Satanists fit right in. You think the bones were some kind of sacrifice?"

I held up both hands. "Down, boy. I'm just looking for a connection. What kind of things do the Satanists do?"

"Depends—they're pretty half-assed, like most people around here. There aren't more than six of 'em anyway. They get together and drink chicken blood or whatever. We found squirrels and shit like that nailed to a front door or two, complete with some weird symbols in chalk. A few cats have disappeared that people claimed were used in rituals. But it's hard to tell what's real from what's paranoia."

"Are there people you could ask? Find out if they've gotten more ambitious all of a sudden?"

He tossed the catalogue onto his desk and sighed. "Jesus—just because of some graffiti on a tooth? Why don't we wait'n see what the lab says? Save me asking a bunch of stupid questions. These people are just dying for a little attention, you know."

His reaction didn't surprise me. "Well—run some names through your head. Think about it for a while. You come up with anything, check it out. Otherwise, we'll wait."

I returned to my office, knowing I'd get what I'd asked for, and probably more. As dismissive as Willy Kunkle worked hard to appear, he was a driven man, compulsively nosy. I knew he would make damn sure he wasn't caught by surprise; he'd have all the names and facts I wanted if and when I needed them. As did many people who'd survived lives of chaos and self-destruction, Willy held dearly to his pride and reputation. That his personality grated on everyone around him was of no consequence—what counted was that he was a cog neither easily overlooked nor replaced.

Still, it was with some relief that I got a phone call from

Beverly Hillstrom a half-hour later, giving me—I hoped—
more than shadowy Satanists to pursue.

Voices over the phone rarely match their owners' appearance, something blind dates discover all too often, but Beverly Hillstrom's brought to mind the exact same tall, patrician
coolness that she presented in person. A slim, blond, immacu-
late middle-aged woman, her diction was grammatical and
precise, her manners distinctly old-world, and her ability to
put veteran cops in their place with little effort legendary.
And yet there was true warmth in her toward those she
trusted and respected, a group of which I was thankfully a
part.

There were proprieties to be faithfully observed, however,
despite a friendship that stretched back years. We never referred to our private lives, never took liberties with social
decorum, and always addressed one another by our respec-
tive titles. With anyone else, I would have dismissed such unstated ground rules as snotty affectations. With Beverly
Hillstrom, I sensed in them a need for order and courtesy, almost a frailty that required nurturing. It was an enigmatic
character trait that allowed me to ponder the personality behind it, and occasionally amuse myself with unfounded wild
images of her life away from the office.

"You sound relieved to hear from me, Lieutenant. Are you
running out of options on this case?"

"You could say that. I just finished telling one of my men to
check out all the local Satanists."

"Ah—the tooth. Is that what that engraving signifies?"

"Supposedly."

"Well, the tooth might be helpful, although perhaps not for
that reason."

"X rays?" I blurted out, instantly regretting that I'd rushed
her.

There was a telling pause at the other end of the line. "No,"
she answered slowly. "X rays have been taken, of course, and
they've revealed a badly decayed, albeit previously treated
tooth. But I can't imagine too many dentists having the time
to compare any X rays we could send them to their patient

inventories of five thousand or so cases each. It would be a near hopeless task.

"What I was referring to was the gold cap itself—which is actually gold-colored aluminum. I've consulted an odontologist colleague of mine up here. She tells me such devices are only rarely used, and then only as temporary stopgaps pending further work."

When Hillstrom had something hot, she tended to drag it out—a touch of vanity I'd come to patiently accept, considering the usually rewarding results.

"They are apparently nicknamed 'tin caps,' " she continued, "and their use has a certain psychological elegance I think you'll find interesting. The X rays have revealed that the tooth was previously filled—extensively—and that the old filling had failed, explaining the return trip to the dentist for the cap. According to my colleague, since the tooth was already so far gone, the dentist probably had two courses of action left to him—he could prepare the tooth for a permanent cap, as is standard, or, if the patient was too short of funds to afford the roughly six-hundred-and-fifty-dollar cost, he could put on a tin cap for one hundred and seventy-five dollars and tell the patient he or she had six months to find the money.

"The trick," and here I could hear the satisfaction in her voice, "is that the tin cap is not only inexpensive, it is also thin-walled, relatively fragile, and not a custom fit. It's available only in a variety of generic sizes, and every dentist has to improve the fit with added cement, which unfortunately does not hold off further eventual decay. Sooner or later, the patient *has* to return to the dentist, if for no other reason than the tooth begins to hurt.

"But the plot thickens—I never thought dentists were so devious. It turns out the aluminum cap is chosen not only for its affordability—about ten dollars each—but because it will only last from six months to a year before the patient eventually bites through it and destroys it. This gives the dentist an even more reliable method of forcing the patient to return for more definitive care."

I searched through the papers on my desk, quickly locating

the close-ups J.P. had given me of the tooth. "So since the cap is aluminum and it hasn't been bitten through," I volunteered, "the implications are that a) we're dealing with a relatively rare dental procedure, and that b) that procedure was done not too long before the victim died."

She rewarded me with soft laughter. "Precisely. I was told that any dentist doing this kind of work would have his patient on a callback list for the next six to twelve months. So if you're lucky, you'll get your identification by asking all those dentists to check not their patient files, but their appointment books."

A sudden doubt checked my own pleasure at hearing this. "But do we know how long the body's been lying around? If it's been years, the appointment book won't be much good."

"Inactive patient files get culled every two years or so, but I was told most dentists keep their appointment books. I wish I could tell you how long these bones have been exposed, and more about the victim in general, but it's too early yet. The information I just gave you was readily available and I wanted to pass it along quickly. Anything else will take more time, I'm afraid, depending on what tests the crime lab conducts. I can't tell you anything definitive about sex, age, or racial origin yet, and I probably never will be able to specify time of death to your liking."

"That's all right. I understand. And I appreciate the tip. We've been thawing the ground where we found those skull fragments. With any luck, we should be able to send you some more pieces soon."

"Everything helps, Lieutenant. Let me know how you fare."

I thanked her again and hung up, gesturing to Harriet through the open door. "Find Ron. I've got a telephone canvass I need him to organize."

*   *   *

North Adams, Massachusetts, lies just below Vermont's southwestern corner. There are several ways of approaching it from Brattleboro, all of them taking a little over an hour, but my favorite—and the one I chose a few hours after my conversation with Beverly Hillstrom—is due west from Greenfield along Route 2, offering a single, spectacular view of North Adams from the crest of the Hoosac mountain range.

It had once been a flourishing factory town, of textiles, I supposed, although I'd never bothered to find out. It lay sprawled at the foot of the mountains, along the winding Hoosic River, like a scattering of toy blocks thrown from the observation platform I always stopped at to appreciate the scenery.

Not that it was an attractive site, even cloaked in a mantle of sun-bleached snow. A jumble of stained, ancient, largely abandoned industrial, brick-clad monsters, enormous even from this distance, the image projected was less aesthetic than one of lasting endurance—a statement of civilization's stubborn willfulness to make its footprints last beyond reason.

I stood on the wooden deck alongside a decrepit souvenir shop, both of which were cantilevered over the edge of the mountain's top, and was once again struck by North Adams's sheer determination. Long deserted by whatever needs had created it in the first place, saddling a road leading to nowhere very important, the place nevertheless hung on, battered and weary, perpetually hopeful. Rumor had it—as rumors often do—that "things were improving." I hoped they were, if only for the faith that had been expended on their behalf.

Since he'd been the one to locate the dentist we were about to visit, Ron Klesczewski was keeping me company. He had saved my life once, several years back, and had stood his ground next to me in a face-to-face shoot-out last year. Yet he remained an enigmatic mixture of timidity and ambition, courage and wariness, intelligence and naïveté. I was becoming used to the idea that while he always looked like he wouldn't make it to the end of the week, he'd probably outlast us all.

The dentist's office was located a few blocks off the main avenue, in a neighborhood—depending on whether the rumors were correct or not—that was either headed for a turnaround, or facing a grim end. It had been the only practice we'd found where a patient had received a tin cap, and yet had never returned for the permanent replacement. According to the receptionist Ron had spoken with, the patient's name had been Shawna Davis, age eighteen, and the tin cap visit had been the only time she'd been in.

We parked next to two other cars in a hand-shoveled lot, and stumbled over ridges of icy debris toward a one-story, flat-roofed, cement building with spidery cracks running along its walls. Inside, the mood was brightened a bit by gentle canned music and the lingering odor of sweet mouthwash. The waiting room was forlornly empty, however, and the hopeful expression of the woman beaming at us from behind a narrow counter wilted as we showed her our identifications.

"You must be the people I spoke to on the phone," she said, her smile lingering as an afterthought. The nameplate on her white cardigan read Alice.

"Yes," Ron admitted. "We're here about Shawna Davis."

"Right." Alice rose from her seat and crossed to the back of her small work area, returning with a thick book. "I checked our patient files to see if she was still there, but we must have dumped her." She sat back down and looked at us apologetically. "We do that pretty regularly. We don't have room to keep them all."

Ron smiled back. "We understand. Were you able to talk to the dentist, to see if he remembered her?"

"I did, but he drew a total blank. He remembered the aluminum cap—they're pretty rare—but he told me he no longer knew if the person he'd put it in was a boy or a girl. You can ask him yourself if you want, but he's going to be tied up for another thirty minutes probably." She dropped her voice conspiratorially. "I wouldn't recommend it anyway. Dr. Williams doesn't have much of a memory."

I motioned toward the thick book. "That the appointment calendar?"

She looked down at it as if it had snuck up on her. "Oh—right." She flipped it open to the correct page, turned it around so we could read its contents, and tapped an entry with her crimson fingernail. "That's her—Davis, S.—that's when she came for the cap."

She placed a Post-it note on the page to mark it, spun the book back around and reopened it at a later page. "And here's where the callback appointment shows up. There's another one a week later, but then we gave up." She handed the book over to us so we could study both pages at leisure.

As Ron returned to the first entry, I asked, "Do you have any memory of her?"

Alice made a face. "Kind of. I've been trying to remember ever since you called, but you know, it's hard. We see a lot of one-timers, and I guess she just didn't stand out much."

I glanced over Ron's shoulder. "What's the date?" I asked him softly.

He ran his finger along the line opposite Davis's name. "November, year before last—about fourteen months ago." He flipped to the next page mark. "And the callback was in May of last year, six months later."

"You have an address on her, maybe in your billing records?"

She sat back, looking embarrassed. "We might, but with records going that far back, Dr. Williams keeps them in storage. That means they're in his attic at home. We're told to say 'storage.' Sounds better."

"You have a phone book?" I asked her.

"Sure." She handed me a medium-sized directory for North Adams and surrounding towns.

Ron read off the number on the callback sheet as I scanned all the entries under "Davis." I finally found a match, predictably near the bottom, next to "Wilma." The address was local.

"Know where this is?" I asked Alice, showing her the listing.

Her face soured. "I should. It took me years to get out of that neighborhood."

*   *   *

Fifteen minutes later, I was sympathizing with Alice's appraisal of her old home ground. The street we were on looked ready to break off from the rest of the town and drift away into oblivion. It was narrow, hemmed in by snowbanks piled between haphazardly abandoned vehicles, and lined with serried ranks of sagging, gray, almost collapsing wooden buildings—remnants of worker housing dating back a hundred years. The few porches still intact were piled deep with snow-covered firewood, the windows were either curtainless, too filthy to see through, or fully boarded over. Occasional wisps of smoke trickling up from a few metal stove pipes were the sole signs of life.

I parked opposite the address we'd found in the phone book. Actually, given the street's condition, I just rolled to a stop and killed the engine. There was no place to park, and no traffic to avoid in any case.

We both left the car and stood soundlessly in the street, staring at the house before us—a patched-together wooden box, single-story, its small windows opaque, a glimpse of tattered blue tarp showing through the snow covering the sway-backed roof. If Shawna Davis had once lived here, it took no great imagination to see why she might have left.

The street was eerily bereft of the usual clatter of civilization. I could hear no dogs, no children, no cars, no voices raised in joy or anger. For all intents and purposes, it seemed like this small portion of hopeful North Adams had missed out on the dream, and simply died.

I motioned toward a narrow, crooked, shoveled trench in the snow, connecting the front door to the street. "Somebody's been at work since the last storm."

We walked cautiously in single file up to the door and listened. I couldn't hear a sound. Suddenly hesitant to make a loud noise in this funereal setting, I finally knocked on the door.

"Who is it?" The question was hostile, immediate, from just

beyond the thin paneling. Its abruptness made us both jump. I noticed Ron unbutton his coat for easier access to his gun.

"Mrs. Davis?" I said to the closed door, "My name is Joe Gunther. We're police officers from Brattleboro, Vermont. We wondered if we could have a few words with you."

"What about?" The voice was cracked and hoarse, as if from underuse.

"Do you have a daughter named Shawna?"

"Maybe."

Ron and I exchanged glances. I chose my words carefully, skirting the truth of our mission. "You're not in any trouble, Mrs. Davis, and neither is Shawna. We're just looking for some information. No harm will come to you."

There was a long pause before the voice came back. "You have a warrant?"

Ron sighed and visibly relaxed. I resisted telling Mrs. Davis that she'd been watching too much TV, and instead used her own preconceptions against her. "We don't need a warrant for a conversation. We can get one, though, if we think you're trying to hide something from us."

The lock snapped angrily and the door swung back to reveal an angular, bitter, pale woman in her thirties with a dirty face and several missing teeth. She was dressed in a pair of tight blue jeans and a red-and-white wool shirt, pulled out to disguise a malnourished, swollen stomach. The hot smell that swept out to greet us made me realize how lucky we'd been to be chatting through a barrier.

"Fucking cops," she said, and turned her back, vanishing into the gloom.

Ron and I tentatively followed, instinctively moving to opposite sides of the door frame once we'd entered. Both of us had spent too many years exploring similar buildings to feel any safety within them.

I narrowed my eyes to see into the darkness, breathing shallowly until I could get used to the stench. I heard the creak of sofa springs as the woman's dim shape folded into a dilapidated couch against the far wall. My vision improving, I saw by the live cigarette in the ashtray by her elbow that she'd been sitting there before our arrival, presumably in the dark, doing nothing.

I didn't bother looking for a seat, not wishing to overexpose myself to my surroundings. "You are Wilma Davis?"

She snorted and then coughed, reaching for the cigarette. "You don't even know that much? This is going to be great."

"And your daughter is Shawna?"

"You already said that."

"She went to the dentist's office under a year and a half ago to have a cap put on one of her teeth. Do you remember that?"

"Sure I do. Figured she couldn't get boyfriends if she didn't have all her teeth. I told her men don't give a fuck about a woman's teeth—not what they look for anyway. Cheaper to have 'em pulled. Cost a goddamn fortune."

She dragged on her cigarette.

I paused, waiting to see if she'd say more, but she'd apparently run dry. I was struck by her lack of curiosity about why we were here. "Why didn't she go back to get the job finished?"

"It was finished enough," she answered disgustedly. "She got the fucking cap. Where did she think the money would come from?"

"You paid for the cap?" I asked.

"Who the hell else was going to? Of course I paid for it."

I thought for a moment, filtering her words from their meaning. Despite the overstated anger, she'd acquiesced to her daughter's desire to get her tooth fixed, and had obviously paid for it at great sacrifice. "You knew it was only a temporary repair—that the tooth would rot unless a permanent cap was put in?"

She crushed the cigarette out as if she wished my eye were beneath it. "I'm no fucking moron. That's what got me so pissed off. I was playing ball with the little jerk. I was going along with the whole deal. I *had* the god*damn* money."

She finished in a snarl, and hurled the dead butt into the darkness of a far corner.

I took a guess. "But by the time the second appointment came around, Shawna was gone."

Instead of answering, Wilma Davis merely dug into her breast pocket for another cigarette, which she lit with trembling fingers.

"Why did she leave, Mrs. Davis?" I asked after a few moments.

Her voice had calmed. "Why do they all leave? I did. Everybody leaves, sooner or later."

"You know where she went?"

"I was the last person she was going to tell. I came home one day, and she was gone. That was it."

"When was that?"

"Late last April . . . What'd she do, anyway? Rob a bank?"

Nine months ago, I thought. I ignored her belated question for the time being, sensing she'd been anticipating the worst from the start. "Did she have any friends we could talk to? Someone she might've kept in touch with?"

She leaned forward in her seat, stabbing the cigarette in my direction, her question already moot in the misery clouding her mind. "I can sure as hell tell you don't have kids. They don't *talk* to you; they don't tell you their friends' names; they don't tell you shit. You look at their faces, looking for the child you knew, and all you see is they hate your guts. They bleed you dry, and then they drop you like shit."

She rose and approached me, still talking as if her rage might stave off the pain we both knew was coming. I heard Ron shift slightly, returning to the defensive. "You want to know who her friends are? Go find them yourself. 'Cause when you do, she'll probably be there, too, doing drugs and getting fucked by men who won't look her in the face. That's what happens to little children, mister. I know. But you can't do anything about it. You can kick and scream all you want, but the more you do, the more they want to leave. You tell 'em the truth—as plain as the shit on your shoe—and they tell you you're full of it."

She had closed the gap between us, her face inches from mine, the cigarette forgotten in her hand. Her breath encircled my head. "You find her, policeman, you tell her I'm dead, just like she is. She won't know what the fuck you're talking about, but she'll find out soon enough."

In the twilight from the greasy windows, I could see the tears in her eyes—the shiny paths they left on her cheeks. "Will you do that? Will you tell her?"

I did look her in the face, and chose not to lie. "We might've already found her, Wilma. And if I'm right, maybe you can bury some of your grief along with her. She's not in pain any longer."

She stared at me in silence for a moment, and then burst out sobbing.

Chapter Five

Gail took a bite of pizza and chewed thoughtfully for a minute. We were sitting at either end of the kitchen's small serving island, late at night, enjoying the novelty of a shared meal, even if it was garnished, I noted wistfully, with vegetables only.

"What did you do then?"

"Asked to see Shawna's room. There wasn't anything useful—no letters or diaries—just posters and stuffed animals and what-have-you. But it was so dark and gloomy . . . and dirty. Tough way to live.

"I thought maybe Wilma's phone records might help—give us a clue of who Shawna was calling her last few weeks at home. 'Course, that was wishful thinking—I suppose I should've been happy she had a phone at all, much less a filing system. I've got Ron pestering the phone company for it instead. We should have something tomorrow. She did have a recent snapshot she let us have."

I paused to eat a slice myself, watching Gail cross the kitchen to refill her glass with milk. It was during small moments like this that I was happiest we'd moved in together.

Despite the crisis that had stimulated the decision, I found myself uncannily comfortable with the end result, wondering why we'd staved it off for so long.

"After that, we went to the local high school," I continued. "Talked to teachers, advisors, administrators—basically anyone who'd known her—and finally we chased down a couple of her old friends. But we didn't get much—she was a loner, a dreamer, someone easily influenced by a smile and a good line. Her grades were lousy, she had zero ambition, her social skills were inept. She was plain and insecure and dying to get away. They all said her relationship with her mother was the pits."

"No ties to Brattleboro?"

I shook my head, and spoke with a full mouth. "No ties anywhere except to her hometown. When we first came up with Shawna's name, we did a complete computer search. Nothing came up. The joke would be if the bones aren't hers at all."

"You see today's paper?" Gail asked after a brief pause.

I gave her a dour look, feeling twinges of familiar dread. "No. What did they do?"

"Nothing bad. They screwed up a little on the details, saying the piece of jaw you found was from the mandible instead of the maxilla, and they pumped up what you found a bit, making it sound like you'd sent a small graveyard of bones to Waterbury, but it was basically okay. They toed the line on the possible cause of death, quoting you that there was no sign of foul play so far, and they kept the little girl's name out of it. Still, it's causing the expected ripple around town."

Given her many political contacts in Brattleboro—she'd served on the board of selectmen for years, among other high-visibility organizations—I knew Gail wasn't referring to local gossip. I also knew she hadn't brought up the newspaper article to make idle conversation. "Who from?"

She shrugged vaguely. "Some of the church groups, the halfway house, a few mental health people—the last two worried their customers'll be hassled by the PD for questioning. And the selectmen . . . I heard the town manager's phone was ringing off the wall with all the official hand-wringing about more violence in our streets."

She turned her attention back to her meal, but I'd caught her meaning. Any political heat was troublesome enough, even as a routine part of the process. The fact that it was building so fast, based on the discovery of a few small bone shards, was unusual. It gave me the queasy feeling there might be something stirring I knew nothing about.

*   *   *

The follow-up story on the "mystery bones" ran on the front page the next morning. I had called Christine Evans— Norah's science teacher—the day before as promised, and she'd been more than happy to talk to Katz and his reporters. A photograph of her appeared beneath the headline, and she was heavily quoted throughout the article, expounding on the habits of scavengers and the aging of bones. I appreciated her keeping Norah's name out of it, but my earlier affection for her was dampened by what I'd since discovered about Shawna Davis. That anyone should benefit from the remains of a girl so neglected in life was an irony I couldn't appreciate.

Except that we still had only circumstantial evidence linking Shawna to our body—an ambiguity we needed to settle.

J. P. Tyler knocked on my open door as I was finishing the paper. "I got a fax from the lab early this morning, and followed it up with a phone call."

I waved him to the plastic guest chair by my desk.

He sat down gingerly, a sheaf of papers clutched in his hand. J.P. was not a "people person"—an inhibition that only worsened when he was faced with someone superior in rank, regardless of how accommodating they tried to be. Still, it made me extremely grateful that while our budget was as anemic as any other department's in town, we could still afford to equip, train, and entertain Tyler enough to keep him with us.

"First off," he began a little ponderously, "most of the bone tissue we sent them was human. What we thought came from animals, did. And the PCR DNA test they ran links the hair to the skull and the teeth. But that's about as definitive as they want to get so far. They *think* the person was a young Caucasian female, but they stress that these are statistically based findings, and have a twenty percent or better chance of being wrong. It might've been better if we'd had more to give them, but even with the other skull fragments we excavated from under the doghouse, it wasn't as much as they would've liked. They favor long bones and the pelvic girdle—that's where most of the aging and sex studies they use for base data have concentrated."

Despite the care and speed the lab had expended on our behalf, I couldn't help feeling a twinge of irritation. I'd put Shawna Davis's face on this cast-off corpse hoping the lab would reward my faith. Now I not only didn't know if I had a bona fide homicide on my hands, I didn't even have a rock-solid identity for the victim.

"What else?" I asked.

He held out half the papers in his hand, all of them long computer-generated printouts with rows of lie-detector-style spikes on each one, accompanied by near-hieroglyphic annotations lining the margins. "These are toxicological analyses of the hair sample. None of them can tell sex or age either, but hair is a good indicator of other things. It grows at a little over a centimeter per month, and retains many of the chemicals ingested by the host."

He leaned forward and began spreading out the sheets, pointing at the various spike patterns. "Some of these are legal drugs—like dextromethorphan—that's found in a cough syrup called Robitussin DM, for example—so we can guess she either had a cold a couple of months before she died, or maybe she took it to get high. Anyhow, there's also some marijuana—at multiple points—and finally," he concluded, extracting a sheet from the bottom, "this: phenobarbital."

"Sleeping pills?"

"Stronger—it's a barbiturate. The longest lasting available. The kicker is that it surfaces right at the root of the hair shaft, implying she was on it at the time of her death, although they tell us to allow a week's margin for error with all this."

"So she committed suicide?"

He shook his head. "I don't think so. The reading indicates a prolonged exposure—like a week or so. Taking a guess, I'd say she was sedated."

My earlier irritation began to fade. "Can you tell if the amount was high enough for that? Maybe she just had a bad week getting to sleep."

Tyler sat back. "I thought of that. Mass spec analyses aren't as refined as urinalyses when it comes to specific amounts, but I checked the *Physician's Desk Reference* for dosage recommendations, and it said that one hundred and twenty milligrams of phenobarbital, three times a day, is the most you'd want to give an adult for sedative purposes. It's true that different bodies metabolize chemicals at different rates and react to varying quantities, but this reading's consistent with that dose—and there're no other indicators along the hair shaft showing prior phenobarbital use. Had there been, it might have explained a growing tolerance for the stuff, and a consequent need for more of it. The hair goes back almost twenty months, by the way."

"But there's no way to say the phenobarbital killed her?"

Tyler shook his head.

"You said earlier the hair had been dyed. You get anything back on that?"

He showed me another printout. "I gave the information to Sammie earlier. She's checking on it now. The infrared analysis pegs the dye to only two manufacturers. If we're lucky, we'll be able to eliminate the hairdressers that don't use this color, and maybe a few others that don't use these brands, and end up with somebody who remembers her." He glanced hopefully at Shawna's photograph I had taped to the wall before me. "One thing that might help is that the hair grew one and a half centimeters after the dye was applied, or about six weeks before she died."

Through my open door, I saw Ron arrive at his desk. "Got the phone records," he said when he saw me.

I beckoned to him, asking Tyler, "That it?"

Tyler nodded and rose. Ron noticed the printouts in his hand. "You get any DNA?"

Tyler looked at him curiously, and then riffled through his collection. "Yeah—somewhere here."

Ron explained his interest. "I was thinking that if we could get any DNA from the bones or teeth, we might be able to match it to Shawna's PKU test on file in Massachusetts."

I stared at him blankly.

But Tyler lit up. "Right. Every child born is supposed to have a PKU test. Stands for phenylketonuria—it's done to check for mental retardation. And the blood sample is usually kept on record at the State Health Department. It's just an identification card with a small dot on it, but it would be enough for us." With rare exuberance, he patted Ron on the shoulder. "I'll get right on it."

Ron watched him leave, a small smile on his face.

"How'd you think of that?" I asked him.

The smile broadened. "I'm a new papa, remember? We just went through all that. Kind of stuck in my mind—all those vital records."

Spoken like a true information nut, I thought gratefully, hopeful again that the identity issue could be settled. "You get a chance to look at those phone records?"

The smile slipped away. "Yeah—nothing to Brattleboro. For that matter, there weren't many long-distance calls at all."

"Okay. It was worth a shot. If you get any spare time, you might want to check the other numbers anyhow. Is Willy around?"

"I saw him talking to one of the patrol guys in the parking lot. Don't know if he was coming or going."

It turned out Willy was going, but I jogged outside and caught up with him just as he was starting his engine. He rolled down his window, scowling. "What?"

"You talk to any of your Satanist contacts?"

His look turned to disgust. "If I'd found anything, I would've told you. Besides, you only told me to think about it."

"And then you went poking around."

"Fuck you." Willy didn't like admitting defeat.

"What did you find out?"

"They're all a bunch of thin-skinned assholes. What I got was a lot of holier-than-you, alternate lifestyle bullshit. As far as I could tell, nobody's contacted them to join up recently, and they haven't been out recruiting. And it doesn't look like they've been butchering virgins lately, either. Can I go now?"

I stood back and let him slither out of the parking lot, his tires spinning on the hard-packed snow.

I didn't share his obvious disappointment. Considering the little we had to work with, and the short time we'd been on the case, we were actually making pretty good headway. That satisfaction, however, was purely professional in nature. Emotionally, I was facing a darker picture. Tyler's report, even with his scientific qualifiers, made it ever more likely that Shawna Davis's death was a homicide.

Chapter Six

Sammie Martens was waiting for me impatiently in the squad room when I returned from the parking lot. "I found the hairdresser who might've dyed Shawna's hair," she said.

"Okay. Let me get my coat." I took a thick, quilted Navy pea jacket from its peg, and slipped Shawna's photograph into my pocket.

Sammie drove us to the south side of town, to Canal Street. An extension of Main, Canal began at one of the town's most confusing intersections. Two parking lots and four roads emptied into this crossroads, which was further boxed in by several large buildings and the bridge over the Whetstone Brook—the town's most significant geographical division.

A hundred and fifty years ago, the Whetstone had been a major power source for a string of grist and saw mills stretching miles away to the west—one of the primary reasons West Brattleboro had started life as the dominant of the two towns. Now, the brook was a social boundary, separating Brattleboro's patrician north side from its more low-brow, commercialized southern half. Whenever we were called for domestic disturbances or alcoholically lubricated brawls, we most often headed south.

The irony was that much of Brattleboro's vitality also resided on this side of the water. The high school, the park, and the old warehouses of the Estey Organ Works—once the world's foremost provider of parlor organs—were all here, along with one of our largest grocery stores, most of the garages, the hospital, and half the town's fast-food outlets. In fact, before the Putney Road was metamorphosed into a "miracle mile," Canal Street, along with lower Main, had ruled the commercial roost.

But it had since acquired a tired, weather-beaten look, especially when compared to the Putney Road's shiny glitz. The interspersing of decaying, multifamily residences, while giving Canal a more human feel, also injected an element of marginal despair. And because it was boxed in by the old wooden reminders of a past long gone, Canal had nowhere to go, while the Putney Road was former farmland, and had acre upon acre left to heedlessly invade.

As a result, Canal was where a business went that either had marginal financing, or hoped to cater to a largely poor-to-working-class population. It was also the home of Clipper Academy—a launching pad for aspiring hairdressers, and a place to go for a very cheap cut, assuming you had low expectations and a flair for spontaneity.

The manager, wearing a miniskirt and tottering on skyscraper spikes, greeted us at the door from under multihued eyebrows and a glistening, curly mass of black hair. She spoke loudly to be heard over the intermittent shrieking of air wrenches from the garage beyond a shared cinder block wall. "Good morning. May we help you?"

Sammie, whom I'd never seen in makeup, nor wearing anything besides pants, practical shoes, and a short haircut, appeared speechless. I gave our hostess a discreet look at my badge. "I hope so. We're from the police department, and we're trying to trace the whereabouts of a client of yours." I showed her Shawna's picture.

She looked at it carefully, holding it with stiffened fingers so her two-inch nails wouldn't get in the way. "It's a terrible cut."

"Does she look familiar?" Sammie asked.

"No. When did she come here?"

"We're not sure," I answered. "It might've been a year ago—maybe six months."

She shook her head, still looking at the picture. "We get so many people, and most of them for just one visit. You don't have a name?"

"Maybe. Does Shawna Davis ring a bell?"

Her face lit up and she returned the photograph. "Well gosh, that makes it much easier. We keep a record of everyone who comes in, along with the student that did the work—it's part of our teaching program."

While she was talking, she circled around to the back of a curved counter and retrieved a fat book much like the dentist's from the day before. "That's last year's." She got out a second one and laid it on top of the first. "And that's the year before." She opened the top one to a sample page. "They're basically appointment books—day by day. You look under this column here, on each page, for the client names. Some of this other stuff is coded, so when you find who you're after, I can translate for you."

She gave both a bright, toothy, lipstick-smeared smile. "Okay? I gotta get back to work before someone gets a crew cut by mistake."

Sammie and I both watched her totter away between rows of mismatching barber chairs, most of which were manned by young, nervous neophytes holding scissors with expressions of wonder and apprehension. It made me happy I'd been cutting my own hair for decades, even if the end result was what Gail called a "prison 'do."

We each took a book and began leafing through its contents, pausing occasionally at some nearly indecipherable scrawl, our eyes preconditioned for anything approaching "Davis."

About a half hour later, I found it, clearly written, along with the date—April 23rd of the previous year. I showed the entry to Sammie. "If J.P. was right about her dying a month and a half after she got her hair colored, that would put her death into June. When did Norah say her chickadees built their nest?"

"Early July."

I caught the eye of the manager, far to the back of the salon, and beckoned to her. "Last June was hotter'n hell. By July, a corpse left in the sun would have decomposed enough for hair to slough off. Ron's PKU test, if he finds it, will make it official, but Shawna looks pretty good as our victim."

The manager approached us, still beaming. "Find what you were after?"

I pointed out the entry. "Yes, thank you. You said you could tell us what all these numbers mean."

"Right. This is the code for the procedure—a cut and dye—purple and orange. The cut was half shave, and half left long—very popular. Let's see, the hairdresser was . . . Hang on a second." She went back behind the counter and retrieved another ledger. After a minute spent flipping through its pages, she announced, her voice flattening, "Susan Lucey."

I broke into a smile. "You're kidding. Is her address still Prospect Street?"

She looked at me with eyes wide, confirming I had the right Susan Lucey. "You *know* her?"

I laughed. "Yeah. I take it she hasn't changed much over the years."

The manager suddenly became guarded. "I don't know. She didn't do too well with us. And she lives on Washington now." She handed me the book so I could read the address.

I shook her hand. "Not to worry. Thanks for your help."

"She's a hooker, isn't she?" Sammie asked me as we crossed the sidewalk to the car.

I caught the disapproval in her voice. In her way, Sammie was quite old-fashioned, and prostitution was one of the things she utterly condemned. But the older I became, the less judgmental I felt—there are a lot of prostitutes out there, after all, and only a few of them are women selling their bodies for sex.

Plus, I genuinely liked Susan Lucey. She'd been a big help to me on a case years before—at personal risk to herself, as it turned out—and I'd never forgotten the favor. And she had spirit—plying her trade in Brattleboro, Vermont, was not the sign of an overachiever, but she carried herself with a pride I respected. As the saying had it, "She walked like she was going places, and looked like she'd been there."

I was struck by the change of address. Prospect Street, where she'd previously lived, followed the crest of a bluff overlooking Canal and most of the town, like a sentry's high catwalk. A few years back, as with the neighborhood behind it, Prospect had been much the worse for wear—a neglected offshoot of a more boisterous commercial age, and now an example of society's frayed edge.

But times had improved, and with them Prospect Street's fortunes. While still no yuppie enclave, it was looking much better. It saddened me to know that Susan had not been able to keep pace, and had instead been forced back—a single, significant block—to the kind of environment where she seemed fated to spend her whole life. Not that Washington Street was a ghetto—it even sported some very handsome, well-maintained houses. But it was also a harbor of endless economic struggle, where a single bad year could mean the loss of a home. Cheek-to-cheek with those occasional gingerbread showpieces were tired, old, patched-together multi-tenant dwellings that stood like reminders of a very thin margin.

Without specifically knowing the address we'd just been given, my gut told me which of the two above options it was going to be.

Sadly, my fears were confirmed. We pulled up opposite one of the dreary, gray-sided triple-deckers, so common to New England factory towns, that looked like the landlord would soon be choosing between a whole new foundation, or complete demolition.

I left Sammie in the car. I had no desire to rub her nose in something she didn't like, nor in subjecting Susan to a scrutiny she didn't deserve.

The manager's ledger had indicated the top floor, so I circled the building, stepping carefully through snowdrifts littered with hidden trash, until I got to the exterior staircase running up the back wall. Switchback on switchback, balcony to balcony—one of which was festooned with frozen laundry—I climbed to the third-floor apartment. There I found a blank door, curtained windows, and an empty porch. The pleasure I'd first felt at hearing Susan's name had by now been corroded by gloom.

I knocked on the door several times before I heard a shuffle of feet, and the sound of something being jarred, as if bumped into. By the time the door swung back several inches, I was braced for the worst.

"Hi Susan, it's Joe."

"No shit. Blind I'm not."

I couldn't see much through the narrow opening, but what little there was didn't look good. Her eyes were bloodshot, her face drawn and tinged yellow, her hair flat and oily. "Can I come in?"

"What for? Can't be a social call, right?"

I suppressed the polite lie forming in my brain. "No."

She looked at me without expression for a few seconds, and then vanished from sight, leaving the door ajar. I pushed it open, stepped inside and closed it behind me. Susan was moving slowly away, heading for a well-used armchair that she sank into with a tired sigh. The girl who'd once walked like she was going places was gone, leaving a giant void behind.

I sat opposite her in a straight-backed chair, my elbows on my knees, and looked at her more carefully. She was thinner than in the old days, when she'd been a compact fireplug of a woman, full of sexual vitality. Her skin now hung on her loosely. At most, she was in her mid-thirties, but she was looking fifteen years older.

"Like what you see?" she asked bitterly.

"I always have, but you don't look healthy. You okay?"

"I don't have AIDS, if that's what you mean."

"I'm glad to hear it. It wasn't what I meant."

She sighed again, and rubbed her forehead. "I'd forgotten what a Boy Scout you are. What do you want?"

"Information, but only after you tell me what's been going on."

"I'm a tired old fuck. What'd you think? I sleep, I eat, I get laid, I have a drink every once in a while. Life goes on—takes its toll—the johns drop off—money's tight. You figure it out."

"You've tried other jobs," I said, telling her I knew at least that much.

She smiled wistfully. "Yeah. Can't seem to concentrate. And I don't like the bullshit. Never liked taking orders. I quit a lot."

"And drink?"

A murmur of the old gleam returned to her eyes. "A lot."

"You doing anything about it?"

"No."

"You want to?"

She stretched in her seat—arching her back like an old cat. She closed her eyes briefly. "Who wouldn't want to change this?"

It was an ambition I thought Wilma Davis had probably lost long ago. "I can help."

She looked at me. "How? Get me into AA? Tried it. Don't like all the God stuff."

"Doesn't have to be AA. I was thinking more of a one-on-one arrangement. Have someone come by to talk with you— figure out a game plan." I cut off her darkening scowl by adding, "You don't have to do anything about it. Just listen and see if it sounds right."

"I let 'em in the door, I can't get rid of 'em."

I rose, bent forward, and kissed her lightly on the cheek. She didn't smell like roses, but interrupting her train of thought seemed worth it.

Her head straightened and her eyes fully focused for the first time. "What was that? You want to get laid?"

I laughed. "No, but I carry a mental snapshot of you in my mind—since the first time we met."

She frowned for a moment, thinking back, and then smiled. "I flash you?"

"You did. It was a sore temptation."

"I remember. You brought me a coffeemaker after that asshole beat me up." She paused. "I offered you a freebie . . . Boy Scout."

She looked off into the distance for a while. I kept quiet, letting her memories fill her mind—I hoped for the better.

Finally, she brought her attention back to me, laying her hands flat against the front of her bathrobe. "Okay, send me your head shrinker. I'll talk to her . . . She better be good, though."

"Thanks."

Without moving a muscle, she seemed to gather herself together then. "What did you want to talk to me about?"

I pulled out the photograph Wilma Davis had given me and showed it to her. "When you were at Clipper's, you worked on this girl—orange and purple dye job, shaved one side, left the other side long."

She studied the picture carefully. "Yeah—Shawna."

I raised my eyebrows in surprise. "That was a long time ago."

"She was special. I wouldn't forget her. We talked. It was like seeing myself, a lot of years ago. The backgrounds weren't exactly the same—but I knew where she was headed." She waved the picture in her hand. "I guess I was right, huh?"

" 'Fraid so."

"Jesus. I didn't even give her a decent cut. How'd she end up?"

I doubted Susan had seen a newspaper or listened to the news in months. "We're not sure. We only found the remains. What made you think she was in trouble?"

She shook her head. "A lamb to slaughter. You know the type."

"But nothing specific?"

A crease appeared between her eyes. "For Christ's sake,

Joe, what do I know? We talked. We never met again. End of story."

"She didn't mention anyone by name?" I persisted. "Where she was living? Who she was seeing?"

She surprised me again. "Mother Gert's—at least we talked about it."

Mother Gert's was the street name given to the William Stanchion Home, a privately funded shelter for the temporarily homeless. "She was staying there?"

"Either staying there or planning to. I might've told her about it—I don't remember. I cut her hair, said a few things, and she unloaded on me like I was a bartender. She talked about where she grew up, her mom, her friends. She was on her own, blowing her last bucks on me, changing her look. 'Course, even there, I screwed her up—not that she complained. She even tipped me."

"But she didn't refer to anyone local?"

She rolled her eyes. "No—nobody local—least nobody I remember. I think that's why Gert's came up."

I stood up. "Okay, Susan. I appreciate it."

I hesitated, about to give her shoulder a squeeze. From that angle, she looked diminished again, like someone dropped from an enormous height.

But she stopped me cold, reading me like an old pro. "Don't push your luck. I'll see whoever you send over, but it could be I'll just throw her out. Make sure they know that."

I nodded and crossed to the door. "I will. Take care of yourself."

"Yeah."

*   *   *

Gert was Gertrude Simmons, a lapsed Catholic nun who had owned and operated her oddly named shelter since the sixties. William Stanchion, she'd once told me, had been an early financial backer—one of the few people from her previous life that hadn't scorned her after she'd left the Church. As far as she knew, he'd never been to New England, much less Brattleboro, but to this day, her feelings for him made her the only person never to refer to the William Stanchion Home as Mother Gert's.

The building was a statuesque Greek Revival mansion on Western Avenue, the heavily traveled umbilical cord tying Brattleboro to West Brattleboro, but the house was set up and away from the road on a tree-lined embankment that offered a sense of privacy and retreat. Sammie and I drove directly there from Susan's in silence—I lost in thought, and Sammie having the sensitivity to leave me there.

The official entrance was to the back, where the original home had no doubt once received horse-drawn deliveries. The trade-off for the building's survival beyond those days had been the carving up of its once splendid but impractical interior into a rabbit warren of offices, dorm rooms, and meeting areas—all of which had doomed the grandiose official entrance hall. It was a sacrifice part of me mourned every time I visited and saw, either hidden under the paintwork or almost covered by later remodeling, a glimpse of the original hardwood, high-ceilinged, stained-glass splendor.

It was not a subject I ever broached with Gert, however. A short, no-nonsense pragmatist, who nevertheless gave both of us the customary hug she offered all comers, Gertrude Simmons was not one to pine over past glories. If queried, I had no doubt she would have acerbically reminded me how the first owners of this house had probably treated those they'd deemed their social inferiors.

She led us into an office the size of a small bathroom, and offered us the one guest chair, which I forced a reluctant Sammie to take. I closed the door behind us and leaned against its frame.

"Two of you," Gert said, perching on an ancient tilt-back that caused her feet to swing free of the floor. "This must be big."

"Actually," I answered, "we're not sure what we're chasing."

"Except that it led you here."

"Maybe." I pulled the picture from my pocket again and gave it to her. "Ring a bell?"

She looked at it and handed it back, poker-faced. "Why?"

The response was typical and expected. Maintaining the confidentiality of her many skittish guests had become one of the cornerstones of her success in this business—something they'd learned to believe in, and we'd learned to respect.

"No strings, Gert. You hear about the bits of skeleton we found? We think it's her."

Her expression saddened, and her response was disappointing. "I'm sorry, then. It doesn't ring a bell. Do you have a name?"

"Shawna Davis," Sammie said.

Gert climbed out of her chair and moved me over so she could get into a filing cabinet by the door. "Do you have any idea when she might have been here?"

Again, it was Sammie who answered. "April or May of last year, give or take."

"Close enough," Gert said, half to herself, and riffled through a tightly packed wad of files, eventually pulling one free from near the back. She brought it with her to her seat and opened it there, where I couldn't see over her shoulder.

After a minute of silently reading, she looked up. "Shawna Davis. Stayed one night only—April twenty-third."

So it looked like Susan Lucey had been the one who suggested Mother Gert's. "Can you tell us anything about her?" I asked.

She closed the file. "What do you think happened?"

It wasn't a question I normally answered from someone outside law enforcement—we, too, liked our secrets. With Gert, however, I didn't hesitate. "She might've taken an overdose of sleeping medicine, but I'm starting to think she was murdered. I don't have anything concrete to base that on, though."

"Are you looking at anyone in particular?"

"We're not looking at anyone period," Sammie answered. "This thing's heading nowhere unless you can give us something."

Gert looked at her sympathetically, and gestured with the folder in her hand. "This contains what we call an 'entrance sheet,' which everyone is asked to complete. It lists things like name, age, address, family, and all the rest, but it's voluntary, and she only gave us the first two. It also has an evaluation form that one of our volunteer counselors fills out if he or she is allowed to by the client. Without actually showing you that form, I can tell you it also contains very little. Apparently, Shawna Davis wanted a place to spend the night, and nothing more."

I tried one last time. "Is there a mention of anyone local, a local address?"

Again, Gert shook her head. "I'm sorry, Joe. As far as we know, she came from nowhere and then disappeared."

*   *   *

I was sitting in Tony Brandt's office, along with the State's Attorney and Gail. Gail's presence surprised me—traditionally, six-month clerks were kept shoveling paperwork. Jack Derby including her was either a sign he liked her, or—more likely to my cynical mind—that as a neophyte SA, he was using her connection to the police department to help smooth his initial contacts with us. Whatever the reason, I wasn't complaining. The novelty of having her in my professional life was very appealing.

The conversation, however, was not cheerful.

"So what you got is slightly less than zero," Derby was saying. "A few bones, an identification, and no idea if she was murdered or not. I liked the earlier bum-who-died-of-old-age scenario better."

"We've got that now, too," Gail murmured, making me wonder what she was alluding to.

Derby ignored her. "What happens now?" he asked Brandt and me. "We better come up with something to tell the newspeople. They're developing an appetite."

Tony Brandt leaned back in his chair. "Why not give them everything we've done so far? They can write about it till they're blue in the face, and we might get something from the publicity. We can tell them about Ron going down to Massachusetts to find Shawna's PKU blood sample, and the lab making a definite match. Might put a slightly better light on it."

"Should we include the etching on the tooth this time?" Gail asked.

There was a noticeable hesitation in the room. "I don't think so," Tony said. "I still want to keep that in reserve, along with the phenobarbital. We're working this as a homicide, even if we can't prove it yet."

Derby nodded in agreement. "You want to use one of those 'Have you seen this woman?' approaches, with a phone number in the caption?"

I glanced at Gail. "If rumors are true that the selectmen are already leaning on us, wouldn't that just turn up the heat? The *Reformer*'s been handling it like an interesting, low-profile mystery."

"The rumors *are* true," Tony answered. "Which is partly the problem. Between the politicians and the bean counters bitching about overtime, we need some kind of a jump start." He looked at me closely. "Unless you've got some other suggestion."

Reluctantly, I could only shake my head.

He rose to his feet. "All right, then. Set it up, Joe."

The tone of Tony's voice made it clear the debate was over. I saw his point, and knew that what Derby had suggested had worked in the past. Shawna's fate had become personal to me by now, precisely because no one had paid it much attention when it counted. I felt badly that my best intentions alone hadn't been enough to reveal what had happened to her.

But such quandaries were a luxury. It was Shawna's death I had to deal with, not the wreckage of her life, and to solve it I would need all the help I could get.

Chapter Seven

Ron Klesczewski found me in my office after hours, catching up on paperwork. "Still at it?" he asked, pausing on the threshold.

I glanced at my watch. It was past nine. "You, too?"

"Yeah. I decided to check out those five long-distance phone numbers on Wilma's phone bill."

"Get lucky?"

A slow smile spread across his face. His dropping by was no casual happenstance. "Could be. One of two calls to Greenfield was to a kid named Hugh Savage. He was a grade ahead of Shawna in school, but dropped out his senior year—got another girl pregnant and had to get a job. Apparently he and Shawna were friends—'fellow outsiders,' according to him. He says she called him out of the blue last year and told him she was going nuts and had to get out of North Adams. She and her mother were at each other's throats."

"What was the date of the call?"

His smile broadened. "April twenty-first."

The month her mother told us she'd left home. "Have a seat."

Ron settled in and stretched his legs out. "Apparently, she angled to move in with him and his family at first, but he told her that wouldn't work. He suggested Bratt. After he moved to Greenfield, he and his wife used to come up here for the live music at the Mole's Eye."

"Did he have any friends up here?"

"One—Pascal Redding, nicknamed Patty. He's supposed to be a musician. Savage told Shawna to look him up."

"You talk to him yet?" I asked.

He frowned. "No. I only talked to Savage a half hour ago. Since then, I've checked every source I can think of, but I can't find Pascal Redding anywhere. The town clerk might have something, but that's a dead end till morning . . . Too bad about that newspaper story coming out tomorrow—I'd like to creep up on this guy."

I reached for the phone, reminded of my own discomfort at having Shawna's picture hung below the next day's headlines. "Don't rub it in."

Gail answered on the first ring. She, too, was still at work.

"How about a five-minute break? Ron and I are playing detective."

She laughed tiredly. "What d'you have in mind?"

"We're trying to locate a musician named Pascal Redding, nicknamed Patty. He doesn't show up in any directories, but he's supposed to be living in town—at least he was. You think any of your artsy crowd might know about him?"

"What kind of music does he play?"

I pushed the speakerphone button and repeated Gail's question for Ron.

"Jazz guitar," he answered.

"That ought to narrow it down. You think he's a guest at someone's house?"

I hadn't thought of that, but it sounded likely. "Could be."

"Try Linda Feinstein. She and her husband put people up sometimes, and they're up to their necks in that world. When do you think you'll be home? I need my daily squeeze."

I killed the speaker as Ron retreated from my office, laughing. "I don't know. I was shooting for ten, but if we get a fix on this Patty character, I might try to check it out tonight."

I could hear the disappointment in her voice. "Okay. I'll keep a light on."

"Thanks. Don't work too hard." I was leaning forward in my chair, about to hang up, when I suddenly stopped. "Hold it. You mentioned something this afternoon in Tony's office I wanted to ask you about—something about a bum who died of old age?"

"They found him last night, under Whetstone bridge. You didn't hear about that?"

"Nobody told me," I answered, slightly annoyed.

"One of your sergeants checked it out. Carol Green signed off on it once the Assistant ME declared it a natural death."

Carol Green was one of Derby's Deputy SAs—the same position Gail was hoping to land after passing the bar. What Gail had just described was mundane enough—most natural deaths were similarly and expeditiously handled. But I was embarrassed by my own ignorance. I hadn't been reading the dailies filed by each patrol shift lately.

"What did he die of?"

Despite her earlier relief at being interrupted at work, I could sense a faint impatience in Gail's response now, exacerbating my own discomfort. "I don't know, Joe, and I didn't get his name. I guess it was a heart attack, or cirrhosis of the liver."

I got the message. "Okay. I'll let you go. Thanks for Linda's name."

I called Ron back in and dialed Linda Feinstein's number, reactivating the speakerphone.

The hesitation in Linda's voice when I asked about Patty Redding told me more than her carefully worded response. "We haven't seen Patty for a while. I think he needed some time to himself."

"You threw him out?" I guessed.

There was a telling change of tone. "We had a disagreement."

I tried a more oblique approach. "Look, I won't tell you my

interest in Patty isn't official, but I want to be straight with you, too. We talk to lots of people in our work. What they tell us is always received in the strictest confidence."

I could hear her sigh. "Okay. We did let Patty stay here for a while. That's something Patty does—live off other people. But we'd done the same favor for other musicians and artists in the past. It used to be our way of saying thank you."

"I take it Patty overstayed his welcome," I prompted, noting that she'd put the entire practice of housing guests in the past tense.

"You could say that. Richard—my husband—went on a business trip several months ago, leaving Patty and me alone in the house. Patty tried to get a little friendlier than I felt comfortable with."

The hairs rose on the back of my neck. I sensed Ron watching me carefully. "Did he assault you?"

"No. It never got that far. But he visited me in my bedroom after I'd gone to sleep. He didn't . . . do anything . . . But it took a while to get him out of there. I called my husband in New Jersey—I was pretty upset—and Richard drove back that night. We asked Patty to leave the next morning. Telling you now, I feel pretty stupid. This won't get Patty into trouble, will it?"

I almost winced at her concern. "Don't worry about him, Linda, and don't ever apologize about some guy coming on to you. It's against the law if they don't stop immediately. To be honest, you ought to press charges—it could stop him from putting other women in your position."

Her reaction was immediate, and sadly predictable. "Oh no. I mean, I did lead him on a bit—I let him make me dinner—and no harm was done. He is a wonderful musician, Joe. He's just got some growing up to do. I'm sure he doesn't make a practice of this."

I bit back the urge to challenge her on that. Neither of us needed me haranguing her over the phone, making her ever more defensive. Instead, I would ask Gail to talk with her soon. I doubted Linda Feinstein had stopped having people stay over because of a small misunderstanding—maybe Gail could get her to admit what actually happened. "All right, Linda. Do you know where he went after he left your place?"

"I know he's still in town. I heard a rumor he's staying with Francis Bertin, the pianist, but I don't know for sure. I wish I could be more helpful . . ."

"Don't worry about it. You've been a big help. And remember, any trouble Patty might be in is of his own making. You did nothing wrong."

"Thank you," she said, obviously eager to get off the line.

"Thank *you,* Linda," I said, but the phone was already dead.

I sat back in my chair and looked at Ron.

"Want me to call Bertin?" he asked softly.

I hesitated, weighing my options. Rationally, his suggestion was sound. It made little sense to drive to Bertin's house late at night, on the off chance Patty Redding was still there, just to ask him if he'd ever met Shawna Davis.

On the other hand, I wanted to meet this clown face-to-face, if only to introduce myself. I got up and killed the lights. "Let's make it a personal visit. Check the computer first to see if Redding's on file anywhere. I'll meet you in the parking lot."

*   *   *

Brattleboro is a distinctly topographical town. Sprinkled over a cluster of hills, ravines, and streambeds, it impresses first-time visitors not with sweeping vistas—it keeps its back to a panoramic view of the Connecticut River and Wantastiquet Mountain—but with the ability of some of its inhabitants to perch their houses in defiance of gravity. Homes and businesses alike cling to hillsides, hover over waterways, and otherwise stack themselves in any nook and cranny available, frequently with a view of the top of their neighbor's roof.

Francis Bertin's address was a perfect case in point. Located on a steep, narrow track named Elliot Terrace, in the heart of town, it had all the accessibility of a Himalayan hut. Furthermore, it was crowded by others just like it—turn-of-the-century, New England–style dwellings that looked as if they'd been dropped from a plane.

Ron nosed the car carefully down the hill, steep enough in parts to make us both wonder if the tires would hold on the compacted, slippery snow. He finally parked to the side of the road, his bumper inches away from a sturdy-looking tree trunk.

"Which house is it?" I asked.

He pointed to a three-story multi-dwelling across the street. "Third floor. Lights are on."

"The computer tell you anything?"

"Yeah. Redding's been slapped for possession twice—both times marijuana; both times minimal amounts. They were party busts—not residential. I think we can assume the guy likes his dope."

We stepped out into the frigid night air, hearing the snow squeak under our feet—as good a sign as any thermometer of sub-zero-degree weather. The sounds of the surrounding town were as sharp as the icicles hanging from the branches, which clicked softly against one another in the barely perceptible breeze.

Access to the third-floor apartment was by an exterior, walled-in staircase, carpeted and warmed by the building to which it was attached. We both stepped quietly, inbred instinct dictating wariness. Also, given Linda Feinstein's admission, I was not inclined to give any advance warning to a man I already disliked. As much as she'd downplayed her story, I knew Redding must have scared the hell out of her. There wasn't much legally I could do about that, but I was perfectly willing to make him sweat.

Guitar music filtered through the top apartment's door, obviously from a recording. We positioned ourselves to either side of the landing as I knocked.

The music was turned down, and moments later the door opened to reveal a thin young man with long hair and a wispy beard, a joint dangling from his lips. The rich, pungent odor of marijuana wafted out from behind him, embracing us all. "Patty Redding?" I asked.

"Yeah. Who's asking?"

Unable to resist, Ron and I reached into our pockets and showed him our badges, like synchronized G-men. "Brattleboro Police."

He stared at us in stunned wonderment, his eyes moving from one to the other. "Does this mean I'm fucked?"

Ron slowly reached out and removed the joint from between Redding's lips, knocking its hot tip off against the door frame and crushing the tiny ember underfoot.

"Could be," I answered. "May we come in?"

I motioned him to precede us into the apartment's hallway. "You alone at the moment?"

"Yeah. Frank's visiting his girlfriend."

"That's Francis Bertin?" Ron asked, "the legal tenant of this apartment?"

Redding's response came warily. "Yeah."

"And you are his guest?"

"Yeah." He'd reached the end of a short hallway leading into a comfortable, pleasantly appointed living room.

"In fact," I added, "you're sort of a professional guest, aren't you?"

An irrepressible arrogance surfaced in his voice. "So what?"

I crowded him, standing almost nose-to-nose, and pointed to a chair with its back against the wall. "Sit."

He sat.

Without stepping back, I looked down at him. "You understand the position you're in right now, don't you?"

He was craning his neck to look up at me, his Adam's apple shifting as he swallowed. "I guess."

"Then you should also understand that feeding us an attitude might not be the smartest thing to do, right?"

"Yeah—okay. Sorry."

"What do you do for a living, Mr. Redding?" Ron asked from one side.

"I'm a musician. Could I have a cigarette?"

"No. Is that a living?"

"It's what I do, all right?"

"Patty," I cautioned quietly, stretching out his name.

"Okay, okay. It doesn't pay all the bills."

"How long have you lived in Brattleboro?" Ron resumed.

I could tell Patty's neck was getting tired, but he didn't want to look straight ahead at my groin. "Five years. I come from Hartford, Connecticut."

"Where were you living last May?" I asked, the emphasis on the month.

"May? I think . . . I guess I was staying with Robbie Messier."

"And spending time with Shawna Davis?"

Genuinely startled, he tried to stand up. By simply refusing to retreat, I forced him back into the chair. "That bitch."

My first thought was that drugs formed the link between them, as they probably did between Patty and most of his "friends." J.P. had told me the lab had found traces of occasional marijuana use in Shawna's hair. But the word "occasional" was what caught in my craw. In the split second open to me, I decided to hedge my bet with a deliberately loaded implication. "Did she tell you she was eighteen?"

He ran his fingers through his hair, his head dropping briefly. "Oh, Jesus."

Ron and I exchanged glances, suddenly unsure of which button we'd pushed—statutory rape, drug pushing, or murder. Whichever it was, I had to make a critical choice. Given his mood, he was liable to confess to something, and I had to ensure it would hold up in court. My two choices were either to make it clear he was free to go—and therefore not in legal custody—and then take advantage of his sudden relief to coax out an indiscretion, or to build on the pressure he was already feeling, inform him of his rights, and let him think we could do more right now than simply give him a tap on the wrist for smoking a joint.

I opted for the latter. "I better advise you, Mr. Redding, that you may be facing criminal charges, and that you have the right to remain silent, and to retain the services of a lawyer if you wish, free of charge if you don't have the money. Do you understand that?"

Now the other hand joined the first in holding his head. *"Man."*

"Do you understand what I just said?" I pressed him, increasingly satisfied with my choice.

"It wasn't my fault—"

"Mr. Redding." I bent over and put my face into his again. "Do you understand what I said?"

"Yes." His voice was almost a croak.

I straightened, backed off, and sat in a chair across from him. "Good. Then do you want to tell us about Shawna Davis, or do you want to wait till you get a lawyer?"

He dropped his hands and slumped back into his chair, looking at me through a scraggle of hair hanging across his eyes. "I don't have a goddamn lawyer."

"We can get you a public defender."

He stared at the ceiling a moment. Regardless of the outcome, I didn't mind stringing this out. If he did opt for the lawyer, we'd take him down to the SA's office, nail him for the roach, get a warrant to search this apartment, and maybe hit him with a felony if we found a big-enough stash. On the other hand, there was nothing quite like the spur of the moment to open a guilty conscience, so if he had something truly incriminating to say, I wasn't about to stop him.

What he finally did say sent a faint chill down my back. "What the hell, it's all over anyhow."

"What is?" I asked, suddenly anticipating the resolution to Shawna's death.

"The deal. It's history, and if she wants to get me for rape, what the hell. She's no fucking virgin, if that's what she told you."

My hopes crumpled within me. This wasn't to be a murder confession.

Ron sensed my disappointment and took the lead. "Let's start from the top. When and how did you two meet?"

Redding let out a big sigh. "Like I said, I was crashing at Messier's place, playing gigs wherever I could. Shawna dropped in out of the blue. A friend of mine named Hugh Savage had given her my address. They went to high school together or something. Anyway, one day she showed up and just kind of moved in."

"What's that mean?" I asked.

"You know. She had nowhere to go, no money, didn't know anybody else in town. I kind of took her in. I mean, she wasn't much to look at, but she was willing and able, and I had nothing else going . . . she *did* tell me she was eighteen."

"What's the deal you mentioned?"

"After a couple of weeks, she was getting to be a drag. Never left the place because she said her mom might've sent the cops after her. She just hung around, wanting attention. I mean, that's okay for a while, but . . . well, you know."

Neither of us bothered commenting.

"So anyway, this guy I hear about's got this good shit to sell—prime stuff at a low price 'cause he's headin' for the joint and needs some fast cash. But I don't have the money, see? I have some friends that might chip in, so I go around, put the deal together, collect a thousand bucks, and that's when that little bitch decides to split—with the money. I couldn't believe it. Fucking cow. She wasn't even a good fuck. Boy, I caught shit for that one. If Messier hadn't backed me up . . . They thought I'd ripped 'em off. Can you believe it?"

I looked at him for a moment, wondering how Kunkle would have conducted this interview—and wishing he was. "Describe Shawna's hairdo," I asked, having left Shawna's photo at the office.

His mouth fell open. "Huh? What the hell . . . It was punk-like. You know, purple and orange, shaved on one side. I hate that shit."

"How 'bout her teeth—anything unusual there?"

He stared at me, totally baffled. "She had a gold tooth."

"Was there any kind of design or inscription on it?"

"What're you guys asking this shit for? No—it was just a goddamn tooth, all right?"

"You're sure?"

"Yeah."

"When did she disappear?"

His eyes narrowed. "What the hell did she do, anyway?"

"Answer the question," Ron said flatly.

Redding scowled. "Middle of May, I think. It was starting to warm up a little."

"During the time you were together," I resumed. "Did she make friends with anyone?"

"I told you. She was paranoid about her mother. She stayed inside all the time."

"What about Messier? What was his relationship to her?"

"They didn't like each other. He told me—just before she split with the money—that she had to go. After she ripped us off, he threw me out anyway. Such a prick. He was talking about how I should start paying rent, so I would've been outta there anyhow."

"You didn't look for her after she ripped you off?"

"Where was I going to look? I called that bastard Hugh—asked if he'd seen her. I thought maybe he'd set the thing up. I knew things were tight with a baby and everything. I even drove down there a couple of times, staked the place out. Never saw nothin'."

"So you dropped it?"

He shrugged. "Hey, you know? It wasn't my money, and once everybody knew Shawna'd done it, things cooled off. I found new digs, life went on."

"How many people chipped in on the money she stole?"

"Four."

"What're their names?"

He looked at both of us with a crafty smile. "Oh . . . I don't think so. You got me on possession—small change. When we get to the judge, there's no way I'm talking about any dope deal gone bad—I got nothin' to win by rattin' on my friends. I gotta live in this town."

I leaned forward, forcing him to bump the back of his head against the wall to avoid touching noses with me. "Listen, you cockroach. You want to know why we're so interested in Shawna? It's because she's dead—you'll read about it in the paper tomorrow. Those bones we found on Hillcrest were hers."

His eyes grew wide. "You're shittin' me."

"We figure she was killed right about when you last saw her—"

"I didn't—" he interrupted.

I grabbed his arm tightly to shut him up. "But you sure as hell had a grudge against her, Patty, and you're the one we got. You catch my drift?"

I could smell the sweat breaking out on him. "You guys are nuts. I didn't kill her. I didn't even know where the fuck she went. This is crazy."

I squeezed his arm harder. "Patty, Patty, listen to me. Maybe you didn't care about the money, but I bet the people it belonged to cared a lot. Am I right?"

"Sure. They were pissed. But murder? For a lousy thousand bucks?"

"People kill for a parking place, Patty. Think about it. You want to keep their names to yourself, it's up to you. But then we got no one to focus on but you."

He nodded jerkily. "Okay, okay. I'll tell you."

I pulled back and straightened up. "You have a phone I could use?"

He pointed across the room. "Next to the sofa."

"Thanks. You give my partner those names. I'm calling the State's Attorney's office. We've got a little paperwork to do. By the way, Shawna didn't lie to you. She was eighteen."

Chapter Eight

I was stretched out on my office floor with the lights off when Ron walked in. In the glow from the outer office, I could see he was holding a Dunkin' Donuts bag in one hand and a folded newspaper in the other. "You sleeping?" he asked doubtfully.

I sat up, crossing my legs, and reached up for one of the containers of coffee he pulled out of the bag. "Not really. Turn on the desk lamp."

It was almost five in the morning. We'd spent most of the night processing Patty Redding and sorting out the details with Carol Green, the unlucky Deputy SA on call. We had gotten a judge out of bed to sign a search warrant and had found enough marijuana and pills squirreled away in Patty's freezer for a felony charge. We'd also hunted down Francis Bertin—Patty's host—at his girlfriend's house, and Robbie Messier, who'd housed Patty and Shawna the previous summer, and had grilled them for a while. Now we had patrol units all over town rounding up the four people who'd financed Patty's dope deal.

It had been an active night.

Ron sat in my chair and handed me the waxy bag. Inside were four creme-filled, sugar-coated donuts, all of which Gail regularly assured me were cooked with animal lard. I sank my teeth into the first one with unrepentant pleasure. A swig of black coffee completed the effect. I groaned with satisfaction.

Ron smiled and handed me the newspaper. "Hot off the presses."

I took it from him and snapped it open. "I'm glad we got to Redding before this did. Made our job a whole lot simpler."

The banner headline, however, was not what I'd expected. It read, "Bank Finds White Knight," and underneath, "B of B saved by local businessman Benjamin Chambers."

I scanned the page below the fold, and found, "Police Give More Details on Body," in much smaller print, along with a dark, one-column-wide picture of Shawna.

The article was short, cold, and to the point. I was surprised by my own disappointment. "Didn't take 'em long to lose interest."

"It's still front-page," Ron countered, "and tonight's activities will keep it hot. But it's a little rough competing with a fifteen-million-dollar bailout."

I looked back to the top of the page. "Is that what happened?"

"Chambers came out of nowhere and took over Lacaille's belly-up convention center project. Lot of people're breathing a whole lot easier today, especially the bank."

My mind returned to the night before, when I'd driven by the abandoned construction site on my way to the *Reformer*, thinking it a monument to the price of greed. So much for my future as an oracle. Benjamin Chambers II, nicknamed Junior, was the semireclusive elder of two local brothers who'd inherited millions from their wily, land-rich father—the man most responsible for turning the Putney Road into the commercial wasteland it was. Junior was reported to be a quiet, retiring philanthropist, but so publicity-shy that very few people I knew had ever set eyes on him—no mean feat in a town this small.

Ron continued, "The article's pretty sketchy, but it looks like Carroll Construction is staying on the site, picking up where they left off, and that Chambers has assumed all of Gene Lacaille's debts."

Gene Lacaille was the developer who'd been forced to drop the project.

"Did it say how much Chambers had to pay?" I asked, still skimming the article.

"Nope. You going to eat all of those?"

I handed him the bag of donuts and put the newspaper on the floor beside me. "Well, I can see why Shawna got second billing—there's probably not a Realtor, landowner, politician, or subcontractor in town who doesn't have a vested interest in this deal."

Ron swallowed a mouthful of donut. "You think one of those four guys Patty fingered will fess up to killing her?"

"For a thousand bucks split four ways? I think Patty was right about that one." I got up and stretched. "I'm going home for a few hours sleep. You going to pack it in?"

He retrieved his paper and the remaining donuts. "Soon. You want Sammie to hold off interviewing those guys until you get back?"

"No, she and Willy can have at 'em. They'll probably just back up Patty's story. My bet is Shawna got into trouble after she ripped them off. Wilma said she left home in late April. She had her hair cut by Susan Lucey on the twenty-third, checked into Mother Gert's the same night, and then appeared on Patty's doorstep shortly thereafter, maybe the twenty-fourth. By his account, she stayed two or three weeks, and then disappeared. J.P. thinks she probably died in early June, which leaves about a three-week gap when she had a bundle of hot money in her hand, and a strong dislike of being seen in public. But somehow, for some reason, instead of leaving town, she met up with someone who pumped her full of barbiturates, probably killed her, and then dumped her in a field."

"Couldn't Patty have killed her after catching up with her?"

Ron asked, turning off my desk lamp and following me into the deserted outer office.

"If you're pissed off at somebody for stealing your cash, you beat the shit out of them. Maybe you kill them. But you don't carefully sedate them for a week. J.P. said it took three doses a day to maintain the drug level they found in her hair—that's no crime of passion. It had to be someone we don't know about yet."

"Maybe Patty kept her alive because she wouldn't tell him where the money was," Ron persisted for argument's sake.

"She couldn't've told him much if she was that sedated," I answered, and paused with my hand on the squad room doorknob. "Which tells us maybe she was being held for some reason."

"Like a ransom," Ron murmured.

"Could be . . ." I pressed my palm against my forehead, feeling a growing pain right behind my eyes. "I may be wrong, but I don't think we'll find an easy answer on this one."

Ron nodded his agreement and put his hand on my shoulder. "Have a nice nap, boss."

I waved as I passed through the doorway, and then abruptly stopped. "Did one of our guys process a dead bum, night before last?"

Ron raised his eyebrows. "Yeah—natural causes. It was in the dailies."

"Who was it?"

"Milo Douglas."

I turned around, startled. "I knew Milo—I didn't know he had any medical problems."

Ron gave me a blank look. "Beats me. The AME said natural causes. He was found under the Whetstone bridge. George Capullo worked the call—talked to some of the other guys down there. They told him Milo had a fit and died, just like that." He snapped his fingers. "The doc found a bottle of heart meds in his pocket, and George checked it out with the hospital. Milo had come in several times this past year complaining of chest pain. The prescription was legit."

"He have a history of seizures?" I asked.

"I don't know. Want me to ask George when he comes on?"

I shook my head and headed back toward the exit. "Don't worry about it. Just being nosy."

I checked my watch as I stepped outside. Despite the hour, it was still as black as night. I knew Gail would be gone by the time I got home—she liked to get a couple of hours in at the office alone, before the phones began ringing. I wondered how long she could keep up this pace. A single all-nighter later, I felt like hell.

I got into my car, its vinyl seat stiff with cold, and cranked over the sluggish engine. The heater would kick in about the time I pulled into my driveway.

I sighed and headed out, letting my mind wander. Where it finally snagged, however, wasn't on Gail, or Shawna Davis, or even on Junior Chambers saving Brattleboro's fat from the fire.

What I couldn't get out of my mind was the death of Milo Douglas.

*   *   *

Sammie Martens was waiting for me at the Municipal Building's rear entrance when I returned later that morning. She was so wired up, she was shifting her weight from foot to foot. "Why didn't you call me last night?"

"Didn't need to. And I wanted you fresh for this morning."

"I could've done both. You know that."

"Yes, and you would've been beating the hell out of the coffee machine by noon." I stopped halfway down the hall and faced her. "Don't start taking being my number two too seriously, Sammie. You're still part of a team. Ron was standing around—I used him, and he was all I needed till this morning. Next time, maybe you'll be lucky enough to get no sleep and chase down a bunch of scumbags all night. Okay?"

She nodded slightly. "You're right. I was out of line."

I smiled at the straight-Army line, and continued through the squad room door, pausing at Harriet Fritter's desk. "Could

you get me the file on Milo Douglas?" I asked her. "An untimely death a couple of days ago."

Harriet nodded without comment. I continued toward my
office, finishing my mini-lecture to Sammie. "You weren't out
of line—you were overly enthusiastic. That's not bad—it just
needs tempering, for your own sake. So how are things with
our guests?"

Sammie outlined the interviews with Patty's business part-
ners. She also detailed what they'd been able to corroborate
of Patty's story from Robbie Messier, and of Patty's current
habits from Frank Bertin. By the time she'd finished, though,
we both knew that apart from a minor drug bust, we still had
nothing useful concerning the fate of Shawna Davis.

"Anyone call in about the 'do-you-know-this-woman' article?"

She shook her head.

"All right. I guess all we can do for the moment is finish up
the paperwork on Patty and hand it over to Jack Derby. But
make sure everything's especially neat and tidy, okay? I don't
want that creep walking because of something we did."

Harriet appeared in my doorway as Sammie left, and
handed me a thin folder. After a few minutes of reading, I
picked up the telephone and dialed the hospital's emergency
room, requesting nurse Elizabeth Pace, a friend of several
years' standing.

"What can I do for you, Joe?" she asked after we'd exchanged greetings.

"I gather you folks recently treated a bum named Milo Douglas for a heart condition."

"That's right. George Capullo was asking about him. Is
there a problem with how he died?"

"I don't think so," I answered honestly. "I just wanted to tie
up a couple of loose ends. The doctor's name on Milo's pill
bottle was Jefferies—is he still on the ER shift?"

"He's here right now—want to talk to him?"

A soft, bland voice came on the line a moment later. "Dr.
Jefferies. How may I help you?"

I identified myself and then asked, "Do you remember a

patient named Milo Douglas? He was a bum you prescribed some heart medicine for."

There was a slight pause. "Right. Nurse Pace just handed me his chart. Mild supraventricular arrhythmias. I put him on the smallest dosage of Inderal available—ten milligrams. I see there's a note he died recently. Is something wrong?"

I sympathized with his implied misgivings. "Not that I know of. I do have some questions, though. Our witnesses reported he had a seizure just before he collapsed. Would that be consistent with his condition?"

"A grand mal seizure?"

I consulted the file before me. "Those words weren't used, but that's the implication. The quote here says, 'He flopped around like crazy.' "

"What were the Medical Examiner's conclusions?" Jefferies asked cautiously.

"He hedged his bets—said 'natural causes.' "

Jefferies thought for a few seconds before admitting, "He may be right, given Mr. Douglas's personal habits. But if you're asking if death was due to the heart condition I treated him for, then I'd have serious doubts. It wasn't that severe. And certainly the grand mal seizure would have had nothing to do with it—that had to have been from another cause entirely. Looking at the chart, by the way, I see I did a pretty thorough medical history at the time I examined him. Mr. Douglas was no pillar of sound health, but there's nothing that would indicate any grand mal seizure activity. It might've been alcohol-related, and misinterpreted by your witnesses. I take it they were people who shared his lifestyle?"

I smiled at the diplomacy. "Yes, they were, and that's a distinct possibility. They may've been more scared than accurate."

My curiosity further stimulated, I hung up on Dr. Jefferies and punched the intercom button. Harriet Fritter picked up immediately. "Which funeral home handled that untimely George took care of a couple of nights ago?"

"Guillaume's," she answered without hesitation. Harriet was what the computer was supposed to be for our squad—the fastest source of information available. I hadn't the slightest idea how old she was—although she was a grandmother several times over—but I knew when she left us eventually, it would be the equivalent of a major system meltdown.

I called Guillaume's, found out they still had Milo Douglas on the premises, and retrieved my coat.

In Brattleboro, funeral homes were employed by the town on a rotational basis. The procedure followed clear and simple guidelines—once the funeral home took possession, an extensive search for next of kin was conducted while the death certificate was reviewed by the Medical Examiner's office in Burlington. Then the body was disposed of in a respectful, inexpensive fashion—all in a few days at most.

The catch was often in finding the next of kin. The state allocated $850 for the disposal of each body, which for a simple cremation wasn't too bad. Embalming and burial cost more and took longer, however, and the state insisted that if no relatives were found, this was the route the funeral home had to take. Guillaume's had informed me on the phone that such was to be Milo's fate.

As with many businesses in Brattleboro, Guillaume's was located in a converted turn-of-the-century residence—this one a true architectural gem, located on one of the town's main drags. Heavily Victorian, replete with an excess of multihued gingerbread, along with the requisite corner turret, the house had long made me ponder the connection between the exterior's pristine appearance—and the efforts made inside to make its clientele look their best.

I parked by the side, climbed the broad porch steps, and entered a huge, thick-carpeted entrance hall—dark, wood-paneled, with stained-glass windows and gleaming brass fixtures. I knew it was meant to both comfort and impress, but it just made me feel self-conscious to be alive. I was relieved when a middle-aged man in a dark blue suit appeared almost immediately through a door beneath the sweeping staircase. His name, much to his chagrin, was Conrad Blessing.

"Joe," he said with a wide smile. "Good to see you again."

We shook hands and exchanged pleasantries while he led

me back the way he had come. His lack of stilted, unctuous manners reminded me that cops weren't the only ones instantly stereotyped by their profession.

"I take it you're having second thoughts about Mr. Douglas's demise," Blessing said, opening the door. The hallway we entered was white-painted, brightly lit, and as functionally stark as the lobby had been theatrically overstuffed.

"Nothing that solid. I just used to know Milo."

Blessing's voice dropped to a more conciliatory tone. "I'm sorry. Were you friends?"

I laughed. "Hardly—the man was a pure opportunist. I used him as a source now and then."

He led the way to a service elevator. "We're running a little behind schedule, so we stored him in a tunnel under the driveway. That's why I didn't take your coat. It's pretty cold down there."

The elevator sank one story, to a large, cool, dimly lit basement with several empty gurneys stationed along the wall. Blessing crossed over to a broad, closed door on the opposite wall, paused to put on a coat he had hanging from a nearby peg, and swung the door open.

The column of cold air that hit us was a surprise, even with his warning, and I shivered as we crossed the threshold.

Blessing closed the door behind us. "Mr. Douglas is down here a ways."

I followed him along a semicircular tunnel, lit by naked bulbs strung along a rough cement ceiling. More gurneys lined the uneven walls, a couple of them occupied by long, shapeless, fully bagged bundles. At about the halfway mark, we stopped, and Blessing waved a hand at a gurney topped by a long cardboard box. "Milo Douglas."

We both lifted the top off the box. Inside was a zippered black body bag, which Blessing, having donned rubber gloves from his coat pocket, expertly opened and peeled back.

Inside, obliquely lit by one of the overhead bulbs, Milo's hairy, filthy face grimaced up at us, his one good eye half-closed as in an alcoholic stupor, the other more open—milky, strange, and as sightless as it had been in life. The hair around his mouth was matted and caked with dried saliva. The stench, even in this natural freezer, was overwhelming.

"You must love these cases," I said. "This just the way you received him?"

Blessing nodded. "Yes. He's scheduled for cleanup and embalming this afternoon."

I looked down at Milo for a moment, struck by a memory so lasting and powerful that seeing a reminder of it hit me with a jolt. I hesitated before saying, "Okay. We can wrap him up again."

Blessing worked the zipper, adding, "It's no problem if you want to move him upstairs for a closer look. It's warmer and we've got very good ventilation."

I shook my head, keeping my thoughts to myself. "That's okay. I mostly just wanted to make sure it was him. Do you have any of his personal effects, by the way?"

He led us back to the warm basement, and to a shelf lined with several brown paper bags, one of which he handed me. I poured its contents onto a nearby table and picked through an assortment of rags, bottle caps, paper clips, broken ballpoint pens, and other assorted junk until I found Dr. Jefferies's orange plastic container of prescribed Inderal. Blessing nodded silently as I gestured putting it in my pocket. "Thanks. I'm going to see if I can get an autopsy ordered. I'd appreciate it if you held him till I let you know."

Blessing returned the bag to the shelf. "No problem. He's not in anyone's way."

I wondered if the same had been true at the end of his life.

*   *   *

Gail was sitting at her desk, to one side of the reception area. Her tired face broke into a smile when she saw me. "Hey, stranger. You get any sleep?"

I crossed over and kissed her. "A few hours this morning. Sorry I missed you."

"Not to worry. My spies told me what you were up to." She waved at the files all around her, covering the desk and floor both. "In fact, Patty Redding is hiding here—somewhere—already. What're you up to?"

"Petitioning your boss for an autopsy. I wanted to tell you something about Linda Feinstein, though."

Gail's eyebrows rose.

"I won't breach any confidentialities, but I think you ought to talk to her. She may have something to get off her chest. You can tell her I told you that much. It's up to her if she wants to spell it out."

She nodded and made a notation in her desk calendar. "You got it. Did you get a decent breakfast—or dinner for that matter?"

"Yeah," I answered evasively. "Ron treated me."

Jack Derby's door opened behind her and he beckoned me with his hand. "Come on in, Joe. You got five minutes."

"Life in the fast lane," I murmured to Gail, and followed him into his office.

"I'm heading for court, so don't mind the distractions." Derby was standing behind his desk, a large briefcase sitting on its edge. He was surveying a snowbank of documents, selecting from among them, and marking his choices off on a checklist by his right hand.

I sat in his guest chair. "I'd like an autopsy ordered on Milo Douglas. He's the bum they found under the Whetstone bridge on Main Street a couple of nights ago."

Derby didn't look up. "Why? I thought he was natural causes."

"He might've been. He had a bottle of heart meds in his pocket for chest pain, but witnesses said he died after a seizure. The Assistant Medical Examiner was a GP, covering for Al Gould, who's on vacation. He combined the cardiac history, the alcoholism, poor living habits, and the fact that Milo was in his sixties, and came up with heart failure. But nobody talked to his actual doctor—both the AME and our own investigator just checked with the hospital."

"And you did talk to his doctor," Derby surmised.

"Right. He said sudden death in such a case was pretty unlikely, and that seizures have nothing to do with what Milo was being treated for."

"Was he part of one of your investigations?"

"Milo? No. I hadn't even seen him in months. I have used him over the years, though, as a less than reliable snitch."

"But he was an alcoholic, right? Couldn't he have died of the DTs? Those could look like seizures, especially given your witnesses."

I considered telling him of my biggest concern—the one triggered by seeing Milo at Guillaume's—but with only my own memories to go on, I wanted some reliable confirmation. The implications of Satanism in Shawna's death were bad enough. No need to add my own unfounded fears to that kind of fire. I opted for a compromise instead. "We'll never know unless we check it out."

He stopped long enough to look me squarely in the eye. "We can't do it all, Joe. We've got plenty on our plates without fishing for more."

"I realize that."

He held my gaze a couple of seconds longer, and then returned to his checklist. "All right—I'll order an autopsy."

"Thanks, Jack." I stood up and moved to the door, hesitating as I placed my hand on the knob, wondering if I should tempt fate. "Why, by the way?" I finally couldn't resist asking.

He stopped again and gave me an enigmatic shrug. "Maybe it's because you've been at this for donkey's years, and from what I heard, you don't ask for special favors. Maybe it's because I'm the new boy on the block and I don't want to piss you off. Take your pick. Anyhow, the ME's office pays for autopsies, so it doesn't dent my budget in either case. Have a nice day," he added with a smile.

Not that my reasons weren't entirely self-serving, but I admired the man's style. It made me happy I'd voted for him.

Chapter Nine

Jack Derby had been right about the Medical Examiner's office paying for their own autopsies—$1,000 each—but when I reached Beverly Hillstrom by phone, she voiced no opposition, despite the fact that she'd already signed off on the death certificate.

I arranged to have Milo shipped to Burlington, but with growing misgivings. Both Derby and Hillstrom had placed their trust less on any real evidence than on my gut instinct, and even there I'd shortchanged them, keeping my worst suspicions to myself.

I couldn't help praying those suspicions were well-founded.

George Capullo, one of our Patrol sergeants, and a veteran of more years than I could remember, had been the one called to Milo's side the other night. He had also collected the witness statements.

I found him preparing for the four-to-midnight shift, reviewing the prior shift's dailies. There were only a few desks in the so-called Officers' Room, forcing everyone to share. It was a situation that led to endless, three-times-a-day shuffles of personal belongings from desktop to allocated drawer,

and—I thought—a slightly disquieting sense of imperma-
nence. In my own squad room, I could see the imprint of its
inhabitants everywhere—from the types of information they
thumbtacked on the walls before them, to the little knick-
knacks that littered their cubicles. There was little of that in
the Officers' Room. A decades-old veteran like George left as
much on its surfaces as a week-old rookie. Neither space nor
budget allowed otherwise.

I perched myself on the edge of the desk he was rummag-
ing through, searching for paper clips.

He glanced up briefly, his first words a commentary on our
department's small size. "Hey, Joe. Nice collar on Patty Redding. He must've shit his pants when he saw you two at the
door."

"Close enough." I chose my next words carefully. As old as
our friendship was, what I'd just done with Milo's body could
easily have been taken as a rebuke for shoddy work. I felt on
thin enough ice as it was without damaging George's pride.

"Tell me something. I'm curious about Milo Douglas's
death. Did you notice any discrepancies—anything that struck
you as odd?"

He stopped poking through the drawer and looked up at
me carefully. "I thought that was natural causes."

"Probably was. I'm just picking at it. I sent the body up for
an autopsy."

Thankfully, he sat back in his chair and nodded. "Yeah.
They don't usually just drop dead like that. But the AME was
pretty sure of himself, and it looked solid on paper. What'ya
thinking?"

"Not much. You listed Danny Soffit and Phil Duke as witnesses. Were they sober?"

"Danny was pretty useless, as usual, but Phil seemed relatively straight at the time."

"What were they doing under the bridge? I thought both of
them went indoors during the winter."

"They do—normally. They got thrown out by the landlord
that morning. Danny wanted to cook something in the room,
so he lit a fire in the middle of the floor. Not much damage—

the smoke alarm went off—but they ended up on the street. They were spending the night in a kind of cardboard cocoon wedged way up where the understructure of the bridge meets the wall, as far out of the weather as they could get. They were planning to find other digs the next day. Probably have by now."

"Where was Milo hanging out?"

"In the storm drain just under them—the one that shoots straight up Main Street. It's clean, dry, stays the same temperature—a few of them use it year round. At the time Milo died, Danny was cooking something on the cement ledge just under the tunnel entrance."

"And Milo was fine up to the time he had the seizure?"

"That's what they said. Guess I should'a pushed a little harder," he finished apologetically.

"I doubt I would've," I comforted him. "I'm just curious why he died so suddenly. The cardiologist he got those pills from says his heart problem wasn't that bad."

"I just took the AME at his word; never occurred to me to chase down the doctor listed on the pill bottle."

I tapped the side of his leg with my foot, once again keeping my own suspicions to myself. "Relax—it's a buddy system. We back each other up. Besides, Hillstrom'll probably tell me I just blew a thousand bucks for nothing. Where d'you think I can find Danny and Phil?"

He looked at me again, this time with determination. "Don't worry about it. I'll find 'em and let you know."

*   *   *

Several hours later, chained to my desk by a week's backlog of paperwork, I found myself growing increasingly restless, wondering why George hadn't called in yet, wanting to settle what was nagging me once and for all.

Had his death better fit his medical condition, and had his physical appearance not been so startling—to me at least—Milo's passing wouldn't have caused me much concern. The lives these men led—and they were mostly men—were case studies for premature death. Virtually all alcoholics, they ate rarely and poorly, were constantly exposed to disease and infection, and lived outside in all kinds of weather. In the wintertime, it was true, when the summer transients were gone, the full-time locals generally abandoned their fair-weather camps along the railroad tracks, the interstate, and up behind the Putney Road, to flock to the town's several fleabag apartment buildings. But it wasn't much of an improvement, and not all of them bothered. Some of the hard-core—as Milo had been—kept to themselves, and chose crannies to live in a stray dog would pass up.

It was lost in these thoughts, my pen ignored in my hand, that Sammie found me close to suppertime. "We may have a new lead on Shawna Davis. Ron's talking to someone right now on the phone."

Ron was just finishing as we reached him. "Thank you very much—you've been a big help. I hope you don't mind if we call you later on . . . Right . . . No, I appreciate that. Thanks again."

He hung up. Still scribbling on a sheet of paper before him. "That was a mailman—Sherman Bailey. He thought he saw Shawna at this address, maybe in late May. It belongs to Mary Wallis."

"Bingo," Sammie murmured.

Mary Wallis was one of the town's most outspoken advocates for the downtrodden—women, the poor, minorities, homeless animals, criminals, children, and a dozen other broad, sometimes conflicting categories.

She was well known to me personally, not only because she and Gail shared many of the same passions, but also because she'd been known to act on them to excess. When Gail was assaulted, for example, Mary Wallis took it upon herself to identify the culprit—inaccurately—and bean him on the head with her shoe.

But Wallis could also be an effective and dogged campaigner. With the zeal of a true believer, she pursued her goals with relentless energy, and had been known to effect the change of an offending policy almost single-handed.

The trade-off was that both her manner and her approach

carried a high personal cost. Few people liked her, including many of those she worked so hard to support. Gail herself, after making much ado about Mary's tenacity and value as an ally, had to admit that she could only take her in short doses.

"He's a little vague on the date," Ron continued, "but he saw her in Wallis's front yard when he was delivering the mail. The hairdo is a match, along with a studded black leather jacket with colored feathers on the sleeves both Messier and Bertin said she wore."

"But he can't get any closer on the date than last spring?" Sammie asked.

Ron shook his head. "He just remembered the weather had started to get hot."

Suddenly remembering one of Mary Wallis's pet causes, I leaned forward and checked a list of telephone numbers Ron had thumbtacked to his wall. "I have an idea how Shawna and Wallis met up."

I dialed Mother Gert's, turned on the speakerphone, and waited until she got on the line. "Gert, who processed Shawna Davis the night she visited you?"

There was a long pause as she went to consult the file. "Why?" came the predictable reply.

I pursed my lips. "Because the girl's dead. Surely you can break a confidence so we can find out why."

"Is the person who processed her a suspect?"

"We're not even sure there is a suspect. We're trying to track her movements."

There was a moment's silence on the other end. "I'm not very comfortable with this, Joe."

I took a deep breath. "Let me try it this way. Will you confirm it was Mary Wallis?"

Gert's short reply bristled with anger, as if I'd been playing her for a fool. "Yes," she said, and the line went dead.

I returned the phone gently to its cradle. "So they met that night."

"Maybe she went to Gert's because she knew Wallis would be there," Ron said.

Sammie shook her head. "Shawna only found out about Mother Gert's that day, at the hairdresser's."

"Either way, she must've sought out Wallis after ripping off Patty Redding," he concluded.

"Looks that way," I admitted.

Harriet Fritter came up behind us. "Joe? There's a call for you—George Capullo."

"I've been waiting for this," I explained and picked up Ron's phone again. "You find 'em, George?"

"Yup. They're camping in a trailer box on Old Ferry Road— Ferguson's yard. At least that's the latest I got. I didn't want to risk flushing them out. I don't know how hinky they are."

I glanced out the window. It was already dark. "They're not going to freeze to death overnight, are they?"

George chuckled. "Oh, you don't know these guys. They give layering a whole new meaning. And if they're there now, they'll be there in the morning."

"Thanks a lot, George."

I hung up the phone and turned to Sammie, remembering her reaction to being left out of the previous night's action. "You ready to pay a visit to Mary Wallis with me?"

*   *   *

Considering Wallis's bellicose lifestyle, her home was a contradictory reflection of bland self-effacement. Tucked away on Allerton Avenue, a short, dead-end street off Western—and within a short stone's throw of the interstate—it was of the same post–World War Two building style that had made Levittown famous and architects shudder. And given her manic concern for the environment, I found it ironic that the singsong throb of high-speed traffic permeated the surrounding air with the same dull monotony of waves crashing on a beach. It occurred to me that either Mary had come to embrace her causes after she'd moved in here—and then couldn't afford to leave—or that she needed the stimulus of a nearby and constant enemy to keep her dander up.

Sammie and I got out of the car, crossed the lawn where the

mailman had seen Shawna Davis, and paused at the front door. The house, though lighted inside, didn't issue a murmur.

But when the door swung open after I rang the bell, Mary Wallis stood before us, white-faced, tear-stained, and so visibly near collapse that I instinctively reached forward and took her by the elbow. "Mary. Are you all right?"

She looked at me in shock and violently pulled her arm away. "What do you want?"

"What happened?"

"Nothing—I just heard a friend of mine had died. What do you want?" Her voice was hard, almost strident.

"Was your friend Shawna Davis?" Sammie asked. Often not the most diplomatic of questioners, there were times when her bluntness was above reproach.

Mary Wallis looked stunned, the hand gripping the door so tightly it began to shake.

"She was last seen here, at your house, sometime last spring."

Mary worked her mouth to say something, but no words came out.

I spread my hands in a gesture of peace. "Mary, can I fix you some coffee or tea at least? Or call someone to come visit?"

More slowly this time, I reached out, took her elbow, and made a motion to escort her indoors. She showed no resistance, and we were able to cross the threshold and cut off the freezing air that had been rapidly filling the house. Mary began shivering only after the door was shut.

I peeled off my overcoat and draped it over her shoulders. "Where's your kitchen? Let me make you something hot to drink."

She gestured vaguely toward the right, and I steered her ahead of me down a short hallway to a modest kitchen facing the front of the house. I sat her in a chair at a small table in the room's center, poured some hot water into a kettle I found on the stove, and lit a fire under it.

"Where did you and Shawna meet?" I asked, sitting opposite her.

Sammie leaned against a counter, watching Mary's face as she spoke.

Her words came out slowly, or maybe carefully, I thought. "At Mother Gert's. I was on duty—volunteering—when she came by looking for a bed. I took an instant liking to her."

"Did she talk about herself much?"

"Not at first. We have a form we're supposed to fill out for every newcomer, and all I could get out of her was her name and age. Afterward, when I showed her to her room, she began to open up. We didn't have much business that night, so I stayed with her, listening—for almost three hours."

My mind returned to Susan Lucey, and to how she, too, had triggered Shawna's need to share her burdens. "What did she talk about?"

Mary took a deep breath, almost a sob. "Her mother, her school, where she'd grown up. She'd had a very hard life for someone so young. She'd suffered badly at the hands of others."

I paused for a moment, looking at the woman before me, and suddenly realized that I hadn't seen or heard from her in a long time, not since her predictable but unsuccessful attempt to derail the convention center project on the Putney Road a half-year ago. . . . And not since the time of Shawna's disappearance—a coincidental piece of timing I hadn't noticed until now.

I ventured a guess. "You must have found much in common with her."

She'd been staring into space, and now raised her eyes to meet mine. "Yes. That's quite true."

The kettle began whistling, and Sammie went about making tea.

"What were her plans when you met?" I asked.

Mary wiped her cheeks with one hand—a gesture of returning self-control that made me think I should have taken Sammie's cue and pushed her harder early on. "She had the name of somebody in town—I forget who—a friend of a friend—where she could stay. But I don't think she had any plans exactly. She just wanted to get away from home."

"Was she fearful her mother might come after her?"

"Yes, although I told her that being eighteen, she was legally immune. But that's not what worried her—the legal threat. She was running from her mother's influence, and there was really no hiding from that."

"You offered to put her up, didn't you?"

Her wan, pale face relaxed into a small smile. "Yes—totally against the house rules and good judgment. Gert would have been furious. But Shawna wasn't interested in any case. She didn't want another mother-figure. I wouldn't have either, in her shoes."

Sammie placed the teacup before her. "You want any milk or sugar?"

Mary shook her head. "No, thank you."

Sammie took advantage of the opening to press on. "But she came back in the long run—about a month later—didn't she?"

Mary lifted the cup to her lips and took a sip, watching us closely over the brim. She then replaced the cup and shrugged my coat from her shoulders, draping it over the chair next to her. "She came to visit once, to say thank you. It was the last time I saw her. She said she was going away . . ."

Her chin began to quiver suddenly, and she dropped her head. "Poor, poor girl . . ."

"The day she was here," Sammie said, almost harshly, "she was carrying a thousand dollars of someone else's money. She tell you about that?"

I gave Sammie a cautionary glance as Mary straightened and fixed us both with a startled expression. "What?"

"Shawna stole a thousand dollars from the man she was staying with," I explained. "That's why we think she was heading out of town."

Mary's eyebrows knit slightly. "I wondered why she was so excited." Her voice then hardened, becoming more business-like. "So you think that man may have killed her?"

"We were hoping you might give us some insight on that," I said.

She took another delicate sip of tea. "She was very vague about her recent past."

"Why would she stop here?" Sammie asked. "Hot money in her pocket—you and she had only talked for a few hours a month before. Seems kind of crazy."

Mary looked at her coolly, now clearly holding something back. "I don't know."

"And she didn't say where she was headed?"

"No."

Sammie scowled openly but remained silent.

"Mary," I asked, "why didn't you give us a call when you read about Shawna?"

A bit of her old combative self rose to the surface. "It's not my job to help you, Joe. I *had* the answer. I knew that a young girl I'd become very attached to—whom I'd last seen full of hope—hadn't even made it out of town before being killed—a town, I might add, that you are supposed to be making safe." She shot a baleful look at Sammie, whose tight, mistrustful expression hadn't changed. "But I know nothing that can help you identify her killer. What good was a call from me going to be? What good has this conversation been, in fact, except to stir up painful memories?"

She stood, skittering her chair across the floor, her eyes narrow with an anger I could feel was being willfully stoked. "Not only that, but you've been insinuating I know something I haven't told you, that somehow I'm tied up in something underhanded. Well, I resent the hell out of that. I resent you barging in on my grief—on my memories of a sweet, neglected, murdered girl—so that you can throw insults at me while you soften me up with tea. That is the height of hypocrisy, and not something I will stand for. My God—what is it Gail sees in you? I think you're a simple bastard, and I want you out of my house. Now." She pointed with a trembling flourish toward the door.

*   *   *

Sammie and I sat quietly in the car for a while—the heater running—looking at Mary Wallis's peaceful, nondescript house.

"Quite a performance," I finally said.

"You think it's all bullshit?"

"Parts of it. Hard to tell which ones."

"You think she killed her?" Sammie tried again.

I mulled that over for a moment. "I doubt it."

I put the car into gear and pulled away from the curb. "But I do think she knows a lot more about all this than she's letting on."

Chapter Ten

I moved a pile of books from one of the chairs in Gail's study and took their place. She was sitting in her armchair again, with her laptop computer back in place, taking notes from the man on the videotape. But this time, despite it being eleven o'clock at night, she wasn't dozing off.

She looked at me warily. "What's up?"

Taking the hint, I skipped the preliminaries. "What do you know about Mary Wallis?"

"Why?"

"Because as far as we can tell right now, she was the last person to see Shawna Davis alive."

Gail shifted the computer off her lap and tucked her legs up under her, hitting the *pause* button on the VCR remote, her veiled irritation becoming concern.

"A mailman saw Shawna standing on her front lawn last spring," I continued. "Mary confirmed this evening that she met the girl at Mother Gert's, and that Shawna came by to say good-bye on her way out of town a few weeks later."

"You think she had anything to do with her death?"

"I don't have any proof of it, but she's not being straight

with us. She was crying when she answered the door. She claimed she had just heard about Shawna's death. But by the time she threw us out fifteen minutes later, she was all bluster and fury, and being very careful about what she told us. She also referred to the death as a murder, with no prompting from us."

Gail cradled her chin in her hand and looked thoughtfully at the floor. "I'm not surprised she struck up a friendship with the girl. From what you've told me, they have a lot in common."

"That's what I wanted to hear more about," I murmured.

"Mary's originally from Pennsylvania—a single child. Her father was a drinker—very rough on her mother and her. I don't know if he sexually abused her, but all the hallmarks are there."

Gail hesitated, obviously uncomfortable. "I normally wouldn't tell you this, but you'll find it out anyway. She killed her father. He was beating her mother, and Mary slammed him on the back of the head with an iron skillet. He was dead before he hit the floor. She was fifteen."

"She do any time for it?" I asked.

Gail shook her head. "No. The mother was in the hospital for a month. The neighbors all knew what was happening. The DA didn't even indict. Everyone figured her father got what he deserved . . . except Mary, of course. She had to live with it, and she didn't know how."

"The mother was no help?"

"No more than before. One of life's born victims. She married again—same type of guy—and this time I know Mary was sexually abused. She left home almost as soon as the new husband moved in.

"She wandered to New York City, began drinking, doing drugs, God knows what else. She pretty much hit bottom. And then she became pregnant."

I listened with growing fascination, reminded of how much we assume we know of other people's lives. I never would have guessed at such a background to the Mary Wallis I thought I knew.

"The baby died a week after birth. Mary was convinced she'd poisoned it with her own drug abuse and malnutrition, and I wouldn't argue the point. But it was the second death she'd played a part in, and she thought she'd better put an end to a dangerous habit."

"By committing suicide," I suggested, familiar with the pattern.

"You got it."

"How?" I asked.

Gail looked at me quizzically. "I'm not sure . . . sleeping pills, I think. Yeah, because she checked into a shelter and somehow or another got into the dispensary and stole the stuff. She almost pulled it off. She was in a coma for a week or more. That, typically, is what eventually saved her. People finally took notice. A women's crisis organization was called in and helped turn her around. She began to fight back. She's been fighting ever since."

"What brought her up here?"

"Her mother's been in a vegetative state for years. Mary heard about the Retreat's geriatric care unit and moved both of them up here about a decade ago. She visits her twice a day. Her mother's the only person I know who gets that much of Mary's attention, even though she hasn't said a word to anyone in all that time."

"Jesus," I said. There was a long silence while I thought about how to phrase my next question. "Her mother, in a way, is permanently asleep. And when Mary tried to kill herself, she took sleeping pills—"

"And Shawna's hair," Gail finished for me, "was full of phenobarbital. Does make you wonder."

I'd expected some reproach for my suggestion, and was surprised at Gail's seemingly detached response. "You think it's possible?"

She didn't smile as she said, "I've come to think everything's possible."

There was a telling pause as we both reflected on the toll of her own recent trauma.

"Shawna was about Mary's age when she attempted suicide," Gail mused. "They met in a shelter, and for all we know, Shawna might've been pregnant when she came to see Mary the second time. She might've killed the girl, except you'd expect some noticeable psychological change—some behavior modification."

I returned to a thought I'd had earlier that evening. "But she did change. Remember how hard she fought the convention center? Tooth and nail up to last spring. Then, all of a sudden, she dropped out of sight. The suit she'd threatened never materialized, and the opposition she'd almost single-handedly organized collapsed."

Gail frowned. "I was so buried in my own problems, I never paid any attention to that, but I guess you're right. And she also missed a golden opportunity to sink the project last month, when Gene Lacaille ran into financial trouble, and the bank ended up holding the bag."

I glanced at the morning newspaper, lying by the wastepaper basket, its headline still mocking my efforts to make Shawna the day's number one item. "Interesting," I murmured, and rose to my feet.

Gail looked up at me. "What're you going to do?"

"For starts," I answered, "I'm going to put Mary Wallis under a microscope."

*   *   *

The new day's first business, however, involved none of what Gail and I had discussed. By dawn's gray light, I was standing in the McDonald's on the Putney Road, ordering enough coffee and food to feed a large horse.

In a car steaming with an aroma no doubt carefully conceived in some sterilized Midwestern laboratory, I then drove north to just shy of the Dummerston town line, and took a right onto Old Ferry Road, past UPS, the dump, and the corporate offices of the Vermont Yankee nuclear plant, to the trailer yard of Ferguson Trucking—where George Capullo had told me Danny Soffit and Phil Duke were camping out.

They were there by permission, more or less. Roger Ferguson had once kept his trailers under lock and key, protected, he hoped, behind a tall chain-link fence. But the attraction of all those huge, empty, romanticized eighteen-wheeler bodies had proved overwhelming. Nightly, people had climbed that fence—bums looking for a place to sleep, teenagers hot to smoke dope or play doctor, and graffiti artists in search of more canvas. There'd been accidents, a couple of small fires, one boy had died of an alcohol overdose. Years ago, Ferguson had finally given up, thrown open the gates, and had left them that way ever since. The boxes, when being readied for use, still had to be cleaned out of bottles, cans, and condoms, but the strategy—such as it was—had worked. No longer on the list of forbidden places to go, the yard had lost its appeal. Now the bums alone still considered it prime real estate, and Ferguson's people were under orders to leave them alone.

George had told me which trailer Phil and Danny were camped in, so I drove slowly over the frozen, rutted yard until I'd drawn abreast of a box with both rear doors all but completely shut.

I killed the engine, got out and paused a moment to listen. Everything appeared utterly still. To the loud moaning of cold-stiffened hinges, I swung one of the doors back and peered inside.

The box was almost empty, its cavernous interior stark and resonant. Far to the back, however, jammed into one of the corners, was a rounded pile of rags, blankets, and cardboard—reminiscent, in a crude fashion, of an oversized cocoon.

"Phil. Danny," I called out. "It's Joe Gunther. Bratt PD. I got breakfast for you."

The vapor from my breath hung motionless before me, glistening in the pale light of the new sun. These people were not early risers, unless they were living in some building's furnace room and trying to avoid detection, so I wasn't surprised that all I got for my effort was a slight shifting from deep inside the bundle.

Encouraged, I returned to my car, retrieved the cardboard trays I'd just purchased, and slid them onto the edge of the trailer floor before struggling up to join them. Once inside, I carried the food halfway down the box, and sat down, my back against the wall.

"Okay, guys, open your nostrils if nothing else. This stuff won't stay hot for long."

Slowly, the cocoon lost definition, coming apart in odd ways—a chrysalis of dubious origin yielding inhabitants not known for their glory. Shaggy heads topped by dirt-flecked wool hats emerged, blinking and bewildered in the intensifying sunlight.

"Who the fuck is that?"

"Joe Gunther," I repeated. "Bratt PD."

Some recognizable forms began to appear—an arm, an outthrust leg, a gloved hand working out the cramps instilled by a night spent in near hibernation. One of them rose unsteadily, leaning for support against the wall.

"Joe Gunther?"

It had been a while since I'd last seen either one of them, and right now they were not at their best. I ventured a guess at the more alert of the two. "Hey, Phil. Tough night?"

"Had worse," he said suspiciously, only his eyes visible between a scarf and a pulled-down watch cap.

"Well, you can refuel with some of this if you want."

The homeless inhabitants of Brattleboro, especially those we called the "regulars," were a pretty predictable tribe. Mostly men in their mid-thirties or older, they kept to themselves, were respectful of us, and largely sought to be ignored. A few of them panhandled, a few—when they had the money—went for a rare meal at a restaurant, much to everyone else's distress, but most of them merely existed on the town's periphery. They ate out of dumpsters, slept out of sight, and lived off what was either given them through charity, or from the money they redeemed for the beer cans they emptied in copious amounts. Regardless of their other sanitary shortcomings, they rarely left a can or a bottle lying around—they were among the best recyclers in town.

They were also remarkably law-abiding. They did their drinking in private, kept their disagreements off the street, and had even been known, now and then, to help us out with some information. Generally, when investigating a burglary, even in the town's poorer neighborhoods, we didn't bother with the bums—however isolated and despairing it might be, theirs was not a life of crime.

All of that, however, also made them wary, and having a cop arrive on their doorstep with a hot catered meal was not something they took easily in stride.

Phil's voice changed to that of a mildly affronted homeowner being disturbed too early in the day. "Excuse me, sir, but what do you want?"

"First, I want you to eat this stuff before it turns to ice. Then I want to talk to you about Milo. George Capullo told me where to find you."

Danny Soffit, the slower of the two, had by now also emerged, but he stayed, splayed out and dazed, on the floor.

"Milo's dead." Phil straightened his neck out, as if to gain a better view of my offerings. The smell of the hot food had already filled the trailer.

"I know that. I guess it was just his time. I went down to the funeral home to pay my respects. Milo and I were friends—at least we were friendly."

"So what do you want?"

"I need to know how he died." I waved my hand at the food. "It's a straight swap—breakfast for a little conversation. No strings attached."

Phil crossed back over to where Danny was still staring at us, and kicked him in the leg. "Move your butt. Food's on."

Danny swiveled around and began approaching me like a shambling bear, on hands and knees. Phil shook his head in gentle embarrassment and walked over to sit opposite me. "He's not too good this early."

I pushed a tray at him. "Me neither. Dig in."

He did just that, as did Danny a minute later, eventually dusting their beards, gloves, and clothing with small fragments of Egg McMuffin, fried potatoes, toast, jelly, and coffee.

I let them eat half the meal in peace before exacting my price. "You told Sergeant Capullo that Milo had a seizure before he died."

"Yeah," Danny spoke for the first time. "He twitched a bunch."

Phil gave his friend a look over the top of his Styrofoam cup, but otherwise kept quiet.

"The three of you were hanging out together, around a fire, and he suddenly up and died—just like that?"

Phil nodded and began to speak, but was drowned out by Danny's, "Oh no. Not like that."

"Shut up, Danny."

We both looked at Phil, Danny's eyes growing wide. "Oh, yeah," he said. "I forgot." Then he looked at me with child-like sincerity. "Yup. He died just like that."

Milo's appearance at the funeral home returned to me once more, along with the memories it had evoked. This was the moment I'd been anticipating and dreading both, and I wanted to make sure I handled it right. "How did his beard get all wet, Danny?"

Danny looked at me in startled silence.

"He foamed at the mouth," Phil answered. "They do that with seizures."

"Sergeant Capullo reported that you two were living under the bridge, and Milo was camped out in the drain tunnel. Is that right?"

They both nodded.

"Why weren't you staying together?"

"Didn't like Milo," Danny blurted.

"So why gather around a fire like a bunch of Boy Scouts?"

Neither man answered.

"Look," I finally said, "let me get something out in the open. The doctor who examined Milo thought he'd died of natural causes—because of your seizure story and the fact that Milo was on heart medication. Turns out the heart condition wasn't fatal, and Milo never had a seizure in his life. I checked on that. I think Milo died of something else. Not anything you did—you were just in the wrong place at the wrong time. But you made up the seizure story to make the whole thing go away. Isn't that about right?"

Danny's mouth fell open, dropping a few half-eaten scraps.

But I focused on Phil. "Yesterday afternoon, I called your old landlord. You can have your room back, as long as you don't start another campfire. But I need to know what really happened."

"We won't get in trouble?" Phil finally asked.

"Not unless you did something against the law."

"We didn't do nothing," Danny complained.

"What happened, then?"

After a long pause, during which the food lay ignored before them, Phil finally said, "We didn't think people would believe us. We weren't all around the fire—that was just Danny and me. We didn't even know Milo was in the tunnel."

"We heard him, though," Danny said, excited now that he could say what he knew.

"Yeah. He was making all kinds of weird noises—shouting and yelling—sounded like he was fighting somebody."

"We were scared."

Phil frowned. "We wondered what was goin' on, so we shouted into the tunnel, you know? We didn't know it was Milo. Didn't recognize his voice or anything. 'Course, the echo didn't help. After a while, the noise stopped, and we could hear somebody moving—"

"Yeah—*shhhhh, shhhhh.*"

"Right, like he was dragging himself along. We weren't about to go in there—"

"Too scary." Danny was alive with excitement by now.

"But that's when Milo came out, crawling on his belly. His eyes were huge, and he had spit coming out of his mouth—tons of it—all thick and gooey. Scared the shit out of us."

"Yeah."

"He looked real sick, and just when we could tell who he was, he started spazzing out, flopping all over, banging himself against the walls . . . and spitting. That was the weirdest part—he kept spitting."

"What did you do?" I asked, feeling the cold much more than I had a minute earlier, a long-dormant horror now thoroughly awake.

"We didn't know what to do."

"I ran," Danny admitted candidly.

Phil made a face. "Yeah, well, I didn't think he was going to hurt anybody—'cept maybe himself. I figured it was the DTs, you know? But I guess I knew it wasn't, too. Anyway, he was sort of reaching out for me, so I offered him a drink—I had a can in my hand—and that's when he just flipped out—"

"He was crazy," Danny said.

"And then he died," Phil added flatly. "Just collapsed, right in the middle of one of those . . . *things* he was having."

"So they weren't really seizures?" I asked.

Phil shook his head. "I had a cousin who had seizures—fall on the ground and get all stiff and then fall asleep—pee all over himself. Milo wasn't doing that. He was gasping and shouting and flopping around . . . Like when you get hit with freezing-cold water—you know how you dance around and breathe hard and slap yourself? It was kind of like that."

"What did you do after he died?" I asked.

"We didn't know what had happened," Phil said. "First I thought we should just leave him there—let somebody else find him. But Danny said that was wrong. So we cleaned him up a little, invented the seizure story, and called you guys." He paused for a moment. "Are we in trouble now?"

I thought he might be, but not in any way he could possibly imagine. "You've done nothing illegal, Phil."

His face relaxed and he looked down at the cardboard tray before him, poking among the fried potatoes.

"But," I added, "I'd like you to do me a favor. Hang out here for a few more hours, okay? I want to make sure your landlord's going to hold up his end of the deal, and I want to know where to find you. Okay?"

Both men shrugged simultaneously. "Sure," Phil said, and motioned toward the two trays. "We're in good shape now, anyway."

*   *   *

I left them and drove straight back to the office. Still wearing my coat, I reached for my phone.

Decades earlier, while in the Army in Asia, we were shown

a cautionary training film about some of the perils of our new environment. It was a silent film, with no voice-over or music, featuring a middle-aged, bearded Indian man sitting on a straight-backed chair in a small, bare room. On a table beside him was a single glass of water.

For twenty minutes, the camera watched as the man, his face contorted and his body twitching, made every effort to take hold of the glass. His eyes huge, rolling, and totally focused on the water, he seemed desperately thirsty—and yet utterly incapable of simply seizing the glass before him. Finally, in a spastic lunge, spilling most of the water, he succeeded, although he still couldn't bring the glass to his lips.

Thick saliva poured from his mouth, impregnating his beard and dripping down his front. His body thrashed against the opposing forces tearing him apart as he fought to bring the now empty glass almost to his lips. Then, finally, mercifully for those of us watching the film, he suddenly stiffened, and rolled off the chair, dead of hydrophobia.

Beverly Hillstrom answered on the second ring. "Lieutenant. You're in earlier than I expected. I was going to call you later. I have disappointing news on Mr. Douglas. I can find nothing to contradict the opinion originally rendered on his death certificate."

"Doctor, I just interviewed the two men who found him. They invented the seizure story to make the whole thing go away, but from what they just told me, I think Milo died of rabies."

Her answer was short and precise. "I'll call you back."

Chapter Eleven

"Okay, everybody," I began, "we might as well get started." I held up a copy of that morning's newspaper. "As you can see, the *Reformer* has nothing to say about Shawna Davis today. Perhaps we can thank Ben Chambers for that. But whatever the reason, it gives us a small breather, just when we may need it."

We were all in the squad's conference room—Kunkle, Tyler, Sammie, Ron, and I, along with Tony Brandt and Jack Derby.

I dropped the paper onto the table we were gathered around. "From our perspective, the crucial difference between what we know and what we're admitting is the phenobarbital we found in Shawna Davis's hair. That distinction makes her death a homicide, at least until proven otherwise. I'd like to keep that distinction under wraps for as long as we can.

"You've all read the internal reports. You know how we've traced Shawna's movements up to a couple of weeks before she died. Last night, in response to a tip we received because of yesterday's article, Sammie and I talked to Mary Wallis, who admitted knowing Shawna, and to last seeing her in late

May. Wallis denied any knowledge of the thousand dollars, claimed Shawna only dropped by for the day on her way out of town, and said she'd only just learned about Shawna's death from yesterday's news reports. Sammie and I think there's a lot she's not saying. Mary Wallis, therefore, has become a prime suspect. But not only," I added with emphasis, "because of her being seen with Shawna in May. Wallis also abruptly dropped her opposition to the convention center project shortly thereafter, just as the groundbreaking was taking place—a crucial piece of good luck for the developers. That may be a coincidence, but it's one we shouldn't ignore."

I noticed Sammie's surprised look at this additional piece of the puzzle—something I hadn't had time to brief her on before.

"Unfortunately," and here I waved a hand in Jack Derby's direction, "by soft-pedaling our findings about Shawna, we also become the only ones treating her death as a homicide. That gives us a break from the press, but it also forces us to tiptoe with the investigation, including our communications with the State's Attorney's office. In the past, we've made it a habit—a good one, I think—to use his staff pretty freely for legal advice on warrants, affidavits, and whatnot. In a situation like this one, however, where the homicide may have wider implications, both the Chief and Mr. Derby have decided that we better use a single conduit to his office—a person who will either directly answer our questions, or pass them on to Mr. Derby. That person," and here I felt my face flushing slightly, "is going to be Gail Zigman."

There was a slight but telling stirring around the table, reflecting the same discomfort I'd felt when Derby had told me of his decision. Gail was not a lawyer yet, not a Deputy State's Attorney, and her contract with the office was only good for six months. The use of a single conduit for sensitive cases was reasonable and routine enough. Using the temporary clerk as such was unheard of.

Derby rose to his feet as if drawn by the unvoiced doubts around him. "I better clarify that. Ms. Zigman, unlike any other member of my staff, has close and personal connections to both this department and to most of the people who make this town tick. Since it now appears your investigation will be touching on aspects of how this new convention center came about—and on who helped it along—I've chosen her as the best suited for the job. Not only is she uniquely qualified, but since she's physically in the office more regularly than I or the deputies, she's much better placed to route your questions to me—unless, of course, she knows the answer herself. This latter case would only apply to situations involving personalities and procedures within town government—not legal questions. If any of you have any problems with this arrangement, I'd be happy to try to resolve them."

Kunkle, not surprisingly, spoke first. "We don't even know what our assignments are, and we're already covering our asses. I don't care if you got some wannabe as your contact. I want to know why the hell you're so twitchy. We got so little to go on here, it seems nuts to start sweating what the media's going to do."

This time, it was Tony Brandt who spoke up. "The media's not the problem, Willy—it's the freedom to move we want. If there is a link between Davis, Wallis, and the convention center job, it'll take a hell of a lot of work to prove it. It'll also kick up a hell of a lot of opposition if some powerful people get wind of it too early."

Willy looked disgusted. "You mean NeverTom Chambers. Jesus, I knew that asshole would pop up sooner or later."

Despite his abrasive manner, Willy had put his finger on the heart of the matter. NeverTom Chambers, so nicknamed because he hated the sobriquet Tom, was Benjamin Chambers's younger brother. Also rich and influential, he was as outspoken and vindictive as Benjamin was philanthropic and self-effacing. Worse—and most relevantly—NeverTom was a newly elected member of the board of selectmen, a position he was fully expected to abusively exploit. Considering that his brother owned the very project we were interested in, one he had vociferously supported even before he'd been elected, NeverTom's habit of throwing his weight around was not a happy prospect.

"Think about it, Willy," I cautioned him. "You really want him, his brother, their allies, the Bank of Brattleboro's lawyers, and a few dozen other screamers all down your throat while you're conducting an investigation that might lead to nothing? Who needs the aggravation?"

He waved his hand at me resignedly. "All right, all right. It just pisses me off. So what're we supposed to be doing while we're creeping around?"

"We've got three general points of focus," I resumed. "First, keep beating the bushes for more on Shawna Davis. That we can do in the open, of course. The second is to focus on Mary Wallis, starting with a canvass of her neighbors—"

"That'll be discreet," Willy said with a smirk.

I stopped. "It can be. The mailman said he saw Shawna at her house. Mary confirmed it. It's not too big a stretch to ask her neighbors if they saw Shawna in the area, and then engage them in a casual conversation about Wallis herself. She's an unusual person, and probably a hot topic on that street. It doesn't have to tip our hand.

"The third area of concentration," I continued, "is to find out if any connection exists between Davis, Wallis, and the construction project. We need to examine how the project came about, and look at everyone involved. It also means we should study this recent white knight maneuver by Ben Chambers. This is where the most discretion will be necessary."

I paused for a moment to let that sink in. "Okay. I've told Billy Manierre that we may be calling on his Patrol for help, but go easy on him. This is going to rack up the overtime, and I want to keep the town manager and the treasurer off our backs for as long as possible—"

"It's not like we don't have a shitload to do already, you know," Willy reminded me.

"I realize that, so that might be a good way to use Billy. Patrol likes to do detective work. Get some of them to handle your lesser cases, and cut yourselves some slack. Shawna Davis is the priority case—bear down on anyone who admits knowing her, and keep after that inscription on the tooth. J.P.,

I want you to chase down the phenobarbital found in Shawna's hair. Since it's a prescription drug, it'll have a paper trail. See if you can find out where it came from. Sammie, you start with the canvass of Mary's neighborhood, then go wherever it leads you. And Ron, you take the construction project. That'll involve a ton of paperwork. Find out if Justin Willette will help you out—he's consulted for us before, he knows his stuff, and he's told me several times he's available whenever we need him."

"I take it I can tell him what we're up to?" Ron asked.

"Absolutely. Also, as each of you proceeds, you might end up with more or less to do. If that happens, Sammie and Harriet will act as coordinators and either get you more help, or reassign you as necessary. I'll try to keep up on what everyone's doing, and I'll also be putting direct pressure on Mary Wallis.

"While I've got you all here," I added, "I think I better mention something else I'm working on—something that may cause some commotion around town. As you know, Milo Douglas was found dead under the Whetstone bridge a few nights back. I had some doubts about the natural-causes ruling the Assistant ME came up with, so I sent his body to Burlington for an autopsy. I also questioned the two bums that were with him when he died. Now, I may be jumping the gun a little, since the ME hasn't called back to confirm it, but I think Milo died of rabies."

A small round of exclamations greeted that, which I quieted with a raised hand. "From what I've been told, only about two people die a year in this country from rabies, so if it turns out I'm right, there're bound to be fireworks. I just wanted you all to know."

"Was he bitten?" Tyler asked.

I hesitated answering, startled by the implications of the question. "I don't know yet, but if he wasn't, we'll have to find out what happened."

*   *   *

Unfortunately, the ominous undertone of Tyler's question was almost immediately given credence. Following the staff meeting, I found a note stuck to my phone to call Beverly Hillstrom "ASAP."

"You were right," she said when I got her on the line. "We did a brain section and found rabies."

"Were there any bite marks?"

"No. Of course, that's not the only way to catch rabies. He might have acquired it via saliva exposure through an abrasion or a skin lesion. There's also the unlikely possibility of a respiratory infection—two people caught rabies by merely breathing the air of a bat-infested cave a few years ago. But that's highly unlikely."

I rubbed my forehead, thinking of Phil and Danny in their trailer, ignorant that I'd asked them to stay put solely to keep them isolated. "If anyone touched the body without wearing gloves, they'll need shots, right?"

"It would be foolish to do otherwise. Saliva is the primary vehicle of transmission."

That very point still had me worried. "Doctor, I know you don't like to hypothesize, but what are the chances of someone catching rabies without being bitten?"

"Statistically? Very slim. I called Fish and Game about this. As you know, there's a rabies epidemic going on right now in Vermont, so the state currently has a rich and current database of disease transmission routes. Of all known cases where rabies was delivered from one source to another, including human victims, every one was through an animal bite."

"What does that lead you to conclude?" I asked cautiously, having heard in her voice a true element of concern.

"Nothing yet, but I'm not finished with my analysis. I'm going to examine this body with a fine-tooth comb, Lieutenant. Human death by rabies is extremely rare in this country, and essentially nonexistent in urban settings. I'll do everything I can to find out how this happened."

*   *   *

I had a patrol car pick up Danny and Phil, and transport them to the hospital to be cleaned, inoculated, and quarantined. Not trusting them to return for the series of five shots required, the county health officials gave them no choice but to remain as wards of the state. It was a far cry from the cheap beds, ready beer, and curbside deposits of secondhand fast food they preferred. I doubted they'd ever want to set eyes on me again.

It was mid-afternoon when I nosed my car into Arch Street, off of Main, and rolled down the steep, downhill curve that ended behind downtown's distinctive twin row of stolid red-brick buildings, parallel to the railroad tracks. Arch Street was a perfect example of Brattleboro's unique personality. Down at the heels, littered, and ignored, it was thirty feet below and a stone's throw east of the town's vibrant business center, cut off by a rampart of intricately joined old buildings. And yet, just across the tracks and beyond a narrow swath of choking vegetation, was a spectacular view of the glittering Connecticut River, and of towering, snow-capped Wantastiquet Mountain on the far bank—the very best scenery the town had to offer, enjoyed primarily by homeless alcoholics and dope-hungry teenagers. Both the contrast and the proximity of these settings spoke volumes about the character of a town at once embracing and bristling, seductive and cranky, charged with staunch conservatives and new liberals. It was not a place conducive to falling asleep at the wheel.

I got out of my car, locked it, and retraced my route part-way up the hill toward Main Street. There, I left the pavement, cut through the tangled weeds, jumped down a small retaining wall, and found myself in a narrow gorge where the Whetstone emptied into the Connecticut. Upstream, the brook echoed loudly under the dark and looming bridge, now high overhead.

Picking my way carefully through the brittle underbrush along the bank, avoiding the ice-slick patches nestled among the rocks, I slowly made for the bridge's gloomy shelter, its darkness emphasized by the dull roar of the water's rush and the rumbling of the traffic above.

The vegetation petered out at the shadow's edge, making progress easier, and I walked to the midpoint under the over-pass and looked north, along the axis of Main Street. Before me was a five-foot-tall cement wall, topped by a narrow ledge, with a cement and stone abutment above it reaching all the way up to the bridge's support beams. Just as George Capullo had described it, a roughly cut entrance, not more than four feet in diameter, was located a few feet above the ledge, looking much like the cave of some wild animal. It was the outlet of the Main Street storm drains, and the last place Milo had called home.

I gingerly placed both hands on the rim of the ledge, watching for broken glass, and hefted myself up. Standing amid the charred debris of Danny's erstwhile campsite, I peered straight into the jet-black void of the tunnel, squinting against a steady breeze of surprisingly warm air.

I dug a flashlight out of my pocket and turned it on. Some ten feet ahead of me, beyond a rough-hewn ice-encrusted lobby of sorts, there was a bifurcation, with a narrow, tile-lined, twenty-four-inch drain angling off to the right, and a much larger, forty-two-inch cement culvert straight ahead, curving up and away, paralleling the street above.

Haunted by Phil's harrowing images of Milo's demented, spasmodic crawl toward the firelight, I headed for the wider of the two drains. There I came to a pleasant discovery. The misgivings I'd been harboring of a smelly, sewer-like environment were displaced by a dry, smooth, clean cement tube, wide enough for me to comfortably proceed in a low crouch.

Locked in the earth's deep embrace, the tunnel radiated a steady, even temperature—cool in the summer, warm right now. And fed as it was by the gutter inlets in the street, the circulating air was clean and fresh. As I moved rapidly along its length, I had to admire Milo's aesthetic pragmatism. Aside from the utter lack of light, this was private, protected, and comfortable.

It was also totally empty. For well over a hundred feet, I followed my flashlight's halo, the monotony of my surroundings only occasionally punctuated by the pain of hitting my spine against the tubular roof. Mercifully, just as my legs were about to collapse from their confined range of motion, I came to a service shaft—a vertical junction of the tunnel I'd been in, and another of the same size, heading the same way, about six feet above it. A manhole blocked an outlet some fifteen feet above. A steel ladder lined one side of the small silo.

I paused to stretch and get the circulation back in my legs. I also killed my flashlight momentarily to get a feel for the dark. The sudden loss of sight was absolute, and oddly liberating. I found my hearing abruptly enhanced, and became aware of new sounds that had been accompanying me from the start—the muffled thunder of a busy town, going about its daily life. I could hear and distinguish the differing types of traffic, the dulled thumps of tires passing over the manhole cover, even the muted scrapings of shovels working to free the sidewalk of packed snow and ice. It was all seductively womb-like, and added to the place's aura of safety.

That, however, was because I was healthy and alert. Had I been in Milo's condition, craving fluids while dreading the taste of my own saliva, my body racked by agonal paroxysms and my head feeling like it was about to explode, this haven must have seemed like a tomb, and the long crawl out of it a hopeless, frustrating, suffocating torture.

Tempered by this new insight, I climbed the ladder to the next tunnel and kept going—essentially up the middle of Main Street—alone, silent, and utterly beyond reach.

Finally, after another 150 feet, I found what I was after—a piece of plywood, laid along the tunnel floor, allowing for the occasional water to pass beneath it. Perched on its edge was the earthly sum total of a man who had slipped from this life with barely a ripple.

Standing my flashlight on end, so that its beam reflected off the pale, curved ceiling, I removed my winter gloves, replaced them with latex ones, and carefully began dissecting Milo's belongings.

As with the contents of his pockets at the funeral home, there wasn't much to see. Clothing for the most part, along with rags, towels, and blankets, in various shapes and stages of disintegration. There were several candle stubs and, surprisingly I thought, a couple of paperback books, albeit on the level of *Conan the Barbarian*. There was also a plastic bag filled with more personal items—letters so old and worn as to be basically illegible, photographs of people who meant nothing to me, a couple of pocketknives, one of which seemed an old and treasured heirloom. There was a stopped watch with a broken strap, a woman's tortoiseshell barrette, a blank diary with leather covers. As I spread these items and more before me, I knew each must have been as eloquent to Milo as they were meaningless and mute to me. I imagined him occasionally laying them out by candlelight, and losing himself in reflection, tucked away in the bowels of a town that paid him no heed whatsoever.

The bottom of the bag was filled with less interesting debris—petrified chewing gum, rusty paper clips, stiff rubber bands by the dozen, odd scraps of paper. There was also an assortment of pencils, long and short, and a hodgepodge of cheap ballpoint pens, some of which had been dismantled as makeshift cigarette holders.

Finally despairing of finding anything of value in all this, I began preparing to bring it to the office where brighter light and more time might yield better results. It was then, almost by happenstance, that I focused on the writing along the shaft of one of the ballpoint pens.

Obviously a promotional giveaway, colored a bright blue, the bold yellow lettering spelled out, "Carroll Construction."

I froze in mid-motion, my brain suddenly filled with more questions than I could grasp. Here again, as with Mary Wallis—and perhaps through her to Shawna Davis—was a connection, however tenuous, to the fifteen-million-dollar convention center that so many hopes and incomes were riding upon.

Chapter Twelve

On a sliding scale, Brattleboro's housing is heavily weighted toward what was once called the lower middle class, a term long since eclipsed by an array of more baffling, disingenuous, but politically correct substitutes. We had our share of grand homes—and of course the odd eighteen-wheeler box or two—but for the most part, we were a town that looked architecturally frozen in the latter part of the nineteenth century, when business was industry, and housing was built for a few owners, their managers, and a great many workers.

The homes of the latter had evolved over time, many of them becoming single-family dwellings, remodeled or rebuilt to look far better than the originals. Others had remained as they were—old triple-deckers, divided into as many small apartments as would fit. Depending on their condition, and where they were located, these catered to anyone from the poor to students to the burgeoning professionals.

There were finally a few housing units that reflected no historical patina, and for which no one kept any nostalgic memories—plain, shabby, decrepit buildings overlooked by most people, but all too well known to us and the town's fire and ambulance squads, who visited them regularly to either investigate odd, threatening odors, or to cart off another piece of human wreckage to the hospital.

The one I was visiting on Elliot Street was among the worst of these, its featureless facade hiding a squirrelly tangle of gloomy staircases and narrow hallways, all servicing a vast number of small, dark, foul-smelling dens—shelters to an ever-changing population, the likes of Phil and Danny.

I was here now, in fact, on their advice, having just visited them at the hospital. After my discovery of the Carroll Construction pen among Milo's possessions, I'd wanted to find out how and where he might have gotten it, or if nothing else, what he'd been up to the last few weeks of his life.

They hadn't been overjoyed to see me, despite my reminding them of their current daily regimen of free food, care, and television. Most people's misconceptions aside, bums do not lie in the gutter, dreaming of such tangible comforts. The "good life" for many of them may not be what they've got— but anything's an improvement over the rat race they fled. In general, Brattleboro's "regulars" were not demented half-wits, flushed out of a state facility because of fiscal constraints. They were erstwhile inhabitants of the middle-class rush to succeed—once married and mortgaged and managed by a time clock—whose hopes and ambitions had suddenly imploded. While the Dannys of this underworld might indeed be utter victims, the Phils viewed people like me as all but trapped behind bars. An enforced return to that life—especially in a hospital setting—was no thrill to them.

Still, life on the streets encourages tolerance, and these people, if nothing else, were experts at handling adversity, even if it came in odd shapes. So after he'd given me hell for the torture he was suffering, Phil had once more become cooperative, trying to remember if anyone might've known what Milo had been up to recently.

The man he suggested, to my chagrin, currently lived in the building I was now visiting.

I'd never heard of John Harris, but according to Phil, he

was one of the few, like Milo, who actively sought his own company. Bums don't tend to favor large groups, but as Willy Kunkle once pointed out, most of them like to know that at least somebody will be close enough—and care enough—to make sure they haven't drowned in their own vomit overnight.

Milo and Harris were loners. They avoided the soup kitchens, the Salvation Army–style organizations, and the summertime camps that sprouted up in the weeds behind Brattleboro's urban facade. They lived off the land, stalking the back doors of restaurants, foraging through dumpsters, and finding out-of-the-way nooks and crannies to sleep. Like cats, they wandered their turfs alone, self-protective, self-absorbed, and silent.

Which was why I wasn't heading upstairs, toward the apartments, but down into the basement, where Phil had told me to look for anywhere warm, remote, and close to a discreet exit.

That proved easier in theory than in fact. Stepping through a once padlocked, now shattered door, I found the building's basement reminiscent of a laboratory rat maze.

The image was reinforced by the floor being dirt, the ceilings low, and the lighting nonexistent. Even with the flashlight Phil had advised me to take, I kept planting my face into cobwebs, and feeling—the farther I went—that somehow, somebody was watching and taking notes.

The "warm" portion of Phil's equation was the easiest to find. The entire building's heating system, as far as I could determine, was based on the same principle applied to hot air balloons. Any radiators above me—whether functional or not—had to be playing second fiddle to the pulsating dry heat pushing up against the floorboards. For all its dank, subterranean appearance, the entire basement had the climate of a desert at high noon.

Locating a discreet exit was more of a challenge. Aside from the door I'd used, and which I doubted John Harris favored, since it led only to the building's front entrance, I could find nothing that served a similar purpose. There were no windows, and the only doors I discovered merely led farther into the catacombs.

I therefore opted for the third condition—remoteness—and began weighting my search toward those areas farthest from either the furnace, the electrical panel, or the staircase, all of which I figured Harris would avoid as being potentially too frequented.

It was following this logic that I discovered an abandoned coal bin, littered with personal belongings, and equipped with a large, waist-high wooden storage box, comfortably lined with bedding. High on the outside wall, an abandoned coal chute showed signs of alternate use—a crudely built platform was strategically placed beneath it, with footprints marring its top, and the walls of the chute itself had been wiped clean, presumably by the repeated passings of a clothed body.

There was no way of knowing if this was in fact John Harris's lair, or, assuming I'd gotten lucky, that he'd be returning anytime soon. But it obviously belonged to someone, and humble though it was, represented all that person's worldly goods. If I had the patience to wait, I knew I'd be joined eventually.

I removed my coat, wadded it up to make a passably comfortable backrest, and positioned myself against the wall opposite the coal chute.

*   *   *

A police officer's life is largely spent sitting—in a car, at a desk, outside a courtroom, even in an interrogation room, facing a suspect, using stillness to undermine the latter's confidence. But it is during surveillance that the immobility becomes most telling—and occasionally most taxing. Whether hidden in darkness or standing in a crowd, straining to pick out one face from among many, the time spent waiting for something to happen has to be made to count. It is a contest of sorts, between the cop and the hours, with each side competing to make the other wither and vanish. The hours take their toll through boredom, discomfort, sleepiness, or a steadily mounting impatience. The cop fights back with a dwindling arsenal of curiosity, endurance, and finally, coffee, cigarettes, and a growing need to pee. It is common for the hours to win.

In the decades I've spent engaged in this struggle, I have tried every strategy I could think of to keep alert, and have failed in various degrees, up to and including falling asleep. But over the past few years, whether through practice or some gift bestowed only on those nearing retirement, I have found a shelf on which I can park my brain, and from which I can merely observe—to the exclusion of all else. I think very little, move even less, and gather my conscious mind around the simple, single task of watching. My claim to Gail is that I have achieved the perfect meditative level she's been striving for her entire adult life. She says I'm merely losing my mind.

Whatever the truth, one trade-off is that I lose track of time, so when the peaceful dull murmuring of the dark basement all around me was suddenly and raucously disturbed by a grating sound followed by a loud metallic clang, I had no idea how long I'd been waiting for just such an interruption.

Despite my eyes being fully adjusted to the gloom, all I could see was the vaguest outline of a body slowly lowering itself through the coal chute, its feet outstretched and groping, until its toes touched the top of the platform. The bulky shadow of a man quickly followed, clambering handily down to the floor.

This was a moment to which I'd given some considerable thought. Hermits like John Harris are not best surprised in the dark, and I had no interest in giving a man I'd never met either a heart attack, or good cause to try to kill me. I had therefore decided to let him discover me, rather than force the issue, and so I stayed as silent as before, watching him place a bundle on the ground next to him, cross the room to a spot near the door, and fumble with something invisible near the low ceiling. A small, bright spark sputtered between his hands, and a lightbulb suddenly burst to life over the tool-box.

His back still to me, he returned to the bundle, removed a six-pack of beer from its bowels, and took one step toward the toolbox.

That's when all my planning went down the drain.

Catching sight of me, Harris screamed, jumped back, dropped the six-pack, and fell head over heels over the low platform behind him.

I leaped to my feet to see what was left of him. He was wedged upside down, between the platform and the stone wall, with his head at an angle I didn't think was survivable. His eyes looked about ready to explode, whether from fright or lack of oxygen, I wasn't sure. The only thing I could tell, if only from the strangled breathing, was that he was still alive.

I helped topple him over onto his side, where he lay thrashing feebly. "Who the fuck're you?" he gasped.

"Joe Gunther. I'm a cop." I was loosening the scarf he had tightly wound around his neck, hoping I had no open cuts on my hands. The smell this man put out was starting to affect my own breathing.

"A cop. Jesus Fucking Christ. You damn near scared me to death."

I stepped back to stop my eyes from watering. "Sorry about that. I wanted to talk to you."

"Talk to me? So you hide down here? Why not walk up to me in the street?" He had struggled to a sitting position by now, and was glaring at me with bloodshot eyes.

"I didn't know where else to find you."

There was a slight pause as we looked at each other. Finally, he pulled his cap from his head and rubbed his neck. "I could sue for brutality."

There wasn't much punch to the comment. "I didn't touch you," I answered. "Besides, you're not in any trouble. I just want to talk."

He considered that. "I'm not wanted for nothin'?"

"Not that I know of."

He gave me a crooked, brown-toothed grin. "Then fuck off. Why should I talk to you?"

I returned to my padded seat and watched him slowly regain his footing. "Because it'll be worth your while."

"How much?"

"I don't know what you got to tell me. A little could get you five. A lot might get you twenty."

He took his coat off, revealing a second one under it. "Okay."

"You know Milo Douglas?" I asked him.

"Sure. I know he's dead, too." Harris removed his second coat. Underneath was a ragged herringbone sports jacket. "You think he was done in?"

"Do you?"

He shrugged and took off the jacket. The next layer was a sweater. "Nah. I heard his ticker quit."

"Were you two friendly? Had you seen him recently?"

Harris sat on the edge of his platform, still breathing hard, and retrieved one of his beers from the ground. "He was all right. Took to the life for the right reasons."

He popped the beer can and drank deeply.

"When did you see him last?"

"A few days ago." Harris paused to belch loudly. "Maybe a week. We were sharing a dumpster. But he'd picked up a bit of money. Was at a restaurant the night before. 'Course, he coulda been bullshittin' me."

"He say where he got the money?"

"Nope." Harris took a second long swallow, finishing the can. He dropped it at his feet and reached for another.

"Did Milo have a regular route?"

"Pretty much, yeah. Up Putney Road early in the week, maybe spend the night at the north end, come back the next day. He'd work Canal end of the week. Sometimes he'd go by the kitchens, dependin' on the weather. He didn't like hangin' around other people." He opened the next can and half-killed it in a swig.

"Did he ever talk about using that new construction site?"

The other man was dubious. "To sleep, you mean? I don't know—he never talked about it."

"Did he say the money would keep on coming? Or was it a one-shot deal?"

Harris considered that for a while. "I don't remember the words exactly, but I thought he'd hit on somethin' pretty good. It's like he had the best of both worlds, you know? The freedom of the life, and steady cash for the necessaries."

He drained his second necessary and dropped it next to the first.

"We didn't find any money on him, or with his belongings."

He burst out laughing. "Well, shit. We get money, the last place we stash it is on us." He smiled as he reached for a third can.

"Would the stash be nearby? Where was he living last?"

Harris drank, wiped his mouth and eyed me craftily. "Where'd you find him?"

"Storm drain under the Whetstone bridge."

He toasted me with the can, obviously beginning to feel no pain. "Bingo. But the stash wouldn't be there—too exposed. Depends. I knew a guy once with a bank account—I shit you not."

"You sure he didn't say where the money came from?"

John Harris killed the third can, and made a pantomime of seeming thoughtful. "What's the meter readin' so far?"

"Twenty if you get this last one, but it's got to ring true."

He smiled and removed his sweater, dazzling me with a red-and-black checked wool shirt. "He said he was set. I said nobody was. He said maybe not, but he wasn't goin' to live forever neither, and this would sure as shit see him that far. I flat out asked him what his scam was. But he just said, 'Wouldn't you like to know?' "

I pulled my wallet from my pocket and removed a twenty-dollar bill. "Did he say *when* he got lucky?"

"Nope. Like I said, it coulda been all bullshit. He *was* dumpster diving, right?"

I got up and handed him the twenty. "Thanks, Mr. Harris. You've been a big help." I motioned toward the door. "By the way, I saw how you got that bulb going—good way to burn the whole place down. I'm going to get an electrician in here to put a switch in, so keep out of sight till he's done."

"I don't want no fucking electrician."

"Live with it or leave—your choice. See you around."

*   *   *

It was cold and dark on the street, and well after 10 P.M. I'd waited almost six hours for Harris.

Elliot Street butts into Main, a ten-minute walk from the Municipal Center. Considering where I'd just been, the fresh air, frigid as it was, had become a near-medical necessity. I walked along the well-lit, mostly empty streets with my coat open, willing the cloying heat and lingering smells to disappear. At other times, it was one of my favorite combinations of weather and time—late night in midwinter. Brattleboro was at its most benign—its businesses mostly closed, its workers dispersed to surrounding towns. It murmured of warm homes, people with their feet up and their stomachs full. Even the John Harrises were settling down, albeit less wholesomely, preparing for a comfortable night's oblivion. When I'd been on patrol, years ago, I'd looked forward to hitting the streets near midnight, less to catch bad guys and drunks, and more to experience the peace of mind I was longing for now.

Instead, with the little John Harris had given me, I was beginning to sense a vague but threatening pattern forming. It was illusory as yet—a fragile linkage of names and events—but it had purpose behind it. A girl had been killed, after being sedated for a week. A bum had been paid off, who'd then died of an unlikely disease. A once outspoken activist had become inexplicably mute. And hovering near them all, vague and yet oddly persistent, was the biggest single real estate deal this town had ever seen.

Somewhere in this quiet, peaceful town, behind a set of windows throwing yellow light upon the snow, there was ambition brewing, and ruthless conniving. I only hoped I could identify it and stop it, before it reached its goal—and disappeared.

Chapter Thirteen

Circling the Municipal Center to reach the parking lot, I had been planning on heading home without stopping at the office. I wasn't anticipating a good night's sleep—I knew how my brain worked better than that. But I thought I might try thinking horizontally, maybe getting lucky around four in the morning, and passing out for a few hours.

Seeing Tony Brandt's office lights on, however, I changed my mind.

He was working at his computer, smoking his ubiquitous pipe, filling the office with a thick cloud of smoke he'd been recently told was now strictly forbidden, under penalty of state law.

I left the door open to air the place out a bit. "Still at it?" I asked, parking myself on a low filing cabinet.

He sat back and pushed his glasses up to rub his eyes. "Yeah—budget crunching. Last year's level funding is looking generous compared to this. I'm considering cuts I would have laughed at a few months ago."

I didn't answer, reconsidering the impulse that had sent me in here.

"So," he added, seemingly out of the blue, "I guess Milo did have rabies."

I looked at him closely. "How'd you hear about that?"

"The ME's office released it late this afternoon, following standard protocol, and the *Reformer* picked it up, along with a lot of other people. It's the first U.S. death of rabies in two years, the first urban death in twenty, and they're going to paint the town with it. Between the Davis remains, the convention center rescue, and this, Stanley Katz's subscription drive is going to go through the roof."

His voice made it clear he didn't share Katz's joy. "I wish someone had asked Hillstrom to sit on the story, until we had a chance to sort it out. It was a little embarrassing handing out a suitable quote when I didn't know what the hell I was talking about."

I was grateful for the mildness of his reproach. We both knew Hillstrom would've honored just such a request—if I'd asked her. "I didn't even think of it. She and I talked right after the staff meeting. That's when she confirmed it was rabies. I asked her to do some more homework on it, but it never crossed my mind she'd release what she had to the media."

"She always does, Joe. It's part of her job."

"I know. I blew it. I guess I was distracted by her saying there were no animal bites. She says that's extraordinarily rare."

Tony gave me a quizzical look. "You think it was something other than an animal?"

"Milo had come into money recently—supposedly enough to keep him going for life—at least his kind of life. But he was very coy about its source. Point is, if someone was paying him off for some reason, they don't have to anymore."

Tony was skeptical, and still obviously irritated with me. "Murder using rabies? Sounds like a movie."

"We're already considering murder using phenobarbital."

I gave Tony credit—he didn't reject the comparison out of hand. "How would you do it? Inject it?"

I shook my head. "I haven't the slightest idea. The body's a big place to hide a small hole, though, and that body especially had its fair share of hiding places—sores, pimples, bug bites, Christ knows what else. I suppose you could smear rabid saliva on a piece of toast."

Tony raised his eyebrows.

"Hillstrom's the one who wants to do more tests," I said defensively. "And you have to admit, Milo's death is hardly clear-cut."

He changed the subject after a slight pause. "Your crew find anything new on any other front?"

I shook my head. "Too early, and I've been out of the office since this afternoon, finding one of Milo's buddies. Willy's checking Shawna's local contacts, such as they were, but I think if anyone's got more to tell us, it's Mary Wallis—assuming we can get her to open up. Her grief is real, but I think it's connected to something she's not telling us."

Tony didn't respond, presumably underwhelmed by how much guesswork I was passing off as substance.

I rose to my feet and left, unwilling to give him any more to think about.

*   *   *

I wasn't really expecting to find anyone in the squad room, but seeing a light radiating from Sammie Martens's small enclave came as no surprise.

I circled the workstations and leaned against the edge of her partition. She was bent over a yellow legal pad, making lists of names. "What're you working on?"

She looked up at me, her expression keen. "Tabulating the canvass—or what I've got so far. Shawna Davis wasn't just there for a few hours, Joe. I've got three people on Mary's block who saw her on different days. And the contexts are interesting, too. Except for the mailman's, all the sightings were either through a window or an open door. Nobody saw her going on a walk, or hanging out on the lawn, or riding in the car with Mary. One of them even said she asked Mary who her friend was, and Mary basically told her to mind her own business."

I smiled at having my suspicions confirmed. "What time span are we talking about?"

"Right now, I wouldn't stick my neck out further than four days. People don't remember dates. I had to ask most of them what they were doing at the time, so they could pin it to a day of the week, but it hasn't been a total success. Two solids are a guy who swears he saw her on a Tuesday; the woman who actually talked to Mary says she saw Shawna on her way to play bridge, which is always a Friday. That gives us the four days, but with no guarantees that Shawna was there throughout, or even that those memories are a hundred percent. Still, the odds of four neighbors witnessing someone visiting for a few hours only are pretty slim. A week or more is more likely."

"I think you're right. How did they say Mary was acting?"

Sammie made a face. "Fine. Totally normal. They all said that, including the one who was told to bug off. Two of them claimed she even seemed happy. Hardly the lurking conspirator."

"She may've been telling the truth about the thousand dollars."

Sammie didn't look convinced. "I suppose, but then why the effort to keep Shawna under wraps?"

I straightened and checked my watch. A little after eleven—not a bad time to catch someone off balance. "Maybe I'll let you know."

*   *   *

My plan had been to get Mary out of bed, putting her at a psychological disadvantage. But as I drew even with her house, I could see her lights were still on.

The response to my knock, however, was a long time coming. And when the door finally opened, her face was neither mournful, sleepy, nor conspiratorial. It was plainly frightened.

"Are you all right?" I blurted, looking over her shoulder into an empty hallway.

Her expression quickly switched to an all too familiar

anger. "What do you mean, am I all right? It's almost midnight. What do you want?"

"To talk."

"Ask my neighbors. I'm sure there're a couple you missed."

"Maybe so," I answered, making no apologies. "They've already made a liar out of you."

Her mouth opened in astonishment, and she made to close the door in my face. I stopped it with my hand. "We know Shawna was here for several days, Mary. We can talk about that now, or I can make it official—and cause you a world of trouble."

She looked at my face, and finally stood aside. "You people are costing me a fortune in heating bills."

I stepped inside and removed my coat.

"Don't make yourself comfortable, Joe. You're not staying that long. So what if she was here? Is there something illegal in that?"

"There might be if you knew you were harboring a criminal."

"I didn't. I told you that."

I was struck at how different she was from the first time we'd talked. Then, she'd floated somewhere between wistful, mournful, and deceptive. It had only been at the end that she'd started breathing fire. This time, the hostility was immediate, but fueled, I sensed, by the anxiety I'd glimpsed as she'd opened the door. Talking to the neighbors may have been even more constructive than Sammie believed.

"We told you she'd stolen some money. Why didn't you tell us the truth then, Mary? A lot of people think you're hiding something."

She buried her fingers in her hair, looking down at the floor, and then walked toward an open archway beyond the hall.

I followed her into a living room not designed for entertainment or relaxation, but more as an ongoing command center, equipped with several long tables holding stacks of leaflets, documents, posters, and books. There were two computers, both turned off, a printer, a copier, a postage meter, and an array of paper cutters and layout tools for making newsletters, announcements, and picket signs, all of which I'd seen her and her colleagues employ in the past. Covering the walls were posters, pictures, and framed newspaper headlines touting over a dozen disparate causes.

Mary Wallis headed for the sole piece of furniture built for comfort—a battered La-Z-Boy recliner—and sank into it with an effort, her eyes closed, her head back. Next to her, on a small table, I noticed a bottle of beer and a telephone.

I straddled an upright chair I pulled out from under one of the conference tables, sensing a small window of vulnerability I wasn't about to let slip by. I kept my voice low and quiet. "What was going on between you and Shawna?"

She opened her eyes and smiled weakly. "I don't really know. Maybe an aging woman's fantasy."

"Seeing yourself in a troubled girl?"

"Partly."

"Did you know she'd broken the law?"

"Not specifically. I didn't know about the money. But it was clear she was hiding."

"From what?"

"She said it was her mother. I guess we know now it was the man she stole from."

I wondered if that was wishful thinking, an attempt to mislead me, or truly what she believed. "You think she was telling the truth about her mother?"

Mary raised her eyebrows. "Just because a girl's eighteen doesn't erase the fear her family might come after her. The law hasn't done her much good in the past—why should she trust it now? You probably know a little about my background by now. When I ran from home, I was scared to death about exactly that, even though I knew damn well nobody was going to come after me. Maybe the paranoia comes from hoping somebody'll actually care enough to chase you—who knows?"

"How long was Shawna here?"

"A week, more or less."

"Why did she leave?"

Mary looked at me for a moment, weighing her answer. I realized then I hadn't been so clever. She'd allowed me a perception of honesty because we'd been treading safe ground. Her next words told me this was no longer the case. "I think my expectations were one-sided. Shawna wasn't like me after all—and she didn't share my hopes for her."

"You had a falling out?"

"Not exactly. She just left one day. I'd been out doing something, and she was gone when I returned."

I read in a book once that a visitor to Paris a hundred years ago stepped out into the street early one winter morning, and was surprised to see that the road wasn't sheeted in frost, but rather criss-crossed by narrow, frozen bands, running at all angles. His companion—a native—explained that the bands of frost were reflections of the slightly warmer sewer lines and drains running under the street, and that given the first glimmer of sun, all evidence of them would vanish. It was an image I'd never forgotten—and one which returned to me now, watching Mary's placid face.

"Can you describe Shawna's teeth?"

Her eyebrows knitted briefly before she said, "About average."

I was struck not by her bland choice of words, but by the fact she'd answered at all. Surely such a bizarre non sequitur would have normally produced a less measured response. The image of underlying calculation sharpened. "Any peculiarities?"

"She had a gold tooth." Mary touched her upper jaw without actually baring her own teeth. "About here."

"Was it decorated in any way?"

This time, her slight bafflement seemed genuine. "Decorated? No—it was just a gold tooth. Like a cap or something."

"She ever show any interest in Satanism or devil worship?"

Her mouth opened slightly. "What? No—of course not."

"One last question," I said, slowly getting to my feet. "What was Shawna going to do after she left town? Did she mention where she might go, or any people she might visit?"

Mary remained poker-faced. "She was born and brought up

in North Adams. It was all she knew. The whole world out-side of there looked good to her."

I walked toward the front hall. "Mary, I'll be honest with you. I still don't think you're being entirely straight with us. I don't know why that is, but I hope you're not into anything too deep. Because we're going to keep digging until we find out what it is."

She surprised me then by the softness in her voice, and the sadness in her face. "I know."

*   *   *

I closed Mary Wallis's front door behind me and took a deep breath of cold air. I frequently interviewed people who were less than candid. Most of the time, I understood their motivations—they were usually lowlifes who knew that talk-ing with me could either put them in jail, or cost them dearly in some other way.

But Mary was not one of those. She was a decent person who saw life as a cliff to be scaled, whose grim determination paradoxically fueled her vitality. As absurd as I'd seen her be, she thrived in her element.

Tonight, I sensed that cliff had gotten the better of her, but that instead of being part of the obstacle, I represented a helping hand she felt incapable of accepting.

Not that such insight was of any practical use. While it was nice to think she might be suffering from some outside influ-ence—it was just as possible she was a nut in denial who'd seen Shawna as some historical alter ego, and had killed her.

*   *   *

I had just touched my car door handle when a shadow slid up beside me.

"Get anything?" Willy Kunkle asked.

"A small heart attack just now. What the hell're you doing here?"

"Got a tip on the inscription you're not going to like."

I opened the door. "Get in. I'll start up the heater."

He circled around and got into the passenger seat. "I just

heard the paper's running an article identifying the tooth inscription tomorrow, quoting some of the local Satanists on its meaning. My source is a devil worship groupie who says her pals're licking their chops over the potential PR."

I adjusted the heater to its highest setting. "Why? The paper'll probably make them out to be kooks."

"To these people, no publicity is bad publicity. Any notoriety—the worse the better—is like a free recruiting poster. Besides, this slant is pretty good. Implications of virgin sacrifice? It'll have 'em coming out of the woods to sign up."

I stared out at the blackness ahead. "Swell."

Willy apparently thought it was. "The kicker is, they didn't bring it to the paper. The paper called them and asked."

I turned to look at his dark outline, struck by the coincidence of two major headlines jockeying for space twice in three days. "Who called the paper?"

"I don't know. Interesting, huh?"

"Yeah," I said thoughtfully. "'Course, it could've been one of the people you've been talking to—you've flashed that inscription around a fair bit, haven't you?"

"Not that much. And, I checked—everybody's claiming ignorance."

I indicated the Wallis residence. "I asked Mary to describe Shawna's tooth. She never saw any inscription, and said Shawna had no interest in Satanism."

Willy grunted, then softly said, "Maybe they're right, then. Maybe it was a sacrifice."

"Oh, come on."

"Why not? If Jeffrey Dahmer can stock body snacks in his fridge, we can rate a single lousy human sacrifice, can't we? All we got is that tooth, but we don't know what the rest of the body looked like. It might've been covered with Satanist shit."

"You told me yourself the locals didn't have anything to do with this. That the inscription was bullshit—to quote you."

"*Might* be legit, though."

I took a deep breath and let it out slowly. The heater was beginning to kick in, making the car more comfortable. "All right. So who benefits by leaking this to the press? The Satanists, following your logic. Could also be someone in the department who wants to feel important. Who else?"

But Kunkle responded by expanding the equation. "What'd you find out on the rabies angle? Is that what got Milo?"

"Yeah—that's going to be tomorrow's other big headline—but there were no bite marks."

"So what d'you think happened?"

"Hillstrom says you can catch it by breathing the wrong air, if you happen to be in a cave with a few million bats. So he *could've* caught it some other way. But she's unhappy not having a credible explanation. What interests me isn't so much the scientific angle, but the sensational method of death—titillating, just like with the Satanist tooth."

Kunkle grunted. "Somebody leaked the Satanist theory just to cause a commotion? Get us off the trail?"

"Or make our lives more difficult," I suggested. "It would be cheap insurance, after you killed someone, to gussy them up ritually, including inscribing a prominently visible tooth. If nobody ever found the body, that would be fine, but if they did, then the suspicion would be thrown onto something inflammatory like a bunch of Satanists."

"Or a hot topic like rabies," Kunkle finished. "Every crank in town would be pounding on our door, demanding we take action."

"You mean, 'will be pounding,' " I concluded mournfully, "'cause planned or not, that's what's going to happen."

Chapter Fourteen

It was an ironically funny front page—a human rabies death shoulder to shoulder with the innuendo of Satanistic sacrifice. In its eagerness to be all things to all morbid appetites, the *Reformer* had wound up looking exactly like the kind of scandal sheet its new owners were fighting not to be.

Unfortunately, I was one of the few who saw any humor in it, excluding, it turned out, the top brass.

Harriet Fritter appeared at my door before I'd even removed my coat the next morning, or gotten beyond the headlines. She didn't look happy—apparently carrying the spirit of her message along with its content. "The Chief wants you— he's got Wilson and Nadeau with him—and Chambers."

I understood her sentiments. Wilson and Nadeau were respectively the town's manager and legal counsel. Their presence in Tony's office usually implied a pending lawsuit or personnel problems. Chambers, on the other hand, was NeverTom, the selectman-from-hell. His being there, without his four fellow board members, was both rare and even ethically questionable—unless he had an explanation, which I was sure he was going to make all too clear.

I hung up my coat with a sigh. "Okay. If anyone else wants me—for anything at all—don't hesitate to interrupt. The sooner the better."

I crossed the building's central hallway to the police department's other half—home of the Patrol Division's shift room, Dispatch, and the Chief's office. Maxine Paroddy, the head dispatcher, gave me a hopeful thumbs-up through her bulletproof window as she buzzed me through the door to the inner sanctum. The allusion to Christian lion food did not go unnoticed.

The four of them were gathered in Brandt's office, its smoky atmosphere of a few hours ago now replaced with a palpable tension. Excepting Thomas Chambers, who sat comfortably sprawled in Tony's best guest chair, the rest of them formed a group portrait of straight-backed reserve, all crossed legs and arms and tucked-in chins.

"Have a seat," Tony said, nodding at the one remaining chair, an armless, wheeled perch he'd stolen from his secretary.

"What's up?" I asked innocently. Whatever it was they were after, I'd already decided they'd have to work for it.

NeverTom laughed good-naturedly, a bad sign to all who'd seen him in action. "I guess you haven't seen the paper today, Joe. They're screaming bloody murder."

I remained silent, although tempted to ask if "they" consisted of him alone.

Wilson, the town manager, cleared his throat. Over the years—and especially since NeverTom had appeared on the board—Wilson had slowly traded whatever authority and integrity he might have had for the ease of simply riding the prevailing current. "Thomas has suggested it might be smart to come up with a damage-control strategy."

"I'm not sure I understand," I said. "What damage are we talking about?"

NeverTom's smile broadened. "Joe, we're thinking ahead. I know you and your people are working hard on this, but you're going to find yourselves trampled by the media before you know it."

"It's never stopped us in the past, and we've been under much worse scrutiny."

"Of course you have," he soothed. "But Satanist rituals and people dying of rabies? This'll be on the national news tonight. We've already had to schedule one press conference for this afternoon just to meet demand."

It wasn't too difficult guessing the source of that demand, which prompted me to blurt out, to instant regret, "Aren't you breaking some kind of selectman by-law, meeting with us? I thought you weren't supposed to act unilaterally."

Tony dove in quickly, just as Chambers was opening his mouth. "Thomas is here at the board's bequest, Joe. Tell me what you were driving at, Thomas. Presumably, you have some ideas on how to help us out."

Chambers, torn between clawing me and opting for Tony's graceful segue, straightened in his chair slightly. "I was thinking you'd appreciate some extra manpower. I was going to suggest the State Police."

"Out of the question."

Tony's flat statement hung in the air, a bitter aftertaste to his smooth words of a moment earlier.

"I would agree with that," I added, returning Tony's favor. "The rabies death is a health issue—it affects this department only minimally. 'Course, if you want to bring in a battalion of Fish and Game wardens to beat the bushes, we won't complain. The governor might not go for it, though."

Chambers scowled at me, his jaw muscles beginning to grind.

"As for the Satanist hoopla," I continued. "That's based on a single scratching on a dead girl's tooth. There is no evidence of Satanism having played any part in her death. Keep in mind that what the newspaper sees of both these cases represents about twenty percent of what's actually there. The other eighty we're keeping to ourselves precisely so we won't be sidetracked by other people's hysteria."

"I'm sorry you see my concerns as hysteria," Chambers said

darkly. "Chief Brandt, is he speaking on your behalf, or just letting his pride overrule his judgment?"

Tony smiled slightly. "I think he's right, Thomas. I can virtually guarantee the State Police will politely laugh in your face if you ask them to bail us out. They've got far too much on their own plate to waste time helping us with some PR problems. In fact, not to be rude, but I don't know why we're even having this conversation, and I certainly don't know why Gary's here."

The town attorney looked as if he wished he could vanish into the rug. He waved his hand vaguely and muttered, "Purely informational."

Tony rose, forcing everyone to follow suit quickly, as if we all knew the meeting had come to a smooth and natural conclusion. "Please tell the board how much we appreciate their concern, but right now there's more thunder than storm to all this. And assure them that if and when we feel the need, we won't hesitate to ask for help. In the meantime, I think you should hold that press conference. We'll keep at our job, and the town manager can be the conduit between us and the board, as usual."

Chambers had little choice but to join the small herd as Tony ushered us all toward the door, but he wasn't leaving without one last shot. "I think you're being foolish. The way to kill this thing is with overwhelming force—take away the opposition's firepower."

By now, Tony had his hand on the door, and was closing it slowly behind them. He'd motioned me to stay. "I think you're talking politics, Thomas. This is just a police investigation with a few media fireworks—no point breaking out the National Guard."

We watched them through Tony's inner-office window, filing by the radio room in a disorganized, disgruntled bundle. I had no doubt the wrath we'd stoked in Chambers was now burning Wilson's ears.

"That was bizarre," Tony said mildly.

I laughed, forever impressed by his ability to dismiss such encounters. "I guess," I agreed. "Why was Gary part of it?"

"He handles discipline and termination matters from the top down. NeverTom had him here to make a point. We screw up, and our asses are up for grabs—or so he thinks."

He crossed over to his desk and sat back down, clearly conscious of what NeverTom didn't yet know about our ever-widening investigation. "Ron's the one looking into the convention center, isn't he? He find anything yet?"

I was sorry I had nothing to tell him. "I could give him more help."

He fixed me with a pointed look. "Do that, but tread lightly. If NeverTom catches wind we're looking into his brother's new business deal, we won't know what hit us. He's powerful and nasty. Not a healthy combination."

I thought over Tony's parting words as I returned to my office. Thomas Chambers was an opportunistic, manipulative, ambitious man. When Gail was on the select board, she'd fed me the inside dope on his quiet but ruthless behind-the-scenes ascent to power. It had been textbook Machiavelli. What most of the public saw, however, was someone else entirely—an easygoing local celebrity, wealthy and connected, who'd quickly mastered the art of the populist sound bite, and been elected to the board by a working-class mandate. It was a dangerous mixture of perception and reality, and would make our job a nightmare if we didn't proceed carefully. So, while Ben Chambers's construction project had only dimly appeared on our horizon, we were going to have to give it a paranoid-tinged priority.

I paused at Maxine's window. "Can you reach Willy?"

She depressed the transit button of the microphone before her. "O-5 from M-80."

There was a short pause. "O-5."

"What's your 20?"

"Green and Whipple, heading north."

"Stand by for a message from O-2."

Maxine raised her eyebrows inquiringly.

"Tell him to pick me up in the parking lot, if he's available."

She repeated the message, and we both heard a "10-4" in

the exasperated tone a tired mother reserves for an obnox-
ious child.

Maxine smiled at me. "He says he'd be delighted to pick
you up, Lieutenant."

"Thanks, Max."

*   *   *

Willy's greeting matched his voice on the radio when I got
into his car five minutes later. "What do you want?"

I refused the bait. The morning had been taxing enough already. "You find any other connection between Shawna and
the building project besides Wallis dropping her opposition?"

"Not yet. Where did you want to go?"

"The building site. I was digging through Milo's personal effects yesterday—found one of those cheap, complimentary
ballpoint pens with 'Carroll Construction' written on it. And a
pal of Milo's told me he'd recently come into money."

Willy's sour face cracked into a smile. "No shit," he muttered, and put the car into gear.

*   *   *

The construction site of the future hotel/convention center
was once again stirring with activity. After a month in moth-
balls, bulldozers and backhoes were cleaning out several
storms' worth of accumulated snow, and crews were milling
around the enclosed shell of the huge building, inside of
which most of the work would be done during the winter
months.

Typically, Willy parked his car under a large sign reading,
"No Parking," and pocketed the keys to make sure it would
stay there.

We showed our identifications to a listless security guard,
and passed through the gate after accepting two visitor hard-
hats. Not far from us, just inside the fence, several trailers
were lined up end to end, housing the managerial and office
staff. I headed away from these, toward the building itself—
an enormous, squat, L-shaped monstrosity that presently
looked either half-built, or half-wrecked. Its gaping windows

and doors were covered with thick, slightly ballooning plastic, in an effort to contain the warmth of the dully roaring space heaters within. It gave the place a vaguely bug-eyed appearance.

"What're we looking for?" Willy asked, as we picked our way gingerly across the newly exposed, rubble-strewn surface.

"I don't know. This job keeps coming up on our radar scope. You tell me."

Willy nodded as if I'd formulated a detailed plan of attack.

We entered through a tall, overlapping plastic curtain, much like what they hang before industrial freezers. Despite the openness of the structure's interior—all girders, steel grids, exposed duct work, and dangling utilities—the atmosphere was comfortably dry and warm.

All around us, people were working, either singly or in small groups, paying us no attention. We were standing in a space big enough for a commercial jetliner, minus the tail. This was the lower of two major convention floors, the upright part of the "L" being the six-floor hotel section.

"His buddy told me Milo usually spent the night at the north end of Putney Road, before working his way back downtown the next day. If I were a bum, this would seem like a perfect place to crash."

Willy looked a little incredulous. "You're going to check this whole place out, just to see where he might've spent the night?"

I began crossing over to where three men were clustered around a worktable covered with blueprints. "With a little help."

"Excuse me," I called out, introducing myself, "I was wondering if there'd been some kind of cleanup crew early this morning, looking things over."

"That would be Larry Amirault," one of them said. "He's one of the assistant supers—downstairs somewhere." He pointed to a door in a wall about a football field's length away.

I thanked them and headed off, Willy in tow.

Downstairs, the scene was similar to the one we'd just left, but without the daylight, the high ceilings, or the sense of burgeoning glamour. This was the building's practical heart, with cement floors and walls, and multiple concrete rooms housing the necessary machinery to fuel the needs of future patrons. Sounds of hammering, sawing, and welding ricocheted off a maze of hard surfaces. The overhead lighting—countless strings of undulating caged bulbs—gave the entire area an oddly disturbing feel.

I stopped one of the first people we came to and asked for Larry Amirault, shouting over the din. The response was the soundless pointing of a finger down one of the wide, gloomy hallways. Eventually, repeating this routine several times, we reached what I took to be the basement of the hotel, where we found a small man standing in front of an enormous, disemboweled breaker panel, a walkie-talkie in his hand.

"You Larry?"

He gave me a slightly weary look. "Yeah—what can I do for you?" The emphasis was on the last word.

I pulled out my badge. "Guess you must be a little under the gun, first day back."

He smiled apologetically. "It's okay. That's what they pay me for. But the place is crawling with VIPs asking dumb questions—slows everything down. What's up?"

I made my answer as low-key as possible. "We had reports the site might've been used by bums during the past month. You seen any evidence of that?"

He shook his head. "Not down here. I found a few cans and bottles in the lobby area—" He suddenly laughed. "And a pair of women's underwear. You gotta be crazy. The place wasn't even heated this last month."

That didn't sound like Milo. "Anything else?"

"What about the upper floors?" Willy asked suddenly.

Larry looked at Kunkle. "No and I don't know, in that order. I haven't had time to check upstairs. I wouldn't doubt it, though. People like crawling around construction sites at night. I did, as a kid."

His radio squawked and he told the caller to hang on. "You

want to check it out, be my guest—just try not to get killed. The stairs aren't closed in all the way up." He hesitated a moment, looking suddenly concerned. "I didn't report what I found 'cause it was junk, you know? Nothing was broken or stolen."

I waved my hand at him. "Not to worry. This is strictly routine."

He nodded, relieved, and showed us to another set of stairs before turning to his radio.

"If we find anything, I bet it'll be up there," Willy said, trudging up behind me. "If Milo's going to break in here, he's going to want a room with a view."

"Good point," I agreed.

One floor up, we came to the future lobby—wide, soaring, with one wall and part of the ceiling, now covered in plywood, obviously destined to receive atrium-style windows. We hunted around for more stairs and found them far to the back, only partially walled in.

The trip took us through a series of variously gutted floors, reminiscent of a model ocean liner I'd seen as a child—large and carefully detailed, protected inside a museum's glass case—in which one half of the hull had been removed to reveal the ship's innards. I'd spent half an hour studying it, trying to memorize it all, and had finally walked away dazed by a blur of uncountable stacked decks. I'd never been able to think of a large ship since as not having one side missing.

Here, as in the model, the normal partitions were gone and I could see as if through translucent walls, from one end of each floor to the other. Farther up, however, things began to change. Walls appeared, hallways took shape, and the vague outlines of the hotel's future look began to emerge. Ironically, in contrast with its more finished appearance, the top floor seemed utterly deserted.

Willy was breathing like a consumptive eighty-year-old by the time we reached the top. His attitude, however, was as solid as ever. "I don't know how that asshole got this far, but I still bet this is where he camped out."

Though dusty, uncarpeted, and raw, this level was essentially completed, making for a huge number of unpainted, sheetrocked rooms to check out. We each chose a wing and split up.

Willy's opinion of Milo's instinct for luxury wasn't just because this floor had the best view. Unlike what we'd bypassed to get here, this one was laid out to appeal to the well-heeled. The rooms weren't just cubicles with bathrooms and closets, but suites, with bay windows and balconies, and fixtures for whirlpools. The fanciest even had a mezzanine overlooking a living room—along with a tidy pile of building scraps, pulled together to form a human-sized sleeping pallet.

I returned to the hallway and shouted Willy's name. It took him under a minute to find me.

"Was I right?" he asked.

"On the money." I ushered him into the room and up the spiral staircase to the half-floor above. No railing was in place yet, so the sense of space—further emphasized by the gauzy, plastic-sheeted, floor-to-ceiling window on the opposite wall—was dizzying. We both found ourselves warily eyeing the platform's edge, even though neither one of us got close to it.

The hammock I'd discovered consisted of a scrap of sheetrock suspended between two stacks of wood, and cushioned with torn cardboard boxes. "*Somebody* slept here."

Willy was not to be dissuaded. "You kidding? Had to be Milo. Probably left a shitload of trace evidence." He pointed around the mezzanine. "Plus there're enough footprints in the plaster dust to fill a scrapbook."

I held up my hand suddenly. "You hear something?"

"People talking on the floor below." Willy smiled. "They better improve the sound insulation or they're going to have some pretty pissed-off honeymooners."

We climbed off the mezzanine, satisfied it had only the one access. At the bottom, I picked up a broken piece of sheetrock, wedged it across the bottom step, and wrote on it, "Police Scene—Do Not Pass—Brattleboro PD." I added my name and the date underneath it, and said, "That ought to hold them for thirty seconds. Let's get J.P. over here."

"You want to check anywhere else?" Willy asked.

"Yeah, but only after we've got this under wraps." I shook my head slightly, looking back up the staircase. "I've got a gut feeling Milo's got something to tell us."

*   *   *

Entering the main stairwell, our path to a phone was interrupted by a peal of laughter from the landing below us, coming from a group obviously heading upstairs. Willy was about to ignore it and head on down, but a recognizable voice made me suddenly stop. Remembering the sensationalist headlines I had no interest in feeding, I felt suddenly exposed—and for a juvenile instant even contemplated flight.

The debate was settled, however, when the first of the party rounded the corner at our feet and fixed us with a surprised expression. He was tall, slim, and well dressed, albeit in jeans and construction boots, with wisps of dark red hair peering out from under his hard-hat, which, under the Carroll Construction logo, was labeled, "Paul."

"Hello?" he said in a politely startled voice. "May I help you?"

The second member of the group—the owner of the voice I'd winced at—appeared by his shoulder, his face split open by the trademark good-ol'-boy, friend-of-the-people grin that had garnered him so much favor at the polls. "Uh, oh, Paul—we better cheese it—it's the cops," he said, after which, Thomas Chambers let forth an uproarious laugh.

"What're you boys doing here?" he then asked, his cold eyes the only harbingers of candor in his artificially happy face.

"We had a report of some vandalism," I answered blandly. "Didn't find much, though."

The man in the "Paul" hat frowned. "I didn't hear anything about that."

"Not much to hear," I continued. "A few cans and bottles—looks like maybe a bum spent the night. No damage. I'm Joe Gunther, by the way, from the Bratt PD. This is Willy Kunkle."

The other man shook my hand. "Paul Hennessy. I'm the

project manager for this job. Glad to meet you." He glanced nervously at Willy, who didn't smile, comment, or offer a hand.

The rest of the group had joined us in the stairwell by now, and were standing awkwardly behind and below one another—Harold Matson, the Bank of Brattleboro's president, Jim Carroll, who owned the construction company, Ted Mc-Donald, of WBRT—no doubt scooping the *Reformer*—and a couple of younger attendants, poised to act on the wills of their masters.

"Where's your brother?" I asked NeverTom. "I would've thought he'd be along on something like this."

Chambers laughed again. "Oh, you know Junior—likes to keep to himself. I'm the family representative today." He jerked his chin in the direction Willy and I had come from. "I take it the top floor is safe to visit?"

Not the most subtle of dismissals, and one I pretended to only half-comprehend. I pressed my back against the cement wall to let them pass. "Absolutely—go on ahead. I might join you, if that's all right."

Willy squeezed by them and continued downstairs while NeverTom's eyes once again zeroed in on me.

Paul Hennessy glanced at his boss, who barely nodded. "Of course," he said. "Happy to have you."

I tailed along, listening to Hennessy describe the upper floor—a series of penthouse suites reserved for the privileged, or for groups pooling their resources. As project manager, he knew the site in more detail than Jim Carroll, who was obviously along as a willing piece of window dressing—as was Harold Matson. This was the town's biggest financial crap shoot yet, and one they'd almost seen vanish into bankruptcy, lawsuits, job losses, and political fallout. The parade I'd hitched onto was a ceremonial victory tour for the conquering hero, Ben Chambers—or at least his self-serving proxy.

We wandered down the hallways, ducking into different rooms. The bulk of the conversation was between Hennessy, Carroll, and Chambers. As relieved as I'd thought the bank president would be by Ben Chambers's eleventh-hour rescue, Matson seemed curiously subdued.

Eventually, Hennessy threw open the door to what I'd mentally labeled "Milo's suite."

"And this is the pièce de résistance," Paul Hennessy announced. "Three rooms, including a bedroom mezzanine—bathroom, whirlpool with a view of the mountains, fireplace, small bar with fridge. It'll have two televisions, with optional sound piped into the bathroom, and phones everywhere. Of course, it's a little hard to imagine at this stage."

He turned toward the spiral staircase and came to a dead stop before my crude sign.

"Sorry about that," I said quietly. "Just a couple of things we want to go over. Our forensics guy should be in and out in an hour or so, and the place'll be all yours again. Hope it's not an inconvenience."

NeverTom's jovial voice took on a slight edge. "I thought you hadn't found anything."

In the corner of my eye, I saw Ted McDonald scribbling furiously in a notepad. "I said we hadn't found much," I answered. "But we like to collect the odd scrap now and then. You never know what might come in handy."

"Interesting use of taxpayer money," Chambers said somberly. "Isn't it a bit unusual for two detectives to be doing this kind of work? I thought you people prided yourselves on the skills and independence of your patrol officers."

"We do," I answered simply.

My lack of an explanation forced him to supply his own. "You just happened to be in the neighborhood?"

"That's right."

Harold Matson filled the awkward silence that suddenly stifled the lofty space. "Well, Mr. Hennessy . . . Mr. Carroll . . . I ought to be getting back. I want to thank you for the tour." He shook hands all around, stopping before Tom Chambers. "Thomas, again, thank you and your brother for your incredible commitment to our town. The two of you make an invaluable team."

The room's invisible spotlight had cynically settled on the

rotund Ted McDonald, the only person there they were all pretending to ignore, who had a small, knowing smirk on his face.

NeverTom pumped the banker's hand. "Nothing to it, Harry. Junior and I are happy we could return some of the good fortune Brattleboro has blessed us with."

I stepped out of the way, ignored in this flurry of mutual congratulations, and let the group file out the door without me. Only Ted stayed behind, stowing his pad, pen, and a small recorder into various pockets.

He joined me by the huge, plastic-sheathed window. "Amazing guy, old NeverTom."

I played dumb, always on the watch with Ted, despite a friendship dating back decades. "How so?"

But he wasn't fishing. He crossed his arms and stared out at the filmy view. "Oh . . . little things, like referring to his brother as 'Junior.' Ben Chambers hates that—as much as his brother hates 'Tom.' Makes you wonder what kind of relationship they have, living together in that big house, both unmarried, both so totally different."

"You know Ben well?"

"No. I've met him a couple of times. I'm not surprised he wasn't here today. Very shy. He's definitely the brains of the family, though. Maybe that's why Tom treats him like shit."

Ted McDonald had been born and raised in Brattleboro, as had his parents and grandparents. There was no one I knew who could better track the town's genealogy.

"What was Ben Senior like as a father?" I asked him.

"Competitive, egocentric, intolerant, judgmental. His wife died giving birth to Tom, and he never remarried, so it was just him and the boys. That's why they both hate their nicknames—their father used them to put them down. Now everyone else does the same thing behind their backs. I always thought they were a little strangely wired."

"Successful, though," I added. "Or are they just spending the old man's money?"

"No—as far as anyone knows." He glanced around. "You couldn't buy this unless you were doing something right. And

NeverTom looks like he'll be taking Montpelier by storm before long."

"State representative?"

Ted shook his head. "Nah—this project is Senate material. If they play their cards right, he could even use it to get to Washington. I think that's what he really wants. This 'blessed Brattleboro' shit is just that. He can't wait to get out of here."

"With his brother funding him all the way?"

"Yup. Each one helping the other—Ben with the brains, and Tom with the balls. Catch is, I don't think they like each other."

He turned to face me, our small moment's musing at an end. "So what's this crap about 'collecting the odd scrap now and then'? What's up there?" he gestured toward the mezzanine.

Figuring the best resistance was none at all, I crossed over to the staircase. "I'll show you."

I removed the sign and led the way up. "Just don't walk around. We want to preserve the footprints."

He reached the top and stood next to me, looking around without expression. "That's it?" he finally said.

" 'Fraid so. We're trying to track someone's movements, and we think he might've spent the night here."

"What's he wanted for?"

"Nothing." I turned and paused at the top of the stairs. "I'll be as honest as I can be, Ted, but you've got to keep it under your hat."

Ted was never one to run the Constitution up the flagpole. "Sure," he said without hesitation.

"We think Milo Douglas—the bum that died of rabies—might have spent the night here."

Ted smiled. "And?"

I shrugged. "That's it for now. We're trying to track his last movements."

He laughed. "I think I can keep that confidential. If you find something interesting, let me know, okay?"

"Will do."

I waited until I was sure he was gone, and then followed

him as far as the fifth floor. I had been wondering how we'd missed Paul Hennessy's tour group when Willy and I had been climbing to the top. Given the echoes supplied by all these hard, flat surfaces, I figured there had to be an enclosure of some kind on the penultimate level that had absorbed the sounds as we'd passed by.

The hallway, as I remembered it, was in rougher shape than the one above. There were gaps in the wall panels, and some of the rooms had no definition at all. There wasn't a single door in place—except at the entrance to one room.

I walked down the corridor, noticing how the dust had been brushed away by heavy traffic, even after a month's worth of downtime, and paused before the door, listening.

Hearing nothing, I knocked, and let myself in.

Beyond was an office of sorts—same plywood flooring as elsewhere, same untreated sheetrock on the walls—but there was glass in the window, an extinguished fluorescent fixture hanging from the ceiling, and several boards spanning sawhorses to make a desk. Blueprints were thumbtacked everywhere, along with artist's renditions of the finished convention center. A row of clipboards, each heavy with paperwork, hung from an orderly parade of nails under the window, near a dusty, well-used office chair and a small table holding a coffee machine. The desk was littered with the expected paraphernalia—a phone, a fax machine, two walkie-talkies in rechargers, a scattering of papers, and a coffee cup filled with brightly colored ballpoint pens, all labeled "Carroll Construction." I slipped one of these into my pocket.

Across several of the documents littering the desktop, the name "Paul" was written in Magic Marker. It was, by all appearances, the project manager's operations center, located not practically in one of the modest trailers by the property fence far below, but ostentatiously, high inside the building he was overseeing. By the assortment of folding guest chairs and dirty cups, I guessed Paul Hennessy had been entertaining his party here, when Willy and I had overheard them.

Which revealed another small connection to Milo Douglas,

much like the cup full of free pens. As best as I could figure, this room was directly beneath where Milo had camped out.

A small point in itself, perhaps, but to me, one coincidence too many.

Chapter Fifteen

J.P. was in and out of Milo's luxury suite within the hour I'd stated to Paul Hennessy. Having made no similar claims concerning Willy and me, however, the two of us took our time checking out the rest of the complex, not leaving until well into the afternoon. Our results, unfortunately, didn't match the effort. Apart from what J.P. had tucked away into a variety of envelopes and recorded on film, we came away empty-handed.

This included a second surreptitious visit to Hennessy's office, where I had J.P. conduct a fast but careful survey, hoping his specialized training might help him see something I'd missed. It didn't. While he did find hair and fiber samples aplenty, we both knew too many people had been through the place to give them any relevance.

My fallback strategy, therefore, became the paper trail I'd assigned to Ron the day before. To find out how he was faring, I had Willy drop me off at the office building of Justin Willette, investment counselor and CPA, next door to the public library.

The address was representative of Brattleboro's frugal solution to an expanding business district. Once an overtaxed, poorly maintained Greek Revival mansion, with a full, deep, wraparound porch, it had been remodeled to house five separate businesses. The only external sign of this potentially destructive invasion, however, was a new, eye-catching, multihued coat of paint.

Willette's offices were on the second floor front, and his own inner sanctum was dominated by a large dining room table in the center of the floor. It was seated here that I found both Willette and Ron Klesczewski, side by side before a spread-out heap of manuals, Xeroxes, faxes, reports, and minutes, all generated by or for the small battalion of committees, commissions, and boards that Gene Lacaille had gradually conquered on his way to obtaining the various permits for his convention center dream.

Justin Willette was small, rotund, totally bald, and equipped with a pair of glasses so thick, they looked like the bottoms of Coke bottles. He was one of an unsung group of citizens who routinely lent the department their expertise. Not a flashy man, he had done well wearing his two professional hats, and had come to my attention through Gail, who'd regularly benefited from his abilities.

Right now, however, both he and Ron were looking a little worn, and I realized without asking that they'd probably taken their task overly to heart, spending more hours than I cared to know about pursuing it. The overtime on what technically remained a low-flying case was going to be a sticky item to defend, especially with NeverTom at the head of the current fiscal clampdown. Maybe that, however, was why I really didn't give a damn.

As I sat down opposite them both, Justin pushed his glasses high up on his forehead, pinching the bridge of his nose between his fingers. "Ah, I was wondering when you might appear, seeking words of wisdom."

Ron smiled apologetically. "I may have pushed Justin beyond recovery."

Willette dropped his heavy glasses back in place. "Nonsense. It's been a fascinating glimpse into how the system works. I never knew there were so many ways for subjective influences to bear fruit."

I smiled at the wording. Justin could be as flowery as he was short. "Meaning what? Corruption?"

He waved his stubby hands in the air before him. "No, no—not at all, or at least not obviously. I'm talking about situations where certain people made choices from among several options, but always to the benefit of the project."

"Someone got to them?" I tried again.

Willette made a painful expression, indicating I'd missed again.

Ron explained. "It's not that cut-and-dried. It's been a little like planning a trip, and then figuring out all the various ways to get from one place to another. We found a few obstacles—Mary Wallis and her group, for instance, or aesthetic concerns that had to be addressed, like how the complex would look from the interstate. But each time an obstacle cropped up, it was avoided—after only a token bit of maneuvering."

"So it's the maneuvering that's got you worried," I finally understood.

"Exactly," Willette said, satisfied at last.

"You've identified all these trouble spots?"

"Well," Ron answered slowly, "all we could see. This only gives you the official view of things. Most of these people are fully aware when they're on the record. There's a lot that has to be going on behind the scenes."

An obvious solution occurred to me. "Would it help to talk to someone who knows both the players and the process?"

Willette tilted his head to one side, considering the point. "Sure. It might tell us who went against their own past principles."

I reached for the telephone.

*   *   *

Gail met us in the reception area and led us down a hallway to a small conference room. "Derby's willing to cut me loose for a half hour or so, but that's it. He's starting to wonder if you'll ever have anything to prosecute."

I squeezed her arm as she pulled out a chair. "Tell him it's in the bag."

She gave me a dour look.

Justin Willette began with a short speech on what we were after. Gail listened without interruption, smiling occasionally at his enthusiastic body language. At the end, she merely asked, "Okay—what or who do you have problems with?"

Willette leaned across the table and laid several sheets of paper before her. "There are three we are questioning. First, when Gene Lacaille brought his initial proposal to the town planner, there was a lot of enthusiasm. Gene was well liked, there was a perceived need to counter Burlington's domination of the conventioneering market, and the land, which Gene already owned, was commercially zoned and bracketed on both sides by shopping malls and stores. It seemed a natural fit. The town planner invited the site-plan committee, and Lacaille bent over backward to accommodate them. Through the committee, the fire chief got his hydrants, Public Works chose where the sewers would be, and Tony Brandt called the shots on traffic layout. Of course, the fact that three of the other members of the committee also sat on the planning commission wasn't missed by anyone. The summation reports were glowing, so Gene started out fast and well backed."

Willette interrupted himself as he came across a separate sheet of paper. "Okay, this is a little off the track, but it did trigger the first of our concerns. All this early enthusiasm was purposefully low-key. No one wanted to alert any potential opposition too soon. But Lou Adelman, as director of community development, *was* tipped off. He came up with the idea of a town loan for the project, financed with state money. There's no indication Gene Lacaille had anything to do with that, which made Ron and me a little curious about how it happened."

Gail was already shaking her head. "That's pretty standard. Once the town planner and the site-plan committee sign onto something, the right people are lined up. Tom Chambers made it very clear from the start he was in favor of the project, and would pull every string he could to help it pass, even before he got on the board of selectmen. By the time the idea of a state-financed town loan was first announced in the paper—with public meeting notices and all the rest—he and his brother and several others, with Adelman in the lead, had already been working on the idea for months. I also doubt Gene was quite as ignorant as it looks. He's got a bit of the politician in him, too.

"Go to Adelman for the details . . . and to the Bank of Brattleboro as well—they were scrambling to be part of the deal, but looking for all the help they could get. This was too big a bite for B of B to take in the first place—one of the Boston or New York banks would've been a more natural choice, but you know local pride . . . So I'm sure they all played a part in the two million from the state. But all that's not unusual."

"Isn't Gene and NeverTom playing footsie a little unlikely," I asked, "given the bad blood between their families?"

"For one thing, the bad blood was between their fathers. The sons never had much to do with one another. For another, who do you think owns the abutting land to Lacaille's property? By having Lacaille take all the risks on the project, the Chambers brothers stood to make a fortune."

"By now," Willette resumed, "Gene Lacaille is pressing ahead for permits." He shuffled the papers before Gail. "Since they all knew they had zoning problems the planning commission wouldn't accept, the project was next taken to the zoning board of adjustment."

Gail interrupted briefly. "That fits the low-profile approach. Few members of the public know or care what goes on at the ZBA—it's too technical and boring. So if you're expecting opposition, it's best to get all your obvious problems ruled on before you hit the commission, which is more in the public eye. I remember the newspaper played a key role here, too, which is why Gene cozied up to Stan Katz early on. When they went to the ZBA, it was noted in the paper, but with no fanfare or editorials. Katz was soft-pedaling to favor the project's passage—not that you'd ever get him to admit it, of course."

"Okay," Willette continued, "as zoning administrator, Eddy

Knox conducts an investigation into how the proposal might conflict with the various by-laws and restrictions of record. He discovered, among lesser problems, that for a building that size, there wasn't enough land left over to meet both landscaping and parking requirements. One or both had to be scaled down. The wording of his report was the second concern that caught our attention. Reading between the lines, you can clearly see where he softens his own findings by citing earlier exceptions in other projects, some of them not even in Brattleboro, and generally bends over backward to stress how minimally he thinks the project steps over the line."

Gail frowned. "That, I'd look into. Eddy's a picky, black-and-white guy. I was still a selectman back then, and although we weren't part of the process early on, I remember seeing that report, and thinking that for a negative finding it was awfully rosy. But I was for the project, too, in the end, so I didn't think much about it. Lacaille had a good track record, the Bank of Brattleboro was backing it, the state was making positive noises about funds for the town loan. I went with the flow like everyone else. But thinking back, the tone of that report was artificially upbeat."

Willette's enthusiasm grew as his suspicions found support. "Right, right, and Rob Garfield, the ZBA head, used that upbeat tone to sell the granting of the variances. That hit us, too, although not hard enough to qualify as a red light. It seemed pretty handy that Garfield was right there being so supportive, especially given his relationship with Knox."

"I agree," Gail said. "The two of them have never gotten along. I even asked Eddy once how he could work with a ZBA head he didn't like. He told me he needed the job, and that as long as he kept his reports straight and narrow, Garfield would never have the ammunition to get him fired. Unfortunately for your theory, Garfield was gung ho for the project from the start, so he didn't need to be bought off."

"Okay," Willette continued, his spirit undampened. "Now the ball ends up in the planning commission's lap." Once again, he shuffled some papers, bringing the relevant ones to the top. "By this time, months have passed, and Mary Wallis has organized her opposition, generating letters to the editor, disrupting commission meetings, circulating leaflets and holding rallies, and getting other groups interested. A couple of selectmen begin to wobble in public statements, and the commission is feeling the heat. On the other hand, Tom Chambers, Lou Adelman, Harold Matson of the B of B, and most of the business community are screaming about jobs and commercial vitality and how the convention center will help put the town on the map."

He paused briefly. "That's when the fight over landscaping hit the fan, exposing the commission's famous quirkiness with a vengeance. Despite the ZBA having granted all the necessary variances, including how much landscaping Gene Lacaille had to supply—to the exact number and type of trees and shrubs—the commission, using its own mandated criterion on landscaping, began talking about the 'feel' of the project—how it looked from the interstate, how the color might jar with the fall foliage, how the architecture looked harsh against the skyline."

Willette riffled through a thick wad of minutes. "Back and forth it went, with Gene trying to come up with affordable compromises, and the commission seeming to change its mind with every shift in the political wind."

He extracted a single stapled sheaf. "Until this meeting, where Ned Fallows, who'd been all but invisible from the start, suddenly stepped to center stage and came down hard on Gene's side. Given Ned's influence on the commission, that did the trick. Even with Mary Wallis screaming from the sidelines, the project was okayed. It went to the selectmen, who quickly passed it three to two, and then Lacaille delivered it to the Act 250 district coordinator, who reviewed it in record time. The final approval was given by the Act 250 board a year and a half after the idea was first proposed to the town planner."

Gail was looking confused. "Who is it you're worried about here? Ned Fallows or the district coordinator?"

Willette was momentarily silent, knowing of Gail's deep affection for Fallows. It was Ron who spoke, for the first time since we'd entered the room. "I'm afraid we think it's Ned. Tracking the arguments on the aesthetics angle, there's no explanation why he suddenly backed this project so hard. The minutes of this meeting show him almost browbeating the other members. And his influence didn't just sway the commission—the selectmen mentioned it as well, when they took their vote later on. Ned made the difference."

There was a stillness in the room as the three of us watched Gail, who sat rigidly still, staring sightlessly at the clutter of documents before her.

When she moved at last, it was to stare directly at me, her eyes narrowed and her face flushed. "*I* was the swing vote on the select board. *I* backed Gene because of Ned . . . You better be damn sure about this, Joe. Don't . . . fuck it up."

She stood stiffly and took in the others. "Are we done?"

Following his flamboyant presentation, Willette looked suddenly pale and stunned at its startling outcome. "Yes . . . of course. Thank you."

Gail turned and left the room.

"I didn't realize . . . I mean, I knew they were friends—" Willette began.

"Ned Fallows was the main reason Gail entered politics," I explained. "He was like a godfather to her—the person who taught her to think beyond her own self-interest. If we find he was dirty, it's going to take a terrible toll on her."

Willette began mournfully gathering his paperwork together. "I should have stressed there might be nothing to all this. These are just things that caught my eye—peculiarities. They may not mean anything."

"She knows that," I soothed him. "People have a bad day, it can influence their vote. The system doesn't work like a machine."

But the words hung in the air like off notes. We all knew what I'd said was only superficially true—integrity was supposed to iron out one's daily mood swings, and usually did.

Gail was not at her desk as I escorted the others out of the SA's office. She returned ten minutes later, her hair brushed and her face fresh from having cold water splashed over it. She glanced at me sitting on the windowsill of the reception area, waiting, but went directly to her chair. Luckily, the secretary was temporarily out, allowing us some privacy.

"We'll treat him with kid gloves, Gail. He's my friend, too. And Justin wanted you to know that what they found might mean nothing at all."

Her voice was tightly under control. "I'm not an idiot."

"You've already jumped to a conclusion."

She looked at me, furious. "Don't preach. I'm not in the mood. We both know goddamn well something's wrong. I should've known it back then—it's not like those meetings were behind closed doors. It's just that the suddenness of Ned's decision got lost in the shuffle. So much was going on . . ."

It was mere weeks after Gene Lacaille's project met final approval that Gail had been raped, her world transformed by pain, guilt, and anger. Ned Fallows had resigned his seat on the planning commission at around the same time, and had left town immediately afterward. Gail hadn't been in contact with him since. It was remorse, I knew, as much as his possible corruption, that was tearing at her now—that in his time of need, she hadn't been available.

And there was resentment, too, aimed at a potentially fallen idol. In a time when she was rebuilding herself from the ground up, driving herself through eighteen-hour days, denying the costs of an unbearable workload, she didn't need to discover that one of her heroes might have clay feet—or that the man she lived with was about to investigate him.

I crossed the room and took her hand. She didn't look up to meet my eyes. "Gail, I know this hurts. I'll handle it myself—go up and see him today. We've got to hope for the best."

Her only response was to squeeze my fingers slightly.

I kissed her forehead and left.

Chapter Sixteen

Ned Fallows had settled near Lunenburg, Vermont, almost three hours by car from Brattleboro. It was a tiny town east of St. Johnsbury, just shy of the New Hampshire border, about as isolated a community as anything the state had to offer. Hanging off the bottom of a 550-square-mile timberland wilderness in the eastern reaches of the state's Northeast Kingdom—so named for its nordic, barren beauty—the hamlet of Lunenburg is a spare collection of simple, elegant, isolated buildings, sitting in an environment as hilly and wooded as any described by James Fenimore Cooper.

Standing in its midst, late at night, when all the lights have been extinguished, it feels little different from how it must have been two hundred years earlier. Ironically, this is not as soothing as it sounds. The mountain lions, marauding raiders, and disgruntled Indians of old may have faded from the scene, but the wild vastness that once contained them remains, and with it an eerie sense of threat.

The setting matched my mood, which had been significantly darkened by the day's work. I ruefully recalled how the morning's twin headlines about Satanism and rabies had struck a humorous chord, when the convention center project had still been a minor, albeit interesting detail. Now, following the meeting with NeverTom in Brandt's office, with its threatening implications, and the looming possibility that the project just purchased by his brother may have been tainted at birth, I was longing for some glint of humor. Given my own friendship with Ned Fallows, and his close ties to Gail, the chance that he'd been corrupted threatened my professional detachment—and I worried that when NeverTom caught wind of where this investigation was heading, that aloofness would be sorely needed.

Although not very late, it was dark when I rolled through town on Route 2. Ned didn't live in Lunenburg proper, but two miles east, on the banks of Turner Brook, off a dirt road that only he kept plowed in the winter. It was an isolated, dark, and lonely spot, which I'd visited just once before, shortly after he'd moved there. I'd wondered then about his explanation that as he'd gotten older, he'd been longing for a little privacy. Now, despite my assurances to Gail, I was frankly skeptical.

He lived in a log cabin he'd built himself with a local crew. It was snug and solid and very small. Its size made it manageable—and clear that any guests, family or not, would be underfoot from the moment they crossed the threshold.

In true Northeast Kingdom style, I hit the horn briefly as I came to a stop beside his pickup, and paused before getting out. It was a courtesy one learned quickly up here, where occasionally armed loners and their dogs took a dim view of surprises.

There was no response, however, although the lights inside cast a yellow veil on the deep snow by the roadside. I got out stiffly, stretched, and shivered in the raw night air. The Kingdom is more thrust up against the sky than the rest of Vermont, and suffers more accordingly from its excesses. Winter starts early, digs in deep, and lasts far into early summer. The region's record cold of minus fifty degrees was logged in Colebrook, New Hampshire, just twenty-five miles farther north.

I stepped carefully through the snow, stamped my feet loudly on the narrow porch laden with cordwood, and knocked on the front door. On the other side I could hear the knee-high snuffling of a dog rubbing its nose anxiously against the thin barrier between us. Ned had a rottweiler—huge, handsome, and silent.

Eventually, I heard footsteps approach, and the quiet soothings of a man's voice. The door opened to reveal a tall, white-haired, heavyset septuagenarian, his face still and harshly lined, his pale blue eyes almost lost in deeply shadowed sockets—a ghostly apparition, emphasized by the light behind him.

"Joe," he said evenly, as if I was dropping by for a nightly card game, and then, to the dog, "Back, Hardy."

The dog amiably put his nose to the back of my proffered hand, but the gentle command was a reminder that for all his peaceful manner, Hardy was trained to attack, without sound or warning.

Ned Fallows stepped away from the door. "Come in—it's cold."

I crossed into the cabin's warm, glowing embrace. The lighting came from an open iron stove and several oil lamps, Ned having forgone electricity. The atmosphere enhanced the impression made by the nearby village, and left me feeling all the more awkward about introducing the vagaries of the twentieth century, especially to a man so bent on letting them be.

It was not a concern I had to consider for long, however. "I figured you might be coming by," he said.

"Oh? Why's that?"

He pointed with his chin toward an easy chair by the stove. Draped over its arm was a copy of the *Brattleboro Reformer.*

"I thought you'd moved up here to get away from all that."

"Old habits die hard—along with a lot of other things. You want something to eat? I got stew ready."

"I'd appreciate that—drove up without stopping for supper."

He indicated a single chair at the small, one-man dining table. "Sit."

I smiled, expecting Hardy to comply along with me, but the dog was already curled up before the stove. I sat. "You been keeping up on our latest mysteries? Satan worshippers and a plague of rabies?"

He laughed gently, ladling soup from a large pot into a bowl.

I considered slowly circling the reason I'd come, but I sensed he already knew. Besides, Gail's anxiety was pulling at me still, and I wanted to get to the point. "Why were you expecting me, Ned?"

He placed the bowl before me, along with a thick slice of dark bread, and settled onto a low bookcase opposite, leaning his back against the rough wooden wall. "I have my reasons. Why are you here?"

His coyness was like the confirmation I didn't want to hear. "Because there's a lot the paper knows nothing about, some of which goes back to your time on the planning commission. Why did you leave, Ned? Gail and I both know it wasn't because you were burned out."

The small smile returned. "How is she?"

I let a little of my disappointment show. "You should find out for yourself. She's tired and overworked and grimly determined to reinvent herself. She's also heartbroken over what we both think you did."

He shifted his gaze to the tips of his workboots, but remained silent.

"We've been examining how Gene Lacaille got the permits for the convention center. One day, after weeks of waffling, you came down like a ton of bricks on his side—"

"Is something wrong with the project?" he interrupted, his face for the first time creased with concern.

"How do you mean?" I asked, startled.

"Are you investigating something about the project that might be wrong—dangerous?"

I considered my options. Instinctively, as a friend, I would have tried to set him at ease. But I was no longer sure where he stood in that light, and his attitude so far had only heightened my concerns. "You trying to soothe a guilty conscience?"

His eyebrows knitted together in a scowl. "Don't."

I rose from my seat angrily, Hardy's eyes watching me carefully. "Don't what, Ned? Don't try to find out what happened, so you can martyr yourself in splendid isolation?" I stared at him. "Jesus Christ. Would you come clean if people *were* in danger? Is that the message? What if I told you your project was tied to murder?"

He seemed to shrink into himself, but remained silent.

I sat back down, ignoring my meal, and spoke in a quiet, measured tone. "For decades, you busted your butt for that town, preaching to others to get involved. You made it a point that integrity and politics were not contradictory. I can't believe that was all a crock. You stumbled, Ned—that's all. I don't know who put the obstacle in place, but I damn well know that commission meeting was the payoff."

"It was a good project," he muttered.

"If it'll help, I'm not debating that. I need to know why you voted the way you did."

He raised those sorrowful eyes. "If the project's sound, what does it matter?"

I played the only cards I had, weak as they were. "Because I think people have been killed in connection to it. If your actions were due to any pressure, then the same person who stuck it to you may've killed them."

Ned rubbed his face with his hands, pressing his eyes against his palms. He crossed to the easy chair, and sank into its embrace. Hardy lifted his nose and touched the fingers of his hand. "It can't be the same man," he finally said in a near whisper.

"How can you know that?" I asked.

"It doesn't make sense."

I almost laughed with frustration. "When does murder make sense?"

He was staring into the flames, and spoke directly at them, as if wishing his words to be cremated. "I did what I did to maintain the belief people had in me—my family, my friends, the whole community . . . Not my reputation—*that* a man has to earn, and if he loses it, it's because he deserved to. But for something bigger—other people's faith in a system they came to personify in me. Like it or not—whether I encouraged it or not—it was no longer my own reputation, which meant it was no longer mine to throw away."

As self-serving as it sounded, this might have been partly true. Ned Fallows had been a guiding light to many, Gail among them. Had he come clean and admitted his corruption at the time, it would have shaken a lot of people, and turned a few into cynics.

But for me, to whom most idealism is suspect at best, his logic only made a mockery of the integrity he'd inspired. Gail had been shocked and saddened by the thought that her idol may have fallen, but she hadn't been corrupted herself. The ideals that Ned Fallows had helped nurture in her were her own now, regardless of what happened to him.

But he'd obviously chosen to turn moral cowardice into a virtue, and no argument from me was going to reverse that choice. I gave up any pretense of debate and flatly asked him, "Who was it, Ned?"

He turned to look at me. "You think the man who fingered me could also be a murderer. Assuming you're talking about the two people mentioned in the paper, can you say for a fact they were murdered?"

I hesitated, my flimsy theory exposed for what it was. "An analysis of the girl's hair showed she'd been sedated with phenobarbital during the last week of her life. She was being kept in a coma."

"She couldn't have died of a heart attack?"

I was outraged by his rationalizations. "She was eighteen years old, for Christ's sake."

"But you have no proof she was killed." He pushed on the arms of his chair and rose. "When you have proof and a suspect, I'll tell you who was responsible for my actions." He ushered me toward the door, barely giving me time to put on the coat I'd removed upon entering.

"I thought a person was responsible for his own actions," I said bitterly, my sense of betrayal approaching Gail's.

"That's not a discussion I choose to have—with you or anyone else," he said, and closed the door.

*   *   *

It was almost three in the morning when I got back home. The moonlight slanting over the bed revealed Gail's dormant shape, suspiciously still for someone who'd become a very light sleeper. Knowing she was awake, I nevertheless undressed quietly, and slipped under the covers.

A few moments later, her hand folded over my wrist. "How did it go?"

I'd been debating how to answer her all the way back from Lunenburg, and had finally settled on the honesty Ned Fallows had denied me. "Disappointing. He basically admitted he'd been compromised, although he'd thought the project was worthwhile, but he wouldn't tell me why or by who. He said he cut and ran to protect the people who'd believed in him—that he didn't care about his own reputation, but was worried his downfall could damage the hope he'd spent his whole life nurturing in others."

I'd tried to sound neutral, to allow Gail whatever leeway she might need to reach her own conclusions.

I needn't have worried. After a long reflective pause, she curled one leg over mine, and murmured into my shoulder with a sigh, "What bullshit."

*   *   *

I didn't have long to enjoy the peace of mind Gail had brought me. I had barely nodded off before the phone next to me began ringing.

"Joe? It's Sammie. Patrol just called. I thought you'd want to know—Mary Wallis is missing. Her house is all lit up, the door's wide open, but she's disappeared."

"You there yet?"

"No—I'm heading out now."

"I'm on my way."

Gail asked me what was up as I replaced the receiver. I repeated Sammie's brief message. She slid out of bed, reaching for her clothes. "I'm coming, too."

I didn't argue. She wasn't only Mary's friend, she was—however marginally—one of the SA's staffers. More to the point, I knew she needed to come. While the loss of Ned Fallows had been in spirit alone, it had been real all the same, and Gail had born it stoically—perhaps overly so. The need for action now seemed healthy and reasonable, and I wasn't about to interfere.

*   *   *

Most of the houses on Allerton Avenue were dark, except for a couple of Mary's neighbors. The patrol car stationed opposite her address, and Sammie's just beyond it, were shrouded by night, only the plumes from their exhaust pipes betraying their running engines.

I pulled over and Gail and I got out, closing our doors quietly. Sammie's familiar slim shadow appeared in the yellow cutout of Mary's front door and gestured to us.

"What happened?" I asked as we drew near.

Sammie stepped back over the threshold. "How're you doing, Gail? Sol was on patrol, saw the door wide open when he drove by. He kept going to the end of the block, but when he came back and saw nothing had changed, he decided to check it out. The place was empty."

"Where's Sol now?" I asked.

Sol Stennis, only two years on the job, but a thoughtful, perceptive man, spoke up from the living room. "Here." He appeared in the doorway. "I haven't had a chance to interview the neighbors yet." He noticed Gail standing behind me. "Hi, Ms. Zigman. I'm sorry about this—hope she's okay."

I looked at both Sammie and Sol. "No signs of disturbance?"

"Nothing," Sol admitted. "The furnace was going full guns when I arrived, and the place was pretty cold, so the door'd been open a while. When I first drove by, I thought maybe she'd gone out to take care of a pet or get something from the garage, but obviously not."

"Her car still here?" Gail asked suddenly.

"Yeah," Sammie answered. "The engine's cold."

Gail crossed over to the hall closet and opened its door, extracting a dark blue quilted coat. "I think we can rule out a walk around the block. This is the only winter coat I've seen her wear the last three years."

"Damn," I murmured, dread seeping into me. I shut the front door. "Sammie, you better call in a team."

*   *   *

In half an hour we'd divided into four teams—one checking the inside of the house, led by J. P. Tyler, the second covering the grounds, and the third conducting yet another neighborhood canvass of people who, especially at this hour, were probably ruing the day they'd chosen this street to live on. The fourth team, under Ron Klesczewski, was back at the office, phoning—and waking up—every person we could either think of or find in Mary's address book and files, to check when they'd last seen her. Additionally, all hotels, motels, rooming houses, hospitals, clinics, drop-in shelters, taxi and bus services were being checked. We also put a covert watch on Mary's mother at the Retreat. If Mary was still operating under her own steam, I doubted her daily visits to her mother would be an easy habit to break.

I set up a command post in the kitchen, with a phone and a portable radio, and directed a wider search to cover both the town and its neighboring communities. Despite the total absence of any signs of foul play, not a single person questioned why an open door and an empty house should generate such a massive response. Such was the consensus that something was seriously wrong. And several fruitless hours later, with Gail looking increasingly haggard but refusing to go home, any concerns that we might have overreacted were quickly fading.

It was then that J.P. came into the kitchen, carrying one of his ubiquitous large white evidence envelopes. "I thought you better see this. Found it hidden in a closet."

He poured the packet's contents onto the tabletop and handed me a pair of latex gloves. It was a woman's purse—inexpensive and gaudy—more a teenager's fashion prop than a practical accessory.

Gail was watching me intently as I donned the gloves. "That's not anything I've ever seen Mary use. She wouldn't be caught dead with it."

I gingerly opened the purse and peered inside, fishing out the two items I found—a wad of old bills, held together with a rubber band, and a cracked, beige, fake-leather wallet.

"You count the money?" I asked him, loath to disturb the evidence more than necessary.

"Thousand bucks even."

I opened the wallet with two fingers. A driver's license stared back at me from behind a cloudy plastic window.

"Oh, my God," Gail murmured.

The license belonged to Shawna Susan Davis.

Chapter Seventeen

By mid-morning Mary Wallis had still not been found. The last sighting of her had been around suppertime the previous evening, when she'd dropped off some papers at a friend's house, saying she was heading home. Her neighbors hadn't noticed the open door, since it was screened by a trellis from all but a straight-on view from the curb. And Mary was known as a night owl, so nobody had thought twice about seeing her lights on when the last of them went to bed. No unusual traffic had been noticed on the street until we'd arrived.

Aside from Shawna Davis's purse, nothing of note was discovered either in or outside the house—no footprints, no scratches on windowsills or door locks, so signs of blood or violence, no significant notes or letters. There was nothing to tell us that this wasn't merely the empty domicile of a woman living alone.

J.P. collected his usual array of samples to send off to the State Police lab in Waterbury, with no great hopes for any of it, but he used an iodine fuming gun to momentarily reveal and photograph the prints on the smooth pale exterior of

Shawna's wallet. The process didn't alter the evidence any—
the prints briefly appeared as clear purple weals, revealed as
if by magic by the iodine fumes blown across their surface,
and then slowly faded back to obscurity. It was a shortcut allowing an instant sneak preview of what the lab would report
in a week or so. In this case, it merely confirmed what the
discovery had suggested—Mary Wallis's fingerprints were
among those on the wallet. An officer was dispatched to
North Adams immediately to collect any items of Shawna's
guaranteed to have her prints on them, so we could compare
them to the others on the wallet. But we weren't holding our
breath for any surprises.

I, however, had more than just this scanty evidence to ponder. I hadn't forgotten how frightened Mary had seemed
when she'd last opened her door to me, nor could I dismiss
the impression I'd been left with of a woman in real need of
help, and yet incapable of asking for it. I was all but convinced that some terrible pressure had been put on her recently, above and beyond her grief over Shawna's death, and
that we were now facing its end result.

Willy Kunkle, never much for similar reflection, gave voice
only to the obvious implications. "She stole the money,
whacked the kid, and then took off when she thought we
were on to her."

Sammie shook her head disgustedly. "Jesus. She's going to
kill a girl for a thousand bucks and then never spend it? And
when she makes her big escape, she doesn't take her coat or
her car and leaves the door wide open? Give me a break."

All the squad members, along with Tony and Harriet Fritter,
were in the squad room by now, sitting in scattered chairs or
parked on the edges of tables.

"You saying Wallis had all her screws down tight?" Willy
shot back. "I don't think so. The girl spends a few days with
her, maybe Wallis gets the hots, makes a pass, gets rejected,
and bam. She doesn't *steal* the dough—she just stashes it, like
she did the body."

"What about the phenobarbital?" Tony asked quietly.

Willy shrugged and looked at Tyler, who admitted, "I

checked every pharmacist we know she did business with. She never had a prescription for the stuff. And the three doctors I found who ever treated her said they never gave her any. It's not the most difficult med in the world to get hold of, though."

"But why use it at all?" Sammie persisted. "Why keep Shawna sedated for a week before killing her?"

Willy waved his hand dismissively at her. "Maybe she wanted to pick her moment, and had to keep the body alive so it wouldn't rot. Pretty slick plan, when you think about it. And the Satanist blind alley was a nice extra touch—pointed the finger at somebody else, and meant she didn't have to bury the body deep, which a small woman like Wallis would've had trouble doing anyhow."

Sammie turned to me. "You interviewed her last. You didn't think she'd killed Shawna then."

"I also didn't think she knew anything about the money," I said. "But I was going on impressions. It's hard to argue with what we've got now. And she did drop out of the political scene at the exact time Shawna died."

"Because she was heartbroken."

Willy laughed. "Oh, come on. She's fighting one of the biggest political battles of her career, and she dumps it because some teenybopper jilts her? Get real, Sam—it makes more sense she knocked her off and then lost her grip. Look at the woman's background—she's a prime candidate for a nut house."

Sammie fell silent, temporarily beaten down.

I gave her a little support. "That's scenario A. But it doesn't take anything else into account—Milo's death and the irregularities surrounding the convention center project. In a town this size, we'd be idiots to assume that two deaths, a disappearance, and the possibility of a corrupt real estate deal are all coincidences. It would be safer to think they *might* be related, and work from there."

Everyone looked at Willy for a reaction, but he kept his peace, scowling. He'd often enough said that anyone who relied on coincidence was a jerk.

I tried to dissipate the tension. "So let's find out if there *are* any connections. Right now, both the Shawna and Milo death investigations are in a holding pattern, pending developments. The Wallis case is wide open, and currently gets top priority, although for the moment, with our own Patrol and all surrounding law enforcement agencies chipping in, we're doing pretty much all we can. The convention center project's looking a little more promising. Ron and Justin Willette came up with a few names we need to look at more closely. Sammie will hand out assignments. We're looking for lifestyle changes or signs of sudden wealth, during the year and a half the project was getting permits. I want to see if we can get enough on these people so a judge will cut us subpoenas for their bank records. But remember to be subtle about it—for our sake. We don't want a lot of thin-skinned bureaucrats screaming to the media and giving whoever's responsible enough time to destroy evidence."

"Is NeverTom on Ron and Willette's list?" Willy asked contentiously.

"No. But if he is involved, he's probably the one pulling the strings," Sammie answered. "First, we need to look at people like Eddy Knox, the zoning administrator, and Ned Fallows and Rob Garfield of the ZBA, and Lou Adelman. They may be the small fry, but if they're crooked and we can get to them, we can use them to lead us to the top guys."

"Don't think we won't look into the Chamberses, Willy," I added. "But we need to take the time to do this right, by the numbers. If we're right about all these cases being interconnected, then we'll be doing a lot more than digging up dirt on a few bigwigs. We might be saving Mary Wallis's life."

*   *   *

Shortly afterward, in my office, I dialed the State Police in St. Johnsbury, and asked for Lieutenant Mel Hamilton, the barracks commander. Several years ago, I'd worked with the Essex County SA's office, and had coordinated with Hamilton on a case. We'd become pretty friendly, and had kept in touch over the years.

"Hi, Joe. What's up?" he asked.

"You don't follow the news?"

He laughed. "Well, I figured it'd been twenty-four hours already—time to add an extraterrestrial sighting to your list, or maybe a tidal wave. Is there any truth to that Satanism stuff?"

"Maybe—it's probably a smoke screen. Unfortunately, smoke is all I've got right now."

"Which is why you're calling."

"I need a favor. Could you have someone pick up a man named Ned Fallows? Lives in a log cabin two miles east of Lunenburg, on the dirt road crossing Turner Brook. I want to talk to him, and he has no phone. Something's come up down here I want him to explain."

"This a bad boy?"

"He's a seventy-year-old retired town planning commissioner who got his hands dirty. I was up there last night, but he wouldn't fess up. I'm hoping I just found the right piece of persuasion."

"Okay. I'll put it on the radio."

"Thanks. Better tell 'em to go slow and polite—he's got a rottweiler. Quiet but big."

"Great."

I'd barely hung up when Harriet buzzed me on the intercom. "Line one, Joe—Conrad Blessing at Guillaume's Funeral Home."

Surprised, I picked the phone back up. "Conrad. How can I help you?"

Blessing's voice was hesitant, seemingly embarrassed. "I hate to bother you. But I think I found something you ought to see."

"Something to do with Milo?"

"Oh, no. I'm afraid it's someone else. We had a customer delivered from the Skyview Nursing Home—an elderly woman who died last night. She has a death certificate listing natural causes, but . . . I suppose this is crazy. I shouldn't have called."

"Don't worry about it. I'll be right over."

I grabbed my coat and headed for the hallway, calling out

to Tyler, "J.P., sounds like I'll need you on this one. I'll be at Guillaume's," I told Harriet. "I'm expecting a call from up-state—the VSP. If it comes in, get the number, and call me at Guillaume's. Tell them not to leave, okay?"

She smiled and waved me out.

*   *   *

Conrad Blessing opened the front door to the funeral home as we reached the top porch step. "I hope this is worth your while. It's just that . . . well, I think there's something strange, and considering how things turned out with Mr. Douglas . . ."

"Why don't you show us what you've got?" I suggested.

Relieved, he led us down the familiar back hallway, and through a wide, locked door into a brightly lit room with a gleaming metal table in its center. The body of a dead woman lay there, dressed in a flowered nightgown.

"This is Mrs. Adele Sawyer, eighty-three years old. Apparently, she had a bad heart—you can see that from the swollen ankles—and I guess the Skyview's attending physician, Dr. Riley, figured nature had taken its course."

We approached the table, and J.P., already having donned a pair of latex gloves, began to gently examine the dead woman's head, face, and neck. "I think I see what caught your eye," he said a minute later.

Blessing moved to the body's other side, and pointed at Mrs. Sawyer's generously proportioned neck. "It seems bruised, doesn't it? I thought at first it might be dirt. Some of the older people have a hard time washing themselves, as-suming they can move at all, but it's not, is it?"

Tyler moved to the woman's mouth, and peeled back both her upper and lower lips, revealing the pale gums under-neath. "No, it's not," he said. "See this piece of tissue stretch-ing between the gum and the inside of the lip, right at the mouth's midline? It's called the frenulum. It's easily bruised when pressure is placed against the lips."

He paused, looking more carefully, prompting Blessing to ask, "What does that mean?"

Tyler straightened and removed his gloves with a snap.

"I'm no pathologist, but from what I see, this woman's mouth was covered with one hand, to stifle any noise, while she was strangled to death with the other."

*   *   *

The Skyview Nursing Home had no view to speak of, the local joke being that the name was literally true, no more and no less. It was located in West Brattleboro, on a street off of Route 9, the town's main thoroughfare, in a large, scooped-out natural depression at the foot of a steeply rising hill. On its other three sides were low-cost, single housing units, mostly painted gray, collectively labeled Skyview Village.

Among homes for the elderly, the Skyview occupied a genteel middle ground—it was neither a clinically supervised resort for the independent rich, nor a medical repository for the abandoned near-dead. Several of its patients had Alzheimer's or a different chronic disorder, while others had simply grown unable to live on their own. Virtually all of them were supported by some form of government assistance. They came to the Skyview to dwindle away in the care of a pleasant, competent staff, which in turn was supported by an outside group of physicians who dropped by for periodic visits. Death here was an accepted part of life, and until now, a matter of evolutionary routine.

Which made our arrival the cause of some excitement.

I had called from the funeral home to have a patrolman guard Mrs. Sawyer's room and possessions, pending a judge's signature on the bottom of a search warrant. By the time I got to the Skyview with Sammie, Ron, and J.P., the lobby and hallways were filled with curious staffers and residents.

On the second floor, a gray-haired woman wearing a white uniform and a very worried expression waited with our patrolman. "Are you in charge?" she asked me as we approached, each of us carrying some of J.P.'s cumbersome equipment.

"Yes—Lieutenant Joe Gunther. Brattleboro PD." I stuck out my hand as the others filed by me into the room.

She gave my fingers a distracted shake. "Janet Kohler, I'm

the head nurse here. What is going on? You really think Mrs. Sawyer was murdered?"

Impressed once again by Brattleboro's amazingly efficient grapevine, I gave her a cautionary shrug. "Right now, we haven't the slightest idea. Were you on duty when she died?"

"No—Sue Pasco covers nights, but I have her report."

"Good. I'd like to see that. I'd also appreciate it if you could call her and ask her to come here as soon as possible. I want to talk to her personally."

Janet Kohler hesitated a moment. "What does this mean . . . if she was murdered?"

I gave her a supportive smile. "Let's take it a step at a time. By the way, I gather Dr. Riley is the attending physician. Has he been associated with the home for long?"

"A few years—seven or eight, I guess. I don't remember right off."

"You two get along?"

She looked surprised, and then guarded. "Of course."

I smiled and patted her forearm. "Sorry—that was a dumb thing to ask. I just wanted to know what kind of a guy he was."

Her face relaxed. "Well, you know doctors. But he's nice enough, and he's always done good work here. We never had any complaints."

"Okay. I'm going to join my crew, so if you could get Ms. Pasco's report and make that call to her, I'd appreciate it. It might also be a good idea to keep any rumors to a dull roar for the time being. No point getting everyone all excited."

She nodded and left. I paused for a moment, watching the patients and a few staffers still standing in the corridor, murmuring among themselves. For a split second, I visualized the same hallway dark and deserted, in the middle of the night, occupied only by someone with murderous intent. It was a sad and sinister image to superimpose on a place already so saturated by decline and death. But despite what I'd told Nurse Kohler about the murder needing to be confirmed, I had no doubts about what had happened. The big question was how to put a face on the "someone" responsible.

And that wasn't our only problem. For a department used to handling one or two homicides a year, this one was going to stretch our resources to the limit. That alone was worth a prayer that we would reach the bottom of it fast and neatly.

Tyler already had the others at work on different aspects of the room—Ron checking the floor, furniture, and curtains, and Sammie the contents of the drawers and the one closet. J.P. himself was bent over the night table, dusting it for fingerprints.

"Anything yet?" I asked him.

He didn't say what I wanted to hear. "Nothing obvious. They stripped the bed. That was too bad. But nothing else seems to have been messed with. Surprising, in a way. Normally, the next of kin clean out a place like this pretty fast."

It was an interesting point, and something else to ask Janet Kohler when she returned. In the meantime, I was more hindrance than help here, so I left the room and went next door—to the room sharing the wall against which Mrs. Sawyer had kept her bed.

The door was open, so I knocked on the frame and stuck my head in. A bird-like woman, thin, small, and with an odd, quick way of moving her head, looked up from the book she was reading in an armchair.

"Yes?" she asked, smiling, marking her place with a gnarled finger.

"Hi—not interested in what's going on next door?"

"Oh, I already know about that—Adele was murdered in her bed last night."

I walked farther into the room, looking around. It was bright and cheerful, something I'd noticed Adele Sawyer's was not, and the walls were decorated with a dozen small, energetic oil paintings of rural scenes. The slight but pervading odor of disinfectant-over-human-waste that lingered throughout the rest of the building seemed thwarted by the room's atmosphere. "You know that for a fact?"

"That's what they're saying."

"Did you hear anything last night—through the wall?"

"No. I sleep like a log."

I introduced myself and we shook hands. Her name was Esther Pallini, and her hand felt like a small bundle of brittle sticks wrapped in smooth, warm cloth. Her eyes glittered with friendly enthusiasm. "What you do must be very exciting."

I sat on the edge of her bed. "Not really. Paperwork and phone calls, mostly." I tilted my head toward the shared wall. "Were you and Adele friendly?"

She shook her head vigorously. "She was a complainer—I don't like that."

"How was her health? Did she get around easily?"

"For a woman her size, she was lucky she could move at all. She was an encyclopedia of every pain known to God, but I think her heart may have been the real problem—she had those fat ankles heart patients get." With forgivable vanity, she tapped her own trim, tiny feet briefly on the floor.

"Did other people like her?"

Her eyes widened and she smiled broadly. "Do I think one of them could have killed her? What a wonderful idea. I suppose so. Most people think we just sit around in a place like this and turn into vegetables. But there's lots of intrigue that goes on." She suddenly lowered her voice and leaned toward me. "And sex. People are jumping into bed with each other all the time. Causes jealousies sometimes."

I raised my eyebrows and matched her conspiratorial tone. "Did Adele fool around?"

Esther Pallini looked utterly startled and burst out laughing. "What a picture. I couldn't even imagine it—oh, think of the poor man. No, no. Adele just liked to talk about it. She usually got her facts mixed up, of course, getting everyone riled."

"Upset a few people?"

Only then did my spirited informant become pensive. "A few. But to the point of murder? I don't really care that she's dead—we're used to that here. But I can't imagine one person killing another." She gestured to a radio situated on the windowsill. "You hear about it all the time . . . I don't know if it could happen here—I mean . . . that one of us could actually do it."

I laid my hand on hers. "I wouldn't jump to conclusions. We don't know what happened yet."

"Lieutenant Gunther?"

I turned at the voice coming from the doorway. Janet Kohler stood on the threshold, holding a file in her hand. "Be right there," I said.

I returned to Esther Pallini. "Thanks for talking with me. I'll see you again later. And don't worry about it, okay?"

"Thank you. I'll be fine."

I stepped out into the corridor with Janet Kohler.

"I called Sue Pasco. She's coming right over. I also called Dr. Riley . . . Was that okay?"

"Sure," I said, although I'd been planning to do that later, after I'd gathered a few more facts. "Is there somewhere we can talk more privately?"

She led me down the hall to a small, cluttered office, and closed the door behind us. I gestured for her to sit at the desk chair while I chose a small bench lining the wall. "Did anyone here contact the next of kin?"

The head nurse looked vaguely insulted. "Of course. Once the doctor's signed the certificate, that's the next thing we do. Sometimes the family likes to visit the body in the room, sometimes not, but it's our policy to give them the opportunity."

"What time did she die?"

She consulted the file she was still holding in her hand. "Dr. Riley declared her dead at two-oh-eight this morning. I have no way of knowing when she actually died."

"Right," I muttered, "but there was no sense of alarm about her death?"

"None at all. She was a heavily medicated congestive heart patient, with both COPD—that's bad lungs—and diabetes complications, and she was grossly overweight. We'd all been expecting her to die for months."

"But she could still get around."

"Oh sure—lots of people can, right up to the end. She wasn't fast on her feet—don't get me wrong—but she did all right."

"I gather she wasn't too popular."

Janet Kohler looked at me steadily for a moment, as if

weighing her options. I was pleased with her final choice. "She was a bitch."

"Thanks for the honesty. Did she have any enemies, or people who disliked her more than others?"

"I'd say the second more than the first."

"I'll have someone get those names from you. How about the home in general—is it a good place to work?"

The tension in her face eased a bit. "I love it here. For the most part, the residents are wonderful, the staff knows its stuff, and management is very supportive. We spend a lot of time coming up with things the residents can do together, and it helps everyone stay young, at least mentally. I used to work in places—some of them pretty famous—where the residents might as well have been animals. All cooped up, with nothing to challenge their minds. We're very interactive here. It doesn't cost any more, and when you think of it, it helps us, too—makes the job more interesting and rewarding. You were talking with Mrs. Pallini—how did she seem to you?"

"Very content," I admitted. "Speaking of her, she implied the patients have pretty free rein to wander."

Kohler smiled broadly. "She tell you about the hanky-panky? It's absolutely true. Some of that goes on. As for the more inno-cent wandering, we do have people that bear watching—the Alzheimers tend to roam, especially at night, and a few others need to be restricted to a single area of the home. It's a passive kind of restraint, though—just so they don't hurt themselves, or somebody else by mistake. Except that we keep a sharp eye peeled for any health changes, all the rest are pretty much free to come and go as they please. The only restriction we impose is that no one spontaneously leave the building."

"You do bed checks, then?"

"Yes, and we monitor the building's exits and access to some of the home's special areas. The residents try to pull a fast one now and then, sneaking around for some late-night highjinks, but we usually know what's going on—we just pre-tend we don't."

"Is there a fair amount of activity in the halls after hours?"

"No. I think we play it up slightly because most of them get such a kick out of it—keeps them young in spirit, anyway. To be honest, we're not talking about more than a handful."

"You said the Alzheimer's patients wandered at night."

"Oh—I see what you mean. Yeah—that happens some-times—it's fairly typical of the disease, but . . . You're not thinking one of them did this, are you?"

I smiled to reassure her. "No, no. I'm not thinking much of anything right now. We've got a lot more digging to do still. I am curious, though, about Mrs. Sawyer's next of kin. Who do you have listed?"

She opened the file and began leafing through it. "It's funny—I've never met them. As far as I know, she's never had an outside visitor—family or otherwise . . . Here it is. Annabelle Tuttle—Spruce Street. You'd think she would drop by every once in a while—must be all of a ten-minute drive." She handed me the file so I could copy the address.

There was a knock on the door as I was finishing up, and the patrolman who'd been guarding Mrs. Sawyer's door poked his head in. "Phone call, Lieutenant—from St. Johns-bury. I think it's line three."

"Thanks—be right there." I turned to Janet Kohler. "I guess that's it for the moment. If you'd like to get back to what you were doing, feel free. I appreciate all your help."

Kohler rose and crossed to the door. "Happy to do so, Lieu-tenant. I'll bring Sue and the doctor to see you as soon as they get here. Shouldn't be too much longer." She pointed at the phone on the desk. "Feel free to use that."

I waited until the door had closed behind her before pick-ing up the receiver. "This is Joe Gunther."

"Hi Joe, it's Mel. Sorry it took so long to get back to you. We had to hunt around for your friend. We ended up just tak-ing him to the barracks—easier than finding a pay phone. I'll put him on. Good luck, buddy."

"Thanks."

A few moments later, Ned Fallows's voice came on the line, sounding cautious. "Joe? What's the problem?"

I decided to play it hard-nosed, hoping that might get me better mileage than the approach I'd used last night—but also because I was tired and angry, and no longer interested in games. "Things have changed down here, Ned. I want some straight answers."

"What are you talking about?"

"Mary Wallis disappeared last night. It's looking like an abduction, and it's anyone's guess if she's still alive. Since the building project's the one common denominator we keep coming across, I need to know who put the squeeze on you. Now."

"It's not connected, Joe."

"I'll decide that. You talk to me now, or I'll charge you in connection to her murder if Mary Wallis turns up dead."

After a long, deliberating pause, he said in a barely audible whisper, "Tom Chambers—NeverTom."

"Why?"

"He'd discovered something I'd done years before—a mistake. I thought I'd buried it, but he'd known all along. He'd just put it in his 'rainy day fund,' as he called it, for future use."

"What was the deal? Vote his way just this once, and he'd let you off?"

"The way things worked out, he got his money's worth."

I couldn't argue the point, although I was hoping the State's Attorney might eventually.

His next comment, however, made that a more complicated issue. "I won't repeat what I just said, though, no matter how many subpoenas you hit me with. Nor will I answer any more questions. I only told you this much so you'd let it be."

I opened my mouth to give him hell, but then realized the futility of it. The Ned Fallows of old had been drowned by self-pity and perhaps self-loathing. I'd gotten what I wanted for the moment. Finding him later wasn't going to be a problem.

"We'll see, Ned. I'll do what has to be done. But if Mary Wallis suffers because of something you're not telling me right now, you will bear the consequences."

"You don't know the half of it," he replied, his voice emotionless. "I'm way ahead of you."

The line went dead.

Chapter Eighteen

Talking with Ned Fallows had both angered and saddened me. In the same way domestic disputes show how love can turn to violence, Fallows had shown me how a man's ego, once used as a beacon for righteous behavior, could be twisted to stand for self-absorption and denial. Now faced with two homicides, a suspicious death, a disappearance, and a corruption case touching the town's leading family, I had little tolerance for Ned's mourning his own fallen image. That his vanity might be impeding our locating Mary Wallis made me furious.

I looked up from these reflections to see a middle-aged woman with her hair tied back, in jeans and a sweatshirt, timidly standing by the half-open door. Her voice was strained with tension. "Janet said you wanted to see me? You didn't answer when I knocked. I'm Sue Pasco."

I rose and beckoned her to sit. "Joe Gunther. Thanks for coming. Please—make yourself comfortable."

She perched on the chair's edge, her legs tucked under her and her hands flat by her thighs, looking like a diver about to spring from the starting block.

"Is it all right if I call you Sue?" I asked.

She nodded tightly. "Everyone does."

"Great—call me Joe. I've been told you were in charge last night when Mrs. Sawyer passed away. Is that right?"

Again, she nodded, her body still frozen in place. "Was she really murdered?"

"We think so. An autopsy's being done right now. How was Mrs. Sawyer discovered?"

Sue Pasco spoke quietly, in choppy sentences, as if fearful that longer ones might be traced back to her. "She was sick. On meds. They get checked. To see if they're okay."

"You do rounds, in other words."

"Sort of."

"Several times a night?"

"Yes. Ten, one, and three."

"So it was during the one o'clock check that you found her."

Her head dropped so I couldn't see her face. "Yes."

"Sue. Are you worried you did something wrong?" I asked, distracted by the intensity of her distress.

Her features were all twisted, her eyes brimming with tears. "I don't know."

"You followed the same procedure you do every night, right?"

"Yes."

I touched her shoulder gently. "Then you don't have anything to worry about. Just concentrate on my questions, and be absolutely honest. A terrible thing has happened, but it won't reflect badly on you as long as you tell me everything you know."

I paused to let her absorb that. "Okay. What happened when you checked on Mrs. Sawyer?"

She collected herself, and then spoke in more measured tones, her eyes fixed to the floor. "We don't knock, so as not to disturb them if they're sleeping, but I thought something was wrong as soon as I opened the door."

"Why?"

"There wasn't any sound. She always snored. That's why we moved her next to Esther. Nothing wakes Esther up."

"What did you do then?"

"I felt for a pulse and discovered she was dead."

"Did you start CPR, or call for help?"

"She had a DNR—a Do Not Resuscitate order. We're not supposed to take any heroic measures with them. Those are the words they use—heroic measures—like CPR."

"So you called for help instead?" I prompted.

She tucked her head again and began to shake. Given both Esther Pallini's and Janet Kohler's casualness concerning death, I wondered if Sue Pasco's sensitivity might not be connected to something else.

I crouched by her seat and grabbed her forearm, forcing her to look at me. I opted for a standard interrogation ploy. "Sue, tell me what's troubling you. If it comes out now, we can try to fix it. The worst thing you can do is let it fester inside."

"I didn't want to wake anybody up. I didn't know . . ." Her voice trailed off.

". . . Didn't know she'd been murdered?"

She nodded, sobbing openly now.

"You're saying you didn't call for help? How did the doctor get here?"

Between sobs, she gasped, "I called *him*. We're supposed to get another staffer. As a witness to the death. It's like a law or something. But we *knew* she was going to die. It was no big deal. So I let them all sleep. It never mattered before. And now it's a murder . . . And I could go to jail."

I squeezed her hand, and reached for the file on Sawyer that Janet Kohler had left behind. I flipped to the back to see where Sue's name and signature appeared, along with someone else's, under the timed and dated heading, "Discovery of deceased."

I showed her the sheet. "You cooked the books, right? Had the other person listed here add her signature early this morning, after she woke up?"

Sue Pasco nodded miserably, slumped back in her chair.

I glanced farther down the sheet. "I take it Dr. Riley played along? His signature's here, too."

"He told me once it was bureaucratic nonsense."

I closed the file and sat back down. "Guess you won't do that again."

She looked up, surprise showing through the tears at my casual tone of voice. "You're not going to tell?"

"Not right now. And not ever if I don't think it has anything to do with the case. What's important to me is that the rest of it is accurate—the time you discovered her, for example."

She slid forward in her seat again, this time eagerly, wiping at her cheeks with the palms of her hands. "Oh no—it's all true. I checked my watch as soon as I turned on the light— one-twenty-two—I still remember. Then I closed the door and locked it, like they tell us, and I phoned Dr. Riley, since he's on the call list this week. I waited for him by the front entrance, took him up here, he examined her, and signed the death certificate. After that, I called Guillaume's so they could get her out before the other residents woke up."

I gave her a supportive smile. "Okay. That's great. Now, thinking back to before you checked on her, did you notice anything unusual in the hallway, or anywhere else, for that matter? Any sounds, any activity? Did you see anyone?"

She paused to reflect. "I always see a few people. Not all of the residents sleep well, so sometimes they wander around— watch TV, read—"

"But nobody struck you as acting odd?"

"No."

"Were any of them on this floor?"

"No. It was empty."

"How 'bout after you found the body? Did you see anyone then?"

"No. And we worked very quietly. By two-forty-five, Mrs. Sawyer was gone."

I thought back to what Janet Kohler had told me. "Did you contact the next of kin? You didn't mention that."

Her face grew suddenly agitated and defensive. "I did, I did. You can check. I just forgot because it didn't matter. Mrs.

Tuttle didn't care one way or the other. She was even a little irritated—asked me why I couldn't have waited to call her in the morning."

"You ever meet her?"

"No. But you could tell they were relatives by their attitude."

I glanced down at the file. "They were sisters?"

"I think so."

I closed the file and sat back. "I've been told Mrs. Sawyer wasn't well liked—that she spread rumors, got into fights . . ."

"I guess so. Being on the night shift, I miss most of that, but she wasn't a nice person."

"Could you list everyone who might have had a grudge against her, for one of my officers a little later?"

"You don't think one of the residents did it, do you?"

"I can't say yet."

"I can come up with a few names, I guess. Some of it would be sort of like gossip, though."

"That's okay. Your list will be confidential. We just need something to get us started. Who stripped the bed?"

"I did. She'd peed all over herself, and I wanted to get the sheets cleaned as soon as possible."

That was disappointing. "So they've been laundered?"

"Oh, yes . . ."

"Is that pretty typical—a patient peeing on herself before dying?"

"Common enough. Sometimes it's worse—their bowels open up."

"But aside from taking the sheets, everything else was left the way you found it?"

She nodded vigorously. "Absolutely, and the door was locked again."

"One last question. What's the security like on the building's exits?"

"All the doors are locked after nine, and the front entrance has a guard to let people in and out."

"How 'bout fire exits?"

"They all have alarms." She gave me a small smile. "And we

know they work, because every once in a while, one of the residents tries them out."

I rose to my feet and thanked her, telling her somebody would contact her later for that list of names. I watched her hurry down the corridor, no doubt to compare experiences with Janet Kohler, or to call the colleague who'd faked witnessing the discovery of the body.

I had the strong impression Sue Pasco wouldn't be bending any rules for a long time to come.

*   *   *

J.P. and his crew were still scrutinizing Adele Sawyer's room, but I could tell from the doorway they weren't happy. Each one of them toiled in silence, obviously going through the motions with nothing to show for it.

"No luck?" I asked.

J.P. looked up. "There're enough fingerprints, hair follicles, and loose threads to start a museum. If you want this done right, I'll have to print and take hair samples from everyone in this place, and even then I doubt I'd have anything to go on."

Sammie was sitting at the small table by the window, leafing through a thin pile of papers and letters. "Nothing here, either. Mostly insurance forms, bills, official correspondence. Some junk mail she kept. There're a few family pictures, including a group shot—looks like a reunion—but no personal letters. The best I could find was an address book. Not too many entries, but I'll chase them all down."

Emerging from the bottom of the one closet, Ron merely gave me a shake of the head.

"Okay," I told them. "I'm going to find Annabelle Tuttle, the listed next of kin. I'll see you all at the office." I checked my watch. "Let's shoot for a noon meeting. Supposedly, Dr. Riley's coming over. If one of you could get a statement from him, that'd be great."

As I entered the building's lobby from the stairwell a few minutes later, a harassed-looking man, his hair tousled and his coat unbuttoned, came banging through the glass-paned double doors.

I took a guess. "Dr. Riley?"

He stopped dead in his tracks. "Yes."

"I'm Lieutenant Gunther—Bratt PD—"

Before I could get any more out, he interrupted me by grabbing my arm, stepping close and asking in a hoarse whisper, "What the hell's going on? I heard Adele Sawyer's death was being called a homicide—that I screwed up the death certificate."

I considered soothing him, pointing out that the postmortem results hadn't come in yet. But then I decided to hell with it. I didn't like the priority of his concerns. "You did."

His face went slack and his cheeks reddened.

I relented a bit. "Look, nobody's going after you. The mortician noticed some bruises around the neck. My forensics guy told me they probably surfaced after rigor mortis began setting in and the blood drained away from the neck area. She normally had a flushed complexion, right?"

"Yes—it was tied in with her breathing problems."

"That's what hid the bruises. The missed cause of death is no big deal—since we caught it—but you might want to be more careful next time."

He stiffened slightly, but took it without comment, which I appreciated. From his opening line, I'd figured him for more bluster. "The problem now," I continued, "is to find out who killed her. Was she one of your regular patients?"

"I've been treating her for about five years."

"A joyride?"

His pinched face cracked a thin smile. "I guess you've heard about her. Pretty unpleasant person."

"How long had she been dead when you got here?"

He frowned. "She'd definitely begun to cool, but there were no signs of rigor. I'd guess two or three hours at most."

"Anything unusual about her medical history?"

"Nothing a little physical self-respect wouldn't have headed off. She smoked, ate poorly, never exercised, and was in a constant rage. Whoever killed her obviously had no patience—another six months and she would've spared him the effort."

"Is that a medical estimate?" I asked.

The smile returned. "Probably more like wishful thinking, if that doesn't put me on the suspect list. She should've been dead years ago, so I suppose she might've lasted a few more. The autopsy will give you the best answer to that one."

*   *   *

Given all of Brattleboro's neighborhoods, Spruce Street was purely middle ground. Shoved up hard against a hilly, wood-choked wilderness area, it contained a few solid, vaguely stately homes, scattered among a wider sampling of more bedraggled, tenacious, middle-class residences, pristine examples of which had been popular in family-hour TV shows in the fifties. Annabelle Tuttle lived in one of these.

I parked across the street from her address and looked at the building for a moment, studying the peeling paint, the odd shutter or two in need of repair, the furrow carved in the snow from porch to driveway, the width of one shovel. I guessed the occupant to be single, living alone, no longer young, and on a diminished income.

I got out, navigated the narrow path to the weather-beaten porch, and pushed the doorbell.

The woman who opened up a minute later was white-haired, slightly stooped, and looked permanently fatigued.

"Mrs. Tuttle? My name is Joe Gunther. I'm from the Brattle-boro police department. I was wondering if I could have a word with you."

She registered no surprise, but stood back to let me in, shivering slightly in the draft of cold air that accompanied me. "I suppose this is about Adele. They called me already."

I stood in the overheated hallway, wondering if I should presume to remove my coat. My hostess made none of the usual gestures to indicate I was invited to stay. "That was last night?"

She let out a tiny snort of derision. "More like two o'clock this morning."

"Right. We were wondering why you hadn't come by the

Skyview to pick up her things, or contact Guillaume's to see about the arrangements."

She was a short woman, and had been gazing at the middle button of my coat so far, but at that, she looked up my frame and nailed me with a hard stare. "That's a concern of yours?"

"It's a source of curiosity. You're the only one listed as next of kin."

"Sisters," she said, as if talking about the flu. "We weren't close."

"All that's left of the family?"

The snort was repeated. "The family's large enough. I was the only one who volunteered to be contacted. The nursing home had to have someone to call. Why are you so interested?"

For the sake of form, I took a shot at solicitude, although I doubted it was necessary. "Mrs. Tuttle, I'm afraid I may have some shocking news. Would you like to sit down?"

"No." Her eyes on me didn't waver, her face didn't change expression.

"We don't think your sister died of natural causes. She was murdered—strangled to death."

I'd added the last bit for effect, but all it registered was a bitter half-smile. "One of her housemates, no doubt." She sighed, and then added, "Maybe I will have that seat. Come."

I followed her into the living room, gratefully removing my coat. We sat on opposing hard, straight-backed couches. She seemed as composed as ever—just a bit more tired. I thought perhaps the brevity that had so offended Sue Pasco on the phone may have been merely weariness and economy.

"My sister," she began, "was an angry, disappointed woman. She married badly twice in a row, had three kids who won't talk to her anymore, and got fired from every job she ever had because of her mouth. Every comment was taken as an insult, every look was an accusation. To say nobody loved her misses the point. Nobody even liked her, including me."

I sat there in silence for a moment, wondering when I'd last heard such an eloquent and devastating tribute. "Apart from you, did she keep in touch with any other family members?"

"No. And she didn't with me, either. The Skyview put my name on her application form—*she* didn't. Who killed her?"

The bluntness of the question caught me by surprise. "We don't know yet. I was hoping you might be able to help us with that."

"I never visited her—never knew any of the people she was living with."

"I was thinking more of outsiders—someone who might have come to see her."

"I don't know who that could have been. I doubt she had any friends, and I already told you about the family."

"How about her possessions? Did she have any property or assets that might benefit anyone?"

Annabelle Tuttle shrugged and sighed, focusing on a distant chair. "No—everything she had was in that room. She had no money. I paid for a few things—a pair of slippers or some new underwear—but it never came to much. To be cruelly honest, she was always a burden, and it looks like she still is, even in death."

I stole a glance at my watch, realizing the time for the staff meeting I'd asked for was drawing near. I stood up. "Are you the only family member who lives in the area?"

She looked up at me. "Oh, no—most of them do."

"Would it be all right if I sent somebody by to collect their names and addresses later today?"

Her eyes slid away from my face and grew unfocused and dull. "That would be fine."

I moved partway to the door, and then hesitated. "Are you all right, Mrs. Tuttle? Is there someone I could call to keep you company?"

She smiled slightly—sadly, I thought. "No. That's all right. I don't really know what to do with company anymore." She paused, and added, "It doesn't seem like anyone in my family was much good at it."

*   *   *

The noise from the people milling around outside my office drowned out Beverly Hillstrom's opening words on the phone. I caught the edge of the door with my foot and swung it shut. "I'm sorry, Doctor. What was that?"

She spoke a little louder. "I said, 'It's definitely a homicide.' Your Mrs. Sawyer was strangled. The assailant used his left hand on the mouth, and his right hand on the throat. I'll be faxing you the details as soon as I have them typed up."

"Did you find anything else? Drugs, alcohol—"

"Phenobarbital? No—I'm afraid not, Lieutenant."

I hesitated a moment before changing subjects, still rankled by the release of Milo's cause of death to the media. "By the way, does your office have a protocol concerning when a cause of death is made public? Some specific time lapse, for example?"

Either I hadn't kept my tone of voice lighthearted enough, or Hillstrom had been adversely hit by this general topic before, because her response was a frosty, "Do you have a complaint?"

"No. I just dropped the ball when I forgot to ask you to sit on the Milo Douglas results earlier, and I wanted to know what kind of time window I have available for future reference."

Apparently mollified, she answered, "There is no protocol. Unless told otherwise, we release our findings as they are completed. In point of fact, I hadn't gotten around to Mr. Douglas before the media contacted us."

I sat dumbfounded for a moment. "They called you? Who did?"

"Your own paper—the *Reformer.* I don't recall who, precisely."

"I'll be damned," I murmured.

"Is there a problem?" she asked, her voice guarded again.

"No, no. I'm just wondering how they found out about it."

Chapter Nineteen

The meeting started late—testimony to the number of people that had been asked to attend. The whole squad was there, along with Jack Derby, Tony Brandt, Gail, our head of Patrol, Bill Manierre, and three of his people—Sol Stennis, Marshall Smith, and a new transplant from the Burlington PD with ten years' prior experience, Sheila Kelly. Kelly was here because much of the last three years on her previous job had been spent on financial fraud cases.

I leaned forward and rapped the conference room's tabletop with my knuckles. The buzz of conversation slowly subsided. "I just hung up on the Medical Examiner. Adele Sawyer is now an official homicide. That means we've got to reorganize and reassign the cases we've been working on. So far we have Mary Wallis—missing under suspicious circumstances; Milo Douglas—dead from rabies, but through no known means of infection; Shawna Davis—cause of death unknown but considered a homicide; the hotel/convention center complex project—possible shenanigans ranging from corruption to blackmail; and now Adele Sawyer. Some of these cases overlap, but for clarity's sake, I'm keeping them separate.

"Given the workload we're facing, I'm moving Milo and Shawna to the back burner. Nothing new has come up on either one of them, and if we're right about Shawna's close ties to Mary Wallis, then I'd just as soon put more heat under the Wallis case, on the chance she might still be alive."

I got up and went over to the white board mounted on the wall, a felt-tipped marker in hand. "Because, despite some differing opinions in this room, I don't think Wallis took off under her own power. I think she was grabbed. She knew something, and someone was afraid she would eventually tell it to us."

I wrote "Shawna" and "Milo" next to each other at the top left corner of the board, but left the spaces below them blank. "Unfortunately, while Mary Wallis is a top priority, we're stuck for options on what to do for her. We've put everything available into motion. Photos and descriptions have been issued to all major agencies in New England, along with the bigger newspapers. The *Reformer* has agreed to play the story big and get it on the wire services. And each of her personal contacts has been asked to let us know as soon as they hear anything. We've been reduced to waiting for a break."

I wrote "Mary" on the board, and left it blank under her, also. "Okay—the building project. This one gets a little more complicated. Ron, Gail, and Justin Willette worked together to come up with a few possibilities here. There's a chance that during the permitting process, the wheels might've been greased to speed things along. One person has claimed he was coerced to support the deal."

I glanced at Gail, who merely nodded her assent. "Ned Fallows," I went on, "says Tom Chambers blackmailed him with proof of some prior malfeasance, the nature of which Fallows won't identify."

There was a predictable muttering around the table.

"Fallows is also saying he won't corroborate that story, no matter how much pressure we put on him."

"Screw him," Willy said. "Hit him with a subpoena and force him to talk."

"About what?" I asked. "Right now all we've got are two

conversations I had with him. His attitude is that if he clams up, we'll have no proof he was forced to vote for the convention project—nor will we find out what crime he committed in the first place. We need to do the same digging Tom Chambers did to force Fallows to spill the beans. And that," I waved a hand in his direction, "is what I want Ron to do."

I put "Chambers" and "Fallows" up on the board under the heading "Project" and drew an arrow connecting Ron's name to Fallows's. "We've also got a few other players we need to look at." I added Eddy Knox, Rob Garfield, and Lou Adelman's names. "These three are only guilty of being unusually supportive of the project so far. We need to examine their lifestyles, bank accounts, past histories, and finally conduct interviews with them. I'd like Sammie spearheading that, working with Marshall Smith."

I wrote all that down, with more arrows, and then circled "Tom Chambers" in red. "Here's the catch. How to dig into the town's richest political hotshot—not to mention one of our esteemed leaders—without his catching wind of it. The answer, I hope, lies in Chambers being the one common denominator between everyone in this group," I tapped Fallows's name and the three men Sammie and Marshall were assigned to. "Plus Harold Matson, the Bank of Brattleboro's president." I added his name to the list.

"The B of B got its fat saved by Ben Chambers. If we think the permitting process was tainted, there's a chance the funding was, too. J.P., find out how the financing was put together. I want you to work with Sheila Kelly—her expertise in this area should be an asset.

"Assuming Fallows is right about NeverTom Chambers being corrupt, my hope is we'll be able to catch Chambers in a pincer movement, between what we can get from the zoning and planning people, and what we can find out about the recent financial bailout. My other hope is that by following this approach, it might lead us to finding out what happened to Mary Wallis."

There was a muted stirring among most of the people in the room. I capped the pen in my hand and let them quiet back down. "For those of you who think we're putting too many eggs in one basket by focusing on the building project, let me remind you how we all agreed earlier that coincidence was a bad thing to rely on." I waved my hand at the board behind me. "Well, if all this isn't coincidence, then what ties it together? The convention center has cropped up—however vaguely—with Milo, Mary Wallis, and through Wallis to Shawna Davis. At fifteen million dollars, it's the biggest real estate deal this town's ever seen, and that sum doesn't include the financial benefits a lot of people are hoping will come their way once the center's up and running."

I leaned on the conference table with both hands. "We have limited manpower we need to use wisely, to pursue the hottest and most available targets we can locate. It may turn out that Milo died of rabies, pure and simple, and that Shawna was killed for reasons we haven't even guessed at. But Mary Wallis is still out there—maybe alive—and everyone involved in creating the convention center is identifiable and can be interviewed. On the chance those two are connected, I think this approach is worth the gamble. If anyone disagrees, let's hear it now."

"What about Gene Lacaille?" Willy said. "He got the whole thing started."

"He's losing his shirt," Sammie countered.

"You know that for a fact?"

I rapped the table again. "Hold it. We should and will look into him, but our caseload is enormous, and we haven't even mentioned our latest addition." I turned and wrote "Sawyer" on the board.

"Right now, Lacaille does seem to have lost out heavily in this deal, and it's unlikely he did that on purpose. So, our priorities and resources being what they are, he's going to have to take a back seat. But," I emphasized, "it should be noted that every lead on this board is subject to change. Names will be removed and added as we go along, and I don't want anyone skipping details just because they don't fit some particular assignment. Either hand over anything odd to the appropriate investigator, or let me know about it. Also, given

the chance that some or all of these investigations might be
linked in some way, and that we may end up with more on
our plate, I want every new case that comes into this office
looked at with a microscope—I don't care if it's a ninety-year-
old cancer patient who dies in the hospital." I tapped the
white board with my finger. "Everything gets a review in relation to this."

I wrote Kunkle's and Sol Stennis's names under that of
Adele Sawyer. "Okay—Willy, find out who knocked her off.
This one's out in the open—it's already on the radio, and it's
going to be front-page news tomorrow. It's a whodunit and it
has a cast of dozens—the lady was not well liked, the night
shift is thinly staffed, and most of the home's residents are
pretty much free to wander. And that's not even considering
someone from the outside. No need to tiptoe—take the place
by storm if necessary and get this wrapped up fast. Billy?"

Manierre looked up suddenly, as if I'd interrupted a com-
pelling daydream. "I know, I know—all the help I can spare,
especially on the Sawyer case. I'll juggle the shifts and see
what I can do."

I smiled at his world-weary voice. "Thanks. One last thing,
everybody. There'll be a slight change in Gail's role as contact
person for the SA's office. As before, if you've got questions
or are dealing with anything involving town government, go
through her first. But if it's a straight legal question, as with
the Sawyer killing, use whoever's available, like we've always
done."

The meeting broke up in piecemeal fashion. I gestured to
Gail and led her across the squad room to my office, closing
the door behind us.

"You okay with how I handled Ned?" I asked her.

She frowned, but gave me a reassuring squeeze of the arm.
"He's going to have to account for it. It's too bad he's doing
everything possible to make things worse for himself."

There was a knock on the door and Willy walked in without waiting for an answer. "I'm guessing," he said, "that you'll
be riding my back on the Sawyer case?"

"I'll fill in where I'm needed—on all of them." Gail got up

and headed out, giving me a small wave. I reached for a sheet of paper that was lying on my desk and handed it to Kunkle. "This is what I found out from the Skyview staff and Sawyer's next of kin. Hillstrom's report'll come by fax in an hour or two, but she told me on the phone that it was a two-handed attack, like J.P. thought. How d'you want to tackle this?"

"Interviews first. We know she was whacked between ten P.M. and one in the morning. That ought to help with check-ing alibis. I don't know . . . I thought I'd play it pretty much by ear. That a problem?"

I caught the defiance in his eye. "Not for me."

He checked his watch. "All right. I'm going to see who Billy can cut loose, and maybe head over there in an hour or so."

*   *   *

I had been up all night, and was planning to stay up a good part of the night ahead, so, despite the flurry of activity I'd set in motion, I told Harriet where I was headed—and went home to bed.

Under similar past circumstances, this had rarely been a successful ploy. When things got this crazy, turning my brain off became a near impossibility, and I routinely sacrificed the hope of some rest to the reality of a few restless, wakeful hours.

This time, however, I surprised myself. As soon as I was under the covers, I fell into a deep and restful sleep.

Part of this may have been due to sheer exhaustion. But I think I was also comforted by having organized our caseload the way I had. Whether proven right or wrong in the long run, it gave order to what had started to become a chaotic jumble of seemingly unrelated cases. I knew the links be-tween some of them and the convention center project were tenuous right now—a cheap pen, the location of a one-night crash pad, the sudden retreat of a firebrand activist. But I was also confident that mere happenstance hadn't conspired to hand us five separate major cases simultaneously. There had to be a common thread linking most of them, and I felt we were on the right track to finding it.

Unfortunately, my peaceful eclipse proved relatively short-lived. Three hours after I'd shut my eyes, the phone dragged me back to a world intolerant of daytime sleepers. Not that this particular caller would have hesitated at any hour.

"You're a hard man to locate," Stan Katz said cheerfully.

I piled several pillows behind me and sat up. "What d'ya want, Stan?"

"We're running dual pieces on Wallis and the Sawyer killing. I was wondering what you had to say about them."

"Talk to Brandt."

"I did. I'm going for more color—a personal angle."

"Not from me, you're not. It's too early on both cases for that. Give me a couple of days to find out what happened. Then you can have your color."

"Come on, Joe. I've got nothing right now. Didn't you guys find *anything?* How 'bout the timing? Do you know if Wallis and Sawyer knew each other?"

"Down boy. If we start hypothesizing in public right now, we'll only do everyone dirt. We'll give you the facts as we get them."

I could tell from the pause at the other end how much credibility that carried. "What about the other cases, then?"

"Look—Stanley—I know what you're up against—"

"Spare me the sympathy, Joe," Katz interrupted testily. "Just because we're operating on a shoestring doesn't make us less viable. We don't need your help—we deserve a little honesty from our public officials."

I shrugged at the phone. "All right, how 'bout if you give me some help? Beverly Hillstrom told me this morning that one of your people called her to confirm that Milo Douglas had died of rabies. Who was your source?"

Katz burst out laughing. "You're kidding, right?"

"You called me for a favor."

"Meaning you'll give me something if I tell you?"

"Soon enough."

There was another pause before he finally said, "What the

hell, I'll play. It was an anonymous call—a man. He said, 'The bum Milo died of rabies—check it out,' and then hung up."

Echoes of an earlier conversation I'd had with Kunkle came back to mind. "Did you get another anonymous call about the Satanist inscription on Shawna Davis's tooth?"

This time, Katz's silence smacked more of embarrassment. "What's going on?" he asked.

"I don't know, Stan. He called you."

"We thought maybe he was a cop."

"I've pretty much ruled that out." I hesitated, and then added, "My personal guess—off the record—is that we're dealing with someone who either thinks the publicity will throw us off track, or who needs the limelight for his own self-gratification. I think we're sniffing around the edges of something pretty significant here, Stan."

"Damn," he muttered. "When will you clue me in?"

"Soon as I can—no bullshit."

He slipped back into his hard-bitten role, like an actor stepping on stage. "I can hardly wait," he said, and hung up.

*   *   *

Unable to get back to sleep, I returned to the office to deal with several days' worth of paperwork. The squad room was empty. Everyone had either gone home or was in the field.

Since almost before I could remember, the quiet of an after-hours office was a meditative tonic for me. It gave me an air traffic controller's view of the world I inhabited—not just the investigations I was working on personally, but bits and pieces of every case currently active in the squad. It supplied me with a sense, however artificial, of being in control.

Nevertheless, by almost 10 P.M., I was sick of the paper shuffling.

In truth, my timing was calculated. Sometimes, when in a jam, I had found it helpful to revisit the scene of a crime at the same time of day it had occurred. I therefore got into my cold-stiffened car, and drove west toward the Skyview Nursing Home.

The neighborhood around the home was illuminated by

periodic streetlamps, so I instinctively cut my lights as I entered it, preserving the sense of stealth that might've been used, had last night's killer been an intruder.

I was amused, if not surprised, to discover I wasn't the only one acting out theories. Parked under the last streetlamp, facing the Skyview's front entrance, was Willy Kunkle's car—a small plume of exhaust trailing from its muffler. I cut my engine and rolled to a stop as silently as a shadow, settling some ten feet behind him.

It hadn't been my intention to actually sneak up on him, even after my stealthy approach, but seeing the back of his head, still motionlessly facing forward after I'd quietly emerged from my car, I was bitten by pure gratuitous impulse. Kunkle was a man who took everything and everyone head-on, with no apologies or mercy. He was so assertively in your face, so stridently claiming control at all times, that I couldn't resist exploiting this one instance of vulnerability.

With no plan in mind, I crept silently forward. I wasn't moved to smack a snowball against the glass, or pound on the door with my fist, like some of the others would have done in a heartbeat. Merely appearing by his side and bidding him good evening seemed good enough, since I knew the effect would be the same.

But I ended up being the one caught off guard. The reason he'd pulled up under the light, and that I'd been allowed my covert opportunity, was that Willy Kunkle was hard at work. Spread across the steering wheel, held in place by two small spring clips, was a broad, flat artist's pad, and appearing across its surface, under Willy's confidently held pencil, was a fanciful rendering of the scene before us—a snow-draped building, half lit by a streetlamp, huddled up against a looming black mass of hills that blended into a star-filled sky. It was beautiful—at once detailed and impressionistic, realistically capturing the night-clad nursing home, and yet endowing it with a grace and charm that escaped the clinical eye.

My astonishment was absolute. I forgot the cold, and my earlier intentions. All was wiped away by this glimpse of a curmudgeon's heart. Hopefulness, serenity, and insight poured from his pencil as they refused to in his everyday life, and with obviously practiced ease. The clips on the steering wheel were evidence this was a long-standing habit. I had often thought he had to have an outlet to keep his inner core quiet, something he could call his own. That it turned out being so utterly out of character made me feel at a loss.

I had never felt myself such a trespasser, and now wished I had warned him of my approach, giving him time to protect his privacy. Moving twice as furtively, I tried to slip away.

But I'd lingered too long. Responding to some territorial instinct, Willy suddenly turned and caught sight of my shadow. His reaction was startling, frantic, and terrifying, leaving me rooted in place with my hands held up in instinctive surrender. He moved in a blur, slipping from my line of sight, knocking the pad from its perch and sending it sailing to the floor, and reappearing through the half-opened door, crouched behind the very wide barrel of a .357 Magnum.

"You fucking asshole," he hissed at me through clenched teeth.

"Relax, Willy," I said calmly, seriously.

"How long you been there?" The gun had not moved—a telling oversight.

"Just got here," I lied. "What're you so twitchy about?"

The gun vanished, the door swung wider, and he got out of the car, closing it behind him with his hip. "You're no cop if you have to ask that."

It was a typical comment—melodramatic, wrong-headed, and hurtful—which I just as typically ignored. But given my newfound knowledge—and his lingering doubts—I felt entitled to return with a veiled warning shot. "I don't have as much to hide as you do."

His eyes narrowed. "Meaning?"

"Nothing." I glanced toward the building and changed the subject. "It's almost ten. I take it that's what you were waiting for."

When he answered, his words were no softer, but his tone had been muted several notches. My generosity, however roundabout, had been acknowledged. "I thought you said I was running this one."

"With as much help as you can get."

He quickly moved into a self-serving compromise. "How 'bout we split up, then? You take the bottom, I take the top."

Sawyer had been killed on the second floor. I accepted without hesitation.

The only unlocked door at this hour was the front entrance, opening onto the lobby with the guard's alcove off to one side. He was sitting there now, and asked if he could help us. We both showed our badges, and Willy left for the stairwell.

We watched him go, the guard scratching his head. "What's wrong with his arm? He bust it or something?"

"It's permanently disabled—sniper bullet, years ago."

His eyebrows shot up. "And he's a cop?"

I didn't bother confirming the obvious. "What're your hours?" I asked him.

"Ten to six. I just got on . . . Little early tonight—had to drop off the wife. Other car's in the shop."

"You were on last night?"

He suddenly looked uneasy. "Yeah, but I never heard a thing and I didn't take a nap, like that other guy said—the one who came to my house."

I didn't inquire who that had been. I would've asked the same question. "What happens when you have to pee?"

He gestured with his thumb. "It's around the corner, but I lock the front door. It's a deadbolt, so nobody can get in or out."

I looked at the telltale bulge of a pack of cigarettes in the left breast pocket of his uniform shirt, and at the "Absolutely No Smoking" sign stuck to the wall behind him.

"You have a flashlight I can borrow?" I asked.

Mystified, he handed over a long, black, metal brain basher. "Be right back," I told him and left the building.

Between the front entrance and the curb was a short, well-shoveled walkway, bordered by hedges on both sides. I played the light along where the bushes met the cement until I found what I was looking for—a five-inch-wide gap, leading off into the gloom. Stepping through it, I followed a narrow footpath along the wall for some twenty feet, to the far side of a darkened bay window. There, the path ended at a well-trampled four-foot-wide circle shielded from view by several tall plants. Around the edges of the circle were a dozen dead cigarette butts, all of the same brand.

I cupped my eyes with my hands and pressed my face against the window. Dimly, I could make out a room with several desks in it, with all the earmarks of a business office.

I collected one of the butts from the ground and returned to the lobby.

"Find what you were looking for?" the guard asked as I returned his flashlight.

"Yeah. Let me see your cigarettes."

His face crystallized. "What?"

I tapped the counter with my fingertip. Slowly, as if hypnotized, he brought his hand to his breast pocket and removed a pack of Marlboros. He put it on the counter. I laid the butt I'd recovered next to it.

"This is a one-time question. Answer it truthfully, and the conversation stops here. Jerk me around, and you can kiss this job good-bye. Got it?"

He nodded, his eyes fixed to mine.

"When you go outside to smoke, do you lock the door behind you?"

"No," he barely whispered.

"How often do you do this?"

"Once or twice an hour."

I picked up the butt and handed it to him. "Thanks."

I left him, and turned right at the back of the lobby, down a wide hallway running the length of the building's east wing. There were several glass-paneled doors on either side, crowned by decoratively lettered signs advertising each office's function. Some twenty feet down, on the same side as the building's front, I came to one labeled "Accounting."

Again, I cupped my eyes and peered into the darkened room. Not only was it the same office I'd seen moments earlier, but I could easily pick out the tall plants outside the bay window, clearly outlined by the streetlamps beyond. A man standing in their midst would cut a clearly distinct silhouette.

I left the east wing for its opposite number, and passed through a pair of double doors leading to a section dedicated to the home's social functions—a dining room with a locked kitchen beyond it, a well-stocked library, an exercise/game room, and—predictably occupied, probably all around the clock—the TV room.

I opened the door and peered into the darkened space. There were six people, either fully dressed or in bathrobes, sitting in sofas and armchairs, all in muted awe of a huge glowing set mounted halfway up the wall. The volume was what I'd expect for a mostly hearing aid crowd, but the door was heavy and insulated, which I assumed was true of the ceiling and walls, too—a thoughtful touch. I retreated and took the elevator upstairs.

Kunkle was in the corridor, leaning with his bad arm against the wall, looking down the length of the empty hall-way.

"Got anything?" I asked him.

He tilted his head slightly. "Just getting a feel for the place—the comings and goings. Fair bit of activity for a dump like this. 'Course," he had to add in the inevitable rejoinder, "most of them just sit there and drool."

Down the hall, I saw Sue Pasco, now dressed in uniform whites, leave one room to cross over to another, a medicine tray in her hands.

Willy stuck out his chin in her direction. "She's in the sec-tion where Old Lady Sawyer died. Most of 'em can get around, but they need their regular meds. At the far end is the hard-case unit—the veggies, the nutsos, and whatever else. What'd you find downstairs?"

"The guard's a smoker. He takes periodic trips outside to feed his habit. He leaves the door unlocked and always goes to the same spot. Getting in is no problem—he can't see the door from where he hangs out. And getting out is even eas-ier—you can see him through one of the office windows."

Willy let out a small grunt. "That's where my money is—an

outside hit. I talked to a lot of these geezers this afternoon—and the staff—and no bells went off. They all thought Sawyer was a grade-A bitch, but she wasn't the first, and everyone knows she won't be the last. It's part of the routine here."

"So why break in to kill her?"

There was a loud shout from down the hall, followed by a distant crash. Sue Pasco appeared in the hallway, and then broke into a fast trot toward the double doors at the far end.

"She's headed for the hard-case unit," Willy muttered, running after her.

I followed, hearing more as we got closer. Ahead of us, Pasco paused to open the door blocking the corridor. It hadn't quite swung to before we reached it. On the other side, the hall was more brightly lighted, the floor uncarpeted, and the overall look more institutional. A small cluster of people stood before us, looking into a room at the source of the commotion.

Willy and I muscled our way past them to the open doorway. Inside, Sue Pasco was kneeling by a bearded man in a chair, talking to him quietly. Across the room, a large muscular orderly was standing almost nose-to-nose with an old man wearing a bathrobe and pajamas.

"Bernie," the orderly kept saying, "Rolly's one of the good guys. You know that."

The old man shouted past him, "Who's the Splendid Splinter?"

Willy smirked. "Jesus Christ."

The orderly's voice was low and gentle. "He doesn't know, Bernie, but he's on our side."

"Who's Yehudi?" The old man shouted.

I crossed over to Sue Pasco. "What's going on?"

She looked up, startled to see me. Rolly, her bearded patient, answered me. "That crazy bastard tried to strangle me, that's what. Says I'm a Kraut spy, that he's going to force it out of me."

"Rolly," she soothed him. "There's hardly a mark on you. I'm sure it was some misunderstanding."

"Yeah. Well, I want him locked up from now on. I was alseep, for Christ's sake. There was no misunderstanding."

"Who's the Splendid Splinter?"

"Shut up, you crazy fuck," Rolly bellowed, rubbing his throat.

"Tell him Ted Williams," I suggested quietly.

Both Rolly and Sue stared at me. "Just tell him," I repeated to Rolly.

"Ted Williams," Rolly said halfheartedly.

"Who's Yehudi?" was the response.

"The guy who turns off the refrigerator light after you close the door," I murmured.

"Do it," Sue urged Rolly.

Rolly unhappily did as he was told.

We heard some muted discussion between Bernie and the orderly, and then they both approached us. Rolly threw his arms across his face in a dramatic defensive posture. "Get him away from me."

But Bernie was all smiling apologies, "Rolly, Rolly. I'm real sorry, buddy. Word was out they'd broken through—more spies. They got Johnnie. They talk better English than we do. Dressed in our uniforms, know who we are and where we are. Only way to trip 'em up—ask 'em stuff only a real American knows. I had to know you were the real McCoy, see? For the rest of us."

His left hand was extended in friendship. The right one was encased in a small cast. After some prodding, Rolly gave Bernie a halfhearted handshake before the orderly escorted the older man out of the room.

"I want him out of here," Rolly repeated with a little less conviction.

Sue Pasco rubbed his shoulder soothingly. "Rolly. Has he ever done this to you before?"

"It only takes one time."

"Oh, come on. Besides giving you a bad scare, what was the damage, really?"

Rolly's outrage climbed a notch. "What'd you mean? You ever been woken up with someone trying to strangle you?"

"If we make a big deal about this, Rolly, he'll be sent to Waterbury, and maybe lose his bed here. You've been to Waterbury . . . You could even go back yourself if things got bad again, like they used to be. You don't wish that on Bernie, do you?"

Rolly's eyes widened at the threatening implication, and he nervously rubbed his bristly cheek. "No, I guess not. But keep him away from me, okay?"

She stood up and patted his shoulder. "You got it. We'll leave you alone so you can get back to bed."

Rolly nodded, lost in his own thoughts, and Sue escorted Willy and me outside. "Let's go into the other section. It's easier to talk there."

We followed her beyond the corridor's double doors. She stopped and smiled weakly. "Sorry about that."

"What's Bernie's problem?" Willy asked.

She sighed. "He suffers from post-traumatic stress disorder and dementia. He's also been an alcoholic for the past fifty years, and has related, permanent short-term memory loss. Bernie is a Battle of the Bulge vet—he's shell-shocked, as they used to call it. He spent years in VA hospitals, was finally let go, managed a few decades as a classic 'normal citizen/closet drinker,' complete with wife and daughter, and ended up abandoned, broke, and mostly talking about a world that's been gone for fifty years." She looked at me gratefully. "Thanks for your help, by the way. How did you know what to say?"

"I've read a lot about World War Two, and what he said rang a bell. The Germans did put troops behind our lines in the Battle of the Bulge, dressed in American uniforms. And he was right—once word got out, the real American troops started inventing cultural quizzes, designed to trip up any foreigners. One American general almost got killed because he didn't know anything about baseball. What did Bernie mean about seeing spies around here, though?"

"That was probably you people," she answered. "All those interviews this afternoon—men in uniforms he's not familiar with. We lead a very structured, protected life here—it doesn't take much to set someone like Bernie off."

"But we didn't go into that ward," Willy countered.

She looked surprised. "It's not locked. We're not that kind of facility. We might restrain a resident now and then, but only temporarily, to see them over a hump. If they ever got really bad, we'd have to ship them out, like I was telling Rolly. The rest of the time, they can move around the building. We keep a closer eye on them than on the others, but that's all. I'm sure Bernie saw you, and took you for German spies."

"You said he talks about fifty years ago—does that mean he just keeps refighting the same battle over and over? Wouldn't that tend to make him violent?"

"Oh, no," she answered emphatically. "I shouldn't have put it that way. He talks about all sorts of things, not just the war—his daughter, animals, the weather—but it's all disjointed, like a scrambled recording. What I meant is that the further back in time he gets, the clearer he sounds. It's still pretty confusing, because he really has no short-term memory at all—he doesn't remember any of us from day to day—so he tells the same stories again and again, thinking they're new. He actually doesn't talk about the war much at all—usually only when he's upset, like after a nightmare. The war's the source of his troubles, so he tends to avoid it. That's why this thing you just saw was such a surprise. I've never seen him do anything like it before. It's almost like something hit a switch inside him."

"If he's free to wander around, couldn't he've taken a whack at the old lady?" Willy asked.

Sue Pasco looked horrified, a credit to Willy's subtle approach. "But he barely touched Rolly. Just because he lost his temper doesn't make him a killer."

"He couldn't've done it anyhow," I said. "He has a cast on his right hand."

"And that happened two weeks ago," Pasco volunteered, slightly mollified. "He slipped and fell . . . Besides, like I said, we keep a pretty close eye on them—room checks every hour on the hour, in fact. That orderly that was talking to him? That's Harry. He's like the den mother up here, and at night he keeps a tight rein."

She paused reflectively. "Something must've set him off. It could've been something you folks did without realizing it—the uniforms, the guns you wear . . . I don't know. And he probably can't tell us."

Given what Bernie might have seen, I wasn't willing to write him off so quickly. And with as many cases as we were handling, I also didn't want to miss the opportunity to wrap up at least one of them.

"Could be we just need to find the right way to ask him."

Chapter Twenty

Willy Kunkle and I watched Nurse Pasco walk back down the hallway to resume her ten o'clock rounds.

"I think there was a reason Bernie flipped out," I told him. "His timing's too coincidental to ignore—acting out a strangulation, exactly twenty-four hours after the real thing. Let's have a chat with Harry."

We found the orderly folding sheets in an oversized linen closet, his enormous frame making the room look cramped. "Harry?" I interrupted him. "We were never formally introduced. I'm Joe Gunther, this is Willy Kunkle, from the PD."

Harry smiled. "Yeah—nice move with Bernie." He pointed at Willy. "I saw you this afternoon, when I was coming on."

That surprised me. "When's your shift?"

"Four to midnight. We got different hours from the nurses. We overlap so the residents don't get a new crew all at once. Some of them are sensitive to that. That was sad about Mrs. Sawyer."

Willy struggled to keep the incredulity from his voice. "You liked her?"

Harry finished folding the sheet in his hands and placed it

on a shelf with a doting gentleness. "Sure. People thought she was a little rude, but you had to know how to talk to her. She didn't mean most of that stuff personally."

"What's Bernie like?" I asked.

The broad smile returned. "He's great. You start asking him about the old days, and he's full of information. Too bad about the war, though—it's like a black cloud he can't get away from. You know anything about the Battle of the Bulge?"

"Enough," Willy said curtly. "How do the others get along with him? Like Mrs. Sawyer?"

Harry looked momentarily stumped. "I don't think she knew him. They sort of kept different hours," he added slyly.

"Meaning what?"

"Bernie's a night owl—we call them 'sundowners,' or 'wanderers.' That's pretty typical of PTSDers—their internal clock gets screwed up. Nights're when the bad dreams come, so they try not to go to sleep."

"I thought Nurse Pasco said the people in this ward were encouraged not to wander," I said. "That they were checked every hour."

"We check 'em," Harry admitted. "But they know the schedule as well as we do, so they pull a fast one once in a while. Bernie's big on that. He'll put his pillow and a blanket under the sheets to make it look like he's asleep—just like a kid. I never told anybody about it—didn't want to get him in trouble."

"And where's he go?" I asked cautiously.

"Around," came the guileless answer. "I see him hiding in the hallways sometimes, in the dark. I pretend not to see him. He's just a harmless old guy who wants to be alone."

"Harry," Kunkle asked in a surprisingly gentle voice. "How was Bernie acting when you came on this afternoon?"

"I saw him before that. As soon as I heard about the murder on the radio, I came in to check up on them this morning. Like I said, they're real sensitive, and I wanted to see how they were doing. Bernie was in tough shape. He was going on about Krauts and spies and people dying—more than I ever heard before. He reminisces a lot, you know? But not about the bad times. This morning, he was really wound up. They finally gave him something to make him sleep."

"You think he saw something last night?" I asked. "Like maybe who killed Mrs. Sawyer?"

Harry looked shaken. "Wow—and him of all people . . . Sure, could be."

"How's he doing now?" I asked.

"Not too good. Talking to himself. He's very tense."

"Not a good time to talk?"

Harry shrugged. "You can try if you want to, but I couldn't get anything out of him, and he usually talks to me most. Right now, he's holding both ends of the conversation, like he was reading all the parts in a play. He did that once before, after he saw two people fighting outside the window—in the street. I couldn't get to him at all."

"Does he have any family in the area?" Willy asked. "Pasco said he had a wife and daughter."

"No. His wife died years ago, and his daughter, Louise, lives in Florida. She's only visited once. He loves her a bunch, though—or at least the memory of her. The best talks we have are about her. He's sort of put her in a time capsule."

Harry leaned against the shelves and placed his hand up to his cheek in an oddly child-like gesture. "That was one of the saddest things I ever saw—the one time Louise came to visit. It was years ago—and he was pretty new here—and all he did was talk to her about herself. But he didn't know who she was, you know what I'm saying? He was talking to a middle-aged woman about her own ghost. She couldn't stop crying, and she never came back."

"Who's his doctor?" I asked quietly.

"His psychiatrist is Dr. Andrews, but I doubt he could tell you much. I hate to say this, but I'm not so sure Dr. Andrews would know who Bernie was without his chart in his hand. Dr. Stover was just the reverse—he loved these people. But he moved to Milwaukee. I guess that's the thing here, you know? The world keeps spinning away—people coming and people going. But here they pretty much stay still—until they die."

I let a small pause fill the room, during which I could feel Willy's impatience beginning to climb. "Harry," I finally asked. "I'd like to talk with Bernie soon. Could you keep an eye on him, and let me know when that would be possible?"

He slowly emerged from his reverie and gave me a gentle smile. "Why not now? I know I said he was a little out of it, but it might do him good to have some company. That way you'll know what he was like when you see him later, after he's calmed down."

I glanced at Willy. "Sure. Why don't we go in just the two of us so we don't crowd him. You mind waiting, Willy?"

He looked at me as if I'd just put a lampshade on my head.

"Right," I said to Harry. "Lead the way."

Bernie was being kept in a room at the far end of the hall. A bedroom much like the others I'd visited, it had a few discreet extras that distinguished its role on this ward—the bed was bolted to the floor, the windows were covered with steel mesh, and there were no loose items lying about that could be used offensively.

Bernie, still in his pajamas and bathrobe, was pacing back and forth energetically, his chin tucked in, his eyes locked on the floor before him. His fists made tiny jabs into the air at waist level.

"Hi, Bernie," Harry said cheerfully.

Bernie whirled around. "Duck, you guys, and keep it quiet."

Harry touched my shoulder and we both crouched down, making me doubly glad Willy had opted out of this one. "What's up?" Harry asked in a stage whisper.

Bernie was back to pacing, apparently not needing to take cover. "They're all around us—we're all on our own now—and they're dressed like us, talk like us. God, it's cold." He continued talking, but in a mutter I couldn't hear. Following Harry's lead, I rose back up and crossed over to the bed, sitting quietly next to the orderly.

"How're things going, Bernie?" Harry asked.

The other man's voice rose in reaction, but he didn't acknowledge us—as if all dialogue in the room was solely contained in his head. "How the hell do you think they're going?
They're killing us. We're dying like flies, killed in our beds,
freezing to death. We got no support, no orders, no ammo,
no front line, no rear. We are fucked, buddy. We are going to
die in this frozen piece of French shit."

"Who died in their beds?" I asked.

"This isn't supposed to happen," he wailed, still pacing, still
punching the air. "We're here on R and R, for Christ's sake. 'A
quiet corner of the war,' they said. Dumb bastards. God, it's
cold . . . Cold, cold, cold, cold. Wish I could light a fire." He
lapsed back to muttering.

I nodded to Harry and pointed toward the door. Outside, I
asked him, "You said he acted like this once before, after seeing a fight. Did he mention people dying in their beds?"

"No—never."

"How long did the episode last?"

"A few hours. He was twitchy for days afterward, but at
least he knew you were in the room. It was the only other
time he got so lost in the war memories."

"Let me know when he starts to climb out of it, okay? And
thanks."

The shy smile returned. "Sure thing."

*   *   *

Willy picked me up outside the ward and escorted me
downstairs and out into the freezing cold. "That was quick.
He spill his guts?"

"He's a little out of it. I do think he saw something,
though."

Willy sighed. "So that's the plan? Wait around for him to
snap out of it and give us a statement?"

"If he saw what I hope he did, we could do worse," I answered simply. "You have any other leads?"

He'd left his coat inside, and crossed his chest with his right
arm in a vain attempt to keep warm. "We just started, for
Christ's sake."

"What's Sol doing?"

"I got him looking into Sawyer's past history." He hesitated, glaring off into the night—not a happy man. "We don't have shit," he finally said.

I stepped into his line of vision, forcing him to look at me. "We've got five major cases so far. Some of them look connected, like Wallis and Shawna. Some of them might be connected, like Wallis and the building project, and others so far look totally independent, like this killing of Mrs. Sawyer. What if we're missing a common link—something we haven't found yet?"

"I'm listening," he said.

"Shawna Davis spent the last week of her life under sedation. Why do that if you're going to kill her anyway?"

"'Cause you're using her for leverage."

"Probably, but you also do it because you can afford to—you've got the time. You've even got the time to make her death look like a Satanist sacrifice, just in case the body's discovered."

"All right."

"Milo's death is looking pretty screwy. Pending what the ME'll say, let's say he was murdered, too—purely for argument's sake."

Willy shook his head but remained silent.

"Again, you've got time—at its fastest, rabies takes a couple of weeks to kill someone—and as with Shawna, you've pointed the finger at someone, or in this case something, else as the culprit."

"What's that got to do with Sawyer?" Willy asked irritably.

"Maybe nothing, except that Dr. Riley said Sawyer's killer obviously wasn't a patient man, since she was so close to dying anyway. What's the other one of our five cases that looks rushed and unplanned?"

"Wallis."

"Right. The same element of time is there, only now you're running out of it. You can't wait to arrange something clever for Wallis, so you just grab her in the middle of the night and hope the cops'll think she split. And you can't wait for Sawyer to die of natural causes, so you strangle her and hope the ME'll miss it."

"Jesus, Joe. You don't have one iota of evidence tying Sawyer to any of the others. And saying Milo was murdered is a pretty big stretch."

"Is it? According to Katz, the Satanist and rabies angles were both leaked to the *Reformer* by the same anonymous caller. Besides, part of our job is fitting various hypotheses to the crimes we're investigating, and seeing if they make sense. I'll concede to leaving Sawyer outside the pattern—for now— but the connections are beginning to grow among the others. We'd be nuts to ignore that."

To his credit, Willy swallowed his criticisms. He merely looked at me for a long, quiet moment, muttered, "I'm freezing my ass off," and left me standing by the curb.

                    *   *   *

Although it was closing in on midnight, I didn't go home from the Skyview. My afternoon nap had thrown off my sleep cycle, so I returned to the office instead. I was also restless with the theory I'd propounded to Willy Kunkle. Coming up with hypotheses was fine early on, but the end result of our job always had to be a solid case, and I agreed with Willy's silent skepticism that I had a long way to go yet—assuming I was even headed in the right direction.

I wasn't the only one who couldn't sleep. Once again, Sammie was hard at work in her cubicle, burning hours she probably wouldn't put on the overtime clock, driven as I was to get the job done, and not bothering to scrutinize her reasons. Across the squad room, I noticed Sol Stennis had caught the same bug.

"How goes it?" I asked her quietly. "Besides the fact you should be home in bed?"

She checked her watch, her face worn and tired. "I'll knock off in another hour or so. I'm just going over what everybody dug up today."

As my second, that was her job only when I was away or on vacation. I didn't protest, however, since I knew it would be useless. "What did you find out about Adelson, Knox, and Garfield?" I asked.

She folded her hands over her stomach. "I'm still digging, but it's already gotten interesting. As director of community development, Lou Adelman handles some big chunks of money. Mostly, they're enough controls on them to make pilfering pretty difficult, but part of his job is to hobnob with fat cats—eat out, go to parties, play golf—so the suspicion that he's padding his pockets basically goes with the job, especially in a penny-pinching town like this. As far as we can tell, though, he's clean. He has been tight with Gene Lacaille for years, which only makes sense, and he's been known to hang out with Tom Chambers, but so have a lot of people.

"Eddy Knox is a different story. I've almost got enough for a warrant to grab his records. His lifestyle has seriously improved since he wrote that glowing ZBA report on the project. I put out some subtle feelers among his friends, neighbors, and acquaintances, and all of them pinpointed last year as the time when his fortunes suddenly improved—a lifetime membership at the fanciest golf course in Keene, a new car, an aboveground swimming pool out back, new clothes. A friend of mine at the Keene PD checked on who sponsored him for the country club—it was Thomas Chambers, esquire."

"Nice work," I said softly. "Eddy works out of the town planner's office. Any indication his boss was involved?"

"None—he looks as clean as Adelman. But Rob Garfield may be dirty. Gail said she didn't think he was bought off, since as ZBA head, he'd backed the project from the start, but I'm still looking into that. He and Tom Chambers go way back, and he lives well. Rumors are his wife is rich, so that may account for it, but I'll find out soon enough."

"Anything more on what Chambers has on Ned Fallows?"

Sammie's face clouded briefly. "Nope—Ron can't figure it out—it's driving him nuts. I did get something on Milo Douglas, though." She smiled at my surprised expression. "During his inquiries into some of this financial stuff, J.P. was told by one of his banking contacts that Milo had a checking account with ten thousand bucks in it. She said she only thought of it because of the rabies publicity—stuck in her mind."

I leaned forward. "New deposit?"

"Yup. Lump sum about two weeks before he died. Milo walked in with the cash and opened the account himself."

The doubts I'd had following my conversation with Willy faded one step back. The circumstances surrounding Milo's death were looking ever more suspicious. "I bet whoever gave it to him never dreamed he'd put it in a bank. Sam, we need to organize a time and date chart—pinpoint as closely as we can every fact we've got on all five of these cases—see if we can find a common link. I want a database we can compare to all the alibis we'll be collecting. When are you starting actual interviews?"

"If I get the warrant for Knox's records and can sort through them fast enough, I might pick him up tomorrow afternoon. I don't know about the others—depends on how much I can dig up on them."

I got to my feet, suddenly more hopeful. "Okay. But don't forget to get some sleep."

She smiled up at me. "Yes, mother."

*   *   *

I walked in on Sol Stennis as he was packing up to go home, his mouth wide open in a yawn. "How did it go today?" I asked him. "Willy said he put you on Sawyer's background."

"That he did, although if today was any indication, we'll have more potential murderers than we can handle. She sure didn't win any popularity contests." A photograph slipped out from among a pile of papers he was stacking, and fluttered to the ground. I bent over and picked it up.

"This is the family picture Sammie found in Sawyer's room, isn't it?"

"Yeah—I've been using it like an index, crossing off each person as I interview them."

But I barely heard him. Scanning the small faces staring unsmiling into the camera, I saw something that spread through me like hot coffee on a cold day—a confirmation that my strategy so far had merit, and that I hadn't been letting some fanciful notions subvert my instincts.

I waited until Sol had slipped his paperwork into the drawer before laying the photograph flat on the desktop. I placed my index finger under the face that had caught my eye—a few years younger, but still easily identifiable, and an undeniable link between Sawyer and the construction project, and thus possibly through the project to our other cases. "You talk to him yet?"

"Nope. Don't even know who he is."

"Paul Hennessy. He's project manager for Carroll Construction. His office is located right under where Milo spent one of his last nights alive."

Chapter Twenty-one

Traditionally, when a cop has zeroed in on a suspect, the actual interview is kept for last, after all available background information has been uncovered. Supposedly, this allows us to know best what questions to ask—and what the answers are likely to be.

That, however, is in a perfect world, after the details of a case have begun revealing a predictable logic.

My problem was that for all its intensity, I didn't know what to make of the link I'd discovered. Had Hennessy killed his own aunt? And if so, why? She was broke, she was dying, and nothing incriminating had been found among her possessions.

Had she been killed by someone else to influence or intimidate him? Then why had her killer selected the one member of Hennessy's family nobody would miss? By the time I returned to the office the next morning, after a restless night's sleep, I had no answers to any of these questions.

Which meant, I finally rationalized, that I would have to interview Paul Hennessy first, since I had nothing else to go on.

*   *   *

Sol and I were at the building site by eight that morning, climbing the same staircase Willy and I had used two days earlier. While the whole place was busier now that construction was back up to speed, most of the work was still occurring on the lower levels. Which made the shouting we heard as we reached the fifth floor landing all the more jarring.

Paul Hennessy's distinctive voice floated down the half-finished hallway. "Look, you tell that stupid son of a bitch to get his act in gear and get that shit here today, or I'll make goddamn sure he never does business with us again."

The response to this was muffled by the office door we were now approaching, but Hennessy obviously didn't like what he heard. "I don't give a flying fuck. Just tell him to do it."

The door opened and a short, round, harried-looking man brushed by us with the speed of a scalded dog.

I poked my head around the corner and saw Hennessy leaning on his makeshift desk, both hands flat on its surface, his head hanging as if he were recovering from a 1,000 yard dash. "Paul?"

He snapped to attention, startled and red-faced. "What?"

"Joe Gunther—police department. Remember? This is Sol Stennis, one of my colleagues."

His eyes widened as if caught by oncoming headlights, making me suddenly happy I'd decided on this trip. "What do you want?" It was more a demand than a question, and distinctly laced with panic.

"Something wrong?" I countered. "Sounds like you're under some pressure."

"It's the job," he answered curtly. He ran his hand through his thick red hair. "A delayed shipment."

"Oh," I exclaimed, as if suddenly enlightened. "I thought it might have been your aunt's death."

He stiffened, caught off guard. "Yeah, that was a real shock. The radio keeps saying she was murdered. Are you people sure about that?"

I was struck by the emphasis to the question, as if her manner of death was more important than the end result. "You were close?" I asked mildly, seemingly admiring the view out the window, but actually hoping the little homework I had done during the half hour before coming here might pay off.

He seized on the question for some conventional camouflage. "Yeah—I haven't been able to shake it. Maybe that's why I'm a little on edge. Who would want to harm her?"

I faced him then, hardening my voice for effect. "Interesting. Every other family member we talked to—without exception—said your aunt was one of the most unpleasant people they ever knew. They also told us you hadn't communicated with her since that family reunion several years ago."

Given his earlier bellicosity, his reaction should have been immediate. What I'd said was at least rude, even outrageous. But Paul Hennessy merely turned red in the face and stammered a few times, as if groping among a variety of inadequate responses.

"Mr. Hennessy," I finally asked. "Where were you the night before last, between ten P.M. and two in the morning?"

"At home," he blurted, and with apparent relief. "My wife'll swear to it."

Sol Stennis silently raised his eyebrows at the defensive tone. "All night?" I persisted. "What time did you go to sleep?"

"Eleven, like always. Before that, we watched TV. I got home around nine, after a meeting with Carroll about getting this project back on track."

There was a pause I let linger for several seconds, during which Hennessy looked from one of us to the other. "And my wife's a light sleeper," he added unnecessarily. "She would've known if I'd gotten up."

The smile I gave him was genuine. Whatever else he was, Paul Hennessy was a man under a great deal of stress—and feeling the weight of some considerable guilt.

"I wonder why you thought you should add that last little detail," I mused aloud. "Of course, you're right. A man under a magnifying glass should try to think of everything."

Not giving him a chance to respond, I crossed the room

and left, Sol Stennis in tow. Halfway down the stairs, Stennis asked, "What was that all about?"

Still feeling the adrenaline rush of a lucky shot in the dark, I laughed quietly. "Damned if I know. I just put on the heat to see what would happen. Doesn't sound like he killed his aunt, but he sure is skittish. From what I've seen over the years, you squeeze a guy like that, he either cooks up an alibi, compares notes with a confederate, or he takes off. They're usually too wired not to do something. I want him tailed. You stay with him until I have you relieved. I'll radio for a car to pick me up here. But keep a low profile. He knows what you look like, and now he knows we're watching."

Linking Hennessy to Adele Sawyer filled me with a sudden sense of movement. After risking the hypothesis that all these cases were somehow interconnected, I'd been frustrated and troubled by their remaining as inert as a pile of logs. Now I was hoping the high-strung project manager would be the loosened cog that would send the entire pile rolling free. For the first time, regardless of where Hennessy fit into the overall scheme of things, I felt that a long-sought opponent might be about to break cover.

As we reached the car I saw two young women getting out of a vehicle farther down the lot. One of them, Nicole, I'd known since her highly precocious high school years. "Call in for someone to pick me up, will you?" I asked Stennis before heading toward them.

Nicole caught sight of me and waved as I approached. "Hi, Mr. Gunther. Wow, I haven't seen you in a long time. What're you doin' here?"

I shook her hand and introduced myself to her friend, who was named Nancy. "Nothing much. You work for this outfit?"

"Yeah—bookkeeping. There's a ton of it with something this big."

"Must be hard to keep track of," I said sympathetically.

Nancy answered. "Oh yeah. They've got four of us here, and a bunch more at the head office. It's like it never stops, especially after a big interruption like what happened."

"So you work mostly for Paul Hennessy?"

"Yeah," Nicole said briefly.

I laughed and gave her a conspiratorial look. "Uh, oh—I know that tone of voice. Sounds like you and Mr. Hennessy don't get along."

The two girls exchanged guilty glances. But before they could think of an evasive response, I added, "He's not my type either. I was just talking with him upstairs. Made me feel like a farmer."

"Yeah," Nancy said disgustedly, despite Nicole's warning glance. "He thinks he's pretty cool—like he's a big wheel. He just works here like everybody else. It's not like he's Mr. Carroll or anything."

"And he won't keep his hands to himself, either," Nicole said softly, reluctantly, and yet not wanting to be left out.

"You don't want to be bending over when he's around," Nancy chimed in. "And I only wear turtlenecks when I'm here." She opened her coat to show me. "I wear anything with a scoop, sure as shit he'll be copping looks. He's married, too," she added in naive outrage.

Nicole had been watching me carefully, more familiar with my ways than her voluble friend. "Mr. Gunther," she finally said, "are you checking up on him?"

I considered the heat I was applying to Hennessy. It couldn't hurt if he caught wind we'd been asking questions. "That's not usually something we talk about," I answered.

"Oh—far out," Nancy laughed gleefully. "That means you are. I hope you nail him—he's such a creep."

"What else does he do?" I asked.

There was a second's hesitation, and I realized I might have pushed them too far. Nicole proved me wrong. "There are rumors he's ripping off the company."

"How?"

"I don't know exactly. I don't know if anybody does, but he lives pretty well."

"He's got a girlfriend," Nancy said, her eyes bright. "She's in Payables at the head office—"

"You don't know that," Nicole protested.

"I sure do. I saw them once. They were all over each other. They didn't see me. I ducked out. They play it really cool otherwise—pretend they barely know each other. I bet they're in cahoots cooking the books."

It wasn't textbook logic, but it worked for me. "What's her name?"

"Ginny Levasseur."

"How could they be cooking the books?"

They looked at each other and shrugged. Nicole said, "There's tons of ways to rip things off. Trucks come in here all day with stuff. There're bills of lading and invoices and whatever, but it's all paper. I mean, nobody actually climbs onto the trucks and counts to make sure every item's on board that's supposed to be."

"And then it sits here forever," Nancy added. "The guard's a joke. Almost everybody's got a pickup, and he never checks to see what's in the back. All they have to do is grab something and throw a tarp over it. I bet they lose a fortune that way."

"How 'bout someone higher up? Like one of the supervisors or the clerk of the works?" I pressed them.

But I could tell before they shook their heads that I'd gotten all they could give me. "Is that what you're looking at him for?" Nicole asked. "Ripping off stuff?"

This time, I opted for caution. "I wish I could tell you. I want to thank you for your help, though. I need all the information I can get."

"Well," Nancy reiterated as they walked away, "I'd go after Ginny Levasseur."

Nicole gave her friend a scolding nudge with her elbow, but it sounded like good advice.

*   *   *

I radioed Dispatch from the patrol car that picked me up and asked them to have Ron Klesczewski meet me at the office. He'd been looking into what Tom Chambers was holding over Ned Fallows. But as important as that could be, I felt spurred by this morning's discoveries to redirect him to better use.

He met me in the Municipal Building's central hallway a quarter-hour later. "If you still have nothing on Fallows," I began, "I think I've found something with more meat on it. Adele Sawyer was Paul Hennessy's aunt. When I spoke to him just now, he reacted all wrong. A couple of on-site book-keepers told me afterward he's rumored to be ripping off the company and has a girlfriend in Payables at the head office. It may all be bullshit, but I put a bee up his nose about our being suspicious of him, and Sol's watching him to see if he makes any sudden moves."

"You think he killed his aunt?"

"Not really, but he fell on his alibi like it was a long-lost puppy, so he might've known when she was being killed. He's connected to it all somehow, and I'm guessing he's the weak link we need. We have to squeeze him hard enough to make him act. The girlfriend's name is Ginny Levasseur. Find out what you can about her, too."

Back in my office, I reached for the phone. It was early yet, and I hoped I could catch the Skyview's attending psychiatrist, Dr. Andrews, before his workday took hold of him. Encouraged by my conversation with Hennessy, I wanted to find out if Bernie *had* seen something that might have traumatized him—and whether or not I could find out what it had been.

I was doubly lucky. Not only did Dr. Andrews answer his own phone, having just come into the office, but he exhibited none of the vagueness about Bernie that Harry the orderly had claimed he might.

"Wonderful guy," said Andrews. "Full of stories. And a fascinating case. In my own experience he's the only post-traumatic stress disorder to exhibit such deep-seated symptoms. Usually, they're either transient or episodic in nature, although they can last for years at a stretch, especially if untreated, but Bernie seems permanently afflicted. He may have an element of what's called Korsakoff's syndrome, which is a classic alcohol-induced memory loss phenomenon. It would exacerbate the PTSD, and may explain why he can't remember much after the early fifties."

"Everything since then is blocked?"

"Well, no. That's why I said he had an *element* of Korsakoff's. There are times he appears more lucid, when I've noticed he assimilates current events into his dialogue. The problem is, I can never be absolutely sure of that. Nursing home life is bland, repetitive, and predictable, which is good—but it makes some forms of clinical observation a little difficult. I often wish I had the time and resources to put Bernie into an environment where I could really study him. As it is, I have a catch-as-catch-can relationship with him."

"Have you seen him since the murder?" I asked.

"No. I haven't had the time—typical, I'm afraid. I heard he was very worked up following the event."

"Do you think he could've seen the murder take place?" I asked hopefully.

There was a long, thoughtful silence at the other end of the line. I expected a speech about the difficulties and dangers of assuming too much from a couple of brief encounters, but he surprised me by admitting, "That's quite possible. His attack on the other resident may well have been an acting out of the event. I also heard that he's been expressing himself exclusively through his warrior persona, which might be another indicator that he witnessed something violent."

"How could I get him to talk? I need a description of whoever killed her."

His response was cautious. "Lieutenant, this man will not be the kind of witness you're used to. If I were you, I wouldn't pin too much hope on getting anything useful out of him, assuming he even saw what you hope he did."

"I realize that. But right now I have nothing."

"Well, I wouldn't look to Bernie for your salvation. For one thing, I can pretty much guarantee you won't get any verbal description. I have a theory—largely unfounded, by the way—that in some cases, one's abilities fade in the reverse order in which they were learned as an infant. Thus, the verbal skills in a patient like this would be among the least reliable. He talks a mile a minute—that's not what I mean—but he doesn't make much sense anymore. Just as a baby's first words are haphazard and often erroneously linked to what it's trying to describe."

"So what's that leave me?" I asked.

"Well, some of the earliest senses are touch and sound. Another is the bonding reflex. I know that Bernie was terribly attached to his daughter, and that he has an affinity for young-looking slender women with long dark hair—the way his daughter looked when he last saw her lucidly. I've noticed he's more relaxed among people fitting that description. Music can be helpful also, as can the touch of a docile animal, like an older cat or dog.

"What I'm saying is that if you can get him sensorially anesthetized, he might be able to express some of what he saw. But it's liable to be very vague, assuming it surfaces at all, and it may demand a good deal of time."

"Is there any harm in giving it a try?"

"I can't imagine any harm, but if he's never met you, there's likely to be a barrier neither one of you could overcome in a single encounter."

"*You* could though," I said flatly, "especially if I supplied the woman, the cat, and some music."

He burst out laughing. "You certainly make it sound easy—a Shake-'n-Bake therapy session. All right, I'm willing to give it a try, but I'll have to think about the approach a bit, visit Bernie myself, and call you back on the timing. Is that acceptable?"

"Absolutely."

"There is one thing I'd recommend in the meantime," he added. "If you do have a specific woman in mind, have her meet him several times before the session, and have her bring the animal. The prior exposure will be important, and while he may not remember the woman from one meeting to the next, he might recall the animal."

"Okay," I said, "you got it. I'll wait to hear from you." I hung up smiling, imagining Gail's reaction.

*   *   *

Unfortunately, my good humor was short-lived. Moments later, the intercom buzzed, and Tony Brandt's voice came over the speaker. "You better get over here, Joe. We've got problems."

With memories still fresh in my mind of the earlier meeting with NeverTom, Wilson, and Nadeau, I crossed the hallway to Tony's office with no small feeling of dread.

But although Tony was alone in his office, his expression was still grim as he waved a letter in the air. "Tom Chambers's lawyer just sent me this, stating that unless we bring formal charges against his client, he's going to sue the PD."

I took a seat, depressed by how fast our stab at discretion had gone for nil. "For what?"

"That's been left purposefully vague, but it obviously has to do with our current inquiries. What's our status there?"

"Sammie got a subpoena this morning to grab all of Eddy Knox's papers. She was hoping to pull him in this afternoon for the initial interrogation."

"Does she think he'll give us NeverTom?"

"I haven't talked to her today. But if Tom Chambers is kicking up dust already, it sounds like Knox caught wind of what's going on and went straight to him for help. Either that, or NeverTom heard through his own sources that we've been checking him out." I pointed at the letter. "Maybe that's a good sign. Why would NeverTom care about the smoke if there wasn't any fire?"

"Possibly because he's a mean-hearted son of a bitch. If he knows he's innocent, this is a perfect opportunity to prove we're out to drag him through the mud. And he'll be able to pull in both Wilson and Gary Nadeau as witnesses to how uncooperative we were just a few days ago. I told you then he had something up his sleeve."

I leaned forward and picked up the letter, scanning its contents quickly. "Does this affect our investigation?"

Tony shook his head. "It's just a threat so far, and a bogus one at that—you can't sue a department for making inquiries.

He's just trying to put us on the defensive. He probably also has more than a few indiscretions he doesn't want us digging up by accident. I just wanted you to know we got his dander up. This is most likely just the opening shot, by the way. He's perfectly capable of calling another press conference and railing at us in public. He'd have little to lose, guilty or not."

I got up, nodding. "Okay. Thanks, Tony—keep me posted."

*   *   *

Back at my office, however, NeverTom's attempt at a preemptive strike against us kept preying on my mind, and gave birth to an idea of how to both feed him some of his own medicine, and help us look into his and his brother's financial dealings. It flew in the face of my professional instincts, and I was pretty sure that if Jack Derby found out about it, it could possibly cost me my job. But I still couldn't shake its appeal. I picked up the phone and dialed Gail for consultation.

"You alone?" I asked once I had her on the line.

"What're you offering, a little phone sex?"

I laughed. "Let me run something by you first."

"That doesn't sound like half as much fun. Go ahead—I'm alone for the moment."

"NeverTom's sicced his lawyer on us, threatening to sue because we're digging into his affairs. I know it's all hot air, but it got me wondering. What if I pull a Deep Throat with Stan Katz? Leak him a little inside information on Tom, get the *Reformer* to do some of our legwork for us, and throw a bit of Tom's shit back in his face all at the same time?"

There was a long pause before she answered. "Why do you need to do that?"

"Because NeverTom's well connected, rich, and not tied down by rules or bureaucracy. We're understaffed, in the dark, and handcuffed by regulations—most of them designed to stop us from doing our job. If I could get Katz fired up enough, it might give us a crucial advantage in finding out what's going on. I know he'd protect my identity, and now that the paper's employee-owned, he's got no outside bosses to tell him what to do."

There was another long silence before she said, "You want my honest opinion? I think NeverTom Chambers has gotten under your skin, and you're going to make damn sure he takes the rap for something, even if it's just bad publicity. From what I've seen so far, you don't have a thing on him. Is that still true?"

I admitted as much.

"You might soon, though, with Eddy Knox coming in. And if the bank is implicated, that could involve some federal charges. The PD gets threatened with lawsuits all the time, Joe. But you keep playing by the rules. That's both the department's strength, and the twenty-pound weight around its neck."

I made no comment, hearing in her comments my own inner debate, and also wondering if she was about to reach the same conclusion I had.

"So now another rich, powerful, arrogant jerk is shooting his mouth off. Only, this time you're thinking, 'What the hell? A few words in the right place, and I can watch the fur fly without getting damaged, and maybe pick up a few insights along the way.' Is that about it? You feeling like rebelling against a lifetime of traditional rectitude?"

I started laughing. "Yeah—that's close enough."

She joined me for a few seconds, took a breath, and then said, "I say, 'Go for it.' If ever there was a guy worth breaking a rule or two to get, it's NeverTom."

She hung up before I could ask her if she knew of anyone with an old cat.

Chapter Twenty-two

Sheila Kelly and J. P. Tyler came by my office later that morning, both hesitating in the doorway as if uncertain on how to proceed.

"You got something?" I asked them, waving them in.

Sheila, as tall and faintly glamorous as J.P. was short and homely, deferred to his seniority. "Yeah," he said, "we may have found a hook on Thomas Chambers."

They both sat down.

"I better warn you," J.P. continued, "this is strictly anecdotal so far. We had to make sure not to do anything that might be thrown out in court later on, so we consulted only public records, and made it clear to everyone we talked to that what we were after was purely informational. I did tape every conversation, though, and had each person sign a release."

I noticed Sheila fighting to hide a smile, and wondered how many times in the last two days she'd been tempted to wring his compulsive little neck.

"From what we were told," J.P. continued, "and from what Sheila obtained from the records, it looks like Thomas Chambers influenced Harold Matson—and through him the Bank of

Brattleboro—to finance the convention center, although neither Chambers nor his brother had any financial involvement in it at that time."

"Aside from owning adjacent property," Sheila added.

"Is that illegal?" I asked.

J.P. looked vaguely uncomfortable. To a man who found pleasure poking through hair samples, bloodstains, fingerprints, and other minutiae, the amorphous world of finance lacked the absolutes he relied on.

Sheila Kelly sensed his dilemma and smoothly took over. "The best answer to that is probably historical. When Gene Lacaille first came up with the idea for a convention center, he had about a million dollars to invest. He already owned the land free and clear—inherited from his father. As we all know, support for the idea was fast and broad-based, including from the Chambers brothers. The biggest problem from the start, however, was financing. Gene was willing to commit to three million altogether, one up front, and two more to be generated from the Keene mall he was just completing. The State of Vermont was sweet-talked into providing two million more, to be funneled through Lou Adelman's office of community development, in the form of a grant that then became a municipal loan. And the Bank of Brattleboro was approached for the remaining ten."

Sheila stretched her long legs out in front of her, settling in more comfortably. "The problem was, for a bank to make a ten-million-dollar loan, it has to have total assets of some two billion, based on a conservative ratio that came out of all those bank failures in the go-go eighties, when people were loaning way more than their banks could afford to lose. The Bank of Brattleboro has nowhere near those kinds of assets. The best it could put up was five million, and even then Matson, the president, was probably pushing it."

"What about the board of directors?" I asked.

"Good question. The board at B of B is the old-fashioned type, pretty rare nowadays, mostly made up of prominent local people with little or no banking background or knowledge. It's almost utterly dependent on the president for its decision-making.

"The obvious solution in a situation like what Matson was facing is to bring in as many additional banks as necessary to make up the difference. That's what he did, but with the unusual proviso that the commitments be made in a tiered fashion, rather than as a pool, so that B of B's five million would be spent before the other banks had to pitch in. This might've been a show of Matson's faith in the project—or it could've been a careful strategy on Chambers's part. In any case, it worked, and once the permits were secured, it was full steam ahead."

"Until the Keene shopping mall project was stopped dead in its tracks," I filled in.

"Correct," Sheila said. "That was supposed to have been completed in time to finance Lacaille's investment in the convention center. But once some PCB pollutants mysteriously surfaced at the Keene site, everything was turned on its ear. Not only was it going to cost Lacaille a fortune to clean up the PCBs, but the revenue he was counting on was history— the EPA and the state of New Hampshire's pollution people saw to that. Matson tried his damnedest to get Lacaille to hang on to the property, but Gene was no longer interested. He was doing all he could just to stay afloat. The convention center had become a pair of cement shoes."

"Enter NeverTom?" I asked.

"Well, yes and no. NeverTom had been in it from the start. We heard he'd gotten Matson to stick his neck out for B of B's commitment of five million, even though Matson had initially been cool to the idea. In fact, that's an area where Matson might have some interesting things to say, since Chambers's public encouragement could easily have become private coercion with nobody being the wiser. The neat coincidence though, is that by the time Lacaille had to pull out, NeverTom was a selectman, and could rally the public to force Matson to come up with a fast solution. You see, normally, when a bank gets handed a white elephant by a bankrupt developer, it takes its time putting together the best substitute deal it possibly can, quoting the interests of the stockholders all the way. But not in this case."

"Because of local political pressure," I stated flatly, reliving the recent past from a whole new perspective.

"Local *and* state," Sheila agreed. "Don't forget that the state had a vested interest, too. The governor picked up the phone a few times to remind people of that. At which point, Ben Chambers suddenly appeared out of the blue, almost as soon as the project got stalled, and offered Matson a fused deal—meaning it was tied to a deadline. His three-part proposal was that the bank, having by now invested four million, forfeit one of them; that the town, having spent both of its million, forfeit one also; and that Lacaille sign over all his interests to Ben, including the land, worth close to another million. In exchange, Ben would assume some twelve million in loans by the date of completion, having acquired almost four million in equity without spending a dime of his own. The catch was that the fuse would burn for one month only—Matson and company had only thirty days to beat the deal, or Ben would retire his offer."

"So Matson sat on his hands for one month and signed on the dotted line?" I suggested.

"No way," she protested. "He would've been crucified. Not only would the other banks have jumped on him, not to mention his own stockholders, but the feds would've, too. No, he and his officers all busted their humps looking for an alternate white knight, but Ben's offer had an element no one else would match, and which was too politically volatile to ignore. His proviso that the town would have to eat half of its two-million-dollar loan was actually a pure gimme—a gift of a million bucks. Any other white knight would've told the town to eat it—why pay for somebody else's mistake? By coming up with that gimmick, Ben all but guaranteed himself success. That one million had nothing to do with the bank, but it had everything to do with good will, and the bank didn't want to look so mercenary that it would willingly stiff the town—and through the town the state and our telephoning governor—for that huge an amount. It was very cleverly done."

"The time fuse also worked in Ben's favor," J.P. added, "because Carroll Construction still had its equipment on site. Had the bank delayed, Carroll would've packed up and left, and the bank would've had an even tougher package to sell."

I was rubbing my forehead. I had never been big on finances, figures, or even talk about banks. "So Ben Chambers got something for nothing. But he did assume twelve million dollars of debt. Why's that such a great deal?"

"Because he'll sell it in the end," Sheila said simply, "and possibly triple his current net worth. In this state, that would transform him from a local rich guy to a major player, especially if his brother keeps climbing the political ladder and ends up in Montpelier or Washington."

The ambition of the scheme filled the room. "All right," I finally said, "but what laws have been broken? Or if nothing else, what rocks do we look under, besides sweating Harold Matson and hoping he fingers NeverTom?"

"We've got some other options," J.P. said with a small smile, "the best being the pollution in Keene."

I raised my eyebrows, and Sheila joined in. "J.P. gets full credit for this one—what caught us there was the timing. Not only was the mall about to open, and supply Gene Lacaille with a steady cash flow, but the B of B half of the funding was about to run out. The partner banks were just about to step up to the plate. Had that happened, the weight of the decision about which white knight to accept would have shifted from Matson to them. Plus, they might've put their investigators to work if they'd smelled something fishy. We called a couple of those banks yesterday, and asked them if they'd gotten sweaty palms at the time. The answer, of course, was no—since they hadn't invested a nickel so far, they wouldn't have cared if it had gone belly-up."

"The kicker," J.P. continued, "is that the Keene mall closed down because someone made an anonymous phone call. No PCB would've been found otherwise, and the quantities the EPA has located are randomly and widely spaced."

"As if they'd been planted," I suggested, caught by the mention of yet another signature phone call to the press.

"Exactly."

"How easy is PCB to get?" I asked.

"It's all over the place," J.P. answered. "Most of the industrial motor oil used fifteen years ago contained the stuff—that means almost every transformer or capacitor made from the early fifties to the late seventies. PCBs were added to oil as a stabilizer so it wouldn't break down in violent temperature changes. Tons of your older motors are full of it—even some water well pumps, if you like irony. Not only that, but because of its very design, PCB is basically permanent—it doesn't degrade. The only way to dispose of it is either through environmentally safe incineration, or legally sanctioned storage, both of which are incredibly expensive. That's what's killing Lacaille right now.

"To answer your question, the reason it's so easy to get hold of is that lots of people—in electrical supplies, for example—have just opted to park whatever contaminated equipment they might have in a back room somewhere, and ignore disposing of it altogether. You could also find an old transformer and drain it, if push came to shove."

"How much are we talking about?" I asked, my imagination suddenly stimulated by this last statement.

"Twenty-five gallons, tops. One man in a pickup, driving around that site for an hour, dropping a little here, a little there, would do the trick. PCB contamination is quantified at fifty parts per million. That's not much. In fact, nowadays, you wouldn't need any at all. PCB is such a buzzword that the phone call alone would've been enough to temporarily stop construction—of course, whoever did this wanted more than that."

"And the phone call was made how?" I asked.

"To the *Keene Sentinel,* on the morning of January tenth."

My smile matched their own. "And if I'd just spent the evening creeping around spiking a building site, I'd make sure people knew about it first thing."

"Meaning the PCB was probably dumped the night of the ninth," J.P. concluded.

"And that if the call was made from here," Sheila added, "it'll appear on somebody's long distance phone bill."

"All right," I said. "Get it all into a report, and tell Sammie about that date. She's putting together a time line, and we can all cross our fingers that one of the alibis we have on file will fall apart right there."

They both stood and prepared to leave. "I also think," I added, stopping them, "if you're comfortable with the idea, that you ought to bring in Harold Matson for a talk—sweat him a little. If you do, make sure he knows he doesn't have to say anything, and that he can have a lawyer present if he wants one. You'll need to coordinate what time you can use the interview room with Sammie—she's pulling in Eddy Knox this afternoon."

They both nodded, their faces reflecting their pleasure at the offer. Interviews of this importance were usually handled by the other members of the detective squad, and rarely by anyone from Patrol. J.P. had always shied away from them in the past, preferring his world of scientific detachment. Reading his expression now, I was glad to be giving him another shot.

*   *   *

Gail's usually cool demeanor fractured at the notion. "Joe, for crying out loud."

"It's got to be an old cat, or a dog—anything that'll just sit there and be petted."

"Are you sure he saw anything?"

"In my gut? Yes. But we've got to get it out of him."

"And my looking like his daughter and holding a cat will do that?"

"No—*he* gets to hold the cat. We've got to win him over as much as possible—make him feel secure."

I could hear her switching the phone from one ear to the other. "Joe, I'd like to help, but there have got to be other dark-haired women with more time on their hands than me right now."

"I cleared it with Derby."

There was a stunned silence, so I added diplomatically, "He said it was entirely up to you, but that whatever you were doing could wait an hour or so."

"Oh, right," she said sarcastically, "that's not what I hear."

I kept quiet, trusting her to look fairly at the issue without further prodding.

"When do you want this done?" she finally said wearily.

"The orderly just called me from the home, and said Bernie had pretty much settled down. His name's Harry. He'll be waiting for you on the second floor."

"And you just want me to be chummy, right? No pointed questions?"

"Right—this is purely an icebreaker. The real meeting will be with the shrink later on, tomorrow if we're lucky. If not, I might ask you to do it again, just to build on the relationship. Would that be all right?"

She let out a short laugh. "Sure, what the hell? Maybe some time with an ancient nut case'll give me a glimpse of things to come."

*   *   *

Harriet's detached voice over the intercom brought my attention to one of the blinking lights on the phone. "Gunther," I answered, punching the button.

"It's Sol," he said breathlessly. "I lost Hennessy. He must've spotted me."

"Where are you?"

"At the gas station where High meets Green. I followed him into the Chestnut Reservoir area, but I had to give him room so he wouldn't—"

"Don't worry about it. Get back in your car, switch to the private channel and stay put."

I ran out, forgetting my coat, and made for my own car as fast as the slippery ground allowed. I noticed for the first time that it must have been snowing for at least an hour—in big, fat, mesmerizing flakes.

As soon as I started the car, I switched over to the closed radio frequency we didn't share with the half-million scanner listeners I was convinced inhabited the area. "M-80 from 0-3. Contact any units in the Birge Street area to be on the lookout for any vehicles registered to Paul Hennessy or Virginia Levasseur. Stol Stennis is standing by with a description of Hennessy's car. Get hold of Ron for what Levasseur might be driving or call it up on the computer. No unit is to pursue. I just want their location reported if spotted."

I dropped the mike into my lap to better negotiate the corner onto Grove Street, heading toward Main, and hit the switch to the blue emergency strobes hidden behind the car's front grille. Without them, I knew the traffic would never let me onto Main, and I had a fair distance to cover fast.

I waited until all my instructions had been forwarded before keying the mike again. "Sol? I'm heading for Birge via Canal. Take Union Street to close it up from the other end, all right?"

"Copy."

Even with a fully equipped patrol car behind them, complete with howling siren, motorists are often at a loss about what to do, assuming they do anything at all. So my demure, silent, flashing blue grille beacons did more to frazzle my own nerves than they did to move any traffic. Nevertheless, mostly through reckless driving, exacerbated by the thickly falling snow, I managed to reach my end of Birge in about five minutes. During that time, the radio informed me that Ginny Levasseur was registered to a '95 dark green Ford Explorer, Hennessy to a red, plow-equipped '96 Ford 350 Custom pickup with dual rear wheels, and that nobody had seen either one since I'd raised the alarm.

Birge Street was one of Brattleboro's significant historical sites, although you had to know the history to believe it. Narrow, nondescript, and located in a ragged section of town, its south side was dominated by a row of ancient, narrow, slate-walled warehouses, each of which nosed into the curb—long, thin, and tall—like oil tankers at a dock. Once home to the Estey Organ Works, they were now the domain of an assortment of diverse businesses, including Carroll Construction, where Ginny Levasseur worked in Payables.

I was here on the probability that if Hennessy had panicked as I hoped he had, his first order of business would be to warn his girlfriend. Now that I was parked at the end of the street, however, having sent the whole department into frantic motion, it suddenly occurred to me that the basis for my action stemmed from a gossiping, gum-snapping, postpubescent clerk I'd met for the first time this morning.

I picked up the mike again, and crossed my fingers that Nicole's friend Nancy was a sound judge of character. "Sol—can you see the parking lot?"

"Yeah, and the Explorer. Fancy car—has all the trimmings."

"It should, if we're right about these two. M-80 from 0-3, we've located the Explorer. All units can stand down and return to regular duties, but keep your eyes peeled for the pickup."

Dispatch responded in flat Chuck Yeager fashion, and I went back to watching the snow build up on the hood of my car.

"Here she comes," Sol said about five minutes later. "He must've called her, 'cause she's moving fast, carrying a man's briefcase."

"Which direction?"

"Hang on. She's still in the lot . . . Okay, she's headed my way . . . I'm on her tail, going back toward Union Street."

"10-4. I'm right behind you," I said, and began rolling down Birge to catch up.

*   *   *

Whatever the pitch of her anxiety, Ginny Levasseur did not set us onto any high-speed chase. The combination of slippery unplowed roads and increasingly poor visibility made her move at an almost leisurely pace. The only indicators of her frame of mind were her car's occasionally nervous sideslips as she overgunned the accelerator.

Not that Sol and I were having an easy time of it. Driving rear-wheel-drive, light sedans, we had our own work cut out for us, especially on Union Street's cliff-like incline up to Western Avenue.

Thereafter, however, things settled down. The Explorer took Western to the interstate on-ramp and headed north. The three of us, mixed in with dozens of other snow-blanketed cars, stuck to the right lane like timid dowagers, relying on the barely perceptible dark double ribbon of cleared asphalt before us for both safety and comfort. One mile south of Brattleboro's last exit, I got back on the radio and told Dispatch to widen the alert for Hennessy's truck to include the Vermont and New Hampshire State Police and the Windham County Sheriff's Department, and to focus on the area north of town.

A few minutes later, after passing the exit, I was glad I'd invited more company.

For most of its length within the state, I-91 parallels the Connecticut River, servicing Vermont and New Hampshire equally. Exits occur about every ten miles, and in between, the views to both east and west rival the prettiest in the country. Today, however, was like driving through a pale gray tunnel, the only things visible being the taillights ahead, and the only sense of motion the sound of the engine and the occasional small bump passing beneath the wheels. This spatial detachment was paradoxically enhanced by the endless, hypnotizing wash of snowflakes against the windshield. For all intents a solid indicator of forward motion, this cone-shaped vortex never seemed to move, dulling the driver's concentration, until his primary impulse was not to steer but to sit back, drop his hands from the wheel, and lose himself in the display. By the time we were approaching exit four in Putney, I felt my eyes might never uncross again.

"She's getting off," Sol reported, much to my relief, and I saw his right-hand flasher begin to wink.

The Putney exit is located south of the village, so we followed Levasseur on a slow parade along the main street, still accompanied by several other cars. I wasn't too worried she'd notice the same headlights had stuck with her all the way from Brattleboro—the nervous, halting way she drove told me she kept her eyes glued to the road—but I was beginning to worry where this little trip might be leading us. If she was going to meet Hennessy, I wanted to make sure I had enough support units to hem him in. But until I knew where that encounter was to take place—or even *if* it was—there was little I could do to coordinate with other agencies. In frustration, I gave Dispatch a geographical update instead, and maintained my twenty feet off Sol Stennis's barely visible bumper.

We continued through town to the junction with the Westminster West Road, took it for a mile, and then veered left again onto West Hill Road, heading back toward Dummerston, between Putney and Brattleboro. We were starting to make a big circle. I began to reconsider Levasseur's ignorance of our presence.

"Sol? She given any sign she knows you're there?"

"I don't know if she has yet, but she's bound to soon. These roads are getting narrower and narrower, and we're about all the traffic that's left."

"When she takes another turn, pass by and double back. I'll pick her up and you can follow me for a while."

"10-4."

The opportunity for this maneuver occurred ten minutes later, when the Explorer turned right onto the Putney Mountain Road—a one-lane dirt trail leading to the crest of a string of steep hills separating Putney from Brookline to the west. In the summertime this road went all the way through, giving both communities a significant shortcut to the thirty-minute run-around through Dummerston. But at this time of the year, it was a virtual dead end. Brookline did not plow its side of the mountain.

Coming abreast of a house, I put on my turn signal, as if pulling into the driveway, and let the car ahead disappear into the veil of falling snow.

"What's up?" Sol immediately radioed.

"I don't want her to feel crowded. She's got nowhere to go, and I can see her tracks in the snow. We can just follow them." I raised Dispatch again and suggested that any additional units should approach from the Putney side.

I moved slowly from then on, focusing on the twin furrows her tires had left behind, my only concern now that we would come upon them too fast, and lose our element of surprise.

I keyed the mike again. "M-80 from 0-3. Does either subject own any known property on Putney Mountain?"

I drove on for a quarter hour before Dispatch came back. "Negative."

The Putney Mountain Road is long, twisting, and steep, with deep ditches on both sides. It is also thinly populated and buried in the woods. The oddness of the situation, the growing sense of isolation, and the awareness of the tightly packed trees pressing in from either side of the car began to heighten my anxiety. Something was going wrong—slowly but surely. In a snail-paced parody of some careening, madcap chase, I could sense we were losing the advantage we'd been counting on. The farther I drove, the more convinced I became that instead of following some unaware suspect, we were in fact heading for a destination solely designed for our benefit.

Higher and higher we climbed, past most of the houses here, past Banning Road, the last feeder trail shy of the mountain's top, and almost to where I knew the road was supposed to be blocked by a season's worth of accumulated snow.

That very thought jogged my memory, and I spoke into the radio. "Sol, doesn't Hennessy's truck have a snowplow on—"

It was all I got out. Directly ahead of me, looming large and fast like the red-eyed monster from a nightmare, the rear end of the Explorer came barreling down upon me, its backup lights blazing. I had time only to throw my arms across my face before the hood of my car crumpled like an accordion, and smashed the windshield, letting in a swirling white torrent of snow and shattered glass.

Chapter Twenty-three

Gail stood at the foot of the emergency room bed, shaking her head. "My God, Joe, you are the most accident-prone man I know. What were you doing running around the mountains in a blizzard?"

I gave her a lopsided smile, tilting my head so the nurse could finish taping a dressing to my temple. "Hennessy took off, his girlfriend took off after him, and we took off after her. I didn't realize till too late that he might've figured we'd follow her."

She came up alongside the bed and kissed me on the cheek. "How is he?" she asked the nurse.

"Hard-headed. He has a bruise and a cut where he should have a concussion." She finished her handiwork. "I'll get some painkillers. Be right back."

Gail watched her leave and then examined me again, her concern more apparent now. "Joe, you've got to stop getting banged up like this. You're not built for it anymore."

I saw the fear in her eyes, and recognized its source. We'd been through a lot in the last couple of years, traumatically and emotionally, and had survived it only by letting go of the

independence we'd long thought was the strongest link between us. But the trade-off was what I saw in her now, and
felt within myself—a more mindful acknowledgment of life's
transience, and a growing dread that what we'd built together,
despite the effort, could be forever destroyed by mere
chance.

She retreated to the safer ground of the here and now,
leaving to time the task of calming her anxiety. "So what did
happen?"

"After Hennessy shook off Sol, he beat it to Brookline
through Newfane, put chains on his tires, and plowed his way
to the top of Putney Mountain. Guessing we might've tum-
bled to his connection with Ginny, he called her on his mo-
bile phone and told her to meet him using the Putney
approach. That way, we'd think she was heading for a dead
end, and tell whatever backup we had to come in from the
east, which is exactly what happened. Hennessy's plan was to
ram the first car that came along with the Explorer, block the
road, and make a clean getaway in his truck. It almost
worked."

She gingerly touched my bandaged head. "Doesn't look
like almost."

"Ginny got nervous waiting in the truck, and got out just
before he rammed me with her car. When he ran back to the
truck, they missed each other in the storm. Neither one knew
where the other one was, Sol was coming up on foot from
behind my car, and Hennessy realized it had all been for
nothing. It was either leave Ginny behind or be caught. Sol
found her on her knees in the snow, crying."

The nurse returned with a small white envelope. "The doctor says to take one of these every six hours, or as needed for
pain, but don't exceed the dose—they're pretty powerful."

I slid off the bed and put the pills into my pocket.

"I don't suppose you're going home to bed," Gail said, not
bothering to phrase it as a question.

I kissed her cheek. "Nope. Too much is starting to come together. We still haven't nailed down our killer, or located

Mary Wallis, but things are beginning to unfold. It can't be too much longer. How did you get on with Bernie, by the way?"

She helped me with my coat and escorted me out the ER's front door. "I like him. I can't say we had any real conversation, but he talks a mile a minute, and he loved the cat. I borrowed it from Susan Raffner—it's so old, it's barely breathing, but it did the trick. His face lit up as soon as I showed it to him. He called it Ginger, which I guess was once a cat he owned."

"So you won't mind doing it again when the shrink calls?" I asked, heading toward a waiting patrol car.

"No." She grabbed my arm and stopped me in the middle of the parking lot, the falling snow dusting her hair. "Joe, I can't make you do anything you don't want to do, but will you at least try to be careful? Take the pills if your head starts to hurt, or a nap if you get tired."

I wrapped my arms around her and gave her a hug. "I'm stubborn, Gail, but I'll try not to be stupid. I love you."

She smiled through her own distress. "I love you, too."

*   *   *

As I'd requested, Ruth Hennessy, Paul's wife, was waiting for me in my office with Sammie when I returned from the hospital. She was pale-faced and nervous, sitting straight in her chair, and had to shift a wadded-up handkerchief from one hand to the other in order to shake mine in an absent-minded greeting.

I sat down opposite her. "Mrs. Hennessy, I'm not going to sugarcoat what's going on here. Your husband is in deep trouble. He's broken the law, and he's decided to run for it. We've got a long list of charges against him, and they may be just the tip of the iceberg. That being the case, the sooner we can get him in here to explain himself, the better off he'll be. If he keeps running, it's likely he'll wind up getting hurt."

I shouldn't have been surprised by her first words. "They said there was a girl."

I didn't hesitate. "Yes, there is, and we have her in custody. They worked together, and she might've been involved with your husband in some of his illegal activities. Whether there was more than that between them, I don't know."

"What's her name?"

"Ginny Levasseur—he ever mention her?"

"I met her once—at a company picnic. Pretty . . ."

I tried to steer her in another direction. "Mrs. Hennessy, do you have any idea where Paul might be right now? A vacation home we might not know about, or with a friend he could trust?"

Her face hardened. "Trust? I didn't even know about the girlfriend. God knows what else he's been keeping from me."

I nodded and rose to my feet. "All right. We appreciate your cooperation. Sergeant Martens here will be asking you some more detailed questions. I am sorry for your troubles."

She ignored me, her eyes fixed, and I left the office for the tiny interrogation cubicle in the far corner of the squad room. As with every aspect of our department, the cubicle was a miniature version of what Hollywood has made common-place. But where the movies show two large rooms, sepa-rated by a one-way mirror, ours was eight-by-eight, and could only be viewed from what had once been a broom closet.

I slipped in there first to join Tony Brandt.

"How's your head?" he asked, his eyes still on the window, beyond which we could see Ginny Levasseur, disheveled, her clothes stained, her makeup smeared by tears, sitting like a schoolgirl with her knees together, her toes turned in, and her hands buried in her lap.

"Not bad. You talk to her yet?"

"Me? No—I figured I'd let you have first crack. Ron got warrants as soon as all this broke, and he and the rest of them are tearing Hennessy's office and home apart right now."

"Any feedback I could use in there?"

"A little. They found an office building in West Bratt be-longing to Adele Sawyer. Looks like Hennessy got her to give him rights-of-attorney several years ago and then hid all his dealings under her name. The building was made entirely of stolen materials from jobs he's managed over the years."

"Enter the girlfriend in Payables," I added. "She been read her rights?"

"Yeah—she didn't want a lawyer."

"Okay—thanks."

Ginny Levasseur looked up as I entered the small room, her face further crumpling at the sight of the bandage. "I'm real sorry—"

I'd already decided not to play that game. "You'll be sorrier soon," I said flatly, pulling up another chair and sitting across from her. "You're already facing charges that'll put you in jail for years."

Her shoulders slumped.

"How long have you been cooking the books for Hennessy?" I asked, having no proof she ever had.

"Six years," she murmured, back to staring at the floor.

"That how long you two have been romantically involved?"

She nodded. "We were building our nest egg."

I resisted pointing out the skewed thinking behind that rationale. "Building his nest egg, you mean. He tell you he was going to leave his wife once you'd stolen enough money?"

"He was."

"And how much was 'enough' going to be? Didn't he keep pushing that deadline further and further away?"

She didn't answer, but began crying softly.

I let a moment pass for the hopelessness to sink in. "Look, Ginny, there's a chance you might not have to serve the kind of jail time you're facing. We both know you were swept off your feet—seduced by a man who promised you everything, bought you gifts, said he'd marry you in the long run. In my book, that makes you more a victim than a crook. He needed you because of your job, and once he'd made all the money he wanted, he was going to dump you."

"We love each other," she tried lamely, in a halfhearted voice.

"He called you at the office. What did he say?"

"That the cops were on to us—that we had to get away— maybe go to Mexico."

"But he asked you to do something, didn't he?"

She looked up at me then, her damp eyes wide, an awareness slowly dawning. "His briefcase, from his office."

"And he's got that now, doesn't he? While we've got you."

She just kept staring at me, a small furrow appearing between her eyebrows.

"Tell me how it worked, Ginny, and maybe we can cut you some slack—no guarantees, but it's the best thing you can do for yourself."

Slowly, in disconnected fragments, I used her shock at a betrayal I'd invented to extract a description of Paul Hennessy's grand plan for the future. As plans went, it was thorough, conservative, and had been nurtured with care. It was also a perfect example of how far corruption can spread inside an organization where too much trust is awarded without any oversight. Carroll Construction gave "hands-off management" a brand-new meaning.

As Ginny slowly detailed it, Paul's skimming had started simply in the beginning. As a brand-new project manager, some ten years earlier, he'd begun inflating his job estimates by fattening line items in the "general conditions" category— telephones, faxes, storage, utilities, "trucking and cleanup," and a dozen other odds and ends all fitting under "overhead." The discrepancies hadn't come to much individually, but they'd begun to mount up.

Next, he'd expanded into rigging the "mechanicals"—overbuying from suppliers, and sending the excess either to a warehouse of his own, to be sold on the black market, or simply to a renegade job site, where the materials went straight into a building—like the one we'd found listed under Adele Sawyer's name.

As the years went by, and Paul's autonomy in the company became near absolute, suppliers were encouraged to make him gifts in exchange for jobs and prompt payments. Also, he began manipulating "direct ships"—sending light loads to the site, where they were accurately logged in, and having bills for full loads sent to Accounting, where they were paid off— the difference in materials again winding up in one of Paul's private warehouses, and the discrepancies vanishing between the cracks.

Ginny was brought in later, as his sense of invulnerability grew. He would tell a bidder that a client would pay, for example, $50,000 tops for sheetrock or whatever, and then he'd tell the client that the bid was $10,000 higher. Ginny would make out two handwritten checks—one for $50,000, which would go to the bidder, and another for $10,000, made out to Paul Hennessy. In the computer, she would enter the $60,000 total as a single check, and bill the client accordingly. Since the handwritten checks were kept in storage at the bank, along with thousands of others, and the auditors were too lazy to actually inventory them one by one, reality became whatever Ginny had put into the computer.

She didn't know any accurate figures—Paul made a point of keeping his cards to himself—but he'd bragged to her once that, over the years, he'd skimmed off in excess of one million dollars.

"Did he ever mention Adele Sawyer?" I asked her, an hour after we'd started.

By this time, the tears had stopped, and Ginny had become fairly matter-of-fact, comfortable with the fiction I'd allowed her that we were part of the same team, merely exchanging information. "Not until she was murdered. He'd told me he had an aunt he was using as a dummy, but I never knew her name."

"How did he react to her death?"

"He went ballistic. This convention center was supposed to be his last job, so he was really milking it. I mean, before, he'd skimmed off little bits, building it up over the years. But on this one, with fifteen million dollars floating around, he figured he'd take them to the cleaners, since we'd both be out of the country by the time they balanced the books. He was hoping for almost half a million. Adele's dying messed up everything—he had to spend all his time just trying to cover his tracks. And when he found out she'd been murdered— that's when he really fell apart."

"Hold it. Explain that."

She stared at me as if I'd fallen asleep halfway through the story. "Sure. First, Paul thought the old lady had just jumped the gun—died too soon . . . He was in a crunch, you know? Had this big deal, where he needed her to stay alive, but he knew she wasn't getting any younger, so he was already real nervous. He'd started turning some of his property into cash, but the timing was bad. So when we first heard she'd died, he was really pissed off—like he'd been stabbed in the back. He kept saying, 'I don't believe this—that bitch had to stick it to me one last time.' He really hated her—I guess they all did. Anyhow, when the paper said she'd been killed, he went crazy, 'cause then he knew, you know, that he'd actually been screwed by his own partner, and he was in real trouble."

I resisted asking who she was talking about, and gave her free rein, remembering Dr. Riley saying that Sawyer's killer must have been an impatient man. "Did they have a falling out?"

"They weren't getting along too good. This guy kept saying Paul was going to mess things up for everybody if he got too greedy—that if he just kept doing things the way he always had, there'd be more money in it for all of them in the long run. But Paul didn't trust him—figured it'd be safer if he got his money up front and then split the country—let the other guy make his bundle on his own. Only the partner didn't see it that way, and I guess he finally killed the aunt to show who was boss. That sure backfired, though, 'cause as soon as Paul heard it was murder and not just old age, he told me he wasn't going to take any raps on his own—that he'd make sure the other guy went down, too . . . Sure is sad—we had a good thing going."

The more we talked, the more impressed I'd become with Ginny's moral compass. I now allowed myself to ask the obvious question. "Who is this partner?"

Her answer was a disappointment. "I don't know. When Paul first told me about him, I was real worried—thought maybe the guy would blackmail us or turn us in, but Paul didn't seem to care. He said the guy was doing stuff a lot worse than us, and wasn't about to blow the whistle. All Paul had to do was help him out a little, and he was free to do what he'd always done . . . except that things got sour between them."

"What did Paul call this man?"

"His partner. That's all I ever heard. I asked him a couple of times, but he said it was better I didn't know. He did say he was a bigwig, though, and that what he was up to really surprised Paul. Paul said there was no telling about people."

"Were you ever there when they got together?"

She shook her head. "No way. He kept all that real private."

"Did Paul ever tell you the favor he had to do for this man?"

"Nope—'cept he said it was the best deal he'd ever made—'course, that was before they started fighting."

"Ginny," I asked hopefully, "would you be able to remember what Paul was doing on the night of January ninth this year?"

She looked doubtful. "We didn't get too many nights together . . . you know, his wife . . . But I could check my diary. I write in it every night—well . . . almost."

I smiled at that. "Did Paul know about the diary?"

"No—why?" she asked, with beguiling simplicity.

I made a mental note to specify the diary in the search warrant of her home and office. "Nothing. Just wondered." I stood up and crossed over to the door.

"What happens now?" she asked.

I paused and looked back at her. "You've entered a system. You're going to see cops and lawyers and prosecutors and judges and maybe the inside of a jail for a while. It all depends. I can tell you, though, that you've made a good start. Keep playing straight and you should do all right—all things considered."

I left her with that faint comfort, knowing better than she that in Vermont, at least, her chances for a light sentence were better than average.

As expected, my office was empty again. Sammie had taken Ruth Hennessy's statement and cut her loose, eager to get things organized for Eddy Knox's interrogation. I got hold of Dispatch on the intercom, and found out Hennessy's wife was back at home, watching it being torn apart by a search team. I dialed that number.

A tense woman's voice answered on the first ring. "Yes?"

"Mrs. Hennessy, this is Joe Gunther again—we met this morning."

"I know who you are, Lieutenant, and I want you to know I resent the hell out of this. I'm not the criminal here—I'm not the one who was stealing and cheating on his wife. But it's my house that's been invaded by your people, and it's me that's being blamed for something I didn't know anything about—"

"Mrs. Hennessy, I know you feel like you've been caught in a car wreck, but it's the only way we can set things straight. Please try to bear with us for just a little while longer. Then we'll be out of your hair—at least out of your house. Do you have any friends or relatives you can call on for support?"

Her voice softened somewhat. "I have someone coming."

"Good—that should help a little. Look, I hate to add to your troubles right now, but I was wondering if you could tell me something. The date of January ninth has surfaced in relation to all this—do you have any way you could tell me what Paul was doing that night?"

I expected another outburst, so I was pleasantly surprised when all she said was, "Hold on."

A minute later, she returned, saying, "We keep a family calendar on the kitchen wall—who's at what meeting when . . . Not that I know what the hell he was really doing anymore . . . What was that? The ninth? Says here he was in Albany, New York, for a meeting . . . God, what a jerk I was."

I waited a few moments, listening to her fight for composure. "When is that friend arriving?"

Her voice was cracked and tearful. "She'll be right here. Thank you, Lieutenant."

"Let me know if there's anything we can do to help." I hung up before the irony of that statement caught up to both of us.

Chapter Twenty-four

The conference room reeked of the pungent, greasy odor of pizza. Several boxes were aligned down the middle of the large table, surrounded by an oval of Styrofoam cups, as regularly spaced as a short, bulky picket fence.

Seated around the room, eating, drinking, or chatting among themselves, were the same people I'd assembled before, but who by now had become an integrated, unofficial task force. The earlier confusion and doubts about what we were up against had by now been washed away by a common desire to nail a single as yet unidentified nemesis.

That this person could only be called "the partner," and that no known connections had yet been drawn between him and Shawna Davis or Milo Douglas or Mary Wallis didn't seem to matter. There was a confidence in the air that we were at last on the right track, and that things would make sense in the end.

I just hoped that trust was well placed.

"Okay," I began. "It's been a full day. I thought it might help to compare notes before we pack it in till tomorrow. You've all read the report on my interview with Ginny Levasseur—or you should have by now—so I won't bother re-peating it. Let's go straight to Sam and Marshall instead, and what they got out of Eddy Knox."

Sammie Martens glanced at her temporary partner, and then said, "A documents search of both his home and office re-vealed a dramatic boost in income beginning at about the same time the convention center project was heading for the zoning board. We talked to his bankers, his wife, other mem-bers of his family, his co-workers, and anyone else we could think of to pinpoint the source of his money, but nobody had any answers. Knox had told them all that he'd hit it rich play-ing the stock market, although a quick check proved that to be totally bogus. As far as we can determine, he's never bought a stock in his life.

"That left the interrogation, which we conducted a couple of hours ago. After telling him we knew he'd been corrupted, and that a direct cause-and-effect line had been drawn be-tween his sudden wealth and his glowing report on the con-vention center project, we got him to fess up, and admit that Thomas Chambers had been the source of the money."

Riding a small murmuring of comments, Jack Derby's voice rose to the surface, "How was that money delivered?"

Sammie allowed a wry smile. "You mean, does it have Nev-erTom's fingerprints on it? No. Knox said they were all cash payments, mailed to him in plain white envelopes. The only connection we could make on paper was that Chambers sponsored Knox for membership in an elite Keene golf club. That's something a newspaper or a rival politician might make hay out of, but it doesn't break any law we know of."

"How was contact made initially?" Gail asked.

"By phone. In fact, all contacts were made by phone. Chambers made it clear that if Knox ever approached him in person on this subject, the money would dry up then and there."

There was a telling silence in the room at this disappointing news, which Gail broke quietly. "There was never an excep-tion?"

"No."

"Great," Derby muttered. "We can basically throw that one out, unless the phone records can tell us something."

Marshall Smith shook his head. "I asked a friend at the phone company to take a discreet look at NeverTom's bills. They must've all been local calls. Plus, Knox told us he was only contacted at the office, when a call from someone like Tom Chambers would've appeared perfectly legit."

My mind suddenly clicked on something obvious. "What about Ned Fallows? He doesn't have a phone, but with Never-Tom nervous enough to threaten suing us, he might've contacted Fallows in person or by mail to keep the pressure on."

"I want to talk to Fallows myself," Derby said darkly. "He's beginning to piss me off." He turned to Gail. "Can you have someone pick him up?"

She nodded, taking notes, her face as blank as I knew her feelings were not.

"If that's all we got on Knox," Tony asked, "do we even have enough to prosecute him?"

"I doubt it," Derby admitted. "Even with his confession, it might be shaky, depending on who he got to represent him. You can get him fired, but you'd have to fight for anything more. Maybe the IRS would be interested."

Willy Kunkle crushed the Styrofoam cup in his hand and tossed it toward the wastepaper basket in the corner, missing by three feet. "That's fucking great."

"All right," I said, overriding a brief resurge in conversation. "Sheila and J.P.—what've you got on Harold Matson?"

"Not much," J.P. admitted. "He got defensive fast and tried to argue various points, all of which Sheila was able to win, but the issues were basically procedural. Without legal authority to get into B of B's records, we didn't have any proof of unethical or illegal activity. When we popped the Chambers brothers on him, I thought we nearly had him—there's clearly a connection between them—but he shut down, demanded a lawyer, and was out the door five minutes later. We just didn't have enough hard evidence to make him bleed."

"Have you been able to look into Ben Chambers?" I asked.

"I was about to ask the same thing," Gail joined in. "Seems he's the most direct beneficiary here."

Sheila answered. "We watched for his name during our paper chase, and asked a few of our contacts, but there's not much there to investigate. He has a checking account locally—not with B of B—and of course a small suitcase of land titles, again with other banks, but the bulk of his assets are out of state, probably in Boston and New York. Again, with no legal muscle, we weren't able to do much. It all sure confirms how private he is, though, especially compared to his brother. An amazing number of people have never even met the man, and the few who have said he's a pretty strange bird—quiet, shy, apologetic. I guess he's a true nerd—happiest in front of a computer, trading stocks and doing deals long distance."

"So all the stuff you dug up points to Thomas, not his brother?" I asked.

"Right."

"All the more reason to dig deeper, then," I said, unsuccessfully masking my disappointment. "On a brighter note, we do have the goods on Paul Hennessy." I leaned forward and retrieved a sheet of paper from under one of the pizza boxes. "Along with a listing of all his properties, courtesy of Ron's diligent spadework. When we do get our hands on him, we'll not only have enough to chuck him in jail for a long time, but we'll have some left over to trade for his partner's name. We have a Be-on-the-Lookout all over New England, so it shouldn't be long before we hear something."

"You wish," Willy said softly.

"It's more than that," I told him. "Whoever this partner is, he ended up giving Hennessy the screwing of a lifetime. We've frozen every asset we can find, so unless he has a Swiss bank account, which he doesn't seem bright enough to have thought of, all Hennessy should have left is a desire to beat the shit out of the guy who put him in this mess."

"Hope he doesn't look in the mirror," Willy said to general laughter.

"All right," I continued. "Everything else seems to be on track. Willy, I take it there's nothing new on Sawyer?"

"Nope," he said with his usual eloquence.

"Gail and I are meeting with Bernie, the patient we think may have seen the killing. Our session with him is going to be orchestrated by his psychiatrist, but we've been warned not to expect much."

I stood up, indicating the end of the meeting. "Let's wrap it up for tonight. Remember, Sammie is putting together a time line tracking everybody's alibis, so any relevant information you get should be handed over to her ASAP. As we've just found out, knowing who the bad guys are and proving it are two different things."

*　　*　　*

It was still snowing hard later that night. Over a foot of it had accumulated on the ground. The sky overhead was as black as a grave, making the appearance of white snowflakes from its midst a little startling, and vaguely magical.

I was standing on a steep hill overlooking Brattleboro from the north, next to one of its oddest landmarks—a sixty-five-foot stone tower built by patients of the Retreat as a therapy project in the 1890s. The Retreat is a famous, 160-year-old alcohol and rehabilitation center, but one of its biggest attributes locally—aside from being the butt of many a teenage nut-house joke—is its maintenance of hundreds of pristine acres within the town limits. Be it farmland or field and forest, this property does much to enhance Brattleboro's distinctly pastoral appearance. Aside from the eccentric tower, the Retreat keeps this vast ownership demure, and does its best to only gently acknowledge its careful and costly stewardship—usually only when it needs to flex a little political muscle. Word had gotten out that tangling with the Retreat was not a great career move.

The tower was part of a recreational area—a crosshatching of trails in a tangle of trees that gave people the pleasures of nature within earshot of downtown traffic. But during the winter, and especially on a night like this, it marked the most isolated of spots—dark, silent, and empty, although ringed by the town's snow-blurred lights, and serenaded by the dulled scrapings of invisible passing snowplows.

Snow has a unique way of isolating everything within its mantle. Early in the morning, before the curtains are drawn aside for confirmation, one can sense the presence of new snow upon the ground. There is a muted quality to the air's resonance all around, akin to the emergence from a deep sleep. Standing in its midst, as it is still falling, that feeling becomes as blatant as the numbing of one of the five human senses—with the added confusion of not knowing for sure which one of those senses has been lost.

Stanley Katz came toward me, dimly lit by the town's residual glow, tramping through the deep snow, his breath escaping in powerful, rhythmic blasts—and yet all without a sound, as silently as a hologram.

He reached the tower's rough, dark, curving wall—an incongruous shaft with no base visible in the snow and its top buried in the black sky overhead—and put his hand against it for stability, his thin, narrow frame bent over from the exertion of his climb.

"Jesus Christ," he said, gasping, "what the hell is so goddamn important I got to kill myself coming up here in the middle of a fucking blizzard?"

"Just a storm, Stan. You should get in better shape."

"Up yours, Gunther. How long did it take you to recover?"

I let him continue in that vein for a few minutes, both hands now on his knees, his breathing gradually returning to normal. Finally, he straightened, took in one last cleansing lungful of lightly powdered air, and fixed me with a baleful look. "All right. I'm here, I made sure I wasn't followed, and I parked my car· the hell-and-gone up the block. What do you want?"

I pulled a plain envelope from inside my coat and handed it to him. "That's a detailed list of illegal—but maybe unprosecutable—activities that Tom Chambers has been engaged in for the past several years, all in the interests of gaining control of the convention center construction project."

Katz held the envelope in his hand gingerly, not opening it, not even looking at it. His eyes were locked on to mine. "What's going on?"

"Not a word about where you got this, Stan—not a name, not the usual 'a confidential police source,' not a murmur connecting us to what's in that envelope, or I take it back and this conversation ends. Agreed?"

"How do I know what it's worth?"

"You'll read it—privately—then you'll check its contents through your own sources. You'll come to your own conclusions."

The envelope moved to his coat pocket. "Agreed."

I paused to collect my thoughts. What I wanted to give Katz was a simple, connect-the-dots story line, linking together most of the headlines he'd been producing over the past week. Some of it would be conjecture, and some of it solid, but all of it was designed to whet his appetite.

"Shawna Davis met up with Mary Wallis at the same time Mary Wallis was protesting the project. For reasons I won't go into, Wallis fell for Davis sentimentally, and when Davis disappeared, Wallis folded her tent. We think she was either physically pressured or blackmailed to back off, and was finally grabbed or killed to guarantee her silence.

"Milo Douglas is connected to the project because he slept above Paul Hennessy's office one night, and possibly overheard something, shortly before dying of a disease to which he had no explainable exposure. We don't know exactly how the two tie together, but we do know Milo was paid a bundle just before he died, and that he was cagey about its source.

"Adele Sawyer comes into it because she's Hennessy's aunt, and Hennessy's been ripping off Carroll Construction for years, using her name on his dummy businesses to keep a low profile. But he took on a partner with this last project, and it was the partner who knocked off Sawyer to curb Hennessy's runaway greed."

"And this partner is NeverTom?" Katz's voice was incredulous.

"We don't know, nor is any of what I just said in that envelope. I only told so you'd know what we're facing. We do know Tom Chambers has engaged in bribery, blackmail, and illegal coercion, but while some of the people he pressured have admitted it to us, they also said all contact was made by phone or mail, so there's no way in hell Jack Derby can do anything about it. That's why I need your help."

Katz pointed at the two of us. "Did Tony set this meeting up?"

"No one knows anything about it—this is just you and me."

The snow fell around us in utter silence as Stanley Katz pondered what I'd told him. My own thoughts were crowded with a dizzying uncertainty. As Gail had pointed out, what I was doing flew in the face of a lifetime of traditional reticence. It felt tantamount to treason.

"What about Ben Chambers?" he finally asked.

"So far, he seems to be Tom's financial source only. But there again, we're still looking."

"Nothing new on Hennessy?"

"Nope, but his girlfriend spilled the beans. My own feeling is he's still in the area."

Katz let out a sigh. "Christ."

I checked my watch. "It's about eight-thirty. Read that over, make a few inquiries, call me at home if you want. You should have enough time to put something in tomorrow's paper if you move fast enough."

"Is that the deal?"

I took several steps away from the tower, heading back the way I'd come. "The *Rutland Herald*'s next on my list if you don't. Have a nice evening."

*   *   *

Arriving home later, expecting the dark and tomb-like silence I'd grown used to over the last few months, I instead found Gail ensconced on the living room sofa, surrounded by pillows like some romanticized pasha, a glass of milk in one hand, the TV remote in the other, and an open bag of chocolate-chip cookies on her stomach.

She gave me a broad smile as I entered the room and patted the sofa next to her, removing two pillows to make room. "Have a cookie?"

I glanced at the TV screen—a hysterically pitched sitcom with too many attractive people speaking loudly and moving fast. "Have we hit job meltdown?" I asked, settling in next to her.

She hit the remote, found a doctor show, gave me a choco-latey kiss, and pushed the cookie bag in my direction. I hadn't had dinner yet, and this seemed an excellent substi-tute.

"A drop-the-books-and-screw-them-all mental health break," she answered. "I intend to finish the contents of this bag—with your help if you're interested—knock off that half-gallon of ice cream that's been sitting in the freezer, and then go to bed at a reasonable hour, where—after about thirty minutes of satiating myself sexually at your expense—I plan to sleep the sleep of the nutritionally poisoned. How's your head?"

I reached up to touch the bandage. "Fine—I'd forgotten I still had this thing. You sure you're okay?"

She punched the remote again, found an old western, and placed her glass on the floor beside her. "Never better—and I have you to thank, twice over. Once because you got conked on the head, which made me realize how much we both give to our jobs, and how little to each other, and the other be-cause you twisted my arm into visiting Bernie at the nursing home—which I did again tonight, by the way—and which has reminded me how wrong-headed it is to take our time on this earth for granted. I have been so wired for so long, I could almost feel my brain leaving my body. I won't say I'm sorry for the last few months, because I did what I had to, but I am going to do my damnedest to keep things a little more in perspective from now on."

She stopped long enough to lean up against me, rubbing my body with hers, and gave me a long, deep, definitely en-ergizing kiss. "I also plan to take more advantage of some of the household appliances I've been neglecting lately."

She kissed me again, her hand roving across my shirt, undoing any buttons she happened across. Dropping my cookie, I fumbled with her blouse, and then pulled her up and along the length of the sofa, probably crushing our dinner beneath us. She paused to concentrate on my belt buckle. "Don't think this lets you off the hook for later on, by the way."

*   *   *

An hour later, still both on the couch, but naked under a soft, thick blanket, we were still watching the western, sprinkling cookie fragments over ice cream, and feeling better than we had in quite a while.

Until the phone rang.

With a one-word curse, I stretched out and fumbled for the receiver, located on a table behind the couch. "What?"

"It's me," came Sammie's voice. "Jack Derby's investigator just called me. They can't find Ned Fallows. His place is empty, the dog's been left with a neighbor, and nobody knows where he went. You want me to set something up?"

I felt a sudden coldness enter my chest. "No, that's okay. It may be time to just let things happen—see where they take us."

I settled back onto the couch, slipping my arm more tightly around Gail's naked waist. She looked up into my face. "Everything okay?"

"Yeah—no problem."

But the coldness remained, along with the feeling that with my visit to Lunenburg, I'd set something dark, sad, and irreversible into motion.

Chapter Twenty-five

The predominant noise in the squad room next morning was the rustling of hastily turned newspaper pages. Everyone, it seemed, was sitting in some corner, silently scanning one column inch after another, utterly focused, I knew, on finding the one thing that wasn't there—the name of Stan Katz's source.

Sammie was the first to broach the subject, following me into my glass-walled cubicle and dropping the paper on the desk. "You see this?"

I removed my coat and hung it behind the door. "Yup—Katz called me at home this morning and warned me about it."

"Did he name his source?"

I laughed. "Right. Who's your candidate?"

"Beats me. The article implies there was more than one."

"I wonder how NeverTom's taking it?" I wondered aloud, amused at Katz's oblique dig at the selectman. "Anything new on Ned Fallows?"

"No. The State Police put a BOL out on him last night, but so far—"

Willy Kunkle appeared at the door. "Got something right up your alley," he interrupted, making Sammie purse her lips in irritation. "Some guy on Deacon Place just called, said his dog showed up this morning with a frozen coon carcass in his mouth—all cut up and weird-looking. Animal Control is on the way already. The guy said he normally wouldn't have called, except that the 'weird' part reminded him of rabies, and the cuts were done with a knife. He's a surgeon, so I guess he would know."

News that somebody had carved up a rabid animal revived the impatience I'd been feeling at Hillstrom's silence about how Milo might have caught the disease. I retrieved my coat and headed back out the door with Kunkle, telling Sammie, "We'll talk when I get back."

It was an extraordinary morning, as bright as a diamond, the snow white and reflective and untrammeled as a new-found beach. The sun on the horizon was the image of an acetylene torch—blazing, blinding, and yet virtually without heat. The air felt cold enough to freeze your eyeballs open.

We took my car and headed north along the Putney Road. Deacon Place is attached to a tiny horseshoe-shaped enclave marking the northernmost reaches of the Putney Road's high-income district, just shy of the short bridge marking the beginning of the "miracle mile" section of the road.

This overlooked neighborhood affords one of the most scenic, peaceful, and expensive views over the West River floodplain, known locally as "the meadows." As we pulled into Vermont Avenue—the southern leg of the horseshoe—I was struck once again at how some areas, regardless of the bustle all around them, manage to appear as sylvan and pristine as a country village.

We didn't talk during the short trip. Willy wasn't inclined that way generally, and I was too busy thinking to bother. The discovery of a dissected, rabid animal, though interesting enough, wasn't the only reason I was making the drive out here. As Willy already knew, the location of this find was as relevant as the animal itself—Tom and Ben Chambers lived on Eaton Avenue, in the same tiny neighborhood.

Animal Control's small dark blue pickup truck, its rear bed fitted out with a cluster of closed cages, was parked opposite the house we were looking for. I pulled up behind it just as Amy Siddons, the control officer, appeared at the house's back door. She gestured to us to follow her inside.

The doctor in question was Michael Brook, a large, bearded, one-legged orthopedic surgeon at Brattleboro Memorial. A skilled physician with an encyclopedic knowledge and a near-compulsive curiosity, he was also a good friend who'd seen me through some bad times in the past. That notwithstanding, my encounters with him had always occurred at the hospital or in his office. I'd never asked or known where he lived, and was startled and pleased to see him now. He greeted us in the kitchen, piled our coats onto a table, and immediately ushered us into a spacious, well-lit pantry, complete with an elegant, highly polished, copper-top counter. There, laid out beside a row of cut crystal glasses and an assortment of expensive liquor bottles, were the sliced-up remains of a frozen raccoon carcass, spread-eagled on its back. I leapt to the conclusion that Mrs. Brook was out of town.

"I knew right off it was rabid," he began, slipping on a pair of latex gloves. "Even frozen, you can see the thick mucus typical of hydrophobia slathered on the coat. And those porcupine quills around the nose are a classic sign of a wild animal being too disoriented to take the most basic precautions. Also, the coat is patchy and unkempt. That's not indicative of rabies by itself, but taken in context, it's a pretty good guess. 'Course, only a brain analysis can prove any of it."

Amy Siddons, hanging back by the door, said, "Dr. Brook, I better get going. Your dog should get a rabies booster, and you should watch it for any unusual behavior over the next forty-five days, but that's about all that needs to be done." She looked at me and added, "I'll leave a special container in the kitchen for that."

Brook turned a dazzling smile on her. "Wonderful, wonderful. Thank you very much." He waited until she'd left the house before adding, "I don't think she likes this aspect of the animal kingdom much."

"Where did your dog find it?" Willy asked, who seemed little more interested than Amy.

"Beats me," Brook answered. He was bent over the small body, poking and prodding with his rubber-tipped fingers. "The thing is, Joe, you can see what's been done to this creature. It's incredible—like some sort of weird science experiment. Made me think of all that Satanist stuff the paper was screaming about a while ago."

He pointed to the head. "This hasn't just been hacked up. Parts have been surgically removed—not with any skill, incidentally—but with distinct purpose. Look here—see? The tongue's been cut out, the insides of the cheeks scraped, and the palate's been split open to access the brain, which looks like it's been scooped out. It's almost as if someone was scavenging for a witch's brew—you know, eye of newt, wing of bat? Really strange."

I had no doubts he was right, and was all but sure I knew what the recipe was for—and who had been the recipient. "Tell us how you got it, Mike."

Brook straightened and peeled off his gloves, dropping them on the carcass. "Cricket brought it in," he said, nodding toward the dog. "I let him out first thing every morning. By the time I've shaved, showered, and fixed breakfast, he's usually back at the door, begging to be let in, especially this time of year. Only today, he had that in his mouth. Given that it's frozen, I doubt it's still contaminated, but I thought you'd be interested by the carving."

"I am," I answered. "Mind if we walk around the property a little?"

He waved his hand toward the door. "Be my guest. I still have a few things to do before I head for the office. You all set on your own?"

"Does the dog roam the whole neighborhood?" Willy asked as we were putting on our coats.

"One end of Eaton to the other, but generally not beyond that. He's pretty territorial."

We thanked him and stepped outside.

"Lucky we got that new snow," Willy said, pointing with his chin toward the narrow track cut into the snowbank—the width of a midsized dog.

We followed Cricket's tour of the neighborhood, meandering, inquisitive, occasionally indecisive. At points, I could visualize him standing stock-still, his nose to the breeze, waiting for inspiration. Willy and I cut across property lines, through hedges, and traveled in circles, hoping the tracks would take us north, toward the Chambers house.

Cricket was obviously a creature of habit, starting with back doors and garbage cans, then expanding to the backs of garages, frozen compost containers, hibernating gazebos, and other relics of summer. It wasn't until we were at the bottom of somebody's sloping lawn, with a sweeping view of a dazzling, flat, white expanse of frozen water that he'd apparently headed in a beeline toward the property I was most interested in.

I picked up the pace then, ignoring my near frozen feet and Willy's increasing complaints behind me, and ran clumsily by ice-bound boat docks and dead gardens until I was standing on the shoreline of Tom and Ben Chambers's property. There, the smooth furrow of a curious dog on his fast morning rounds was replaced by a wide, trampled, dirt-strewn half circle, attached like a soiled snow angel to the side of a fallen tree trunk. Here, Cricket had found his sought-after reward, stuffed under the log, and wrapped in the remains of a now eviscerated dark brown trash bag.

"You got your portable?" I asked Willy, whose voice had been stilled by our discovery. "Get J.P. here—now. And I want a search warrant for brown plastic, thirty-gallon garbage bags, surgical instruments, any animal parts, hair, or remnants, and any surfaces stained by or utensils used for the handling of said parts, hair, or remnants. Probable cause is the possible use of said animal in Satanist rituals, the nonburied disposal of a potential health hazard within one hundred feet of a water source, the killing of a fur-bearing animal out of season, and anything else you or the SA can think of that a judge'll sign—tell them to be creative."

"You want the *bags* included?" Willy asked incredulously.

"J.P. showed me a *Journal of Forensic Sciences* article about how garbage bags from the same box can be microscopically linked to one another, even if they weren't in sequential order in the box—something to do with how they're made at the factory. Anyhow, I'm hoping that even if NeverTom cleaned up the rest of his mess, he won't have thought about the bags."

I turned and looked up the long, curving lawn to the enormous home perched at its top. "Find me a way to get into that house, Willy."

*   *   *

Ron Klesczewski located me in my office pretending to shuffle paperwork while I waited for Willy to produce the search warrant. "I got it," he said, closing the door behind him. "At least I think so—what Tom Chambers has on Ned Fallows."

I let him grab a chair. "I started thinking," he resumed, "maybe it wasn't related to the zoning board, so I broadened my research, looking in every town record I could find for Fallows's name. Remember several years ago, that fire in the Cotton Mill Hill warehouse? Gutted part of the building? Most of the damage was on the first floor, to an upholstery business, but upstairs, in the back, there was a big storage room—all stereo equipment and electronics—easily damaged by smoke and heat. Everything was declared a total loss. The arson report was inconclusive, but the investigator made a note about how the smoke got into that upper storeroom—a door was left open that should've been shut, and a window was conveniently broken to draw the fire in the right direction. But the fire showed no suspicious origin, the upholsterers were way underinsured, and so nobody pursued it.

"Here's the trick, though. The electronics represented the entire stock of a small, pricey, unsuccessful stereo store on Main, owned by Ned Fallows. His banker just told me Fallows was having problems meeting his mortgage payments. The equipment was mostly out of date—basically unsaleable in a trendy market—and there was a lot of it. But since the insurance was for replacement instead of current value, Fallows got top dollar to buy brand-new, cutting-edge stock. After which, and after spiffing up the store, he sold the whole business within a couple of months of the fire, making him either real lucky, or someone who pulled a fast one and got away with it."

Ron moved to the edge of his chair with enthusiasm. "Digging a little deeper, the lucky-guy picture begins falling apart. Fallows didn't run the store—he had a series of managers instead, the latest one being someone named Ricky Steves. Steves had been on the job for about four months before the fire, and had come to Brattleboro from North Carolina, where he has a criminal record for arson.

"My banker contact told me that after the sale of the store, Fallows paid off all his debts, retired the mortgages on the business and his house, and went back to being a Realtor and a teacher—as well as a member of the ZBA. The kicker is that according to town tax records, only a few months after the store was sold, Steves got a high-paying job for BTC Investments as a 'consultant,' although the low-level BTC workers I talked to never saw or heard of the man. BTC, of course, stands for 'Benjamin and Thomas Chambers.' "

"Son of a bitch," I murmured.

"Right. After collecting a paycheck for about a year, Steves left town without a trace. I couldn't find him in any computer we're hooked to."

Ron sat back in his chair and crossed his legs. "So, what can we prove? Nothing. But I bet Tom Chambers is holding some sort of documentation laying out how Ricky was hired by Fallows to torch the business for the insurance. That's the leverage NeverTom must've used to get Fallows to cheerlead the project through the ZBA. The irony is, rumors at the time said Fallows would back the project anyway, given his past voting record. Makes you wonder if Chambers twisted Fallows's arm just for spite—to show he could knock him off his pedestal. That must be a bitch for Fallows—knowing that voting his conscience had made him look like he'd been corrupted.

"Of course," Ron added, "there's no way in hell we're going to get all this confirmed, not unless Tom Chambers finds religion and bares his soul. But at least we've got enough for a little leverage."

I didn't argue the point, but I dearly hoped we had more than that. Not only was I concerned about Ned's wandering around loose, his intentions vaguely ominous, but Mary Wallis's disappearance continued to pull at me like a chronic ache. Despite the consensus that she had either fled or been killed, I couldn't suppress the feeling that she was still alive— but that like Shawna before her, her time on this earth might be running out.

*   *   *

By mid-morning, Willy Kunkle and I were at Tom and Ben Chambers's door, armed with a warrant and accompanied by a search team.

NeverTom was not happy to see us. "What the hell do you want?"

Willy handed him the paperwork and gestured to the others to file in. "For you to get out of the way."

I could see Chambers considering whether to block the door with his body. Instead, to my relief, he moved aside, waving the warrant at me. "God *damn* you. I want to know what's going on."

I stepped inside and closed the door. "I won't expect you to like this," I began, "but we have reason to believe a raccoon was killed and dissected in this house, parts of its body removed, and the rest wrapped in a garbage bag and illegally disposed of on your property. Since the raccoon showed signs of being rabid, we felt the need to check this out. I suggest you read the warrant for the details."

Tom Chambers's face, never placid at the best of times, grew red to the point where I became mildly concerned for his health.

THE RAGMAN'S MEMORY 287

"You bastards. It's not enough you libel me in the newspaper, and skulk around town asking questions and smearing my reputation. Now you come up with some weird little scam to invade my home. You and your Chief and that arrogant crippled asshole in there had better start looking for new jobs, buddy." He stabbed my chest with his finger. "Because I'm going to have every one of you fired."

I snatched up his finger in my fist, watching his eyes widen slightly in alarm. "Mr. Chambers, you are entitled to do anything you want, under the law. Threatening me and denigrating my officers is not included in that. If you want to call your lawyer, go ahead. I don't give a damn. But if you so much as think about getting in our way while we're working here, I'll bust you so fast you won't know what hit you. Is that understood?"

He retrieved his hand and held it against his chest, as if giving it comfort. "You're history," he snarled and retreated to another room.

I took a deep breath and turned to see Kunkle looking at me from a doorway, a grin on his face.

*　　*　　*

Surprisingly to me, J.P. and his team found several items beyond the half-empty box of dark brown garbage bags I'd been hoping for. A small bonanza was located in the basement, where under a strong fluorescent light, and alongside a washer and an old-fashioned sink, a wooden worktable, scarred and worn, displayed a large oval pale spot in its center.

J.P. pointed at it. "Bleach—fresh, too. And there were animal hair shafts on the floor, and stuck to this sheetrock knife." He opened an evidence envelope to show me. "Found it hanging on the pegboard over there with the other tools. Trash has been picked up several times since this was done, so we didn't find anything there, and the sink doing double duty for the washing machine means the trap's been cleaned of any residue I could get. Still," and here he held up a small plastic bag, "I did find a couple of additional hairs caught in the drain grate."

He moved over to the far side of his large evidence-gathering case and picked up a small cardboard box. Inside was an old metal ricer, popular for making mashed potatoes. "Interesting, huh? The only kitchen tool down here. It's been hit with bleach, too."

I merely scowled in response.

"Here's something else," he said with satisfaction, and pulled out an open box of coffee filters. I still didn't say anything, so he prompted, "Filters and a press . . . the raccoon had its brain scooped out, remember?"

I finally reacted. "You saying he made cider out of the brain?"

"Seems reasonable. That's where rabies resides—there and in the saliva. The other part of the coon that was scraped was the inside of its mouth and tongue. It's not a scientific way to harvest a virus, but there's no reason it couldn't work . . . In fact, I guess we know it did."

My memory returned to an earlier hypothesis I'd shared with Tony Brandt. "Hiding the injection site somewhere among all the sores, flea bites, and acne."

Tyler finished the thought. "All he had to do was get Milo comatose on booze. By next morning, he never would've known."

"You find a hypodermic?"

He shook his head sadly. "No—this is all pure conjecture. Except for the hair and the bags, we don't have anything, and I doubt they'll be able to match the hair to the specific dead animal. They'll probably just confirm it came from a coon."

"You checked everywhere?"

He raised his eyebrows equivocally. "We did a reasonable search—by the book. For all I know, we're standing on enough evidence to put him away for life." He tapped his foot on the earthen floor. "But we may never find out." He hesitated a moment, and then added, "We did bump into something upstairs, in the master bathroom, but it wasn't on the warrant, so I didn't even touch it—a prescription bottle of phenobarbital, made out to Thomas Chambers."

*   *   *

At the top of the basement stairs, I found Connor O'Brian, NeverTom's lawyer, waiting for me, fussily dressed as always, and equipped with a superior smirk.

He tapped the folded warrant against the palm of his open hand. "I hope you had a good time touring the house, Joe, because a tour is all you're going to get out of this blatant invasion of privacy. This," he held up the warrant, "is a joke, as you probably know. If Judge Harrowsmith had been in town, instead of the twinky you hoodwinked, you never would've gotten it signed."

"But I did get it signed, Connor."

"A temporary inconvenience—worse for you, since I see you actually collected something. Now it'll all be thrown out, along with the warrant. I thought you were more professional."

"I wouldn't expect you to know the difference."

The smile flattened slightly, to my satisfaction. Connor O'Brian had always soured my stomach. "Joe, there is no weight of law behind the recommendations of how to dispose of dead animals, rabid or not."

"Take me to your master, Connor," I said, not bothering to debate.

Walking stiffly, he led the way to the door through which Chambers had vanished two hours earlier. It opened onto a truly magnificent library—wood-paneled, with leaded windows and leather furniture—straight out of *My Fair Lady*. Tom Chambers was standing by a large fireplace, lit, I noticed, by gas jets behind decorative ceramic logs. In a far corner, looking like a child in an oversized chair, Ben Chambers sat watching the three of us, pale, withdrawn, and nervous. I nodded silently in greeting, and he responded in kind.

"Have you finished?" Tom demanded petulantly.

"Yes, thank you. And collected some evidence." I gave him

a handwritten receipt. "I should warn you, Mr. Chambers, that despite what your lawyer may say, you are in trouble."

He glanced down at the receipt, and to my disappointment, a look of genuine amazement crossed his face. "What the hell? A *ricer?* What in Christ's name is a ricer? And coffee filters? What do you people think you're doing?"

I glanced at his brother, who was looking with baffled alarm at Tom. I began to feel slightly queasy, as if some vast and expensive structure of my own design had just begun to crack at the foundation.

Tom Chambers was advancing toward me, his face back to its familiar shade of purple. "Get out of my house. Now. I'll see you in court, Gunther, and it won't be over some fucking ricer. It'll be to sue you for every penny you fucking own. This is the last time you'll ever play the Gestapo in this town."

O'Brian slid between us, placing his hand on Chambers's chest, murmuring calmative phrases I couldn't hear over his client's bellowing. I left, closing the door behind me.

J.P. and Willy were waiting for me outside the house, stamping their feet against the cold.

"I guess Mr. Big took offense," Willy said with standard grace.

"Yeah," I agreed, heading for the car. But I was no longer sure Tom Chambers's outrage was so misplaced.

Chapter Twenty-six

"Bring the time line into my office," I told Sammie as I passed her desk.

She did as requested, surprised at my tone of voice.

She sat down opposite me and opened a file folder on her lap. "This is as much as I have so far."

"What've you got on Tom Chambers?"

"Specifically? Nothing. There are three dates we know for sure—when the PCB was dumped in Keene, when Mary Wallis disappeared, and when Adele Sawyer was murdered. Tom Chambers was in Montpelier on the first, at home on the second, and at an all-night poker game on the third."

"Who's vouching for him being at home? His brother?"

"Yeah."

"So that one's up in the air."

Sammie continued. "We're pretty sure Hennessy did the PCB. Neither his mistress nor his wife can give him an alibi, and the meeting he claimed he was at in Albany never took place. Also, just for the hell of it, we had Keene PD check their records for that night. Hennessy was given a ticket for burning a red light at two in the morning. He was driving a

Carroll Construction pickup with an oil drum in the back. He was also so hyper they gave him a breath test. He passed."

I thought a moment, my apprehension growing. "Did J.P. hear back on the raccoon carcass?"

"Ten minutes ago—there was too much damage to the brain to do a test, so we can't categorically say it was rabid. Not only that, but he checked the ricer and the wood samples he removed from the worktable. He couldn't find a trace of anything except bleach."

"And the phenobarbital?"

Her expression lightened. "There we might have something. The prescription was filled by an out-of-town pharmacist, which is why we missed it the first time around. J.P. got a warrant based on what we found in Shawna's hair, and took a look at the pharmacy's records. Tom Chambers has a standard prescription there—has had for the past five years, for difficulty sleeping and nerves, and there was a spike in the purchase pattern at about the right time, as if he'd had to replace a bottle. 'Course, that's pretty circumstantial—he could say he dropped them down the drain by mistake."

I tossed the pencil I'd been holding across my desk. "Shit. Without Hennessy, Wallis, or Fallows, we don't have a goddamn thing, do we?"

"We will," she said softly.

"What about Ben Chambers?" I asked suddenly.

She shrugged. "Nothing—and nothing to use as leverage, either. He's a loner who keeps to himself. BTC is a privately held company, so its records are closed without a warrant. We have been asking around, but where NeverTom goes everywhere and sees everybody, Ben either stays at home or visits the office. He doesn't date any women, go out to restaurants, travel anywhere, belong to any clubs. At business meetings, he either phones in or shows up late and leaves early so no one can chitchat. He's not a recluse, but he comes close."

I had moved my chair while she was talking, and was now staring out the window at the cobalt-blue sky.

"We've got a problem, don't we?" she said quietly.

I shifted my gaze to her. "Yeah. We focused on NeverTom

fast and early. He's a loud-mouthed creep, he obviously deals dirty, and we had people like Fallows and Eddy Knox to help prejudice us. But I'm worried we missed the boat . . . Still, how can you dig up as much as we have and still wind up with nothing? It doesn't make sense."

"Unless you're digging in the wrong direction."

"You mean Ben Chambers?" I asked. "Where're the connections? Aside from buying the convention project, he never comes up."

"Maybe Ben's using Tom as a front."

"So why can't we nail Tom then? It should work out that if we can get one, we get the other. My God—with three dead bodies and a possible fourth, and a fifteen-million-dollar con game going on right under our noses, you'd think we could come up with some solid evidence. What the hell're we missing?"

*   *   *

Ted McDonald filled his tiny studio. A truly huge man, planted on an all-but-invisible swivel chair, he could reach every knob, switch, and button on his various pieces of equipment without having to do more than bend forward slightly. Ted was WBRT's news director, not a DJ who read the news, so the two of us were on our own until the top of the hour, when the rock-'n'-roll diet was regularly interrupted for a five-minute informational update.

Not that all he did was sit and wait. He got out quite a bit, sniffing around for material, often filing his reports by remote. Less obviously, he kept in touch with probably a thousand informants, from street cleaners to selectmen to state legislators, all of whom he treated with the same generous equanimity. Although restricted to five minutes every hour, McDonald had enough in his brain to monopolize the air all day.

"So . . . you did a Deep Throat with Katz," he said, smiling.

I didn't bother denying it. On such matters, he was a listener, not a talker. "Hope you didn't mind."

"Mind? Christ, no—made perfect sense. I'm a headline service. You needed something in depth to shove under Never-Tom's nose. Did it work?"

"I don't know. We're pushing pretty hard, and we've got nothing to show for it. I was hoping you could expand on that portrait you drew for me at the construction site."

"Of the Chambers boys? What do you want to know? I've only met Junior a couple of times."

"What about when they were younger, when the old man was still alive? You said Tom had the balls and Ben had the brains, and that Tom got his kicks putting Ben down all the time. Can you build on that a little? Seems like everyone else we talk to either doesn't know or is too scared to say."

McDonald smiled cherubically. "Works that way a lot, doesn't it? All right, I suppose I could do that. Keep in mind, though, this is all rumor, okay? Quote me and I'll play dumb."

I merely nodded.

"The old man was a traditionalist parent, and since his wife died when Tom was born, he was free to do what he wanted. So, traditionally the elder son gets the inheritance, and the younger one gets to screw around and become a drunk, and that's the way things started out. Except neither son cooperated. Ben was a slow learner—retiring, intimidated by his overbearing father, who was a real tyrant. The more the old man pushed, the less Junior was able to achieve.

"NeverTom, on the other hand, blossomed. Ignored by his father, a witness to what was happening with his brother, he took all the old man's lessons to heart, without the old man knowing he was even there. Tom became the athlete, the socialite, the popular one—*and* a son of a bitch—until his father finally took notice. Then, typically enough, Benjamin dropped Junior like a hot rock, and turned all his attention to Tom, who ate it up. Conversely, Junior was able to get up from under the heat lamp, sorted himself out, and became the scholar of the two boys.

"He turned into a bookworm, almost an intellectual, even though his brother got the higher grades. You seen that library they have at home? I doubt Tom's read a single book in it. That's Junior's room—his sanctum."

"Isn't Ben the one who really runs things? You implied he's the reason they still have all that money."

Ted laughed and gave me a Machiavellian look. "I may have misled you slightly the other day—rumor is there isn't as much money as people think. From what I heard, Junior's taking the gamble of a lifetime with this convention center."

I scowled at him. "Wouldn't the bank know that? They had to have checked Junior's books when he came riding in as the white knight."

I could tell Ted was enjoying being the source for once, instead of the mouthpiece. "Harold Matson looked at the books, sure."

I stared in stunned silence. How many times had we talked around the same subject—a single item lost among dozens—without seeing it in just this way? "Matson cooked the information, and then sold it to his board and the other banks?"

McDonald shook his head. "I said no such thing. For all the proof I have, this might as well be a fairy tale."

"All right, all right," I retreated. "Let's go back. So Junior may not be such a hot businessman after all. What're the rumors specifically?"

"That while he's been a wheeler-dealer, he's lost more than he's made. He's still got money—both of them do—but it's less than what the old man left them. That brings up one of the weird wrinkles about the relationship between the two brothers, in fact. Despite the old man's disenchantment with Junior, he insisted on keeping the eldest son at the helm of the business. That's Junior's hold over NeverTom—he controls the cash flow. That's one of the reasons all of this was kept quiet—politically, Tom couldn't afford to appear dependent on a recluse loser of a brother, so they've both worked well together at hushing up the truth and making Junior look like a winner."

"So all that stuff that was leaked during NeverTom's run for the select board, about how Junior'll do anything to pave his brother's political future, is bullshit?"

"I don't know," Ted answered. "But I don't think there's any love lost between them."

"How does NeverTom treat him?"

"I haven't the slightest idea, but Tom could be pretty awful when they were young. Word was he tortured pets, pulled cruel jokes on people, and once 'accidentally' broke the arm of a rival football player so he could play first string. Pretty sociopathic behavior, all in all. I wouldn't guess he's a great guy to live with."

Ted smiled at my expression. "You seem disappointed."

I stood up in the small room and ran my fingers through my hair. "I am. We've been getting nowhere trying to nail this on NeverTom. I was hoping you could give me something on Junior."

Ted gave me an apologetic look. "Sorry. From everything I know about them, Junior's just your classic repressed nerd."

*   *   *

Beverly Hillstrom was uncharacteristically jubilant. "Congratulations, Lieutenant, your hunch was correct. We located an injection site at the base of Milo Douglas's skull, just above the hairline. He was definitely exposed to rabies artificially. You can rule his death a homicide."

"Thanks, Doctor. I appreciate all the hard work."

But she sensed the flatness in my voice. "Is this not good news?"

"It is. I'm sorry. I'm just not sure how to use it anymore. Things have been unraveling a bit down here. We're trying to regroup."

She tried to fill the awkward pause that followed. "I hope it's not a major setback."

Painfully aware of the effort she'd made, I tried to lighten up a bit. "It's not. We'll get this nailed down, and what you just gave me will be a big help. I'll keep you updated."

*   *   *

I shifted my weight from one foot to the other and checked my watch for the fourth time.

"Don't tell me," Gail smiled at me. "He's still late."

I gave her a sour stare. "Typical doctor—and he even chose the time."

She returned to the lawbook she'd brought along, and I began another tour of the lobby's paintings and citations. We were waiting at the Skyview Nursing Home for Bernie's psychiatrist, Dr. Andrews, who'd finally called to schedule "our little experiment," as he phrased it.

With a sudden bang of the front door, a tall young man, athletic and wild-haired, came striding in from the night. He was carrying a briefcase in one hand and a sheaf of loose papers in the other. A wide smile split his face at the sight of us, defusing my irritation.

He marched by without pause, talking as he went. "I'm so sorry—had somebody on a bender, couldn't pull out before she landed. Let's duck into one of these offices here. I want to bring you up to snuff on a little of Bernie's history."

Gail and I exchanged glances, both of us struck by his congenial energy, and fell into step behind him. He stopped at a door about halfway down the hall, fumbled in his pocket for a key, and ushered us into an office whose blandness suggested a large number of short-term tenants.

There were three armchairs grouped around a low coffee table, across the room from a more formal arrangement of a desk and three ladder-backs. Andrews chose the former, dumping his paperwork on the coffee table.

"Sit, sit," he urged, and took his own advice, not bothering to remove his coat. "What did you do to your head?"

I unconsciously fingered the bandage. "Just a cut."

He absorbed that with a nod, enigmatically adding, "Might come in handy tonight. Okay—I'll make this fast so I won't waste any more of our time. I visited Bernie this afternoon, just to make a quick appraisal, and found that the recent snowfall has set him back a little, which could be to our advantage. Fresh snow reminds him of the war, and therefore throws him into his soldier mode, as I call it, but since that's the mode in which he chooses to reflect on Mrs. Sawyer's death, that may be good news." He looked intensely at Gail, his smile broadening. "You're Gail Zigman? Thank you for all the time you've spent with him. It's had a great impact. He keeps talking about the cat. You have it with you?"

"Harry's got it upstairs. Seemed easier to let him keep her."

"Right. Well, the 'lady with the cat' is a big hit. He can't place you in time—keeps thinking you're either his daughter or wife or an old girlfriend—but I like the fact that he's taken a current image—you—and placed it back in the historical time frame he's comfortable with. It shows he might've done the same thing with Mrs. Sawyer's murder."

He picked up the papers and settled them in his lap. "Right. Either of you know much about the Battle of the Bulge?"

"Hitler's last-ditch effort to stall the Allied invasion of Germany in December, nineteen forty-four," I answered, feeling like I was back in school.

"Right—that's the big picture. From Bernie's perspective, it was an eighty-mile-wide patch of dense forestland, flat up against the German border, where green troops were supposed to get a gentle introduction to being on the front. They called it the 'Phantom Front,' because everyone knew the Germans were basically whipped, and that even if they did put up a fight, it wouldn't be in a thick forest with a few narrow roads.

"Bernie was a seventeen-year-old PFC, attached to the Hundredth-and-Sixth Division. He'd been in place five days, had only fired his rifle on the range, and was part of a combat group that was way understrength. When the Germans attacked, they did so with a massive one-hour artillery barrage—complete with batteries of searchlights to both blind and light up the American positions. For the GIs, the result was instant bedlam—not only because of the incredible noise, but because the shells knocked out many of the telephone cables they depended on for communications. Before they knew what was going on—or could figure out if this was a 'spoiling attack' versus an all-out counteroffensive—German tanks and troops were suddenly mixed in with their own. Inexperienced American officers found themselves giving orders

to German soldiers and getting shot at for their trouble. In-
fantrymen ran for cover behind tanks from the wrong side.

"Bernie was a part of all this.

"Unfortunately for his mental health," Andrews continued,
"he didn't get captured along with most of his buddies. Somehow, he slipped through and ended up as part of the retreat,
without a unit, without leadership—lost, confused, and par-
don my French, scared shitless. This was when the roots of
his PTSD took hold.

"Needless to say, no one knows the exact details of his life
for the next two weeks. There were more American casualties
in that battle than in any other we've been in before or since,
including both sides at Gettysburg. So Bernie was swept
along like a snowball in an avalanche—cold, abandoned, ter-
rified, not knowing who to trust, not knowing the local language or geography. The weather was terrible—freezing and
snowing hard. Artillery or tank shells exploded in villages and
among the trees making shrapnel out of bricks and wood.
Frozen body parts were found for weeks afterward, tossed
about like confetti. Some soldiers used stiff enemy corpses as
benches when they sat down to eat.

"In the end, after the Americans had gained the upper hand
and were pushing the German bulge back to the border, they
started finding people like Bernie—wide-eyed, shell-shocked
ghosts of their former selves, walking around like robots.
They called them 'ragmen,' which may be the best description
I've ever heard. Many were brought back to some form of
mental stability, others were less lucky. Bernie was a mixture
of both—long-term hospitalization, a few years of supposed
normalcy, during which he hid his symptoms in booze, and a
final surrender to his condition, where he is to this day. We
have a bunch of fancy-sounding terms for what may or may
not be ailing him, from PTSD to Korsakoff's to alcohol-
induced dementia—and they may all be right—but the final
result is as unique as his own personality."

Andrews stood up abruptly. "Anyway, that's his history in a
nutshell. I'm hoping it might help you follow some of his references if he takes that path. The soldier mode is sometimes

acted out, sometimes loud, but I've never heard of him doing anyone harm. Even that pseudo-strangling scene the other night was mostly hysteria on the other guy's part. Bernie's war is inside—he was a nonviolent boy then, and he's the same now. Okay—let's go."

He moved quickly toward the door and then stopped. "You bring the pictures of your suspects?" he asked me.

I patted my breast pocket.

"Good. I'll let you know when to pull them out."

Upstairs, we met Harry beyond the double doors separating Bernie's ward from the rest of the home. He was holding the cat in his arms.

Andrews, who apparently never saw a detail he didn't take an interest in, leaned forward and thrust his face into the cat's. She peered back at him with a sleepy, almost drugged expression, purring loudly. "She's great. What's her name?"

"Georgia," Gail answered. "Named after Georgia O'Keeffe."

Andrews straightened back up. "Perfect—she looks half-dead. How's he doing, Harry?"

Harry showed his gentle smile. "Pretty quiet, doc. He killed the lights in his room to see the snow better. He's been sitting by the window for an hour, talking to himself."

Andrews patted the other man's arm. "Good. The mood sounds about right." He turned to face Gail and me. "Dark room, his focus on what's outside—let's lead in with Gail and Georgia first, then me. Joe, if you could stay in the shadows at first, that might be best, until we can gauge what he's thinking. Don't hide—just don't make a big deal of being there."

Given what we knew of this man—a traveler lost in time, using stray, unrelated signposts as references, his faulty memory damaged by disease—the setting he'd created for himself was downright eerie. The snow outside the darkened room had taken on the glow of the streetlights and was reflecting it back with an energy all its own, lighting the ceiling and walls with a ghostly iridescence, and backlighting Bernie with a thin, shifting corona.

Quietly, as if entering a church, the three of us filed in, Gail going directly to the window and taking the chair opposite Bernie's. She placed Georgia in his lap without a word.

He took his eyes off the snow and looked down at the cat, smiling. "Hello, Ginger—where did you come from?"

"I thought you'd like some company," Gail said softly.

Andrews quietly lifted a chair and placed it nearby. Bernie glanced at him, but otherwise kept his attention on Gail.

"I always love your company, Lou. You know that."

I moved within his sight, so he knew I was there, but settled on the bed across the room—a mere shadow in his peripheral vision.

Gail took her cue from the name he'd given her. "How are you doing, Dad?"

His hands began to unconsciously stroke the cat. He went back to gazing out the window. "Too many dreams."

"Bad dreams?"

"Uh, huh."

She waited for more, got nothing, and so prodded him with, "What are you looking at?"

"Anything—anybody."

I could almost feel her trying to follow, remembering what Andrews had told us. "Are they out there?"

"You bet. They wear white uniforms, so we can't see 'em."

Georgia stretched in his lap. He looked at Gail. "Is Lou here?"

After a split-second hesitation, she said, "She'll be here soon."

Very gently, Andrews leaned forward and removed the cat from Bernie's hands, placing her on the floor, where she wandered off in my direction, her job done. The psychiatrist took a short, blunt, smooth stick from his pocket, and placed it across Bernie's palm. The old man's fingers curled around it and he lifted it to his cheek, his expression darkening.

"Gotta have a gun," he murmured. "Gotta keep alive."

"When did you last sleep, Private?" Andrews asked.

Bernie snorted gently. "Who knows?" He shivered.

"Cold?"

Bernie nodded. The shivering intensified. He stamped his feet. "Wish I could feel my feet."

"And you're hungry," Andrews stated. "And scared."

Bernie's voice was pitiable. "I want to go home."

"Gotta keep alive to get home."

"Right—keep alive." Bernie's eyes were now glued to the view outside. Suddenly, he sat bolt upright, the stick gripped in his hand like the butt of a pistol. Instinctively, we all looked outside and saw a dog cut across the snowy ground, barely at the edge of the light.

"What was that?" Andrews asked. "Was it them?"

Bernie slipped off his chair and crouched by the windowsill, barely peering over the top. "Yeah."

"But they're dressed like us."

He placed his finger against his lips. "Listen."

Andrews got down next to him, in front of Gail's knees. I noticed her face was frozen, her eyes intense—almost fearful. "That's German they're speaking," he said.

"Right," Bernie agreed. "The spies."

"Who're 'Dem Bums'?" Andrews asked in a whisper.

"Brooklyn Dodgers," was the quick reply.

"Where's L'il Abner live?"

"Dogpatch, USA."

"They don't know any of the answers."

"Damn Krauts—why do they have to dress like us?"

" 'Cause they're out to get us, Private—just like they got Johnnie."

I stretched my own memory back to when I first met Bernie, right after he'd attacked the other patient. "They got Johnnie," he'd said at the time. I was impressed Andrews, with all his other patients, had remembered that small detail from Bernie's file.

An important detail, too. Bernie grabbed Andrews's sleeve. "God damn you, Johnnie. I told you not to sleep there. You gotta hide. They look for you where it's warmer. They know where we'll be."

"I'm tired," Andrews said in a sagging voice.

"You die, I'm all alone, you bastard . . . " Bernie's hand

dropped, and his gaze shifted to me, far across the room. "I'm all alone."

Andrews gestured to me to come forward slowly. "But you saw the man who killed Johnnie, right?"

Tears were flowing down Bernie's face. "I was so close, I could've touched him. I was scared . . . so scared. I didn't want to die."

Andrews pulled Gail off her chair so she would be kneeling with them in a tight group. "Johnnie's mom needs to know, Bernie, so she can get some peace. She needs to know who killed Johnnie. We all need some peace. We all want to sleep."

Andrews motioned to me to crouch before Bernie, who stared at the bandage on my head with wide eyes. Andrews nodded and I silently removed a stack of pictures from my breast pocket and handed them to Bernie.

"Krauts, Bernie," the doctor suggested. "Which one of them killed Johnnie?"

Bernie looked at the stack in his hand, hesitating. The light from the streetlamps was strong enough to see the pictures, but I worried the leap from memories to reality might prove too wide. In his mind, Bernie had transformed a stick into a gun, and Gail into three completely different women. What would he do with what I'd handed him?

Andrews seemed intent on the same problem. He gently removed the top picture from the pile—one of Eddy Knox. "This him? The one who killed Johnnie?"

Bernie touched the photo with his finger. "No."

Andrews replaced it with another, this one of Willy Kunkle. "No."

A third came up. Bernie shook his head.

Andrews put the whole stack in his hands, his voice firm. "Look through them, Private. Find Johnnie's killer—the man who strangled him as he slept."

Slowly, reluctantly, Bernie did as he'd been told, peeling off pictures one after the other, moving faster, shifting his position so I could no longer see which ones he was looking at.

And then he stopped, one picture held out before him, crying openly now. "Johnnie . . . God damn it . . . " He took the photo and placed it, facedown, against Gail's breast. Her hands closed on his and he bent over, his cheek against her stomach.

Andrews began rubbing Bernie's back, mouthing instructions soundlessly at Gail, who by now was crying also, a victim of her own nightmares. "Thank you," she said with difficulty. "Thank you for helping me. Thank you for letting me sleep again."

She raised his head in her hand and kissed him on the cheek. Andrews rose and helped Bernie to stand, and then escorted him to the bed. "Lie down. Your job is done. You've brought peace to yourself and others—peace and quiet. The war is over, Bernie. Time to sleep."

He helped Bernie stretch out, smoothed his bathrobe and arranged his pillow. Bernie looked up at us all for a moment and smiled. "My friends," he said quietly, and shut his eyes, sighing deeply.

Georgia, who'd been curled up at the foot of the bed, rose, stretched, and resettled into the crook of Bernie's arm. Instinctively, his fingers lost themselves in her fur.

We crept out, followed by the sound of her purring.

In the hallway, squinting in the glare of the overhead lights, we stood a moment in a tight circle, emotionally spent. Then, without comment, I extended my hand to Gail. She gave me the photograph.

I looked at it for a moment, trying to untangle the emotions it stimulated—the questions, the arguments, the doubts, and finally the acceptance that it might all be starting to make sense.

The picture was of Junior Chambers, NeverTom's reclusive brother.

Chapter Twenty-seven

I was pacing the floor of the squad room when Ron Klesczewski entered, a concerned expression on his face. I had called him at home from the nursing home and told him to meet me at the office. Ever since the birth of his first child, I'd grown reluctant to disturb him at home. Tonight, however, I had no such concerns. After so many frustrations and false hopes, I was angry, elated, worried, and most of all anxious to move forward.

"What's up?" he asked.

"You've been digging into Hennessy and Levasseur. I need to know if Ben Chambers's or BTC's name ever surfaced in any of Hennessy's black market dealings—*before* the convention center came up."

He raised his eyebrows and removed his coat, draping it over the back of his chair. "How long before?"

"Could be years. I'm looking for some initial contact."

He unlocked his desk and slid open a full filing cabinet. "You got it."

I retreated to my office and called Tony Brandt at home. "Bernie pegged Ben Chambers as Adele Sawyer's killer."

Brandt remained silent for a long time, letting me twist in the absurdity of what I'd just said. I was glad I hadn't broken the news to Jack Derby yet. Mercifully, Tony merely pointed out, "Maybe not the ideal witness. What else do you have?"

"I'd like to try something. Part of the reason people haven't been willing to squeal on the Chambers brothers is fear of reprisal. But if word got out that their boat is sinking, that might change. Newspaper articles like this morning's are not lost on people like Fallows and Matson, and even Hennessy. If they see that Tom and Ben are under fire, they're going to be a lot more eager to cut a deal with us, not only for their own advantage, but to make sure both brothers get properly declawed."

"Funny you should mention that article. Nice piece of timing. I never did hear back from NeverTom's lawyer."

"Yeah," I said vaguely. "Lucky break."

Brandt left it at that. "So what're you after?"

"I want to bring Garfield, Knox, and Matson in again, tell them they either testify against the Chamberses now or go down with them. If it works, they may give us the evidence we'll be pretending we already have—at least enough to stimulate a warrant."

Brandt barely hesitated. "Okay. I'll call Derby. I want him here for this."

*   *   *

I chose to interview Harold Matson, the bank president, playing good cop to Sheila Kelly's bad cop. And since Matson had a lawyer stuck to his side like a pilot fish, I asked Jack Derby to stand by as well, in case I needed some quick advice.

But Sheila had done her homework well. Showing no emotion beside a surprisingly implacable toughness, she took Matson to task, point by point, through a tangled web of intrigue involving both Chambers brothers and the Bank of Brattleboro. Matson's lawyer ran interference at first, until the brothers were shown to be exposed and vulnerable. Then he began fishing for ways his client might escape prosecution with the least possible damage. As I had hoped, two hours later, we'd gotten Matson to agree to testify against Ben and Tom Chambers in exchange for the loss of his job, a probationary sentence, and a modest fine. To my private satisfaction, Matson mentioned that the article exposing NeverTom in the *Reformer* had been a major influence in his decision to come clean.

Sammie and Marshall Smith fared equally well with Eddy Knox. In exchange for leniency, he gave a chapter-and-verse reading on how to corrupt a public official. The biggest difference between Matson's and Knox's testimony, however, was that while the latter still maintained that all clandestine communications between NeverTom and him had taken place on the phone, the former owned up to having face-to-face meetings. This, as we all knew, was a critical distinction—as it would be to the judge we'd be asking to sign our warrants.

The zoning administrator, Rob Garfield, proved a dead end. Increasingly angry at being put under our microscope, he denied any knowledge of skullduggery, and further informed us that if we bothered him again without presenting hard evidence, we would be made to regret it. Tony Brandt, when he heard, merely rolled his eyes.

The final piece of truss work we tacked into the affidavit for search warrants of all and any paperwork of both Ben and Tom Chambers, was Ron's discovery that four years earlier, Paul Hennessy had built a small rental property for Ben using one of his dummy fronts, thus establishing a connection between the two men that predated their mutual involvement in the convention center project.

By ten o'clock that night, I was on a private phone to Stanley Katz, telling him what we had, and what we were about to do with it.

He took everything down without comment before finally asking, "If you've got enough for a warrant, why're you giving me all this?"

I was bluntly honest with him. "Because we might not find anything. I want Fallows and Hennessy to know it's safe to come out of hiding, and I want other people who might've been screwed by these two creeps to know that now's the time to speak up."

"What about the Sawyer murder? Does she tie into this?"

I hadn't told him about Bernie's revelation. Tony's reaction earlier had been all the encouragement I needed to keep that one under wraps. "We're making progress, but it's still too early. With any luck, and if we can get this Chambers avalanche rolling, all sorts of things will show up in the debris."

"Are the Chamberses implicated in the murder?"

"Off the record? I can give you a strong 'Maybe.'"

To my surprise, he dropped it. "Well, I got enough for now anyhow. I sure wish you'd stop calling me so close to deadline. This late-night-crunch routine sucks."

I took that as a thank-you and hung up.

*   *   *

As the affidavit was being prepared and a judge rounded up to sign it, I had patrol cars check out both the Chambers residence and the BTC offices on High Street, to see if I could locate both brothers. From the reports that came back, it didn't seem that anyone was at the house. The lights at the office, however, were still burning brightly.

"Damn," I muttered to myself.

Tony, still in my office, picked up my concern. "Is that a problem?"

"Could be. Ted McDonald told me once that NeverTom had informants all over town. If he caught word we brought Matson in again, he might've decided to cover his ass and destroy all the evidence. I'd like to move with that warrant as soon as we get it signed."

Tony stood up, a small smile on his face. "Mind if I join you?"

It was an unusual request. The Chief was less a cop than an administrator nowadays, but he had come up through the ranks. I also knew that for this bust in particular, he wanted to be there when the tables were turned on one of the most antagonistic selectmen he'd ever had to deal with.

"It would be a pleasure," I told him.

* * *

BTC Investments owned one of the old brick buildings that stood on High Street's steep slope, just before it T-boned into Main. Tall, narrow, and unremarkable architecturally, these structures looked painfully jammed together, as if the first one at the bottom of the hill had suddenly ground to a halt at the traffic light, and forced all the others to collide and compress like passengers in a bus wreck.

It was an abandoned wreck at this time of night, however—dark and silent. In midweek, midwinter, and after hours, Brattleboro tended to fold up like a backwoods village. Glancing up at the address as I got out of the car, I could see why the patrol unit earlier had made such a quick and accurate assessment of BTC's occupancy—theirs were the only lights on in any of the surrounding buildings.

There were four of us—Tony, J.P., Sheila Kelly, and me. The other team, led by Sammie Martens, was already on its way north, to Eaton Avenue and the Chamberses home.

"Front or back way?" J.P. asked as we gathered on the sidewalk.

I looked at the door facing us. "Might as well go through here. I don't even know where the back door is. Most of these buildings have been turned into mazes."

We trooped inside, located the ancient, phone-booth-sized elevator, and rode creakily to the top floor. Just as we were almost there, Sheila sniffed the air. "You smell something funny?"

The door slid open as if in response, and the small space we were in filled with the acrid tang of smoke.

"Damn," I swore, running toward the door marked "BTC Investments," around which I could see thin, gray tendrils leaking into the hall. "J.P.," I called back over my shoulder, "find a fire alarm."

With the other two close behind me, I paused only briefly at the door, checking it for heat, and then threw it open and burst in. Ahead of me was a large, high-ceilinged room, possibly once an enormous storage area, now segmented into office cubicles by interlocking waist-high panels. A wide, central walkway led straight from the front door to the back of the room, and it was there, as if lost in a fog, that Ben Chambers stood grabbing papers from a row of open filing cabinets, and stuffing them into a burning metal trash can, a wet handkerchief tied across his mouth and nose.

I broke into a run.

I was about twenty feet away when he saw me, a thick wad of paperwork clutched in his hand like so much laundry. But instead of bolting for a back door, or merely yielding to overwhelming odds, he caught me by surprise. Ignoring what must have been excruciating pain, he dropped the papers, grabbed the hot metal trash can in both bare hands, and threw it at me with all his strength.

I instinctively dove to my right, behind one of the cubicle panels, and crashed heavily onto the floor against a desk. The can sailed overhead and exploded in the middle of the walkway, in front of Sheila and Tony. Sheila let out a scream as her momentum carried her right into the flames.

I scrambled to my feet and saw Chambers vanishing toward a far corner of the room. Tony had already grabbed Sheila from behind, pulled her free of the flames, and was stripping his coat off to extinguish the few flickers on her clothing.

Seeing me hesitate, he shouted, "Go, go, go. Get the son of a bitch."

I turned on my heel and gave chase.

Chambers had disappeared down a narrow, dimly lit hallway. Pausing on its threshold, I closed the door behind me to cut off the noise and listened. Vaguely, as if from very far off, I heard the clattering of footsteps, half-running, half-falling down a set of stairs.

I moved quickly along the short hall, checking each door until I found the one opening onto a brick-walled stairwell. There, the sounds I'd heard so dimly echoed clearly from below. I headed down, three steps at a time, just barely keeping my balance. "Chambers—stop where you are," I shouted. "This is the police."

My words sounded tinny and futile against the fear I knew was driving the man ahead of me. I didn't bother repeating myself.

Like two magnetized toys with similar polarities, we sped downstairs, never closing the distance between us, never setting eyes on one another. We ran as if isolated and alone, both of us stimulated by the pounding of the other man's feet on the metal-edged steps.

Near the bottom, a loud crash killed the effect, and suddenly the only sounds left in the stairwell were my own. I descended the last two flights to find a second hallway, this one wider and longer, at the back of which was a wide, heavy fire door. Again pausing only briefly, hearing the muffled din of approaching sirens from outside, I pulled open the door and found myself looking down a last set of stairs, and into a dark, cold, and very quiet cellar.

Using the light spilling out of the corridor behind me, I groped for a switch, flipped it on, and slowly, gun drawn, began edging my way down. Reminiscent of the cave-like, dirt-floored basement in which I'd interviewed John Harris, this one was strung with intermittent bare bulbs, casting as much shadow as light, and heading off along a labyrinthine selection of passages.

Pausing on the last step, however, I began thinking the choices facing me were perhaps of little concern. Chambers had not used the light switch, and upon opening the fire door, I hadn't heard a sound, both of which implied he had gotten himself cornered—or that he wasn't far from where I was standing.

I placed my back to the nearest wall, suddenly aware that our roles might have just been reversed, and silently cursed my forgetting to grab a radio on the way out of the squad room.

But backup would be on the way eventually. If I was right about Chambers being boxed in, my staying put wasn't such a bad strategy. Nevertheless, acutely aware of the dark niches and shadows confronting me, I began looking around, plagued by the concern that he might have somehow gotten away, and that the basement was silent for good cause.

My eyes went to the dirt floor, and there found the explanation. Scratched into the greasy soil was a fresh quarter-circle arc, radiating out from what appeared to be part of the wall. Crouching down, I studied the wall, actually a rack of wooden planks spanning two ancient brick pillars, and found where it was discreetly hinged. I moved to the other side, looking for a door pull or handhold, and heard the tiniest of noises—just enough to make me move my arm up defensively—before I was catapulted backward by the door flying open against me.

My left arm absorbed what would have been a direct shot to the head, but I was thrown against the opposite wall, and had the wind half-knocked out of me. Sprawled on my back, I saw Ben Chambers loom briefly before me, a two-by-four in his hands. I aimed my gun in his direction and fired.

Unharmed, he turned and ran into the darkness behind him, the sound of his retreat increasingly muffled, dull, and subterranean. As I struggled to my feet, dazed and with my arm throbbing with pain, I realized where it was he'd been hiding. The back of this building faced the Harmony parking lot, a block-sized quadrangle enclosed by a ragged wall of banks, businesses, and apartment buildings. In the days before oil, coal had been used to heat several of these places, and I had heard of at least one tunnel, supposedly long since filled in, designed for the distribution of coal throughout the block. As I stumbled down this narrow, musty, utterly black void, my arms outstretched before me, a tiny detached part of my brain marveled at the fossils left in the wake of a town's march through time. I wondered at the happenstance that must have led to Ben's discovery of this curiously convenient relic—and at the personality that had chosen to keep it secret.

Following the sounds ahead of me, I continued running blind until a dull glimmer of light and a blast of cold air from another door being thrown open indicated I wasn't just nearing the end of the tunnel, but approaching the outdoors as well. Where I ended up, after passing through a second disguised panel, was a large, dark, former coal bin, filled with cardboard boxes belonging to the businesses overhead, and equipped with an ancient iron ramp leading up and through a gaping bulkhead. Through it, I could see stars, a streetlight, and part of an alleyway wall.

Wary of a second surprise as I surfaced to street level, I climbed the ramp gingerly, to be greeted by the angry bellow of a car horn somewhere down the alley to my left. Emerging into the night, I saw Chambers waving his arms in the middle of Elliot Street, in front of a pickup truck now skewed crookedly across the road. As I began running down the alley to intervene, the truck's driver exited angrily from his cab and was smoothly laid out by one swipe of Chambers's club. Barely breaking stride, Chambers threw the weapon aside, slipped behind the wheel, and gunned the engine.

I reached the street just as the wheels spun back to life, slithering wildly for a grip on the snow-clad surface of the road. The truck slid past me, just missing its former driver. Without thought or plan, I threw my gun into the bed and grabbed the tailgate with both hands, hoping to vault grace-fully into the truck and put an end to this frantic idiocy. Instead, I was instantly pulled off my feet, and ended up hanging on for dear life, watching the road speed by below my nose.

Slowly, fighting the pain in my left arm and the lurching motion of the truck, I chinned myself up to the gate and after several attempts managed to get a knee onto the rear bumper. There, hanging on grimly, I paused, gasping for breath.

Chambers was speeding west along Elliot, away from downtown, and parallel to the Whetstone Brook. Elliot is only a half mile long before it becomes Williams beyond a four-way intersection, and it was only here, where Chambers had to slow briefly, that I was able to hook my leg over the tail-gate and begin to work my way forward.

This, however, was still not easy. Chambers had seen me hitch on, and began jerking the steering wheel back and forth, trying to throw me off. Clutching on to the siderails, my feet wedged against the wheel wells, I impotently watched my gun as it careened around the truck bed like a gravity-resistant pinball.

Such maneuvering, however, was ill-suited to the road conditions, and eventually Chambers overdid it. The truck began sliding sideways down the street, the spinning of its wheels now only exacerbating the loss of control. All thought of catching this man was overwhelmed by the desire to simply survive.

The end of our madcap journey came with merciful grace. Bypassing all guardrails, utility poles, parked cars, and trees, we plowed into a thick, soft, energy-absorbing snowbank. The impact sent me flying through the air like a basketball, but even in midflight, I was glad to be free of the truck. I landed half in the freezing water amid a thick cluster of dead reeds.

My anger overwhelming any remnants of caution, I scrambled up the stream bank, vaulted over the half-buried hood, and wrenched open the door. Ben Chambers, small and frail, his eyes wide and his sooty forehead smeared with blood, stared at me plaintively.

"Please—don't hurt me."

I stared at him in stunned silence, torn between responding and tearing his head off, and finally managed instead, "You're under arrest."

Chapter Twenty-eight

I emerged from the interrogation room after an hour and a half with Ben Chambers, my adrenaline pumping, the end of the case in sight, finally having heard the answer I'd been hoping for since the night Mary Wallis disappeared.

J.P. Tyler met me in the tiny hallway outside the viewing room, where he'd been videotaping the interrogation. "Get it all?"

"Yup."

"Do me two favors. Round up Smith, Lavoie, and Stennis for SRT duty, and call Gail at home and have her meet me here. Tell her Mary is still alive and that we're about to launch an operation to free her."

I saw Ron sitting at his desk, phone in hand. He swung around at the sound of my voice and pointed at the receiver, "I'm lining up a no-knock warrant for the trailer right now."

I gave him a thumbs-up and took Dr. Andrews by the elbow as he followed Tyler out of the viewing room. I had asked him to observe the interrogation to give us what insight he could. "Doctor, would you walk with me down to the basement? I'm assembling the Special Reaction Team, and we've got to change into our gear downstairs. I was wondering if I could ask you a few questions about Junior on the way."

Andrews looked slightly startled at all the sudden activity. "Of course."

I steered him out of the squad room and toward the stairs leading down. "Why did he do all this? It made more sense when we thought NeverTom was the crook."

Andrews smiled slightly. "Don't sell NeverTom short. He got where he is through a combination of blackmail, corruption, and intimidation that he's practiced his entire adult life. That and the ghost of their father's influence was what Ben was reacting against. People thought that after Ben Senior rejected Junior and turned his attention to Tom, Junior happily sought refuge in his books and philanthropy and making more money. In fact, he went into a slow simmer of rejection and envy, building up steam over the years until he finally blew. It was less obvious than NeverTom's sociopathic personality, which found a therapeutic way to vent itself against political enemies, and in the end, as with anything that's been penned up for too long, it was much more destructive.

"The classic love-hate twist to it all," he continued, as I opened the door at the bottom of the stairs for him, "is that Ben set out to get his revenge on his brother by becoming his ally—he's the one who recognized that more could be made from the convention center than just a little political mileage. To him, it was a way to make a fortune, and ride his brother's coattails as high up the social ladder as possible, all the while knowing that it was he, and not Tom, who was responsible for that success."

"But by saying Ben blew his cork, how do you explain the care and time he took in killing Shawna and Milo?" I asked.

Andrews shook his head apologetically. "For Ben, it *was* a sudden release of sorts, even if it was meticulously planned. He basically took his father's and brother's behavior, and exaggerated it to make it his own. Where the other two plotted and planned and killed people figuratively, Ben did it in fact. As he said during the interrogation, his killing of Shawna was an experiment. It was a maiden voyage into a new lifestyle. Look at all the complexities of that crime—the Satanist overtones, in case the body was discovered before it totally disintegrated; the fact that he kept Shawna alive for a week so he could show her to Mary Wallis and prove his absolute power. That worked so well, Mary didn't know Shawna wasn't still alive until the skeleton was positively identified. And even then, Ben had a plan in place. He not only triggered the Satanist diversion by making an anonymous phone call, but when he grabbed Mary, he threw suspicion onto her by planting Shawna's wallet in her house, even forcing Mary to put her fingerprints on it.

"This signature pattern is repeated with the Milo killing. During the interrogation, Ben simply said Milo tried to blackmail Hennessy and him, and therefore was taken care of. What he didn't dwell on was the complex methodology, which again was less appropriate to the task than to satisfying his own psychological needs. Why use rabies? Because it's arcane, experimental, takes brains to pull off. Anyone could've knocked Milo over the head and dumped him in a ditch. He would've been frozen solid by morning. But to use rabies was a sign of genius. A genius who needed recognition, of course, which is again why he made another anonymous phone call.

"The same pattern of camouflage and deflection is evident even while he was ostensibly helping NeverTom's cause," Andrews continued. "He used his brother's phenobarbital on Shawna, cut up the rabid raccoon using his brother's worktable and tools, and made it appear Tom was Eddy Knox's sponsor at the Keene country club. Not only would all that get Tom into trouble if everything fell apart, but it imbued Ben with a secret power over the very person who had mentally tortured him his entire life."

I paused near the end of the high, dark, basement hallway we'd been traveling. "Let's back up a bit. Why did he grab Mary Wallis and put her under lock and key? Why not kill her?"

"A couple of reasons, as I see it. First of all, he had to do something after Shawna was proven dead, because his hold over Mary had suddenly vanished. He tried threatening her at first, which is why she seemed so secretive and fearful to you, but he soon realized that would yield only short-term results—that Mary would probably tell what she knew if you promised her protection. As to why he didn't kill her, that's a little less practically motivated. People who kill in this fashion need to justify the act in their own minds. That way, they aren't so much butchers as unappreciated servants of society—it's a form of vigilante mentality. Remember how he described Shawna, Milo, and Mrs. Sawyer?"

"A hooker, a bum, and a bitchy old woman with one foot in the grave."

"Right—blemishes on the face of society, in his view. But Mary Wallis, regardless of politics, wasn't a blemish—she was a community leader. That's why Ben had to stop her in the first place. She was powerful enough to halt the construction project, so killing her created a moral problem. Also, I think in his demented way, he was hedging his bets in case he got caught. His whole demeanor changed when he told you about Mary still being alive, as if she had now become proof of both his good will and his rationality."

I stopped beside the door to the locker room, letting some of the people J.P. had summoned file by us. I offered Andrews my hand. "Thank you for your help—with Bernie, too. We probably couldn't have done this without you."

Andrews smiled but shook his head. "Oh, I doubt that. People like Ben Chambers just think they're invincible. It would have caught up to him sooner or later. For one thing, he wouldn't have been able to keep such a success to himself. Being caught allows him to finally bathe in the limelight."

*   *   *

"So what role did Hennessy play in all this?" Gail asked, after I'd brought her up to date.

I slowed for an upcoming curve in the road, the blue lights on top of the car flashing off the snowbanks on either side. I was leading a short caravan of vehicles, including an ambulance, to Sunset Lake Road in West Brattleboro, where Ben

Chambers had told us Mary Wallis was being held captive in a trailer.

"It was purely financial. He'd been skimming Carroll Construction for years, which Ben discovered early on. When Ben hatched his plan to take over the convention center project, he needed someone dependable to remove Gene Lacaille from the picture. Hennessy supplied the answer—the PCB—and even salted the Keene construction site. Problem was, Hennessy was promised a piece of the action once Ben sold the project a few years down the line, but Hennessy was a short-term thinker, and maybe a little nervous about Ben. He decided to milk the deal up front by embezzling from Carroll like never before. Ben got pissed. That was the fight Milo overheard, and which got him killed. Hennessy's greed was why Ben killed Adele Sawyer—to get his partner back under control."

"And NeverTom knew nothing about any of it?" Gail asked skeptically.

"According to Ben, he knew only the bare necessities. Tom applied the pressure to Eddy Knox, Ned Fallows, and the others, and he was fully aware of the squeeze being put on Harold Matson and the bank, but he had nothing to do with the killings, and thought the PCBs that stopped Lacaille's Keene project were just a stroke of good luck. We've had him picked up by the State Police in a Montpelier hotel about an hour ago. Politicking to the end. They'll be delivering him to us in the morning."

I slowed down, killed the blue lights, and got on the radio. We'd turned onto Sunset Lake Road, and were now minutes away from the trailer Ben Chambers had told us about. "0-3 to all units. SRT assemble at the lead vehicle. All other units stand by for backup as assigned."

I saw the string of headlights behind me die as I pulled over. I stepped out onto the frozen dirt road, grateful for the cloud-covered moon and the night's total stillness. Appearing from the gloom like menacing ghosts, the rest of the Special Reaction Team gathered around, dressed as I was in black watch caps, black BDUs—Battle Dress Uniforms—and Kevlar vests.

I put my hand on Gail's shoulder. "You wait here. Once we give the all-clear come to the trailer. Okay?"

She nodded, her eyes narrow with tension.

Moving soundlessly in rubber-soled combat boots, I led the team up the road another quarter-mile. Just shy of the small clearing surrounding the trailer, whose anemically glowing windows we could just make out, I signaled the five people behind me to stop.

Sammie came up and handed me an infrared night-vision monocular. I scanned the area slowly, studying every pale, green-tinged detail for any anomalies, any movements. There were none.

"Okay," I murmured. "It's a go."

Sammie, Sol Stennis, Marshall Smith, and I crossed the thick snow to the front door, making no more noise than the creakings in the trees nearby. The two remaining members of the team spread out to cover the far corners. In the reflected amber glimmering from the small, grimy windows, we could just make out a trailer whose traveling days were over—patched, sagging, and surrounded by insulating hay bales. The wispy smoke of a wood stove escaped into the night air from a crooked metal chimney. At the rear of the rig, plywood panels had been bolted to the windows of the room we'd been told was Mary Wallis's prison.

Marshall Smith and I positioned ourselves to each side of the rickety door, located to the right of the long wall, while Sammie and Sol stood slightly back and to the center. All of us except Marshall were armed with thirteen-inch shotguns with powerful flashlights strapped to their barrels. Marshall had a pry bar which he quietly fitted between the door and the jamb. From inside, all we could hear were the muffled exclamations of a TV set.

At a nod from me, Marshall threw his weight against the pry bar, springing the door open. Following his own momentum, he fell away from the opening, allowing me and the two others to pour past him, while he circled around to bring up the rear, a pistol now in hand.

I went straight across the narrow space to the opposite wall, quickly checking to the right where there was only an empty sofa and table. Sammie and Sol came in covering the left, from where we'd heard the TV, she in a crouch, and he standing.

"Don't move—Police," we all shouted simultaneously.

Before us, sitting in matching upholstered rocking chairs, their mouths open in astonishment, were an elderly couple, their eyes as wide as the three shotgun barrels facing them.

"Tim and Bernice Walters," I said, "you're under arrest. Is there anyone here besides the woman you're holding in back?"

Speechless, both of them shook their heads.

Sammie and Marshall moved farther into the trailer, checking all the doors, including the only locked one at the end of the narrow hallway. "Clear," she reported. Our assault had taken about eight seconds.

I nodded to Sol, who pulled his radio from his web belt and forwarded the all-clear to the others. Sammie had Tim and Bernice Walters sit down on the floor next to each other, and cuffed their hands behind their backs.

Gail arrived moments later, and I escorted her down the narrow hall, leaving Sammie to read from her Miranda card.

"You ready?" I asked her.

"Go on," she urged.

I worked the heavy lock and pulled the door open. It was dark inside, and utterly airless.

"Mary?" Gail asked tentatively, squinting to see better.

"Who's there?" came the tired, confused reply.

A light flashed on, and Mary Wallis was revealed sitting up in bed, one hand on a small lamp, the other shielding her eyes. She looked dirty, haggard, and weak. "Gail?" she said incredulously.

Gail crossed the room and held her in her arms. I faded back to the front room. The old couple were being led outside by two patrolmen. Sammie glanced at me expectantly.

"She looks like hell," I told her, "but she's alive. Might as well bring up the ambulance."

*   *   *

The next morning was overcast, the sky as gray as the now-gritty snow. There was a dampness to the cold, making it difficult to ward off. After the satisfaction of escorting Mary Wallis to the hospital and from there to her mother's bedside, I'd returned to the office to bring the paperwork up to speed. What we'd stopped Ben Chambers from burning in his office had amounted to a gold mine of evidence against both him and his brother.

In addition, without fanfare or drama, Paul Hennessy had turned himself in at the dispatch window three hours earlier, having heard of our arrests on the radio—a special irony, I thought, considering how much I'd relied on the newspaper. Now, Stanley Katz's "exclusive" on the case's wrap-up would trail Ted McDonald's reports by a full day. Sweet revenge for Ted, not that Katz had much to complain about—Hennessy would produce enough copy to keep Katz content for weeks.

Maxine Paroddy's voice came over the intercom. "Lieutenant? State Police just called—they're about five minutes out."

I rose and grabbed my coat. "Willy?" I shouted across the squad room, "want to help with the honors?"

For once, there was no grousing. Kunkle appeared from around the corner, dressed for the weather. I wondered how long he'd been waiting. Although neither one of us had ever referred to it, I knew how NeverTom's reference to Willy as a cripple had hurt, which was precisely why I'd asked for him now.

We went outside and stood around the parking lot for a few minutes. Willy had slept no more than I had, and was in no mood for conversation. Eventually, the crunching of tires on old ice announced the arrival of the dark green State Police cruiser. We waited for the car to roll to a stop, and then Willy bent forward to open the back door.

Thomas Chambers sat in the rear, his eyes fixed straight

ahead, his handcuffed hands nestled in his lap. Two troopers emerged from the front.

"Quiet ride?" I asked the driver.

"Yeah—snowing a little up north."

"Coffee's fresh inside."

Willy reached into the car and grabbed NeverTom's arm. Chambers jerked it away angrily. "Get your hands off me."

Willy laughed and dragged Chambers completely out of the car, landing him on his knees. "Not this time, asshole." With his one good arm, he lifted the other man up as if he weighed no more than a child. The two troopers looked slightly alarmed.

"Not to worry," I muttered. "He had it coming."

The driver nodded and went around the car to park it properly, while his companion joined us as we walked toward the building.

It was the slight crackle of ice underfoot that caught my attention. Otherwise, the dark shadow appeared from around the building's edge with all the sound of a gentle breeze. I glanced over casually, expecting to see one of our officers walking toward the parked cruisers. Instead, it was Ned Fallows who stood there, legs slightly apart, a semiautomatic pistol held in both hands. Willy Kunkle, oblivious to all but his prisoner, was directly between Fallows and his target.

"Gun," I shouted, diving in front of Chambers and pushing Willy hard in the chest with one hand.

The explosion went off just as I hit the icy ground, Willy's startled cry still in my ears. I heard the trooper who'd been walking behind us shout, "Freeze," and looked up to see Fallows standing, hands high in the air, the pistol at his feet. I rolled over to check the damage he'd done. Willy was struggling to get up. Tom Chambers lay spread-eagled on his back, motionless.

Willy's face was twisted with humiliation and outrage. He looked from Fallows to Chambers's prone body. "God damn it," he yelled at me, "I could've handled it. What the fuck did you push me for?"

A pool of blood was rapidly expanding from the gaping

wound in Chambers's head. I slowly got to my feet and walked tiredly over to Ned Fallows, taking him by the arm. I looked him in the face for a moment, studying its familiar, haggard lines. "You did this because of what I told you, didn't you?"

His eyes flickered to mine for a moment, but thankfully, he didn't answer.

*   *   *

I sat exhausted in my office, my head throbbing. Instead of the elation I'd hungered for, especially with Mary Wallis being found alive, all I felt was sorrow and loss and depression. The motivations I'd recently witnessed—Ben Chambers and his amoral brother, Paul Hennessy and his beguilingly dissolute girlfriend, Ned Fallows, whose life of good work had grown twisted and bitter with pride—had shaken my trust in human nature. I thought of their victims—Shawna, Milo, Mary Wallis, Adele Sawyer, even poor old Bernie, who'd been forced to revisit the battlefield that had crippled him—and wondered how it was that they should have been singled out for such wanton destruction. It seemed so carelessly capricious. The irony was that NeverTom—who'd killed no one—had wound up the victim of his own devices.

Unfortunately, that gave me no solace. Too much damage lay in the way.

"Joe?"

I looked up and saw Gail standing in the doorway, the smile on her face oddly fitting the tears in her eyes. We silently embraced, lost in each other's arms—the mutual harbor we'd nurtured over the years. She knew of my troubles as if by telepathy, and after a few moments, unhooked my coat from the back of the door and said, "Let's go home."

"It's the middle of the day."

"And other people can finish it—for both of us."

I sighed at the sense of relief that gave me, and let her slip the coat over my shoulders.

Outside, I held open my passenger door for her and circled around to the other side. As I slid in behind the wheel, she handed me a large sheet of paper. "This was on the seat. What is it?"

I held it up. It was a beautifully rendered pencil sketch of the Skyview Nursing Home, huddled against a looming black mass of hills, vanishing into a star-packed sky. "I think it's a gift."

"Anyone I should worry about?" she asked with a smile.

I laughed and carefully placed the picture on the back seat. "No . . . not in the least."